THE SPERLING CHRONICLES 3:

NO TEARS FOR DEAD MEN

by

Dilsa Saunders Bailey

Good Show Publications, LLC

The Sperling Chronicles 3: No Tears for Dead Men

All Rights Reserved.

Cover Design by Derek Omo

SAN: 920-0533

ISBN Print: 978-0-9995505-0-2

ISBN ePub: 978-0-9995505-1-9

ISBN Mobi: 978-0-9995505-2-6

Library of Congress Control Number: 2018937278

Good Show Publications, LLC

Dedication

Thanks to my great friend, Lynn Suruma. You are the best, keeping me motivated and inspired to follow my dreams. So, to you, Lynn, and the wonderful ladies in my mastermind group who helped keep the Sperlings alive during this long journey, thank you!!!

You ROCK!

A SHORT HISTORY

KALI'S CONTEMPLATION

THE DRIVEWAY WAS still the same. Kali heard the gravel popping as she drove up the slight incline. The sounds reminded her of the last day she had lived there. That infamous day that she tried not to think about, tried to hide from herself. But, it hadn't worked. After all these years, she would still awake from dreaming about the blood-splattered walls, and the gaping, gushing hole in the middle of her mother's chest. She had covered it with a pillow and tried to apply pressure. But, her mother was already gone. So was her father. His head was a mess. A shotgun will do that to you.

She sat in the car and looked around for a while. The swing set was gone. The crepe myrtle trees were bigger. To her surprise, the house looked almost exactly the same. She wondered who lived there now. Somebody was maintaining it. The white trim glistened in the morning sun. Putting her hand on the door latch of her car, she took in a deep breath. Her new therapist had recommended this trip hoping it would help put those dreams to rest, though Kali didn't agree. How can you put a scene like that to rest — ever?

Kali went to the front door and rang the doorbell. There were a few cobwebs around it, so she realized it wasn't used often. Whoever lived here, and their visitors, most likely used the door by the garage. She took a step back, thinking of going around to that side door when she heard movement inside. The door swung open and a tall, brown woman broke into a wide smile and then grabbed her. Kali almost fell into the door over the stoop. The woman hugged her tightly, rocking her.

"Kalina, oh my God, Kalina. It's really you. It's really you. You don't know how many times I pictured you walking up to this door. Oh, thank God. You finally came home. You finally came home," the woman said and then let her go.

Kali stood there staring at her, then past her. The place was even smaller than she had remembered.

"You don't know who I am, do you?" the woman asked, stepping back and waving Kali toward the small living room.

Kali shook her head, but followed her into the living room. She stood in front of the sofa, but not before turning and taking in a full view of the room. She remembered stumping her knee against a coffee table that used to be there and a large color television set that her dad was so proud of used to be here, she thought as she looked toward the space. Now there was a big screen television on the wall and only a sofa and a loveseat. Her father's recliner that had helped to cramp the room was gone.

"Mandy." the woman reached out and touched her arm. "Kalina, I am Mandy. Your best friend from when we were little all the way through high school." Mandy's voice faded a little. "You do remember me, don't you? I know you have been through a lot over the years. I wanted to reach out to you, but your husband said you didn't want to hear from us. He asked us to give you your space. He said you would reach out when you were ready. I guess you are ready now," Mandy said with a nervous laugh that suddenly sounded a bit familiar.

"You knew Ashton?" Kali asked, not surprised the woman was Mandy. She did sort of look like her. She was much heavier, but Mandy always had been a little plump, even as a child.

"Yes, of course. He owns this house; well I guess you own it, technically. It's in your name, of course. But, he had everything that belonged to you stored. It's still in storage. He lets me and Rudy stay here to keep it vital, he says. He said an empty house dies fast."

"Did you have the baby?" Kali asked and eased down onto the sofa. The fact that Ashton had a hand in this house knocked the air of her. She had to sit down or fall down. There was no getting away from that man, dead or alive.

"Yes, I had a little girl. She's grown now. She will be graduating from USC-Columbia in a few weeks. And I had a boy. He's in college, too. And you, girl, I hear you have four children. I never imagined you with children. Heck, you didn't either when we were younger," Mandy said smiling down at her friend. "How are your children? How are *you*? Ashton's death was all over the news down here."

"They are doing well. So am I," Kali said as she looked toward the stairs.

"Do you want to go up there? If you do, it's okay. You can look all you want, and if you want, I will get the keys for the storage unit and we can go over there. I did keep a few little items around, just in case you knocked on the door one day."

Kali took three deep breaths, rose from the sofa and dropped her purse on the table. The steps leading upstairs were only about four feet away in reality, but her eyes thought they were much, much farther. Her mind teased her that she would take too long to reach them, and her heart commanded her, "don't go."

Mandy stood at the bottom of the steps watching Kalina make slow deliberate movements, as if she were preparing for something dreadfully important. "Would you like some water or something?"

Kali shook her head no and took the first step away from the sofa. Her first instinct was to sit back down, but she took another step and then another until her hand rested on the bannister. There were only a few steps up to the next landing, nothing like the stairs in the penthouse or the house in Jersey. She could be at the top in a couple of seconds, but she couldn't move. Perspiration burst from her cells as if someone had just sprayed her with one of those water guns her children played with growing up. She lifted her hand and rubbed the moisture in it on her pants leg. She didn't want to slip. Then she noticed that her legs felt as if they were wrapped in weights and her knees felt as if they were splintered in place. She tried to lift her foot, but her legs were too constricted to move. Kali took another deep breath.

Mandy's warm hand rested on her lower back in support, "It's okay. You don't have to go up there right now. Take your time. Take all the time you want."

Kali shook her head and then gently pushed Mandy's hand away. She was going up there. Prying her foot from the floor, she lifted it to the bottom step. Her whole body began to shake, and in her mind, she heard the loud boom of the shotgun. Her foot dropped back. She looked at Mandy who didn't seem to be alerted to anything unusual, realizing the sound was more a memory than reality. She took another long, deep breath and lifted her foot again. It still shook with fear, but it moved. Holding onto the bannister, she moved up one step at a time until she was at the top of the landing. A memory of her mother pleading with her father caused her heart to pump loudly in her ears.

"Rudy and I have your parents' room. We didn't keep any of the furniture. It's in storage though, if you want it. Ashton said your mother's vanity was an antique and may be worth a lot of money. But, your bedroom set, that was real quality furniture. My daughter loved it as she grew up in there. It's still there, if you want to see it."

Kali held onto the wall as she made her way down the hall. She had to see it. She had to see her parents' room. That was where her nightmares took place at least once a month, now twice a week after all that had gone down with her husband recently.

Mandy opened the door for her, and then walked in. The bed was different, but it was in the same location where her parents' bed had been and Kali's knees began to buckle. She could see her mother's lifeless, bloody body staring at her. She closed her eyes and opened them again, seeing a lighter colored bedroom set with lavender bedding and with Christian-like pictures on the wall, which almost seemed funny to Kali. She wondered how much lovemaking took place in this room under the watchful eye of a pious figure suffering and bleeding. It was obvious this family had never suffered any violence or tragedy. If they had had a reminder of someone's suffering, that wouldn't be something they would want to see at night before going to sleep. Kali walked over to the window and looked at the same forest she had seen on her last day there, and all the days before growing up. The trees hadn't been taken down to make room for a subdivision or anything like that. It was as if the place had been stuck in time.

Kali had seen enough and went back down the hall with more control over her legs now; her knees were bending without thought. She opened her bedroom door and smiled slightly. Mandy had been right. Her four-poster bed stood where it always had, along with her vanity, her dressers and her bookshelves. The furniture was well cared for and didn't look old or dated; it just shined as if it was expecting her. Kali walked in and slid her fingers across the top of the vanity and then checked her face in the mirror. It was done, she thought. She had faced her fears, but she wasn't feeling any differently. Maybe, just maybe the nightmare of her parents' murder-suicide would fade. But, what would take its place? The rapes, the murders, the loss of her home, loss of her husband? She had no idea what else she could withstand and she didn't want to know. All she knew was that she could cry no more tears for dead men.

"CAST"

Ashton Taylor Sperling – Intense by nature, spoiled by his wealthy grandfather, a man who takes what he wants and believes it belongs to him regardless of anyone else's claims. That is, until he meets the woman of his dreams and must fight everyone else who wants her, too. **(AKA – Lazarus Smith)**

Asa Thomas Sperling – Ashton's identical twin. The creative photographer, once a lighthearted and playful man, who wanted nothing more than Ashton's approval. But, then Ashton took everything he ever wanted from him and ignored him. At least, that's how he felt as he let his father and his lover, Redd, drive them tragically apart.

Kali Sperling aka 'Kalina Denise Harris'– Briefly and illegally married to Marcus Roberson. Later becomes and continues to be the wife of Ashton Taylor Sperling. She is the mother of four children, Katie, Ash Jr., Adam, and Kacie and the matriarch of The Sperling Family. Kali Sperling knows exactly who and what she wants out of life and nothing is going to stop her.

Micah Sperling – Bald, tall, chocolate, and beautiful. The loyal, loving brother of Ashton, his best friend, and confidante. They will do anything for each other, even share each other's wives. Micah has fallen in love with Kali, and the consequences could be life-changing for all of them.

Jordan Banks – Famous saxophone player, Philadelphia's King of Music. Loved by the public for his soulful sounds, but loved more by his wealthy and high-powered patrons for his underground business. Jordan's sale of beautiful bodies trained by him and his favored grandson, Ashton, is the source for his legacy of wealth.

Billy Banks Sperling – Jordan's only son, ungrateful and angry, pits his twin sons against each other. All he ever wanted from Jordan was his wealth and privilege, not his name. Whether he wants to admit it or not, he follows in Jordan's footsteps by keeping his sons who have been born to different women. All but one discarded, he raises Ashton, Asa, Micah, Chico, and Ricky with the one that he married, Micah's mother.

Ruby Sperling – Though she was the first true love of Micah's life, his loyalty remained with his brother and not to her when he realized she was a part of a plan to destroy Ashton.

Elizabeth O'Reilly Sperling aka 'Redd' – Ashton's first wife, the supermodel whom he helped to create, but who he also stole from his twin brother. She was the love of Asa's life. To Ashton, though he loved her, it was more about status until she hurt him to his core by trying to deny him fatherhood.

Tawny Elliott aka 'Elliott' – The only woman that gets Ashton, she was hired to be his executive assistant. But she became more than that. Elliott was his confidante, his children's play grandmother, and his wife's advisor as well. She was their rock in the many bad times. They all looked to Elliott for answers, and Elliott's answers dated back to the days of Jordan.

Elinor Rutherford Banks aka 'Ms. Elle' – Billy's wife and Micah's mother. She was the only woman Jordan trusted to be a part of the inner family, long before Ruby, and long before Kali.

Detective Troy Lucas – Ashton's old friend who worked for the Philadelphia Police Department. Troy is overly loyal to Ashton because he almost cost Ashton his life. He had blamed Ashton for the untimely death of his sister and put Ashton in a predicament that changed his life and his family's lives forever.

PART ONE

PROLOGUE

1950

TALL, DARK, AND not so handsome. The first thing people noticed about Philadelphia's most prominent and well-loved saxophone player was his dark skin, and then they noticed his dark suits. Jordan Banks was always attired in a black suit with a dark gray shirt and a red tie. Everybody knew him and there were plenty who didn't want to know him. That's why it shouldn't have been a surprise how successful his businesses outside of the music business were doing.

It was already summer time, and he had been home off the road for only three weeks in the last three months. He enjoyed his jazz tours, hanging out with his band, picking up more beautiful women across the country, whether they were white, black, and everything in between. It was the life. But, he had a home and a growing side business that had nothing to do with music and everything to do with a warm babe. He couldn't leave that alone too long, especially with his son, Billy, at the helm.

Billy was both fickle and defiant. He had announced Christmas morning that he was changing his last name from Banks to Sperling, a move that had cut Jordan to the core. His only offspring was going to willingly take his mother's last name. Billy was planning to change the boys' last names, too; there was nothing Jordan could do to stop him. This was going to end the Banks legacy, by name anyway.

Jordan owned a little storefront café in North Philadelphia on Ridge Avenue that shadowed as a speak-easy upstairs in the back, Thursday night through Sunday morning. In addition to selling unlicensed liquor, he sold women's bodies belonging to some of the prettiest women you'd ever seen. It wasn't exactly a secret, not by far. He had as many officials, politicians, and police officers buying his wares as anyone else. And they weren't cheap either.

Jordan walked into the sparkling clean café highlighted by the sunny day through its large glass windows, making it look larger than it was with just five tables. He looked over and waved at Mrs. Goines. She was a regular who was sitting across from an older gentleman Jordan didn't recognize. Mrs. G. was smiling politely over her heavy ceramic mug, probably filled with lukewarm coffee and a splash of bourbon from the flask she carried in her over-sized pocketbook. She looked up and winked at Jordan. He nodded as he didn't mind if she kept the chair warm all day. She helped to make the place look legitimate.

He turned toward the counter and saw Tawny Elliott leafing through a newspaper looking bored behind the counter. He nodded toward her and headed for the back office where he found Billy at the old wooden desk going over some paperwork and sipping a cup of coffee.

"Why is that gal out front? How many times have I told you to send her packing? Besides, she's not even paying attention out there. Someone could walk away with the register and she wouldn't even notice." Jordan walked over to the desk and saw his three-year-old grandson, Asa, sitting in the floor with a bunch of crayons in his lap. As Jordan looked closer, he saw scratches of some unidentifiable picture on the light colored tiled floor. He grabbed a piece of paper and put it in front of Asa who seemed thrilled at the new possibility.

"There's nothing in the register. The only customers this morning are the ones you probably saw out there flirting with each other. I don't think they are thinking of getting their change back at this point," Billy, who was a stark contrast to his father, answered without looking up at his father.

"Suppose other customers walk in? The kind to take advantage of the situation."

"Mrs. Goines will let me know. She always does. Besides, we don't have anything anyone wants today. It's not Thursday." Billy shuffled the papers together and pushed back in his chair. "Besides, you need to just close this place down until your real after-hours place opens. I'm not going to be here much longer to police this place or keep up with the weekend funds. Your daytime cash flow is little or nothing. Everybody goes over to the five and dime for their coffee in the morning."

"What do you mean?" Jordan had heard that song before.

"I am accepted. Penn accepted me into their law school."

"And, how do you propose to pay for it?"

"You have always wanted a lawyer, Dad. You will."

"I wanted a lawyer with the Banks' name. You are too confident that I am going to keep shelling out money to you, especially now. The only reason I am helping you is because of these two beautiful babies," Jordan said looking around the room for the other twin. "Where's Ashton?"

"Isn't he down there on the floor?" Billy got up and leaned over the desk.

"Ashton," he called. "Ashton, get back in here right now."

Jordan walked over to the bathroom and peeked in and didn't see the little boy anywhere. When he turned, he saw Billy examining the closet.

"He wasn't out front?"

"Not unless he was hiding behind the counter. You know how he likes to play hide and seek. Tawny's probably got him hiding under that big skirt of hers." Jordan smiled and started back into the restaurant area. Before he could reach the counter, he heard a loud, thunderous collision just outside. Then he heard women screaming.

"Ashton," he called panicking and stuck his head behind the empty counter, where now even Tawny was not in sight. His heart sank, where was Ashton? God, he pleaded, don't let him be outside.

Jordan turned to see Billy holding Asa tightly and probably thinking the same thing.

"Don't move. Stay right there," Jordan ordered as he had to shove Mrs. Goines aside to get out of the door. Traffic had come to a halt and a small group of people were in the street just a few yards away.

He walked slowly trying to survey what had happened. He noticed a small white boy standing on the sidewalk, his eyes looking as if they had been painted wide open with big blue dots. Jordan walked past him and into the street, just as he recognized Ashton's cries. He was wailing at the top of his lungs.

"Oh, my God," Jordan said as he moved people aside following the wails he knew so well, but this one was different. Ashton was frightened. When he arrived in the middle of the group, a woman had Ashton in her arms holding onto him as he struggled as hard as he could to get loose. As Tawny reached him a few steps ahead, the boy turned and saw Jordan. He fought both women even harder.

"Thank you, Miss," Jordan reached over Tawny for his grandson whose face was beet red and pulled him from the woman's arms. Tawny stepped back and went to join Billy.

"Don't thank me," the woman said, gesturing toward the woman on the ground. "Thank her. I saw the whole thing. He was chasing a ball. Came running out of that door full-speed ahead and ran straight for the street. He ran right in front of her and her little boy. She grabbed and pulled him back. He fought her and she lost her footing. Fell right in front of that old Buick."

Jordan followed the woman's eyes and spied the young white woman pinned beneath the wheel of the Buick. It had run over her just below her hips.

"Thank you, again." Jordan walked back to Billy and looked down at the little boy again.

"Here, take Ashton," he said to Billy. "Don't let him out of your sight. Take this little fellow with you, too."

"What little fellow?"

"Hi, my name is Jordan. What's your name?" Jordan knelt down in front of the little boy.

"Jack," the little boy answered.

"Are these your groceries?" Jordan saw the spilled bags around Jack as he clutched one with a clenched fist.

Jack nodded.

"Don't worry. We will get some more, okay?"

Jack nodded again.

"This is my son, Mr. Billy and this young lady is Miss Tawny. Do you want to go inside with them and have a soda?" Jordan asked, and the little boy nodded again.

"Go ahead."

Tawny took the little boy's hand and looked around. Both Ashton and Asa had wrapped themselves around Billy in such a vice he wouldn't have been able to shake either of them loose. The group disappeared into the café.

Jordan made his way back into the crowd and sat down on the ground next to the woman trapped beneath the car. He was surprised that she was awake.

"Thank you," he whispered to her. "I promise you, you will never want for anything for saving my grandson.

"My son," she whispered back. "Where's Jack?"

"He's inside. Don't worry I will take good care of him. But, right now, we need to take good care of you." Jordan got up and dusted himself off.

"Did anybody call an ambulance?"

"I did." Mrs. Goines was right behind him. "They on their way."

"Can some of you men help me get this car up?" Jordan inquired around.

"I'm the driver," said a tall, hefty, sallow-looking man with a greasy head of blond hair as he walked up to him. "I'll help you, if you think that's what we are supposed to do."

"I think it's going to have to come off," Jordan said.

As he and the driver began to lift the car, a couple more men pitched in and they pushed the car back and away from the woman's body.

"Oh, Lord," Jordan heard Mrs. Goines scream behind him.

"She's crushed," another woman yelled.

"Somebody should have been watching that child," another woman's voice lamented.

"You are right about that," Jordan said audible only to himself. It was then that he made up his mind that if Billy ever left his household, those boys wouldn't be going with him. Neither of them would ever wander around unattended again.

CHAPTER ONE

KALI – PHILADELPHIA
(PRESENT YEAR – TWO DAYS EARLIER)

SHE HEARD A light tapping on her bedroom door as she emerged from the shower. Kali slipped her soaking wet, golden brown body into a robe, her feet into her dainty little terry cloth slippers, and then waltzed across her large bedroom toward the tall wooden double doors. With five kids and three brothers-in-law in and out of her home, she was always on call. Somebody couldn't find this or somebody needed that. Being the only woman in the house was exhausting. Even though her excessive wealth relieved her of the worries of a typical woman, the constant needs of her family were still taxing. Thank God for money, she thought. No ordinary woman would survive this family. But, it wasn't just her money that helped her through it all, it was her strength. Kali Sperling was a formidable woman with a definite mind of her own.

Kali had kept her family in the penthouse in Philadelphia, still living on the entire 15th floor of the Banks Building in Center City. Every time she had thought about moving back to their rambling, Victorian house in South Jersey, something had held her back. No, not something – him, Ashton. That was where they had been their happiest. It had been a little more than ten beautiful years in Jersey or, at least, *she thought they had been.*

Kali was trying to run a towel through her heavy, dark curly hair as she unlocked the door to see which child, or child in a man's body, was looking for her now. It was her brother-in-law, Micah, and sometimes like now, she didn't want to admit it, her best friend.

"What do you want?" she asked, turning away from him. He was at the top of her shit list these days. The whole family knew it. The friction between them was hard to hide. For a while, it had been obvious that she and her brother-in-law had become more than just best friends, the term they had used frequently to describe their relationship. But, people knew instinctively they had crossed that line long before her husband had abandoned her to go to Europe.

"We need to talk about tomorrow night," Micah said as he let himself in and locked the door. He loved the view of the city from this room, especially at night when he used to visit her so they could comfort each other. He crossed the expansive bedroom to the sitting area facing the floor-to-ceiling patio windows and doors. The sun beamed brilliantly off the surrounding tall buildings, no evidence of the impending storm except a few clouds in the distance. The sight relaxed him a little bit and gave him a little of the courage he needed this morning.

"What's to talk about? You are bringing her, aren't you?" Kali asked, rubbing her hair more vigorously than usual.

"Let me help you with that." Micah pried the towel from her hands and she sat obediently on the ottoman in front of him. He began to gently dry her hair, knowing well that pampering Kali was the easiest way to get her to be still long enough to listen to him.

"Lazarus is getting on a flight soon. He will be here in a few hours."

"So," Kali retorted as he tried to relax her with his hands, massaging and rubbing her head.

"You are going to have to let me go, Kali. There's no place for me, not like we were, anyway. My, my," Micah spoke gently trying to avoid the use of the word *brother*, "my friend, my best friend, my other best friend, will be home soon and his heart is with you. Will always be with you."

"Could have fooled me. I haven't talked to him in months and, even then, he sounded distant. Like I was the last person he wanted to hear from. Even had the nerve to tell me never to call him again. I don't call that love, darling."

"You know why he said that. Plus, I think it went more like *'let me call you.'*"

"Well, he hasn't called yet. Funny, he can still keep in touch with you and Ash. I bet *you* call him whenever you want him."

"Ash? When did he talk to Ash?" Micah took her by the shoulders and turned her toward him.

"Oh, I don't know. But, I know my son, and I know when he puts on his Ashton Senior manners he's had contact with that man in London. That man influences him in that way, you know it. He gets his swagger on and that look with an *'I know something you don't know'* attitude.

Micah laughed, "That's your evidence?"

"It's enough. I know my child like I know you," Kali said as she gazed into his deep brown eyes. "I know you love me, Micah. I don't know what you feel for that other woman though. I think you are settling. You are too good to settle."

Gazing back at her, it was easy to understand other men's obsessions with her, he thought. Everything about her exuded sex, or a sense of *get closer to me, if you can.*

"Is there another you out there that I don't know about?" he asked, as he pinched her chin playfully.

"Probably. But, her name is not Anjuli Wyatt. Trust me." Kali turned away from him and snatched the towel back. She got up to get her big-toothed comb to tackle the tangles. He followed her to the vanity in her dressing room.

"Why? Is it because she resembles Ruby a little? Why? Why do you dislike her so much? She likes you, Kali," Micah said, thinking of his dead wife only briefly. It was hard not to notice Anjuli's resemblance. She had the same milk chocolate skin, and those eyes, wide and alert and curious, so curious. He tossed the thought of Anjuli's similarities aside for a moment and took the comb from Kali's hand, while making her ease down on to the bench. Her robe fell open exposing her moist skin and her bronze, plump breasts. She made no attempt to cover up, and smiled at him slyly in the mirror. He reached around her and closed the robe before he began to untangle her hair. She let out a sad sigh.

"Stop it. Behave yourself. Anjuli is stopping over this morning and the last thing I want is for her to walk in on us."

"Doesn't she know? If she really loved you, she would have already figured out that you are in love with me, not her. Besides, I don't think she loves you, Micah. I think she wants something from you. I just haven't figured out what yet. I don't trust her. All her grins and solicitations come across as false. She's not natural. She's just, eww!"

"You just make her nervous, that's all." Micah looked around the dressing room. He wanted to take her somewhere they could talk earnestly. The last sweep of the penthouse had picked up a couple more listening devices. He had taken Kali and the kids to the park to ask them to watch their conversations until they could track down the source, just in case more had been planted.

Kali saw the momentary concern in his eyes. They had all been on edge for the last three weeks. Something in the air had changed and it wasn't just the listening devices. It was all Lazarus. He was coming back. And that uneasy feeling that somebody was still after him, which meant after *them*, had been alerted.

"I'm really tired of this," she whispered. "What does anyone else want with us?"

Micah snagged a tangle.

"Ouch," she squealed, but she got the message not to say anymore. She knew the answer. Just didn't know who, or maybe she knew that, too.

Ever since that shooting two years ago on the campaign trail that supposedly claimed her husband's life, his old friend, Detective Troy Lucas, was still digging around to see who was responsible. And of course, the absurd part of it was that he was pointing his finger at her husband. Poor Ashton had returned home with amnesia after surviving a murder attempt on his own life. He had reappeared looking like a different man, shrunken to mere bones with a huge scar on his face and a brand-new identity: Lazarus Smith.

He had found his way back to Philadelphia, searching for himself, only to find his twin brother, Asa, impersonating him and wreaking havoc on her and his family. Since Troy wasn't privy to that fact, he was pointing fingers and trying to pin the fake Ashton's murder on the real Ashton. It didn't seem to matter to him that Lazarus had been on the stage with fake Ashton when he had taken the bullet to his head. That fact hadn't swayed Detective Lucas from his one-man mission to bring Lazarus to justice. None of it was because he had any real evidence but, more than likely, because Kali had shunned Troy's affections after Ashton's supposed death and, instead, appeared to have chosen Lazarus over him.

That was the one and only thing about Troy Kali had admired. His instincts were good when it came to identifying criminals, even in this case. But, in this case though, the problem was all he had was instinct; he had no evidence. But, if he only knew what was truly behind the assassination, what crimes had actually been committed, he would be justified in his pursuit of her husband, no matter what name he was living under. But, that was only one of the reasons Troy could never know that his closest friend, the one to whom he had once sworn all his loyalties, still walked the face of the earth, just not in Philadelphia.

"What did you want to talk to me about?" Kali asked.

"I have invited Anjuli to Katie's opening tomorrow," Micah said, holding a length of hair to begin untangling it from the ends.

"You have mentioned it. Several times. Why bring it up again?"

"I want you to get to know her. Try to spend some time with her at the after party."

"Ha. Ha. Ha," Kali smirked. "Why would I have more than two words to say to that woman? You know the two I would like to say. Good Bye."

"Kali, seriously, you and I are, well, we are still a team. Will always be a team, but I need my own woman. Don't you understand that?"

"Hmmm. What a concept." Kali turned and pushed back. She stood up and let her robe drop to the floor. She was about to turn 40 in a body that had produced four children and she looked damn good. She knew it. Micah knew it, too. He backed nervously into the shelves loaded with shoes and folded his arms. He shook his head.

"Stop playing, Kali," he said, tilting his chocolate bald head to the side looking at her as if he was just seeing her for the first time.

"I'm not playing."

"I'm trying to tell you something."

"What? That your girlfriend is stopping by this morning. That you invited her to my family's celebration tomorrow night. That she will be sitting in one of the family boxes at the theater. Or just that Lazarus is going to show his delinquent ass up, too?" Kali walked up to Micah and touched his chest.

"I bought a ring," Micah said, taking her right hand into both of his. That was the one he knew she would swing with first.

"How lovely." Kali stepped back freeing her hand. "Katie loves jewelry, too. I am buying her a charm bracelet. I plan to add a charm for every play she is in. Which reminds me, I need to get dressed. I have to pick it up." She snatched the comb away from Micah and picked up her robe. She was sliding back into it when he pulled her into his arms.

"I plan to ask her to marry me."

"Go, Micah. I have a lot to do today. I don't have the time to talk about your fantasies. You are not marrying her, babe. Go ahead and ask her. It will never happen."

Kali tried to walk around Micah out of the dressing room. He grabbed her right arm.

"Why, Kali? Why won't it happen?" He made her turn toward him. He lifted her chin to look her in the eyes.

"I know you are lonely, Micah. So am I. But, I promise you, I would never, ever stand in your way if I thought you had found the right woman. She's not the one, Micah. There are too many things. Too many," Kali said, pulling away from him, escaping a few steps into the bedroom.

"Too many what?"

"Things. Questions she asks. Questions she doesn't ask. I don't know. Things. Lurking things," Kali answered, looking around the room to give him a hint that she didn't want to verbalize them.

"I will see you at the office today?" Micah asked, giving up, realizing she wasn't going to or could not say anymore.

"I'll get there in time for the board meeting. Now I need to get dressed."

CHAPTER TWO

"MRS. SPERLING," RECK said. He moved away from the doorway as she stepped out into the hallway from the penthouse.

"Reck," she acknowledged him as she turned left heading for the rear elevator instead of the one facing them.

"We are not walking to the office?" asked the tall, blond bodyguard with the close-cut hair. The little light spikes of hair were cut so close to his skull, from afar he appeared bald, especially in the sunlight.

"No, we are driving to King of Prussia Mall. Are you up for the ride? Or, should I just meet you later?" Kali asked, though she already knew the answer.

"You are a very funny lady," Reck said as he took a few extra steps to get ahead of her. He stuck the key into the elevator lock to call it.

"I can't believe we are still using a key. Remind me one day that we need to get more high tech in this building."

"We have discussed this several times, and several times you have changed your mind," he said, stepping into the elevator ahead of her.

"Shouldn't you have held the door for me?"

"And, have you tell me that I should have stepped in to make sure it was secure for you first?" Reck smiled, his blue eyes twinkling.

"You think you are so damn smart," Kali said smiling. This was the first bodyguard she had ever had that she even conversed with beyond giving a few orders. She liked this one. Micah teased her saying she liked him because he was her first white bodyguard. But, that wasn't it. This one was just comfortable. She had no other explanation for it. It was almost as if she already knew him from some place.

He reached over her and pushed the button for the garage and she caught a whiff of him. He smelled good, reminding her of her husband's smell. The smile on her face died at that thought.

"Where to, Princess?"

"Princess? You mean Your Majesty the Queen, don't you?"

"Oh, yes, I forgot, you were elevated."

"Elevated in the descending elevator," she said, letting a little silliness rise up within her. The thought of Ashton was not going to ruin her day. Kali walked past the vintage Mercedes that Ashton's grandfather, Jordan, used to own and that Reck was obsessed with driving. She headed for the driver's side of her new BMW.

"Oh my. You are driving today?"

"Yes, I am," she said jingling the keys playfully.

"Okay, whatever you say, Boss Queen." Reck jumped into the passenger side of the front seat, which was something none of her other bodyguards had been allowed to do. They would have trailed her in another vehicle and then she would lose them if she didn't want to be bothered. Or, she would sit in the back seat of whatever car or SUV they were driving. She hated doing that since she had gotten so good at evading them when she was in her own car. She could, at least, credit her skill in evasive behavior to her husband and his bald-head brother. Again, she reminded herself that she didn't want to think of those Sperling brothers.

"Reck, hold tight," Kali said enthusiastically, as she gunned the engine and haplessly merged into traffic on 17th Street, sailing the streets of Philadelphia heading for the expressway. Reck gripped his seat to keep from bouncing around too much, but sat there smiling at her. That's one of the things she liked about him: nothing she did frightened him nor did he admonish her too often for many of her wrongdoings. Most of the time, he seemed to revel in her recklessness as much as she did. At times, he even encouraged it helping her to put herself in danger when she was dying to feel anything except boredom.

"Turn the radio up. I want to hear Luther loud and clear," Kali said as they merged onto I-76.

"In one of those moods?" Reck obeyed and cranked up the volume which made her scream with delight.

Kali sang some of the lyrics with Luther Vandross.

"Anyone ever tell you that you have a beautiful voice?" Reck asked.

"What?" Kali asked and then pointed toward the radio.

"Anyone ever tell you that you have a beautiful voice?" Reck yelled as he lowered the volume.

Kali deflected her eyes from the road for a second too long and swerved a little bit. "My mother. My father. Even Jordan. Lots of other people, but they didn't matter."

"Those three did, I assume."

"I am who I am because of those three."

"Was Jordan your grandfather?"

"No, my husband's."

"Mother's side?"

"No, father's side."

"We are talking about Jordan Banks, right?" Reck asked.

"Yes."

"Not Sperling?"

"No. Ashton's father, Billy, didn't carry on the Banks name. He used his mother's last name, after he decided to become a lawyer, I believe."

"Oh, that explains it. I always thought the Banks name belonged to you somehow."

Kali glanced at him. In the three years she had known Jordan Banks, he had molded her more than anyone had other than Ashton. She was who she was because of them: a woman who knew what she wanted and who she wanted in her life.

"No, I met my husband while working for his grandfather."

"But, the old man, I heard, left you a fortune. You must have a meant a lot to him. I mean, since he left money to you specifically and all. Rumor has it, he gave some of his own family members less than he gave you and some nothing at all, right?"

"He was good to me, alive and dead, you could say," Kali said, pressing down on the gas leaving behind all the other motorists on the road and the bad parts of Jordan with them. "So, who molded you, Reck? I mean, who was your greatest influence? Was he or she a bodyguard? Your parents? Did they teach you to protect?"

Reck turned his face away from her as if he were checking out the traffic. "There was someone, a mentor. I used to wish he was my father. He was everything to me. Then I grew up and I didn't need a father anymore," Reck said, laughing as he turned back to her. "You are going to get another ticket."

"I'm suddenly in a hurry to get back home," she said. The thought of her parents and their influence on her life made her want to see her kids.

"Did you enjoy your date last evening?" Kali asked as she floored the gas to pass a few more cars. The day before, she had overheard Reck making a dinner reservation for two.

"Yes, she might be the one," he answered, lying. It had been his intent to get more information about tonight's board meeting, but the woman knew nothing useful. She had been such a waste of his time. And, he was running out of time.

"Good. Don't forget to invite me to the wedding," she said, speeding off the exit to the mall.

"Are you upset about something Mrs. Sperling?"

"Of course not. I just want to get out of here and back to the office, then home. I don't know why I bought the damn thing way out here."

"Oh, Mrs. Sperling," Reck said, shaking his head, as they took a steep curve off the exit at a racer's pace. "You drive really well, but... it's the cops you attract that I am not very fond of. Do you think we can get to the mall and back without any backseat conversations with the cops today? You know, you may have enough tickets now to get us both put behind a cell door for a few hours."

"Don't worry, I don't plan to do anything to make me miss Katie's play tomorrow or the board meeting tonight."

"Thank God," Reck laughed. "But, I think we must slow down a bit."

"Just for that," Kali said and sped dangerously into the parking garage of the mall. She looked over at Reck and smiled. His crystal blue eyes smiled back. Nothing she did shook him, not even almost killing him. She had fun with him, her little white boy. That was what Micah called him, though there was nothing little about him. He was as tall as Micah and Ashton. From his resume, she guessed he was about their age, late forties to early fifties, too.

He had come to her highly recommended by a former client and, so far, things were working out well. Instead of going to formal training classes for self-defense, the two of them would go to the gym at the Banks Building and he would teach her different ways to protect herself. That was the other thing about Reck, he had given her the confidence to fear no one. No man would ever be able to rape her again. And, since he was teaching her girls, too, no man would ever have the opportunity to do the same to them, not without a fight.

"You seem a little tense today. Anything special going on?"

"Huh, you have to ask. My daughter is debuting as a professional actress in a play most likely headed to Broadway in a few months. And you are asking me if something special is going on? You are on duty tomorrow night, right?"

"Yes, ma'am. I will be walking the perimeter keeping the Sperlings safe," Reck said as he reached for the car door.

"You can stay here, if you like. I have to run into one store to pick up a piece of jewelry I had made for Katie. It won't take but a few minutes, I am sure."

That was another thing she liked about Reck. He took the hint and leaned against the car without trying to convince her otherwise. He reminded her of Ashton again, her fearless Ashton. Maybe it was because she was going to see him tonight, or maybe it was because she was feeling lonely, she couldn't stop thinking of their home in Jersey.

On the huge property they had bought in South Jersey, Ashton had come across a cave inside a ravine that was adjacent to a waterfall flowing into a river. It was beautiful. In the summer, the whole property turned into the deepest, plushest green you could ever find anywhere. Topped by the cool mist of the water being forced over and through to the river basin below, Kali used to feel as if she had moved her family to heaven. Often, they had wondered out loud if the original owner even knew about the little waterfall, it was so remote.

Her adventurous husband had gotten everyone out of bed early one Saturday morning to go exploring. In the rear of their property, which was surrounded by an expansive forest, was a large stable, the selling point for buying the house in the first place. Ashton had always wanted a horse, now he had eight. Some of the most beautiful animals she had ever seen. His horse was a stallion, a magnificent beast he had named Nightmare, who shared Ashton's temperament. After many episodes of who had the strongest personality, they had finally become soul mates. Ashton and Nightmare looked like they were one when they galloped through the bushes and trees. Kali remembered being a little jealous of the two sometimes. They were so perfectly matched.

She smiled remembering that day. As usual, Ashton and Nightmare were racing ahead of everyone else. She was on her horse, trying to keep her youngest daughter, Kacie, from spooking hers. Animals and Kacie didn't sync very well, but she was managing okay. Micah and the three boys were somewhere up ahead, their voices filling the air with laughter, probably at someone's expense. She was guessing it was Adam's, her youngest son, who was always getting himself into weird situations. Pulling up the rear was Katie, her sulking, oldest and now teenaged daughter who hated nature. She referred to her new home as "the wilderness." For her, leaving the city had been worse than if she had lost all her teeth at once. At least, that had been exactly how Katie had described it.

But, the odd thing about this cave and the waterfall was that they had been in that house almost seven years before discovering it. They had ridden those horses and taken those trails hundreds of time but, on that morning, there it was, as if someone had painted it into a picture. In an instant, everyone heard Nightmare's loud neigh and then a crash. That was before the rushing sound of the waterfall made itself known. Kali held onto her own reins and Kacie's as she hurried toward Nightmare's sounds of distress. When she arrived, A.J, her oldest son, was holding the reins trying to calm Nightmare down. He had dismounted his own horse and was stroking Nightmare's face, leaning his head into Nightmare's mane, and talking to him gently.

"What's going on?" Kali called to Micah who was looking over the edge. "Where's Ashton?"

"Where's Daddy?" Kacie echoed her.

"Down here." They heard Ashton's voice through the sound of the rushing water.

"Down where?" Kali slid off her horse and handed both reigns to her nephew, Artie.

"Down there," Micah said grinning. "Nightmare was smart enough not to go over. Looks like someone else didn't get the hint."

Kali ran to the edge of the ravine and looked down to see a cliff jutting out from beneath. It had been just big enough to catch her six-foot-two husband and stop him from falling onto a rock bed adjacent to the river; to the left, and a little below, was a very tall waterfall.

"Are you hurt?" she shouted. "Did you fall all the way down there?" Kali couldn't believe her husband was walking around.

"I didn't fall down here. I fell off the horse up there," Ashton yelled back. "Look at this. This is amazing."

"How did you get down there?" Kali was getting a little dizzy standing so close the edge. She noticed grass and mud on the back of Ashton's shirt and on the side of his jeans.

"I slid down here," he said pointing toward a group or rocks embedded into the side of the ravine. "It's sturdy. Come on down."

"Hell no," Kali said.

"Ooh," said a couple of the kids.

"Mommy cursed," another child said.

"Mommy did not curse," Kali replied. "I just emphatically said no."

Their children giggled.

"Look at this," Ashton called out. Everyone peeped over the side, but no one could see him. The kids had long ago let go of the horses; they were grazing in a group nearby under a large tree standing alone on the hill.

"What's down there?" Micah was already making his way through the rocks, holding on and sliding and maneuvering in a manner that had Kali holding her breath.

"Wow." AJ started down right behind him.

"AJ, get back here now," Kali screamed.

"Mom, Dad is already down there. It has to be alright."

"Get. Back. Here. Right. Now," Kali yelled at her oldest son, the other half of the teenaged twins. He and Katie had entered the world together and, for the most part, had been inseparable — until recently. Now, they fought more than anything.

"You heard, Mom," Katie yelled at him in support. "She said get back here now."

Kali turned around to see Katie standing dangerously close to the edge with her hands on her narrow hips. It hit her: both twins had not only inherited their dad's looks, but his mannerisms, temperament, and daring as well. Where was she in either of these people? Who were they?

"Move back from the ledge," Kali said, and reached up and tugged Katie's arm. Katie willingly stepped back, but leaned forward making Kali even more nervous.

"What's down there?" Katie shouted.

"A cave," Micah and Ashton shouted back.

"A cave?" Kali was astonished at the find. She had looked at the plat carefully. It didn't mention a cave. She knew the river was nearby. They had been to it several times, but they had never taken this turn. But, here they were and there it was. She could tell from the excitement in her children's eyes, she was going to have to go down there to that darn cave one day. But, not today.

"Okay, everyone, get your horses. Now. We are going home."

"What about Daddy?" Kacie cried.

"He will make it home just fine," Kali said, waving her children in the direction of the horses. "You, too, AJ."

"Ah, Mom."

"Don't give me the "ah mom" line. Get on your horse. Take Kacie with you. I

will bring her horse."

Kali folded her arms and watched the children walk away begrudgingly to gather their horses, all but Kacie's. AJ sat his younger sister in front of him on his horse and kicked the horse into a gallop. She squealed.

Kali lay down on the ground and peered over until she saw the two brothers, now completely covered in dirt, walk back to the jutting rocks grinning.

"Come on down," Ashton said, waving her down.

"No," she said. "You can take pictures and show me later."

"Kali, don't be a scaredy cat. You know I am going to bring the kids down here soon."

"No, you are not. It's too dangerous."

"A little danger never hurt anybody. Don't worry, it's safe. This is a good place for them to learn how to be careful wherever they go."

"No," Kali protested. "You are not taking the kids down there."

"It's safe enough, Kali," Micah chimed in.

"I'm not listening to you either, Molasses," Kali protested. Molasses had been his grandfather's nickname for him. He had always said that Micah thought things through, but he was as slow as molasses thinking them.

"I'm going to come up there and get you," Ashton started back up the rocks. "I want you to see this. Trust me, I want you to know every step, every inch of this place before I bring the kids down."

"Then I suggest you do the same before you bring me down," Kali sat up and looked over at the waterfall. It was beautiful. She was going to go back and check the property plat to see if this belonged to them or if they were on someone else's property.

"Come on, Kali. You are a country girl. You can do it. I just want you to see it before we clean up down here."

"Clean up?"

"Yeah, there's brush and stuff. I want to make sure we don't have any slithery friends around."

"That's it. I'm definitely not coming down there," Kali said as she got up and brushed herself off. She peered over and waved the two men good-bye. She threw Ashton a kiss and went straight for the horses.

"What are you smiling about?" Reck was getting back in the car, putting his phone back into his pocket. The bracelet had been ready and waiting. He found Luther Vandross on another of the stations and left it there. He knew he was Kali's favorite artist. Any song Luther sang, Kali knew all the words. He had even seen her slow dance to Luther all by herself, belting out the lyrics in a voice almost equally as moving as Luther's. He wondered why she wasn't a professional singer, but then he remembered. She had been one of Jordan Banks' concubines. There wasn't anything else for her to be, except kept and beautiful.

"I have been thinking about home a lot lately," she replied rocking her head to another one of Luther's melodies.

"South Carolina?"

"No, I haven't thought of that place as home in years. No, I was thinking of our home in South Jersey. We were in walking distance, or should I say riding distance by horseback, that is, from the river and the most stunning little waterfall."

"Sounds like you miss it."

"I do. I have been thinking a lot about it lately. Been thinking about how happy we were as a family back then."

"Are you telling me you are not happy, Mrs. Sperling?"

"First of all, if I wasn't, I wouldn't tell you."

"Of course, not. Who am I?" Reck looked at her with a curious grin on his face. Kali grinned back and chuckled.

"You are Reck," Kali laughed, "my irreplaceable Reck."

"Why are you thinking of home today?"

"Oh, I guess maybe it's the new woman in our lives that made me think about some of the previous ones."

"I don't follow."

"Anjuli. She is the new woman. She's coming to Katie's play tomorrow."

"Is she from Jersey?"

"Actually, I did some checking and she is from Jersey. She's from a suburb outside of New York called Linden. Have you ever heard of it?"

Though Kali was driving, weaving and speeding on the expressway toward home in what was now pouring rain, she saw a slight change in Reck's expression as he turned away from her.

"I've heard of it."

"You're from Jersey, aren't you?" she asked, noticing his face was a little flushed when he looked ahead.

"I went to school there. I am from here."

"That's right," Kali replied. She knew that. She had perfect recall. He went to Rutgers before going into the military. He hadn't completed his degree there or anywhere else. For a moment, she wondered what else he hadn't finished, but she didn't have time for that conversation right now.

"So you checked her out? Huh? I told you I would do that for you."

"I run a security firm, remember? PDSI. Personal Defense Systems Incorporated. Where your paycheck comes from. I have access to everything. What makes you think I need you to check someone out?" Kali asked as her car dashed in front of a large truck.

"Mrs. Sperling, if you want to make it to Katie's play or to your board meeting, you need to drive a little more steadily, please. After all, the roads are getting slick. You have noticed it's raining pretty hard."

"Did I scare you?" she asked. For a moment, she thought she had finally frightened him with her driving or something.

"I have no fear," Reck said as he started messing with the radio again. "So, I get that you don't care for the new woman in your brother-in-law's life. Is there a reason? I mean, one that makes you think of home, especially?"

"We all used to live together in Jersey. It was sort of like the family compound. I found the place shortly after Ashton began to recover from that fiasco that sent him to prison."

"I'd read about that during my research on the company. That was a shame how his brother framed him for murder. Even more of a shame that his brother died before paying for it. His identical twin, right?"

"Yes, Asa. Asa and Ashton were doomed, I think, by their father and even more so by their grandfather. But, that's another story for another day," she said, wishing Asa had really been dead the first time around instead of coming back to torment them.

"As I was saying we all lived together. First, Ashton and I moved there with our then, three children. It was the only home Kacie had ever known." Kali laughed for a moment. "She was the only child born in a hospital and the only one not born in Philly. Then, Micah and Ruby and their son, Artie, moved in. Before we knew it, his younger brothers Ricky and Chico were calling the place home. It was wonderful. We were always doing something together. It was good.

Everything was good. Then we moved back to Philly when Ashton started having issues with his memory." She wanted to say because he wasn't Ashton. "You know the rest."

"Yes. While campaigning for the mayor's office, your husband was murdered in front of hundreds of people," Reck added.

"Yes. And we stayed in Philadelphia. We stayed. But, we lost Ruby before we lost my husband. Something should have made us run back to Jersey then. But, we stayed."

"Why don't you like Anjuli? You hired her, didn't you?"

"No, hiring her was Micah's idea. He thought it would be good to have a forensic psychologist on staff to help develop our products. Maybe even to help some of our clients solve their internal security issues. I agreed."

"You signed off on it."

"I signed off on it. That was before I met her, before I realized she was going to be Ruby's replacement. I saw it coming as soon as I laid eyes on her though."

"He's a widower. Didn't you expect him to find another woman eventually?"

"Eventually." Kali held back the fact that she had been that woman for the past few years, off and on, and she had been comfortable with that. Maybe too comfortable, since her husband wasn't dead.

"Why don't you like her?"

"She reminds me of Ruby in a myriad of ways. Ways that spook me, sort of," Kali got off the exit back to Center City while thinking she had said more than she should have. Reck had that effect on her. She could talk to him. He was her sounding board. These days, Kali had so many things she wanted to say out loud to convince herself she wasn't totally crazy. But they were things that should never be uttered for his ears or anyone else's.

"Would you like to elaborate on that?" Reck probed.

"No, it's nothing concrete. It's all just spooky. I have yet to put my finger on it." Kali was happy to see the Banks Building looming ahead. The kids had already left for school. She was going to have to check in with them tonight.

CHAPTER THREE

LAZARUS – LONDON

EVEN LAZARUS REALIZED bench pressing 400 pounds alone was insane. He had done it anyway, praying he wouldn't get caught. But, of course he did. The grocery bags jarred onto the hardwood foyer of the small flat with an astounding sound. He was glad the bar had already been placed over the rack to settle in or he may have been startled into losing his focus and possibly crushing his larynx. All he had wanted to do was prove that his body was in its greatest shape ever, even better than when he was 20 years younger.

He slid down the sweaty bench and sat up just in time to face her protruding, pregnant belly.

"You no train yourself," she said in her thick Bosnian accent, pointing her long red fingernail.

Though her huge belly eventually blocked his view of her finger, he knew her well enough to know it was still in action.

"What?" He feigned ignorance.

"You know what I say. Trainer said no. No by yourself. You kill you," Natasha said as her belly pushed him back into a prone position. He smiled up at her reddened face as genuine anger spread across it.

"No laugh me. Not funny. I come home. You dead," she said, shaking her head whose hair was layered with multiple colors since he would no longer let her dye it. As she began to walk away, he caught her hand, and then he sat back up and pulled her into his lap.

"Oooh, scared of you," Lazarus kissed her on her forehead. "I promise. No more weightlifting alone. You are right, that was pretty stupid of me. But I survived. See?" He held up his big, muscular arms and flexed. "I'm in good shape, no?"

She squeezed his bare upper right arm and smiled, then put her hand over her mouth and nose. "You stink. Take shower."

Lazarus lifted his arms and smelled under each one.

"I've been very active today," he said, lifting her up to her feet. "I ran seven miles this morning. I was going to run ten, but I realized I was getting short on time."

"Oh, so you run seven and then try kill you?" Natasha said as she went back to the bags whose contents were half-spilled all over the floor.

Lazarus ran over and scooped up the groceries carrying them into their little kitchenette.

"Wow, woman. How many groceries did you buy? You bought enough to feed an army. Are you sure there's only one baby in there? That tummy is awfully big." He stepped back and examined her with his dark hazel eyes. "And awfully low. I think you have dropped, Nat."

"No be silly," Natasha answered as she smoothed the yellow tunic over her belly. The trip to the grocery store had been more taxing than usual. Her legs were feeling as if rocks were tied around her ankles. Her body's energy was ebbing and spiking simultaneously. One minute she was tired and the other she was ready to conquer the world.

"Ah, are you sure about your due date? I mean, I would hate to be out of the country when your little brat arrives."

"No call my baby brat. You no know him. He good baby," she said, putting the groceries away.

"Son," Lazarus said, using his favorite nickname for almost anyone he spoke to, "I will call that baby 'brat' and whatever else I want to call him because he is not going to help but be a brat if I am around."

"No make my baby brat."

"I am going to spoil that little booger, make him bratty, and baaad," Lazarus laughed.

"No bad. No bad. Stop talking 'bout my baby and go shower. Leave clothes," she ordered.

Lazarus stopped at the bedroom door and began to peel out of his clothes. They did reek. He rubbed his hands through his long hair and realized it was as drenched as the rest of him. As he leaned over to pick up his clothes, she stepped into his space and put her arms around him.

"I thought I smelled," he hugged her back.

"You leave me. No want you leave me," she said, burying her head into his chest.

"Nat, I will be back. I will only be gone for a week. It will fly by fast. I promise."

"What if she no let you come back. What if she say no leave her? You stay?" Natasha stepped back and let her hand run down his warm, wet chest. He was a beautiful man, no one like she had ever seen before and he was even more beautiful now that he was healthy again. She had envisioned him as a work of fine art the first time she had seen him in his hospital bed only eighteen months ago. Most people probably only saw him as a long skeleton lying in that bed unable to lift his hand to get a cup of water, but she saw a magnificent sculpture moving in slow motion.

Lazarus took her hand and kissed it. He started to back into the bedroom when she ran into his arms again.

"She take one look at how big your tree trunks are and won't let you go. I know this. You leave me for good," Natasha said, fighting back tears. She knew she had no right to this man, but she claimed him, nevertheless.

"I need to get dressed. I don't want to miss my flight. Stop worrying, Nat. I will be back. I promise," Lazarus said, blowing her a kiss.

Natasha stood at the end of the kitchen counter watching him as he closed the door. Here he was fully nude in front of her, but he still closed doors for privacy. That made her smile behind her tears. She noticed the picture of the woman with the head of massive curls staring at her from the windowsill and wondered if the woman knew about all the scars or even the surgeries, since she had never once come to visit him. If it hadn't been for her, Natasha, he would have died alone in a foreign country. Nothing could be worse, she thought.

Natasha walked over to the windowsill and stared at the row of pictures, all of them surrounding the curly-headed one. There were kids of all ages, but she could tell that some of them were the same people just at different stages of their lives. There were men, too, but the curly-headed one was the only woman.

Natasha looked back at the door as she dared pick up the hefty picture frame. He never talked about any of these people, not with her. All of them appeared to be of different ethnicities. She still wasn't sure what Lazarus was; whenever she asked, he would just say "human." A burning sensation ran through her fingers as she held the woman and stared into her eyes. It was as if the Curly One screamed at her to put her down. She did just that and walked away from those piercing eyes as she looked back over her shoulder. The woman frightened her, not only with her beauty, but with the intensity she displayed in those devilish green eyes.

After throwing together a healthy bowl of stir-fry with bits of chicken, his favorite, Natasha opened the bedroom door to find him moisturizing his body like a vain woman. He even had his own special oils made. Said the recipe for those oils was a family secret. All she knew was that the concoction made him smell delicious and sexy.

"Don't miss raindrops on back," she said as she picked up the bottle of mixed oils he used on his long physique. She sniffed the bottle. The smell triggered a memory, but she wasn't sure what it was. She had smelled this concoction a million times because that was what Lazarus used every day. But today she breathed it in deeply. Who else did this smell like?

"Go ahead," he turned his nude back to her and let her gently massage the raindrops on the back of his torso; on his front, he had similar scars that looked more like leaves blowing around bare-limbed tree trunks. She wondered what had happened to him. How did he get so many of them? He had hundreds of these little keloid scars.

"Want to make love?" Natasha loved the feel of his body under her hand.

"And chase that baby out? Heck, no. I'm good."

"It's been awhile. Long time. You no touch me. You 'fraid of my baby boy?"

"Yes. I am," Lazarus laughed as he finished getting dressed. She watched him slide into a pair of slacks. He never wore slacks. He was a hard-pressed jeans and t-shirt man.

"You dress up."

"I am going straight to a board meeting. Gotta look the part, don't I?"

"What board meeting?"

"A board is a group of people that oversees other people who run a company. The board meets to hear reports from them. I haven't been to a meeting in two years. Now they are demanding that I show my face or get kicked off the roster. So, I go to meeting."

"Is she on board?"

Lazarus grabbed a small piece of luggage and an armload of clothes as he walked out to the small living area. She noticed how meticulously he packed everything in it, wordlessly. He was the neatest man she had ever seen, but she hated that belt he was packing, the one with the crazy looking belt buckle he said he bought in Germany.

"You eat lunch, get cold."

"Lunch, you mean breakfast." He looked at his watch.

"You miss lunch on plane," she said.

"They will feed me." Lazarus looked at the two plates on the counter loaded with food. "Okay, I will eat lunch." As he was passing the windowsill, he stopped and adjusted the Curly One's picture frame. Natasha's heart stopped. How did he know she had been moved?

"What are you going to do while I'm gone? Just feed bratty boy?" He asked, thinking of all the food she had just hauled in.

"I go see my sister," she whispered, hoping he didn't hear her response.

"You what?"

"Go see my sister," she answered.

"No, no. We had that conversation already. You stay here or in the neighborhood or on this side of London. You no go to the Badlands. You stay away from your sister."

"I no hear from her. She could be sick. Could be dead," Natasha pleaded. "I have to go see her. And stop calling my home Badlands. You said you take me see her last week, then this week. Now you go. So I go. I don't need be here to fix your meals or clean up after you. Or make you behave. No kill yourself," she said pointing to the workbench that he still had to fold up and put away.

"No. But, you don't go to see your sister without me. I promise I will take you the day after I get back. I swear. You stay away from your sister."

"My sister need me. You no know what family means. You have no family."

Lazarus played with the bland food on his plate. He didn't know if it was the progressing pregnancy that was causing the sudden interest, but Natasha was getting more and more curious about the pictures on the windowsill and more and more obsessed with him. For her own safety, and for his own secure mind, she would never know about his life before London, not from him. Now she was insisting on visiting her crackhead sister. What next?

"Nat, your sister is in her own world. A world that is harmful to you and your baby," he said as he pushed the plate away and stood up. "I can't stop you from associating with her, but I can stop you from living here. You have to make a choice. You wouldn't be sitting here about to burst from being raped, if you had listened to me back then. You can't help a crack addict and you can't circumvent old pimps. If he gets wind you're anywhere in the vicinity, he is either going to kill you or fold you back into the stable. Next time he won't just rape you. Don't you get that?"

"He no even there no more. My friend told me he gone to America."

"Your friend? Are you telling me you are still in touch with those people? You promised me you would keep your distance. I have told you this on more than one occasion, I do not want that type of drama on my doorstep."

"I no tell them where I am. I just try to see who see my sister, if she okay."

"I know you love your sister, Nat. But, the last time we saw her, she was too far gone to care about you. Let her go."

"I love her. She only family me and baby have. You can't take her from me."

"Fine. Fine." Lazarus slid into a suit jacket. "Go live with her."

"No, Lazzie, don't say that." Nat ran into his arms. He kissed the top of her head.

"Natasha Kurjak, I want only what's best for you, but I can't have you here melting down while I'm gone. Stay away from your sister. Go to the movies, go shopping. Eat all this food you just bought. Keep your mind on a healthy baby. When I get back…."

"I know you take me see her. I promise, I promise to stay away from her. But I still call her to see if she answers."

"I don't believe that's a good idea either. Just keep your distance until I get back." Lazarus let her go and grabbed his bag, turning around he saw her hands positioned in the small of her back.

"No crossing your fingers behind your back. I'm taller than you, I can see down there. Don't make me promises you are not going to keep. Seriously, stay away from her. And, don't bring her here, if that's why all the food."

"But, she could be somewhere starving to death. She forget eat."

"She survives, trust me." Lazarus backed out of the door. "Will you be here when I get back or are you moving out?"

"Stop it. Go." Natasha waved at him, wanting to tackle him and chain him to the bed.

"What if I take you to a hotel down near Buckingham? You can explore the scenery, eat that nasty pudding and stuff down there. Relax," Lazarus said, standing in the doorway. Time was short, he had to get to Heathrow, but for some reason, he didn't want to leave her. If only she had a passport. He was going to have to talk to Micah again to see what was taking so doggone long with that.

"No, go, Lazzie. I promise to behave. You promise to come back."

"I will come back." Lazarus pushed her hair behind her ear and gave her a short kiss on the lips. He didn't know how he was going to explain her to Kali, but he had no plans to abandon her. She was the only reason he was returning to Europe. That other business that brought him over here was done. He no longer cared. All he wanted now was his family.

CHAPTER FOUR

LAZARUS BEFORE LONDON

IT SEEMED AS though time had no beginning or end. He knew it wasn't going to be easy finding Redd's second husband, that is, if they were really married. But, the only lead he had was that she had lived in Munich, the same place she had been stranded in before they were divorced. He still wasn't clear on what had happened there, and now there was no one who could tell him the truth. They were all dead and, so far, his family was still safe. But, this second husband thing was nagging him and Micah. Somebody other than Asa had tried to tie him to two murders he did commit, but would never have been suspected of, and that someone had to have been close to Redd. He was sure of it. Who else would have carefully placed a book bag with cash at the waterfall where he had murdered Brady, his old friend and Redd's accomplice.

And how did a prison identification badge with his fingerprint conveniently get discovered at the crime scene where he had murdered Scully, the security guard who had helped him with his contraband business before turning on him for profit? Asa could have been responsible for the latter, but not the first one. Again, everyone who had wanted him dead was accounted for, except one. All of them now resided underground, but most likely not this one, he was still above ground. That made Ashton nervous. Who was he? Or she? Was he done now that Redd was no longer here? His gut said no.

Micah had hired an interpreter and investigator to help him as soon as he had arrived in Munich. They met in an outdoor beer café on a very busy, cobble-stoned street near the university in Munich. At first, he was shocked. She was someone he had not expected to even find in Germany. The woman was a tall, thin-framed woman of Nigerian descent with almost blue-black skin. He smiled, she was too stunning to be working as an investigator.

"I speak five languages fluently," the woman said as she extended her hand and smiled back. The shock on his face must have been obvious. "You are Lazarus Smith?" The woman pulled at a chair as Lazarus jumped up to pull it out for her.

"Yes, yes," Lazarus said a bit sheepishly. He chided himself for thinking of her soft, willowy silhouette and laughing at himself for not expecting anything but a German bulldog of sorts.

"You can call me, ChiChi. I won't bother you with the rest of my name," she said leaning forward on the table. "Where do we begin, Mr. Smith?"

That had been the on the second day he arrived. The first day there he had slept in. One, he had been exhausted by the trip, two, by the goodbyes, and three, something was wrong with his internal plumbing. He wasn't feeling well, not at all.

As he sat there discussing his needs with ChiChi, he began to feel feverish. He wiped his forehead with the back of his hand, surprised by how wet the perspiration was, but he kept talking and ChiChi kept making notes.

"Are you well?" ChiChi asked, noticing that Lazarus was beginning to pale. "Would you like medical care?"

"No, I just need to get some fresh foods, fresh vegetables and such. Can you show me where to shop?" Lazarus answered hoping this feeling could be attributed to his near lack of food for the last few days. He did have an apple this morning, but then he began to wonder about the water he had washed it with.

"Come, let's get you settled properly," ChiChi put her portfolio in her bag and then got up. She put her arm around him as he didn't appear to be too steady. "You need a doctor. Come, let's go back to your hotel. I will call someone."

That was the last thing Lazarus remembered until he awakened in a hospital bed listening to the fluid conversation in German above him. What were they saying? His eyes tried to focus on one of the people, and they latched onto ChiChi in a light blue sweater. Something's wrong, he thought. Wasn't she wearing a silvery thing with straps at the restaurant? He sucked in air, startled as he tried to move his arms. They had been restrained.

ChiChi noticed him and rushed to his side.

"You were delirious with infection. They had to restrain you. You kept screaming you didn't want a colostomy bag."

"Bag?" Lazarus tried to sit up, but couldn't. "What the hell?"

"The nurse has gone to get a doctor to explain everything. It appears you are very ill. I brought you here to Martha-Maria Methodist Hospital. I have a friend from America here. I will call him, too. We want to make sure you are well."

"I was fine when I got on that plane," Lazarus said, lying. He hadn't felt right in the last few weeks. He knew something was wrong, but he had convinced himself that he didn't have the time for that.

"It's okay," ChiChi patted him on the arm. "While you were resting, I did a little research. There are no electronic records of Redd Sperling's other marriage. I have hired a few people to research the hard copy records. But, I did find someone who may have known them as a couple. I can't see him until Saturday though. He's incarcerated at Toytown. I had to get special permission and an appointment to visit him since I am not a relative or legal counsel. But, I was told by a woman at the courthouse that she used to see the couple all the time and then she mentioned who she used to see them with. It turns out this man was involved in the sex trafficking trade years ago. I looked him up and he's serving a life sentence for murdering a few of his girls. Does that sound like the kind of man she would hang with?"

Lazarus was still processing the word *'resting.'* "How long have I been in the hospital?"

"Two days," a man in a pair of scrubs walked up behind ChiChi and answered. "As you can see we have been feeding you intravenously. We all know you are very adamant about no colostomy bag." The doctor laughed. "Honestly, Mr. uh Smith," he said, double checking the medical record. "You need a whole new set of works. My recommendation is this: that we get you well enough to get back to the United States and get a transplant done stomach, intestines, the whole GI tract. I don't know who pieced you together, but the job was only a temporary fix. Do you understand?"

Lazarus nodded his head, yes, but he wasn't ready to go home just yet. He had come here for a purpose.

Just like in the States, they wanted to discharge Lazarus from the hospital as quickly as they could, but he was experiencing a dilemma. What was he going to tell his wife, his brother? How could he go back not knowing what they were faced with? So, he made a deal with ChiChi's doctor friend and they shipped him to London to a doctor he knew who would perform the transplant. All of this had happened within two weeks of arriving in Europe. He saw ChiChi one more time but, for the life of him, he couldn't remember a word she had said. Then it was too late. By the time he was able to look her up again, he'd found that she had been murdered. Though he had no proof, he knew it had something to do with what she had found in Munich. It was then when his life became a series of freeze-frames. For the first time in his life, making decisions became hard. He wanted his family safe, but the gripping fear that his presence among them would cause them harm went into overdrive. He stopped calling Kali. He tried not to call any of them. He wanted them to forget him.

By this time, Natasha had come into his life and it was as if the Universe was supporting him in his decision to break clean from his old life. Telling him it was okay to accept that he was no longer Ashton and that it was better that his family live in peace and security without him. Though a small nugget kept tugging at his heart, he tried to focus on a healthy Lazarus and the new woman in his life. That was the decision he regretted the most.

CHAPTER FIVE

NO SOONER HAD Lazarus stepped onto the street, Natasha's phone rang. She looked at it excitedly.

"Marja, where you been? I been call you every day for over week. You scare me."

"Not scare you enough," a male voice on the other end of the line said. "You have a choice. Either you come to me or I come to you. I bet boyfriend wouldn't like it if I come to you. I know his type. He could double back any minute."

"How you know?"

"Jocko knows everything. You knew that, didn't you? Come on. I know your boyfriend just stepped into a cab. Now all you have to do is go downstairs and catch a cab yourself. You can do that for me, can't you love?"

"How you find me? Where Marja?"

"You don't think I know your address? I sent you to him, remember? I knew where he was then and I know where he is now. I know everything. Marja, say hi to Natasha," said the harsh voice as Natasha heard a lot of scratching noises in the background.

"Natasha." The slur in her sister's voice was obvious.

"Marja," Natasha called, but got no response.

"What you do her?" Natasha paced in front of the counter looking down at the dirty dishes sitting there.

"I will do nothing to her, if you come here. You don't show up in the next two hours… two hours Natasha… No show. Well, no sister," the voice said as the phone went silent.

Natasha looked at her watch and looked at the dishes. It wouldn't take two hours to get there and she needed to think. What did Jocko want? She started crying as she put the food away quickly. Jittering with nervousness, she scraped the dishes and threw them in the dishwasher.

She knew what he wanted. He wanted the baby. She touched her belly. Lazarus was right, she had dropped. Somehow Jocko knew that, too.

Natasha checked her watch again. It had only taken fifteen minutes to clean up and her hands had been shaking through the entire process. Maybe she could call Lazarus and have him double back the way Jocko said he might. Then he could save her like he did before. Natasha grabbed her bag and marched down the stairs slower than any of the slugs she used to torture with salt as a kid. When she reached the sidewalk, she unwillingly lifted her arm to hail a cab.

She started to giggle anxiously after getting into the cab, because the radio was playing a Bob Marley song telling her not to worry. If only she could believe that. She settled in and gave the cab driver the address in Brixton. He gave her an odd look as if wondering why someone from this beautiful neighborhood would want to go to Brixton, let alone the neighborhood where her sister lived. For a moment, she thought the little dark man was going to refuse her. Instead, he flipped on the counter and sped into traffic.

She checked her wallet to make sure she had enough for the hour trip and began to cry as she saw that her wallet was bulging. Lazarus had struck again. He was always surprising her, putting extra money in her wallet. He had already given her a large wad of bills the night before. Now there were more. Who was he, she wondered? Why was Jocko so fixated on Lazarus? There had never been any unsavory people or criminal activity that she was aware of around him. He wasn't a pimp or a drug dealer like Jocko. Heck, all he did was run and exercise, and take a few phone calls. Those phone calls were always private though. If someone called while she was around, he would leave the flat.

She had followed him one day. He had only gone to sit in his car to talk. Sometimes, when she would walk into the flat unannounced, he would shorten his phone call. She had not once heard him utter anyone else's name, other than hers, as an acquaintance. All she knew about her friend and employer was that he was kind and generous with a horrifically scarred upper torso. Other than that, she knew he cherished those pictures on the windowsill. He had even stopped on his way out of the door earlier and looked directly at those pictures.

"Are you alright, Miss?" the cab driver asked in a Jamaican-British accent, noticing Natasha was rubbing her belly as if she was in distress. "Need hospital?"

"No," Natasha said through a few sniffles. "I'm just having hormone issues, I think." The sniffles turned to a torrent of tears.

"Do you want me to pull over?"

"No, I don't want be late. Thank you. Keep driving."

Natasha pulled out tissues and began to clean up. She began to think about the first time she had met Lazarus and why they had even crossed paths.

"Where are you going?" a nurse asked. Natasha was doing the best she could to make her way to the intensive care area where Jocko had told her to go meet this man. Every nerve in her body shattered with pain with each step she took, especially the ones in her face where he had landed several blows hard enough to break both her nose and her jawbone. She could barely see beyond the gauze on her face.

"I go see friend," she spoke awkwardly between the appliances on her face and kept moving, holding unsteadily onto her IV stand for support.

"One, you just don't walk up on this hallway, and two, looks like you need to be in one of these beds."

"My friend need me. I need him." Natasha kept moving until the nurse blocked her with her entire body.

"Now, Miss, I don't think it would be a good idea."

"Please. I need see him," Natasha said, not lying. Jocko had beat her and delivered her to the emergency unit of King's College Hospital where this man was staying.

"What's his name?" The nurse reached over and looked at Natasha's plastic arm band.

"His name Lazarus. Lazarus Smith. From America." Natasha tried to hold her head up high, but it was weighing heavily with each shooting pain. She needed to sit down, preferably next to the bed of this Lazarus Smith.

"Oh," the nurse answered, looking back down the hall.

"Lazarus isn't doing too well. And since no one else has been to visit him, I guess you can go. Maybe you will give him something to hold onto." The nurse smiled a little. "Let me help you. Stay here. You need a wheelchair yourself."

The nurse wheeled Natasha into the small room. It was quiet except for the hum of machines attached to the man. He lay there like a polished sculpture surrounded by lots of hair, his eyes closed.

"Closer," Natasha said. She wanted to get close enough to see if his body was as cool and hard as it looked. The nurse complied until Natasha's face was near Lazarus's.

"I okay now," Natasha said, lifting her hand to touch his face. He opened his

eyes and they stared at each other.

"I will leave you two. Push the button, if you need anything." The nurse backed out of the room.

"You okay now," Natasha said stroking his face. "You okay now. Natasha here to take care you," she said and saw his eyes well with tears.

He whispered, "Water, please."

"You sure you drink water?" She asked, afraid she would break him if she touched him too hard.

"Yes," he whispered, nodding toward the pink pitcher and cup that sat on the tray next to him.

Natasha found a straw and stuck it into the cup, though it was way too long. She bent it and put it to his lips. He took two sips and sighed, "Thank you."

That's how their friendship had begun. She took that stroll down the hall several times a day until they had to release her. Then, she had camped out in a nearby alley overnight, washed up in the hospital's public bathroom every morning, and visited him until he was finally released. Even though she would have done it anyway because he intrigued her, she did it, too, because she had no choice in the matter.

Every other day or so, her sister would visit her in her hospital room, or in the hospital lobby after she had been released, to ask for a report on this man. She had never asked Marja why. She knew her sister was following Jocko's instructions just like she was. It didn't matter. In the back of her mind, she worried for her sister and increasingly worried for Lazarus, but she was developing a strong attachment to him. The man was smart and kind. And, he was very giving, especially that. He had already given her all kinds of things.

One day, before she had been released, as she braided his hair into two long, thick braids, one on each side of his face, he had reached up and touched her hair.

"You need to wash it, you know. It smells a bit, and I bet when it's clean, it's as beautiful as the rest of you."

Natasha had never been so embarrassed. She went straight to her room and found the shampoo supplied by the hospital. She asked the nurse for fresh gowns and she jumped into the shower, scrubbing her hair and her body. She didn't want to smell bad when she was near him. When she limped out of the bathroom, she saw clothes on the bed. She found new underwear and a pair of sweats she could use as pajamas. Hurriedly, she put them on before someone came to claim them. Then she found the flimsy comb in the hospital drawer and began to comb her hair.

The nurse came in as Natasha was sitting on the bed. "Oh, I forgot these. He had me pick these things up for you, I hope everything fits," the nurse said as she sat a pair of brand new flip flops on the bed. They were leather and expensive looking. Natasha kicked off the paper-like slippers on her feet and slid her toes through the thongs.

"They fit," she exclaimed.

"Good. I will let him know." The nurse closed the door.

"I let him know. I thank him," Natasha slid off the bed and grabbed her cane. She was getting stronger and better every day. That scared her. The last thing she wanted to do was to go back to her life with Jocko. What she wanted now more than anything was a life with this man, Lazarus Smith. That's when she decided she would never leave his side. No matter what the cost.

CHAPTER SIX

LAZARUS WAS DISAPPOINTED that his flight was delayed once again and for two more hours. He had been sitting at the airport most of the day. At this rate, he was going to miss the board meeting. But, maybe, just maybe he would be able to make Katie's play. Per all reports, the weather in the states had not improved and all flights were either being re-directed or not allowed to land at JFK at all. He had even checked to see if there were any open flights directly into Philadelphia, but there were none. Everything was booked and everybody was waiting.

With nothing else to do, he decided to go to one of the Premium lounges for a drink and to see if he could relax a bit. He had a feeling it was going to be longer than another two hours before he left England.

Lazarus stepped up to the bar and slid onto a stool beside a woman in a flight attendant's uniform. He did a double-take, she looked very familiar. Her hair was a nappy, dry-looking blonde nest pulled up into a bun. She was already nursing a drink; from the look on her face that wasn't her first. He signaled the bartender who sped by him more than once.

"Let me," the woman said. She held up a finger and the bartender responded immediately. She pointed to Lazarus.

"Sorry, it's crazy in here today," the bartender said. "I was coming back. What will you have?"

"A scotch on the rocks. No, just scotch, don't water it down," Lazarus said, then pointing to the lady. "Get her another one, too."

"Thank you." The woman smiled and it struck Lazarus that he did know this woman from somewhere, but there was no use in trying to figure out from where. She would probably only know him as Ashton, the man who was supposed to be rotting in a grave in South Jersey.

"You look darn familiar," the woman said shocking him.

"I get that a lot," Lazarus answered. He already knew he favored his old self a little too much these days. The plastic surgeries done on him by his brother and the doctor in Colorado had only been done to fix the scars on his face after the attack. At the time, he had lost so much weight from having his stomach torn apart and being nearly starved to death by his kidnappers that he had looked nothing like himself. Kali had taken to calling him her stick man. Because of that it had been an easy transition into Lazarus Smith, his new alter ego. But now he was healthy again. His face was fuller and, though his jaw had been reset, his face had been skewed only a little bit. Even he recognized Ashton again in the mirror. That was one of the reasons he had grown the full beard that obviously wasn't doing enough to hide who he was from this woman.

Going back was going to be a risk to him and to his family. He could feel it in his bones, but he couldn't stay away forever. He thought about his children and how they were moving on with their lives without him. It wasn't fair to them and definitely not fair to Kali. But, he dreaded it. He dreaded having to set foot on that airplane. His mere presence was going to get his buddy, Troy, investigating again, asking questions, probing for things that needed to stay buried. How was he going to call off Troy?

"Well, maybe it's because you look a lot like someone that used to be in the news a lot," the woman said, gaining his attention again.

"Really, who?"

"He was this rich guy, married to this big-time model. Everybody used to think they were the perfect couple. But, he dumped her and she went crazy. I mean really crazy," the woman said as she lifted the glass to her cracking, pink-stained lips. "I don't think people knew much about that part. But, I did. I used to be sort of friends with her."

"Sort of friends?" Lazarus looked at the woman closely. Who was she? He should know since she was referring to his ex-wife, Redd, the woman responsible for his current predicament. It was obvious she knew Redd, since she mentioned she had gone crazy. The press didn't know about that. The worst thing that the news had reported was that she was washed-up as a supermodel. Back then, it was an age thing. Supposedly, she was being overlooked for jobs because she was starting to look older. Today, it would have been a different story. She would probably still be working, that is, if she hadn't gone bonkers, he thought.

"Well, in the early days, she and her husband used to fly a lot, especially on my route. I used to help her make sure she was on my flight or I would make sure I was on a flight she chose."

"Yeah," Lazarus stopped himself from saying more. He

remembered her. She was one of Redd's old friends. The woman had even spent nights in their home when she laid over in New York.

"My name is Nancy," the woman offered her hand.

"Lazarus," he said taking her hand. But, he noticed her eyes had a sad, defeated look in them.

"What's wrong, Nancy? Been waiting around here too long today?"

"No," Nancy said taking the drink from the bartender and then gesturing toward one of the tables that had just freed up. Lazarus grabbed his drink and followed her as he signaled the bartender where they were going.

Both dropped their bags and took the small table next to the window where they had a great view of all the planes lined up.

"This is my last flight as an attendant," Nancy said, as she adjusted her seat. Then she took a big sip of her scotch.

"Retiring?"

"Yes, it's been over twenty years in the skies. And, too many years in and out of Europe. I can't wait to get away from this place. Get home. Settle down. Maybe adopt a kid or something," she snickered after the word 'kid.'

"Are you married?" Lazarus had no idea why he asked that. A woman didn't need a husband to raise a kid. Kali certainly didn't and she was raising five.

"Hell, no," Nancy answered laughing. "No man in this world could deal with me or my schedule. I was always on the go. I could never be pinned down in one place. I liked traveling and partying too much. Now, I am too old to party and too tired to travel. I have seen the whole world. All I want to see now is a quaint little backyard in a quaint little house somewhere in South Jersey. Somewhere I can drive to the beach in about a half hour, come home and plant some tomatoes. Do the things my parents used to do when I was younger that sounded so boring. Now I crave it."

"Well, I wish you luck." Lazarus drained his drink. "You think you could get your friend over here again?"

"Sure." Nancy raised her hand. "It helps to be a regular in here."

The bartender sent over a couple of more drinks and the two of them stared for a while at the dormant planes.

"It's going to be longer than they are saying, you know. I talked to a friend in New York. The storm hitting the east coast is pretty bad. It's coming up from the south with hurricane force winds and torrential rains. She said they don't expect it to die down until tomorrow morning. The worst of it was getting ready to hit New York. It was pouring down heavy already in the Philly area according to her. Those planes out there are just going to keep stacking up. They don't fly into winds like that."

"Damn." Lazarus shook his head. "I'm going to miss the meeting that I was flying out there for."

"Well, you can either cancel the meeting or cancel your trip," Nancy said.

"I still need to go. Haven't been back in over two years. Can't avoid it any longer."

"Wow, sounds like you are dreading going back."

"No, I just have to pay the piper. Not looking forward to that. But, on the other hand, I'm a little excited." Lazarus flung the whole scotch down his throat at the thought of the potential consequences for going back at all. He had considered fading completely out of his family's lives. But, it was those haunting pictures on the windowsill that kept calling him home.

"Why aren't you dreading going back? I mean, I like it over here."

"I used to like it. Then I got mixed up in some things," her voice trailed off. "Well, I think I will be safer at home, better off at home."

"Some things?"

"You know, I was young once and, like I said, I liked to party. Started partying with the wrong crowd, and well, I have this creepy feeling coming back. I just want out of here." She looked around apprehensively. "I'm kind of glad you started talking to me, you know. I was feeling a bit out there. Kind of alone. Maybe, it's because I'm finally leaving this place. I tried not to come back. Hadn't been over here in years and the company asked me to take this route for my last few months. Boy, it was creepy coming back, especially going to Munich. I hate that place. But everything's been quiet. Nothing happened or anything. It's just that…I will be relieved to get home."

"Can I ask?" Lazarus waved to the waiter who had brought over their drinks. "Maybe we need food after all this drinking."

"Yeah, wouldn't be nice to take my last flight drunk, now would it?" Nancy muttered. Her face had changed over the last few minutes.

"You look a lot like her first husband, you know? And, you sort of remind me of him, too."

"What?" Lazarus took the menu from the waitress.

"You made me feel calmer as soon as you walked over and sat next to me. I think he used to calm her down, whether she would admit it or not. I know, I know she treated him like shit most of the time, but he was what anchored her. Not that spineless twin brother of his. She only used him because she could manipulate him. They were so opposite," she sighed.

"Because I look like him, I am calming you down?" Lazarus smiled. He had never thought of himself as having a calming effect on anyone, especially as Ashton.

"Maybe. Maybe I am just being little anxious. You see, I was in a Tesco the other day and I saw someone that reminded me of someone else. It wasn't him, just like you aren't Redd's ex-husband, but everything about him worried me. It was like bad voodoo Deja Vu. Ever since then, I just wanted to get out and stay out."

"Who did you think he was?"

"Well," Nancy looked behind her and around very carefully, "as I said, Redd and I were friends, of sorts. After that gorgeous hunk left her she started going a little sideways. Not only that, she was starting to lose out on those big modeling contracts. Their excuses were references to her age, but I think she was hitting the bottle a little too hard. She never wanted to admit it, but I think she actually loved the one she lost. She always claimed she was in love with the goofball photographer brother that she dragged around. But her heart was with Ashton. It really was because when he left, well, she just started going downhill fast. And then, there was this guy. We both met him on a flight to Munich. Called himself Jocko."

For a moment, it was as if his eardrums were about to explode from a sudden lack of air, the woman's lips were moving, but he failed to hear her for a few seconds. He remembered ChiChi's full lips as she had leaned over his hospital bed at King's College during her only visit. *The inmate had said Redd's husband had a nickname that started with a J. It was a nickname that was taken from a deejay in America. He had used it as his deejay name on a US military base in Germany and it stuck when he came to work with roving parties in Germany. I am working on matching the deejay with a name. The old man didn't think he had ever been arrested, not in Germany, but the military should have something. I will let you know as soon as I can."*

As his eardrums kept pounding, all he could hear was Jocko. Jocko was also the name of Natasha's old pimp, the one who had raped her and gotten her pregnant. There couldn't be that many Jockos in the world. There had been only one prominent one, the deejay he grew up listening to on WDAS in Philly. Now there was another one? In Munich? Had to be connected to Philly, his home. He shook his head slightly to get his full hearing back and tried to focus on what Nancy was saying. There weren't that many coincidences in the world either.

"We thought it all sound so exciting, these parties he was talking about. So, we agreed to meet him at one. And that changed our lives. The first time…" Nancy stopped talking and took another sip of her scotch, "the first time was right before Redd's husband had her served with the divorce papers. We got stuck over there. I almost lost my job. I had to come up with some fake medical records to save my ass. I got out before she did though. Somehow, Jocko's people had gotten their hands on our passports. Thank God, the airlines had a copy of mine. They were trapped, Redd and her husband's twin brother. He was supposed to be her manager, but he didn't act like a manager. Asa let her get away with everything and gave into anything. That's how he ended up there, too."

"Trapped?"

"Yeah, trapped in the circuit and no way to get out of Munich." Nancy leaned over and whispered, "The sex circuit, I mean. In Munich, they have these wild sex parties that travel. Beautiful women, lots of drugs, lots of filthy rich guys, some corporates, some thugs. It's a big thing. This guy, Jocko, was one of the higher ups in the organization that ran these things. I heard they were busted a few years ago and finally shut down. But, I know for a fact, that some of those girls didn't make it out alive."

"So why are you still afraid, if that was years ago?"

"From what I heard, Jocko was still busy quieting anybody involved with his side of the business. You won't believe this, but when I heard Redd died down in South America, the first person to come to mind was Jocko."

"You think he followed her down there to kill her?" Lazarus asked, knowing full well that he was the one who had committed that murder, or at least, set it up to happen.

"He wouldn't have had to follow her. They were together. Somehow, some way, he lured her back into the circuit after her husband dumped her. Then, supposedly, she helped him run the damn thing. I ran into her on a flight going to New York one day and we decided to hang out, just for old times' sake. She told me she had married Jocko, of all people, and that they had a little boy. But, there was something wrong with the kid and he was confined to a hospital. She was on her way back to Philly, she said, to ask her family for money toward expenses. Apparently, after the bust, she and Jocko couldn't afford the child's health care costs outside of Germany and they wanted to go back to the States. Not only that, they didn't think he was getting the right care or something. I don't know the details, but she was concerned. Very."

"How old was the kid?"

"He was about four or five when we talked. It was only a few months later that she was dead."

"How long ago was this?" Lazarus asked, remembering the vengeance in Redd's eyes as she stabbed his torso a thousand times. Asa had tied him down and Lazarus had been too helpless to fight her off.

"About, maybe, a little over two years ago. Maybe only a month or so before her ex-husband was murdered. I guess tragedy just followed them."

"Is the kid still alive?"

"Word has it, he died about the same time she did."

"So the guy you saw, you thought it was this Jocko dude, her husband?"

"Yes, but he was much younger, so it couldn't have been him. Had that same dead look in those blue eyes though. Wouldn't be surprised if they were related. Maybe he was his brother, although by his age, I'd say a much younger brother, but definitely related or something. It was uncanny."

"Wow, that is some story. I understand why that would frighten you. But, you are going home now. Stop worrying. Let's eat."

"Aye, aye, Captain," Nancy smiled. "I never told anyone about that before. I wonder what made me open up to you?"

"Fate. My grandfather used to tell me I should have been a priest. I don't know why but people have always opened up to me about their darkest secrets" Lazarus picked up his sandwich and sighed wishing his own twin, Asa, had been one of those people. He was still having a hard time with processing Asa's desire to hurt him mortally. He had almost believed Asa had no intent of killing him the first time around, but the second time, during his resurrection, he almost didn't recognize him anymore. There had been something about his eyes that morning Asa and Redd had kidnapped him. It was almost as if he and his brother were meeting for the first time.

"There are just some things in life I have learned that we just shouldn't question," he answered absentmindedly. "Sometimes we just have to go with the flow."

CHAPTER SEVEN

"WHAT DO YOU mean he's going to miss the meeting this evening?" Kali was walking into her office with a stack of messages her assistant had handed her because she hated checking her own voice mail. She put down the stack and looked up at Micah for a response.

"Have you looked out the window? You did pay attention when Reck was driving you in, didn't you?" Micah shrugged his shoulders dismissing Kali's complaint.

"I understand it's raining, but I thought his flight was supposed to arrive in plenty of time. Didn't we take additional delays into account when we found out his flight was today and moved the meeting to 7:00?"

"You changed your mind. The meeting is still scheduled for 5:00." Micah looked at his watch. It was 4:30 pm.

"Cancel it. He has to be there. Reschedule it for another day this week. I didn't want to go through this today anyway. I'd rather be home helping Katie prepare for tomorrow night."

"Doing what? What would you have to do to help her get ready?"

"I don't know. Hair. Nails. Listen to her rehearse, maybe." Kali plopped in her chair, realizing that wasn't true. The makeup artist for the play would be doing hair and nails — all of that tomorrow. And Katie had long ago stopped rehearsing with her.

"Okay, I have nothing to do," Kali confessed. "Is he going to make it to the play?"

"Only, if the weather doesn't prohibit it. You know there will be a lot of flight catch up going on. There are a lot of people stranded everywhere," Micah said, sounding extremely formal. Kali lifted her head toward him and saw their executive assistant, Geri, walking through the door. Kali had suspected Micah had a crush on this one but, instead, he was dating that ogre, Anjuli. Kali sat back in her chair and crossed her arms.

"Better yet, he will be here Monday, Tuesday of next week, right?"

"Yes, Kali, but you can't play with people's time. I'm sure some of them are almost here."

"Three of them have already arrived and I am sure the others are closing in," Geri walked over to the desk. She was a sharp one, mentally and physically. Kali was always asking her about her shoes, her hair, and her clothes, like where and when. But, that wasn't the only thing that impressed her. Geri was almost as good as Tawny Elliott, the woman who used to be Ashton's right hand, and hers too. Elliott had even evolved into the kids' unofficial God Grandma. She had been the all-encompassing executive assistant, assisting them in every aspect of their lives, even the bad ones. Initially, Elliott had left them during the Asa impersonation era, and had decided not to return after things became normal again. On the upside, she had been introduced to Ray Rivera, the man who befriended Lazarus when he had no memory. Ray had fallen in love with Elliott, then married her and whisked her away to Colorado. Kali missed her although she still talked to her every other week or so. Thinking about her made Kali smile as she was looking forward to seeing her tomorrow. Elliott was coming to town to see Katie's play, which was probably just an excuse to see Ashton again. That woman loved Ashton like a mother. In her eyes, he could never do anything wrong.

"Make it worth their whiles. Were we planning to feed them?" Kali asked.

"Of course," Geri answered with her hands on her hips. "We could feed them better, though. I know the owner of that five-star restaurant that is opening across the street."

"It's not open yet," Micah chimed in. "How do you know it's five-star?"

Both women laughed. The chef was famous and he only launched five-star restaurants.

"No, I know it's not yet open but he's trying out chefs as we speak. Wouldn't you like to be one of their guinea pigs?"

"You think you can swing it?"

"You know I can." Geri gave Kali a wink.

"Ah, you go girl!" Kali got up and gave her a high-five. "If they aren't happy after that, give them a check for $1,000 a piece, in addition to their expenses."

"Yes, ma'am. Do you want to see the ones who have arrived?" Geri stood at the door with her hand on the doorknob. Kali was shaking her head no as she sat back down in her chair. When she noticed both Micah and Geri staring her, she nodded yes and got up.

"Five minutes."

"Ten," Geri recommended. "That's how long it will take me to get across the street and back. What's the excuse?"

"The chairman of the board is stuck in the airport in London due to weather. His calendar is full, but he will be available to reschedule anytime Monday or Tuesday. And, it's still mandatory that we all attend," Kali said, checking her makeup in the mirror on her desk.

"Got it," Geri answered as all three of them looked at their watches. "Ten minutes."

"First thing, tomorrow. Well, maybe not first thing. Let's shoot for noon to run over to see your mother, Micah," Kali said, walking past him.

"My mother? Why? I was just over there yesterday. I will go on Friday. You go. She'll like that."

"Seriously, Micah. Tell me you didn't forget. What good is that girlfriend of yours if she can't help you keep up with your mother's birthday?"

"Are you sure?" Micah asked, looking at his watch again for the date. He closed his eyes and shook his head. She is expecting us for dinner tomorrow, isn't she?"

"Not tomorrow night. The play, remember? Noon. Lunch. Stick with me."

"Yes, how could I forget? I guess you are right. We have to have lunch with her?" Micah asked as if he dreaded the idea. That struck Kali as odd. He never missed a chance to dote on his mother.

"That's right. Something wrong?"

"No," Micah answered, toying with his phone as if he expected it to ring any second.

"Good. So let's get these civil hellos over with so we can get home in time to make sure everyone is going to be ready for the play tomorrow night. You know I have to make sure, at least, that the boys know what to wear."

Micah laughed and opened the door, and then he stopped. "You go play nice. I have to get my mom a gift. Or, did you get one for me?"

"Why would I do that? I'm not your other half as you keep reminding me. Besides, you know you have to put a personal touch on your gifts for your mom. You know her better than I do. She didn't start liking me until she came down with Alzheimer's. Now she thinks I am her daughter, God forbid. I thought about waiting until this weekend so we could take all the kids over. But I know, somewhere in that warped little brain of hers, she will know that it's her day."

Micah called Kali the next morning. He wasn't quite ready to tell her about the noise-laden conversation he had just had with Lazarus who was calling him from the airport. He could only make out half the details between the noise interference on the phone and the loud announcements in the background. But, he culled enough to know he was supposed to find someone from their past.

"Where are you?" Kali said as she answered her cell. She was just getting out of the car with Reck, outside of the assisted living facility in Abington where Micah's mother lived.

"I'm running a few minutes late, but I will be there. Trust me, it won't matter what time I get there. She won't know whether it's lunch or dinner just as long as we show up."

"Don't make me sit too long by myself over here. I don't know a third of the people she talks about," she said as Reck held the building's door open for her.

"Oh, the gift," Kali pointed back toward the car. She went ahead inside, still fussing at Micah over the phone.

When the nurse let Kali into the apartment, she wasn't surprised to see Elinor Sperling sitting in her white leather, high-back chair, waiting. The woman was dressed in a pink suit with a lace pink top underneath. Her dark skin gleamed under the big matching pink hat embroidered with pearls that matched the pink-tinted pearls around her skinny little neck. Ms. Elle was still a diva. Kali had never ever seen the woman dressed down, not even in the middle of the night when she had first met her many years ago. Ms. Elle was one of those women who always spoke perfect English, even her curse words sounded proper. Everything about her exuded a natural elegance. That used to be the only thing that Kali had liked about her.

Kali and Micah had searched far and wide to find the right care for Ms. Elle because Billy, Micah's father, had just thrown her into a nursing home when Elle started going a little bonkers. Not a very good one at that. But after he died, they decided she deserved something better than a small room with a bed and a chair. They found her a snazzy assisted living apartment and hired additional, around-the-clock care. She was looking ten times better than that first time Micah had dragged Kali over to see her, pleading with her to help him, even though he knew their history. Elle had always been mean to Kali, except for that first night, when she was busy luring Kali into Jordan's nasty sex trafficking trap. But, how could she say no to Micah, her lover and her protector, and the stand-in father for her children? There wasn't anything she could deny him and she would fight anybody to protect him, including protecting him from himself and his new love interest.

"Oh my God, you even have on the shoes to match. I'm scared of you, Mama. You look beautiful this morning on your birthday," Kali said as a wide grin spread across Ms. Elle's face. The old woman reached for her and Kali reached back. Elle gave her such an eager and tight embrace that Kali thought for a moment the woman may have been grasping her for the last time.

"My baby girl," Elle said, kissing and patting Kali on the checks. "How's my baby?"

"I'm fine, Mama," Kali said, falling more easily into the role as daughter with every visit, especially since she had found out Elle had had a baby girl once. No one knew what had happened to the child. There weren't any records of her birth so, whatever the situation, it must have been hard on Ms. Elle. Kali pulled up an ottoman to sit next to the older woman, so she could touch her.

Elle loved touching her. She would first do the same thing all the Sperlings seem to do instinctively to her: they would move her rogue curl from her face and try to anchor it behind her ear. Kali smiled. She wondered when any of them would figure it out. If she didn't cut it off, it was going to do what it wanted to do whether she pinned it, slicked it, rubber banded it, or anything else, that curl would find its way right smack into the center of her eyes, just lollygagging away. It was such a part of her, she never noticed it. She figured it was akin to people who wore glasses. She wondered if they paid attention to that object on their faces.

"You look like a pretty picture. Wait, let me take one." Kali pulled out her digital camera and started snapping pictures. Elle's eyes lit up with each one. As she was about to ask Elle's caregiver to take a picture of the two of them, the doorbell rang.

"Oh, I wonder who that is," Kali feigned surprise.

"I don't know," Ms. Elle leaned away from her to get a close look at who was being let in. It was Reck with a big box in his arms.

"Oh, my, I wonder what that is?" Kali kept playing the game, but when she looked back at Ms. Elle, there was a stern, almost frightened look on the old woman's face.

"What's Jordan's little white boy doing here?" Ms. Elle yelled at Kali.

Reck was so surprised by the outburst, it looked as if he were going to drop the box. No, Kali thought for a second, it looked as if he were going to throw the box down in anger. Then Ms. Elle grabbed her attention again.

"What are you doing with Jordan's little white boy? I told all of you children to stay away from that child. He's evil. He reminds me of death," Ms. Elle ranted. "Get that little white boy out of here," she yelled.

"Mama, Mama. It's okay, Mama. He's my bodyguard. He brought your present up for me. He's not who you think he is," Kali said, trying to hug her, but Elle pulled away.

"I would know that little white boy anywhere. I know those eyes. Those eyes are dead eyes. All they see is death. GET HIM OUT OF HERE!"

"Of course, of course. Reck, I'll set this thing up. Just put it down over there. You can leave, Micah is meeting me here. He'll take me home."

Kali noticed something about Reck when she walked to the door. It was the same thing she noticed yesterday in the car: an ever-so-slight change in his demeanor or expression and here it was again. Maybe he had just taken offense for being yelled at by an old woman. But, normally, that wouldn't have caused a man like him to flinch.

"Are you alright? You know she has Alzheimer's, right? She didn't mean what she said. She thinks you are somebody else, somebody from when her boys were children, I guess."

"Do you know who she is talking about?" Reck asked, his body language more familiar to her now.

"I don't have a clue. Besides, trust me, ten minutes from now she won't even remember you were here. And if I ask her about Jordan's little white boy, she will say 'who'?" Kali snickered and Reck nodded and winked at her. He left.

"Look what I bought you, Mama," Kali marched back into the room. Elle was staring at the box as Reck backed out of the door watching the old woman.

"What is it?"

"It's one of those combo music centers, the little ones, see. You can play albums and CDs and cassettes. All kinds of stuff. You can even listen to WDAS."

"Is Jocko still on the air? I used to love listening to his show. He was the best deejay in Philly," Ms. Elle said, trying to pry herself up out of the chair. Kali went back to help her when the doorbell rang again.

"Happy Birthday, Mama," Micah walked in with a big blue box wrapped with a big pink bow in his arms.

Ms. Elle bounced a little bit and threw her arms wide open. Her heart had arrived. No one ever doubted how much she loved her son. The way she would say his name just shouted to the heavens, 'This is my baby boy and I love him so much.' Micah picked up his mama and spun her around as she happily protested.

"Are you almost, no, you can't be 79 years old? Can you? You look 50."

"Younger," Kali added. "You see how pretty she is today. Mama is all decked out."

"Mama is beautiful," Micah said, gently setting his mama back in the chair. He went back for the box he had put down on the ottoman where Kali had been sitting.

"What do you have there?" Ms. Elle tapped the box lightly.

"Go ahead. Open it," Micah urged.

Ms. Elle tugged at the big ribbon and it fell away easily. She lifted the box top and then covered her mouth in delight.

"Look, baby," she said to Kali. "Your brother brought me some albums to go with your record player. I can play music and listen to Jocko whenever I want."

"You have such a sweet boy. I know you are going to have so much fun listening to the music, Mama, but I am not sure if Jocko is still on the air," Kali laughed. She had been hoping Micah was going to stop in his office before running out for his mother's present last night.

Apparently, he hadn't gotten anything else even after he had abandoned her with the board members. As usual, she had taken care of all the details. Elle's apartment was covered in white roses. Her favorite chocolates were sitting beside her on her little table with her other favorite stuff, and now she had fifteen vintage albums from her heyday to play on her new record player. Not to mention sitting around looking pretty in a pink designer suit, shoes, and hat. Kali had bought it all. And, next to Elle's chair, was a matching purse, too.

The things Kali was always doing for his mother didn't go unnoticed. He loved her for that and more than anything it made him want Kali to be his significant other. But, he knew how things had turned out when Ashton had stolen Redd from Asa. The repercussions were still vibrating and wrecking their lives daily. He blew Kali a kiss wondering what life was going to be like after today when Ashton walked back into the penthouse, even as Lazarus.

After lunch, Ms. Elle started nodding off on them and they took it as a sign to leave. They both hugged and kissed her before leaving. The rain had finally turned from short periods of downpour to a steady drizzle.

"It's supposed to be gone by five o'clock," Micah pointed at the raindrops on the windshield.

"I wonder if that boy is in the air yet," Kali said, talking about Lazarus. "Now he is going to miss the play, too."

Micah shook his head. No matter how old they got, she always referred to him and his brothers as boys. Probably had something to do with her being in the presence of their grandfather for so long. She talked a lot like him whether she realized it or not. Ashton had once said that Jordan had imprinted on her more than he had on any of them. Kali had picked up a lot of the old man's character traits, good and bad.

"I don't know. I'm sure he would have called if he was boarding."

"Yeah, well, he's not really good at that now is he, calling?" Kali folded her arms and looked up at the breaking clouds and then squealed at the first sight of the sun. "Sunlight. Great. Maybe the theater will be packed tonight."

"Oh, it will be. Weather never stops anybody here. Not unless it's three feet of snow." They both laughed. "Not too many people are going to fight through that. Let them clear the streets first."

"Yeah, I don't like that white stuff myself. And apparently, your mom doesn't like white people, either. She went off on Reck."

"What?" Micah looked at her with surprise.

"The mother I have known all my life never had a prejudiced bone in her body. Heck, if she didn't like white people, she sure married the whitest black man she could find." Micah laughed at his own joke because his father was half-white with pale skin, gray eyes and straight hair.

"Well, she didn't like Reck, not even the sight of him. She started calling him Jordan's little white boy."

"She called him what?" Micah turned toward her so fast the car veered a little bit.

"Micah, are you okay?" Kali touched his hand which was gripping the steering wheel as if he were pushing it down into the dashboard. "She called him Jordan's little white boy," Kali repeated as Micah's hand loosened a bit.

"Are you telling me my mom called your white boy Jordan's little white boy?" Micah asked.

Kali chuckled. "Do you and your mom think alike or what?"

"There was this kid, one time," Micah began to wonder out loud. "He showed up at the penthouse right after Jordan and Ashton had moved in. He was a couple of years older than Ashton and much older than me. His name was...."

Micah could hear his brother's voice breaking up on the phone yesterday. Lazarus had said, *The only lead I have is the nickname, Jocko, like the deejay on WDAS. Remember him? When I heard it this time, it reminded me of Jack, the kid Jordan used to take care of. His name was Jack. Jack Pulaski. And he used to love to listen to Jocko, anything DAS really. But, he used to try to imitate Jocko.*"

After that, Micah had missed most of the conversation. There had been too much noise in the background. But now his mother may have given them another potential lead. Who was Reck? What did they really know about him?

"Anyway, my mother and my father didn't like the kid," he said deciding not to scare Kali by telling her about Ashton's call last evening. Not yet. He wanted her to enjoy Katie's play this evening without worrying.

"I'll have to ask Ashton about him. Ricky and Chico were even younger than me. They probably wouldn't remember much about him, either. But, he was white. That's all I remember. But..." Micah shook his head. "I don't know. Maybe, maybe we should find out where that kid is. I mean, my mother may be crazy, but she is not insane."

"Well, I am going to be insane if those kids aren't getting ready when I walk through the door."

CHAPTER EIGHT

LAZARUS SLID HIS phone into the inside pocket of his jacket. In the last three hours, he had tried to reach Natasha four times and she wasn't answering her phone. He and the friendly flight attendant had moved to a more comfortable section of the lounge area. She was slumped over in a big leather chair across from him. But, her story had made him too anxious to sleep. He started reading through some of the PDSI company documents he had been carrying around. He was going to need to sound like a board chairman — especially with his announcement so, he had better be prepared.

The reading was too dry. The numbers were not making any sense because his mind was on home and his family. He pulled out his phone again to call Micah to see if he had come up with anything on Redd's second husband. Every cell in his body was telling him it was Jack Pulaski. Still no answer; so, he decided to try Nat one more time. But, then, his phone rang.

"Well, there you are. I have been trying to reach you all damn day. I'm still at Heathrow." As he said that, Nancy's phone started ringing and she jumped up at attention. Lazarus smiled hoping she would be getting good news about the flights.

"Hello. Who am I speaking with?" asked a very heavy, British-accented man on the other end of the line.

"Excuse me." Lazarus looked at his phone to make sure he had seen Nat's name on the caller ID. "You called me. What are you doing with this phone? Who are you?"

"I am Inspector Duncan from Brixton Police Station. May I ask who you are?"

"We could keep going around in circles, Inspector, if that is who you are. Tell me, what are you doing with this phone?"

"The phone belongs to a young woman, kind of dark hair with some light strands here and there, slight build, very pregnant. She's here at King's College Hospital."

"In Brixton? What the hell is she doing down there?" As soon as Lazarus asked the question, he knew why. Nat had gone to see her sister.

"Is she alright? Did she have the baby? I told her she looked like she was close. Oh, my God, I will be right there. Tell her I am coming." Lazarus hung up the phone and began grabbing his things.

"Are you alright?" Nancy asked. She was checking her face in a compact mirror. "The flights are back on. The storm is moving out. Your flight leaves in about an hour. Mine is out in a half. Thank you for staying with me. That was the best sleep I have had in a long time."

"Glad I could help," Lazarus answered, more grateful for the news she had provided about this Jocko character. "Listen," he said as he pulled out a business card that only had a number on it. "If you continue to feel frightened once you get back to the States, call this number. I won't be the one to answer, but just say Zebra. Don't write that on this card now. Just remember to say Zebra. I have some security friends that would help you out immediately. Okay?"

Nancy nodded her head and a slight frown crossed her face. She got up out of her chair and moved close to him. He thought she was going to kiss him on the cheek.

"Are you him?" Nancy whispered. "I didn't know him well, but I know people and I just feel like you are him."

Lazarus stepped back and looked at her.

"I'm just a concerned fellow American," he smiled as he touched her chin. He walked away realizing that going home was going to open an even bigger hornet's nest. Maybe he shouldn't go back at all. It was going to be kind of hard for people who knew him even better than one of Redd's old hanging buddies not to recognize him. But, that was going to have to be put on hold a couple of more days. He tried to call Micah again as he jumped in the cab. He had already missed the board meeting and was without a doubt going to miss his oldest daughter's professional debut as an actress in her own hometown. Maybe they were all better off without him. Maybe it was fate, not getting on that plane.

Lazarus didn't know where he was supposed to be going when he arrived at the hospital. It was the same hospital where he had first met Natasha. She had helped nurse him through his second transplant surgery after the first one had failed badly. He was standing there, partly because of her. He didn't have any other choice but to be there for her.

The name, he thought, he wondered if she had named the baby already, and whether she had chosen Aaron or George. He hated the name George, but she liked it for some strange reason. But, then again, Nat was strange. He smiled imagining her talking to a baby, poor kid. His English was going to be messed up right out of the gate.

The thought of another baby boy in his world made him a little sad, no matter what his name was. It had been over two years since he had seen or touched his own little boys, whose bodies were getting them closer to manhood every day. How much they must have matured in those years.

He walked up to the information booth and asked for Natasha Kurjak. The woman searched her records and shook her head.

"Are you sure that's the name she would be registered under?"

"Yes, she just had a baby. She would be in your maternity ward."

"How do you know this?" The woman asked impatiently.

"I received a call from the police. They had brought her here."

"Then you need to check the emergency department. The two could still be there. Down the hall to your right. Follow the signs," the woman said, without looking up at him.

Lazarus followed the directions and walked up to another information desk where a gentleman was hunched over a keyboard, biting his nails and swearing at a computer screen.

"Excuse me," Lazarus interrupted his swearing. "I'm here to see Natasha Kurjak."

"Who?" The man was typing fast and switching screens. "We don't have anyone registered under that name."

"Are you serious?" For one second Lazarus thought he had been lured out of the airport, but why?

"I received a call from an Inspector Duncan, not an hour ago, telling me she was here," Lazarus said, trying not to raise too much attention. But, he was getting angry.

"Oh," the clerk said, putting his hand over his mouth. He then stood up and looked around the room. He held his hand up and waved to someone. Lazarus watched as a short man in a crumpled dark suit began walking towards them. The man took out a small pad, a pen and something else as he walked toward him.

"Hello, sir. I'm Inspector Duncan," he said flashing his badge, putting it in his pocket and then removing Natasha's pink metallic phone from another pocket.

"Do you recognize this?"

"It's Natasha's phone."

"Natasha," the Inspector started writing. "A last name?"

"Kurjack. Where is she? What's going on?"

The inspector stepped around him and leaned over to the clerk. "Is there a room or someplace this gentleman, Mr. Er…?"

"Smith, Lazarus Smith," he said, feeling an arrow zipping into his torso, penetrating deeply. He told her not to come down here, he thought with dread.

"Over there," the clerk pointed to a wooden door with a narrow strip of a frosted glass pane in the middle.

"Let's talk in there," the inspector said. He opened the door and let Lazarus go in first. He stood by the door. He doesn't want to get trapped in here with me, he thought. The man's hand was still on the door knob as he pointed to the visitor's chair, making no effort to sit behind the desk himself in that little room.

"Why do I get the feeling you are not about to give me any good news? Did the baby make it? Is she okay? Why doesn't she have her phone? She had a baby; she didn't lose her voice, right?" Lazarus tried to stop his left knee from shaking, an old childhood habit that would pop up now and then. Jordan had broken him out of it with hard whacks across the legs multiple times.

"I'm sorry to tell you, Ms. Kurjack passed away within minutes of me contacting you. They thought they were going to be able to save her, but she had lost too much blood by the time she arrived here. They couldn't get enough pumped back into her to help. It was too late."

"Blood. I don't understand. She was fine this morning. She was healthy. She was happy. She was…alive," Lazarus swallowed hard. "Why was she losing blood?"

"Someone tried to remove the baby from her and didn't do a very good job or didn't get a chance to finish. Whatever happened, someone found her crawling in an alley. They went inside to call the police, came back out and she was gone. About an hour after the call, one of the hospital workers found her in the trash dump behind the hospital."

"What the hell?" Lazarus started rocking. He wanted to rip that little office apart. "No. No. This did not happen to her. Why would someone want to do that to her? The baby, the baby. It was supposed to be a boy. Where's the baby?"

"Here, the baby survived," the Inspector said.

"Can I see him?" Lazarus asked. "Can I see her?" He was shocked to feel a warm stream of tears dampening his face.

"Yes, but I'm afraid I need to ask you a few more questions first. You could start by telling me about your relationship, and then you can tell me where you were when this happened?"

Lazarus looked up at him in disbelief. "I have been at Heathrow for most of the day waiting for a flight to Kennedy Airport in New York. I was supposed to connect to Philadelphia. He pulled out his boarding pass and showed it to the officer.

"I'm sorry. The reason I called your number is I see that you had tried to reach her several times."

Lazarus nodded. "I was trying to give her updates on my progress. My flight kept getting delayed. Plus, I wanted to check on her. I thought she was carrying awfully low this morning. But, she assured me she had at least three weeks left. And the first ones are always late, right? I never would have left her."

"Mr. Smith, I have no reason to suspect you at the moment. The investigation has just begun. All that I can ask is that you delay leaving London. Can you do that?"

"Yes, of course. Of course, I will be here. I want to know who did this. I want to know why they did this." Lazarus was being honest in a roundabout way. His gut was urgently telling him this had everything to do with unfinished business with someone from his past. Someone from way back.

He tried to call Micah again while he was waiting for the staff to take him to Nat and the baby. Still no answer. What the hell was going on in the States?

"Mr. Smith," a woman in scrubs approached him. "I'm told you are here to see the young lady that just passed this evening."

"Her name is Natasha." Lazarus fell into step behind the woman who seemed to care about his grief. She was quiet and low key. As she put her hand on the door, she stopped for a moment and turned to him.

"Are you sure you would like to see her?"

"I'm told someone has to identify her, plus yes, I need to see her."

"She hasn't been cleaned up yet. The coroners are here to remove the body. They need to…," the nurse hesitated at a loss for words.

"I understand," Lazarus answered quietly. The woman opened the door. Nat was still on a hospital gurney, probably the one they brought her in on. She was covered in multiple white sheets, but they were all soaked thoroughly with her blood.

"Try to focus on her face. They didn't touch her face," the woman said.

For the first time in his life, Lazarus wanted to drop to his knees and wail. He didn't know if it was because he knew, just as certain as he was standing there, he was the reason she was dead or because he feared who else was going to die because of him. Should he stay or should he go back to the States? Would he harm his family by returning or save them by staying here? Too many questions, too much blood. But, the blood was far from the problem. He had seen death up close before; blood was just an inconvenient by-product sometimes, a necessary evil.

Unknown to many, his grandfather had an even darker dark side. Jordan never hesitated to eliminate the young women who threatened to put his business in danger. He had even made Ashton help him dismember one when Ashton was only fifteen. After that, Ashton sped up his studies in school so he would have an excuse to leave for college early. He hadn't wanted to stick around for that kind of life anymore. It used to scare him to death when Jordan would get angry with Kali. Thank God, she stole his heart and saved herself.

What made him want to melt down most was the little smile on Nat's face. That smile used to greet him every morning and put him to bed at night. Why her? Why butcher her? For the first time, real fear settled into his very being. What was frightening him was the possibility of facing this kind of bloody scene with another one of his own soon. Nat may not have been one of his family members, but she had been counted as one of his own. Somebody was going to have to pay for this.

"Can I just be with her for a few minutes?" He wiped at his tears with the back of his hand and the nurse handed him a box of tissues.

"I will be right outside," the nurse said, putting her hand on the door. "If it helps, and I don't know what would help in this situation, she said you would come back for her and your son. She said to tell you she knew you were coming back."

"I was," Lazarus choked as he spoke, but not missing the words 'your son,' "I was coming back to take them back with me. I wanted to get her out of this country."

He turned to the nurse. "She was going to go to nursing school. She was going to make a good one. Just the right touch. Compassionate. This does not make any sense at all," his voice began to rise. He choked back more tears and held his hand up. "I'm sorry. Just let me have a moment, please."

"Of course." The nurse left the room.

"Nat, whoever did this to you will pay. I'm sorry I got so complacent that I didn't pay attention to what was going on around me. If this has anything to do with me, I swear they will pay triple for this. Don't worry, I am going to take Aaron back to the States. Sorry, but I just can't raise a George." He tried to laugh but choked instead. "I won't let him out of my sight. Never again, I'm so sorry." He kissed her on her forehead and, like the nurse advised, tried to keep his eyes off the bloody sheets, but that was nearly impossible.

It was surreal following the nurse into the nursery to find a little boy with a tag with no name screaming at the top of his brand-new lungs. Lazarus scrubbed his hands, dressed in the garb only allowed in the nursery then followed a new nurse to the wriggly little thing swaddled in a blue blanket. He sat down in a rocking chair and she handed the child to him. Lazarus cried again and swore to himself that this would be his last cry. It had to be. He had come to London, broken and alone, too sick to keep his promise to his family and then so depressed, he almost hid from them. It wasn't until he had left for the airport that he realized what he had done these past two years. All he had to do was pick up the phone. Kali would have been by his side, not Nat. And maybe, just maybe, Nat would still be alive. He would have healed faster and found Jack before Jack found him. Or, at least, take him on, man to man. No, he became complacent and shallow, hiding behind his Lazarus moniker. Avoiding Kali and even, sometimes, Micah. He knew what he had to do now. But he had to get the facts first, and he had to have a sound plan. He was going home and he was going home as Ashton Taylor Sperling, a whole man. And, he was going to wreak havoc on Jack Pulaski.

CHAPTER NINE

K ALI AND MICAH walked into the penthouse only a few minutes after the children. The living room was complete chaos with book bags, yelling, and snacks being shoved into their mouths. The two of them looked at each other for a moment and then Kali charged in.

"Hey, hey, hey." Kali walked into the middle of the living room and turned full circle. "Everybody listen to me. In less than three hours we are going to leave here for the theater. Where's Katie?"

"Right here, mom. I can't find my blue hairbrush. I need my blue brush." She was running down the steps full throttle. "I'm late. I need my brush."

"You left it in my dressing room this morning when we were talking about the schedule. I will get it," Kali said, not wanting Katie to discover any of the gifts that she had bought her over the last few weeks. Even though Katie was in a hurry, knowing her she would take a second or two to snoop. Kali had watched her do it too many times. She was just like her father in that respect, as well as having inherited many of his other traits.

Kali started for the stairs. "Does everyone know what they are wearing tonight?"

Kacie started whining about Kali's assistant, Mona, who was usually in charge of the children when she wasn't there. Unfortunately, Mona, a college student, had an emergency and wasn't around to defend herself from Kacie's objections. "She laid out something red. She must have bought it. Cause you didn't. You know I don't wear red, Mom, you know how much I hate red. And, it's a dress. I hate dresses."

"I'll help her find something," Ash stepped up. It was funny how her children had paired themselves off. Ash had fallen in love with Kacie the minute she was born. He was always looking out for his baby sister. If she or Ashton stepped out of the room, there was big brother Ash watching her every move. He was the one to see her take her first steps. When everyone else was busy, Kacie was right under Ash. After their father's departure, it had been Kacie who had decided Ash should no longer be called A.J., for Ashton Jr. She said he was no longer considered a junior if their father was dead, so they both decided that Ash was a more appropriate nickname.

In the same manner, Katie had taken the nurturing, big sisterly role with Adam very seriously. She had acted as if she wanted to be his mommy, Kali thought, from day one. Katie was always trying to dress him and give him advice. Now that he was older, he spent as much time running from her as he did with her. But she could still manipulate him in the funniest ways. Adam was at his most gullible when it came to Katie. She could make him believe or do just about anything.

And, then there was Artie, Micah's only child. After his mother passed, Kali had taken the then ten-year-old under her wings and wouldn't let him go. The two of them had a special bond, so special they could finish each other's sentences. Kali looked around the room for him.

"What are you wearing, Artie? Did you decide on the tan suit or the blue?"

Artie hunched his shoulders. She knew it. He was the most indecisive one out of the bunch. "Come on," she waved to him, as she saw Micah stepped back outside the door. She wondered if he was getting a call from Lazarus.

Micah had gotten a call alright, but it was from Anjuli. She was waiting for him in front of the main elevator.

"You and those luscious lips." Micah embraced her and kissed her deeply. "What are you doing here? I thought we were meeting at the theater."

"Oh, work got boring. There was nothing urgent, so I thought I would come over and keep you occupied."

"Sounds like a plan." Micah led Anjuli back into the penthouse. She helped him peel his jacket off, hinting that she wanted more than just to wait patiently for him. As he led her to the study, kissing the back of her neck lightly, she dropped his jacket on the table in the foyer with his phone in it. The phone began to buzz as soon as he closed the door to the study. No one was around to hear it.

CHAPTER TEN

KALI WAS FEELING both exhausted and excited all at once. After years of hauling Katie to acting classes, small plays, and even smaller venues to get her ready for this moment, the night of her professional debut as an actress had finally arrived. To make it even more worthy of all the sweat, tears, and hard work memorizing scripts and dance steps, her baby had landed the lead in a play that was sure to be destined for Broadway. Philly and then DC were its test runs.

Kali looked around to make sure all the family was seated. The three boys and Katie's boyfriend, Roderick, were seated in the box next to them. She and Micah had the first box, along with Kacie and what's her name. Kacie sat on the end, and Micah sat behind her with Anjuli. Kali looked at her, and the woman waved at her as if they hadn't entered those seats at the same time. Kali hated the woman's grin. It reminded her of the Joker on the old Batman TV series, a wildly painted, fake grin.

Kali turned to see if the other Sperling brothers, Ricky and Chico, were there in the box beside the boys. Then she noticed the other seats in it were empty.

Kali interrupted Micah's conversation with Anjuli. "Where's everyone else? Did you hear from them?" He shook his head at Anjuli and smiled. Then he turned his body to give Kali his full attention, knowing that if he didn't give in, the rest of the night would be uncomfortable, to say the least.

"What?"

"Ray, Elliott. They are not in the box with Ricky and Chico. Where are they?"

"Oh, that." Micah turned and gave his younger brothers a wave. They waved back.

"Oh, that what? Nobody called me to tell they weren't going to make it. Or, are they just late? What's going on?"

"Ray had a sudden family emergency and Elliott went with him to Montana, I think it was. That just came up a few hours ago. They had to get back on a flight as soon as possible."

"When were you going to tell me this?"

"Now, I guess. I just got the messages before coming in here. Oh, and have you checked your messages? Lazarus is going to be delayed a few days."

"Is the weather that bad?" Kali sighed.

"No, I will fill you in after the play. You knew at this point, he wasn't going to make it, right?"

"Yes, I had made peace with that."

Kacie tugged at Kali's jacket sleeve. "Mom, mom, what else did you get Katie?"

"Oh, let me show you," Kali said excitedly. "It's a beautiful platinum charm bracelet. I only got one charm for tonight with the date on it. You will love it. It has the two faces.

Kali started digging around in purse.

"Oh, my God, where is it? I didn't take it out of my purse."

"What?" Micah leaned over to see what Kali seemed to be stressing about.

"Katie's bracelet is missing. It's not in my purse."

"Maybe you forgot to put it in there when you changed purses. You do that a lot you know," Micah reminded her.

"No, I didn't have time to change purses. I was busy ironing the right shirt for Artie while you were getting busy in the study." Kali caught herself before Kacie overheard any more.

"Yeah, don't look at me like that, I know. I was on my way in there to get a card to put with Katie's gift," she whispered in Micah's ear as he leaned in closer.

Micah patted his forehead and closed his eyes. He wondered how much of the getting busy she had witnessed and was hoping Anjuli couldn't hear the conversation clearly. He kept his voice low, but Kali's voice was carrying upward even as a whisper.

"I'd left my purse in the foyer. I picked it up and took it upstairs with the intention to change purses."

"Was it in there then?"

"I don't know, one of the kids called me and I got distracted. As usual, I was on my own."

"Don't say that," Micah protested.

"Why not, it's true," Kali said as a funk hit her hard. Ashton was gone and it seemed he was doing everything in his power not to return.

That hadn't been the plan. The plan had been for him to find out who else was in cahoots with Redd and Asa when they tried to bring him down. Who else, other than whom they suspected. Everybody in the family suspected Troy Lucas, his one-time best friend. Good old Troy, a Philly police detective who had — and for all they knew still — blamed him for Troy's sister's death years ago. That's why Ashton had ended up serving time, almost a year, for a murder he didn't commit.

But, they also believed that someone else had been linked to Redd in Germany. That's why Ashton had gone over in the first place. He and Kali had planned sexual trysts in romantic places in Europe between his investigations. But, something had changed before there was even a first visit. Within two months, his life became a blank to the family. He had left Munich and gone to London with no explanation. It was as if he was trying to disappear.

The music started and the curtains fell back bringing her attention to the real reason she was in a dark theater. Whether Ashton/Lazarus or whoever he was today was here no longer mattered. She was a proud mother. Her children were healthy and, as far as she could tell, relatively happy. She couldn't deny that Ashton's brothers, Micah, Ricky, and Chico, had been helpful in keeping them under control. Yet, it was she who did all the heavy lifting, was ultimately responsible, not just for the children but for them, too. Between her family and her job, some days she thought she was going to go insane. Grimacing, Kali touched her forehead. There it was again, that gnawing little ache. She had been trying to ignore it all day and, until now, had almost succeeded.

The last curtain call after three standing ovations was the most exhilarating one of them all. Kali could hardly contain herself in the box. They all kept hugging each other. Ricky and Chico had joined them in the box standing on the steps leading back to the outer lobby.

"Oh, my God! Oh, my God, she was wonderful." Kali was surprised by the excitement in Anjuli's voice and the big hug she pulled her into.

"Yes, she was," Kali said, tears pouring down her face. This had been another life changing event for her and her baby. Deep down within, Kali knew Katie was going to be the first to leave the nest. She could feel it; already an emptiness was creeping up inside her. How was she going to let her go? Ashton had snatched Katie and AJ away from her at birth, never giving her the chance to even smell them. They were three years old when she finally got a chance to be their mother. She had never known how much she had longed for them until she had touched their soft little faces for the first time. Now, that emptiness was going to rear its head again and be more evident than when Katie began to go away for more than a night or two for school trips or a sleepover. This was happening. Kali took a deep breath; the show was over and their lives as a family had just changed. The audience was exiting the theater. They didn't have to rush as Katie was going to be awhile and they had been invited to come to the dressing areas a little later. Right now, the cast would be getting ready to talk to the press.

Kali sat down in her seat and methodically searched her purse for the little aqua blue box with a silver ribbon tied around it. Not found. She had rushed to the Mall to pick it up and had gone straight to the office yesterday, then to Elle's this afternoon, and then home in Micah's car, all with the same purse. There were no other stops and not once had she left her purse unattended, unless she considered the foyer. Had it dropped onto the table behind the tall flower vase? Kali listened to the chatter and banter of everyone around trying to remember if she had removed it when she took the purse upstairs. She had planned to write a special note on a cute card, but Micah had blocked that with his amorous acts on the sofa under the spiral stairs in the study. Silly, how a grown man and woman thought they could hide behind an open stairwell.

Kali shook her head. This is not funny, she thought, gently rubbing her forehead.

"Still having headaches?" She looked up and saw Chico smiling down at her.

"Yeah," she answered, reaching up to him for a hug.

"Wanna stop by and see me tomorrow, or my partner?"

"Probably your partner," she giggled.

"Oh, is he better looking than me?"

"Straighter." The two of them laughed together. Chico took the seat beside her, and Kacie sat in Ash's lap while they waited to go join Katie.

"Something wrong?"

"Can't find the gift I drove all the way to King of Prussia to pick up yesterday. I was there when the store opened. Haven't changed bags or anything since. It should be in here."

"Are you sure you didn't take it out and forget? I know you are a bit overwhelmed by a lot of things, right now." Chico didn't want to mention his oldest brother's name, not in public anyway. He hugged his sister-in-law again. She didn't deserve this aggravation, especially not being drawn into their whacked-up family.

"Seriously, let my office do some blood work tomorrow to see what's going on with those headaches. You are drinking lots of water, right?"

"Probably, too much. Maybe that's the cause of the headache."

"Excuses," he said and leaned around her to his brother.

"So, when were you planning to tell me what's going on overseas?"

"What?" Micah shrugged.

"The girl. The girl that works for Lazarus. She's dead. Right?"

"When did you hear that crap?" said Micah, "I haven't heard a thing about that."

"Oh, well, I was doing a little snooping to see why he was going to miss Katie's play and his flight was not the reason."

"What?" Kali leaned back as both of their big heads were almost forehead to forehead and close to her breasts. But she could hear them just fine. "How do you know she was someone who worked for Lazarus? Why hasn't he called to tell us what's going on?"

"I called my friend of a friend, you know?" Chico answered.

"He said it's all over the news. The girl was butchered. Somebody tried to remove her baby from her."

"What?" It looked almost as if Micah was kissing his younger brother, they were so close.

"Haven't you talked to him?"

"No, we keep missing each other's calls." Micah sat up and pulled his phone out. There was another message that he had missed. He waved Chico out of his seat and stepped out of his box. The two of them exited the area. Their youngest brother, Ricky, followed them. Kali got up to follow them, but Micah motioned her back to her seat. She stood there torn as she caught a glimpse of her children huddled together, smiling, clueless to the latest event in their father's life. She was, too, Kali thought when a sharp pain raced across her temple. What girl? Was she the reason her husband had dropped off the radar?

"What's up?" Anjuli asked shifting over to Micah's seat. "Did I miss something?"

"No, you didn't miss anything. It's the norm around here, especially with those three." Kali turned around to see where they went, but they had completely disappeared.

"I thought *my* family was close." Anjuli leaned her body completely toward Kali as she pulled her knee underneath her. Kali thought that was very manly of her and smoothed out her own dress to distract her from the woman's look.

"Have they always been this close, or did they become closer after their older brother died?"

"Always." Kali considered the woman's big, dark eyes. She was having a hard time reading them. Maybe that was another reason she wasn't a fan of Anjuli's.

"I saw you digging in your purse several times. Did you forget something?"

"No, I misplaced my daughter's gift." As soon as Kali said that, she turned around to Ash. "Ash, could you do mommy a big, big favor? Please." Kacie was sitting on his knee facing Katie's boyfriend, Roderick. Kali could only hope Kacie wasn't getting a crush on the boy. But, then again, that would make sense. It was darn obvious why Katie was attracted to him; he looked like Ash's clone. What made matters worse was that it was the first thing people would mention when they met the poor kid. How much he looked like Ash. Kali glanced over at the tall, lanky boy who, at the moment, was making Kacie giggle.

"Yes, mother."

"Don't mother me. I need you to go to the penthouse pronto and find Katie's bracelet for me. Look for a light blue Tiffany box"

"That's eight blocks away," Ash complained.

"Take a cab."

Ash held out his hand.

"I can take him," Anjuli offered.

"The boy's a minute or two from eighteen years old. He can take a cab and let himself into his home," Kali protested as she pulled out a wad of cash and handed it to Ash.

"Can I go?" Kacie leaned down toward her mother.

"No, you stay here with me and the rest of the family." Kali stood up and looked at her watch. "They should be out of costume by now, don't you think?"

"I have to go to the bathroom, mom," Kacie added.

"Can you wait until we get upstairs?"

"No, I've been waiting."

"I'll keep an eye out for her before I leave," Ash said, getting up and motioning Roderick to move out of his way.

The boy stood up and Kali hid her mouth to cover a smile. Roderick was sporting the exact same hair cut as Ash. There was no doubt in her mind that Katie had something to do with the young man's new look. She could tell Ash had already noticed too. She saw him take a long, hard look at the boy, giving the impression he was about to say something. But instead, he walked around the boy as fast as he could. A tinge of pity raced across her heart for the Ash look-a-like because her son was not happy. And, he had the body language of his father when he was about to take full control of things. That's how she knew Ash was going to break up that relationship. She didn't know how, she just knew it would be done and most likely, before morning.

Ash led the way with Kacie and with Roderick close behind. "Where are you going?" Ash asked the boy.

"I was just going to stand out in the hallway with you."

"If you really want to do something," Ash said, looking past the boy's shoulder recognizing a young woman he knew, "you could run to the penthouse and pick up Katie's gift for my mom."

"I don't know," Roderick answered, "that's a long walk."

"Take a cab." Ash pulled out the same wad of money his mother had given him and gave it to the boy. They both looked toward the tall window panes of the theater overlooking the street.

"And it's raining," Roderick added as an excuse.

"Here, take my jacket." Ash peeled out of his soft leather, gray jacket that Roderick had been admiring all evening. It looked expensive. He hoped and prayed that, one day, he could afford something like that.

"Are you sure?" Roderick took the jacket. Touching it, he thought it would melt between his fingers.

"Sure, the keys to the elevator and the apartment are in the inside zipper pocket." Ash patted the boy hard enough to make him sway, but not to hurt him. He could tell from the look on his face that the boy liked that. For a minute, this kid was feeling accepted. Ash shook his head. Poor kid would never survive the Sperling family.

"Where is it?"

"I don't know, check my mom's room, check the living room. She said it's a light blue Tiffany box."

"Okay," Roderick said, sliding into the jacket, almost elbowing Kacie in the face.

"Oh, I'm so sorry," he said when, just in time, he saw Katie's younger sister out of the corner of his eye. Kacie grinned. She liked the fact that Roderick was always so polite. He would make a good brother-in-law, she thought.

"Why are you wearing my brother's jacket?" Kacie asked in her typical, investigative way.

"I'm borrowing it. I have to go to the penthouse to pick up something for your mother."

"Why?"

"It's a gift for Katie. She forgot to bring it."

"She has a lot of gifts for Katie. Do you know which one she wants you to bring?"

"No, just a Tiffany box in the living room or her bedroom."

"You are going into my mom's bedroom? She never lets anyone in there. You had better let me go along to help you get in and out of there fast."

"Okay, but don't you have to let someone know?" Roderick was beginning to feel real special now, if he had the chance to watch Katie's little sister and enter the penthouse without an escort. Heck, maybe marrying Katie one day wouldn't be totally out of the question.

"I'll let Ash know," Kacie backed away from him and ran over to Ash who was very close to a young woman in a very tight short, black dress. Kacie gasped when she noticed Ash's hand resting on the woman's butt.

"Go back into the theater with Mom," Ash said as soon as he saw her.

"No, I'm going to the penthouse with Roderick," she said. "If not, I am going to tell Mom."

"Kacie," Ash cut her off as he could feel the young woman pulling away with concern, "go with Roderick. I'll tell mom."

Roderick and Kacie caught a cab out on the Avenue of the Arts side of the theater and arrived within minutes at the penthouse. Kacie had to help the young man with the keys.

"I'll check Mom's bedroom. You check down here." Kacie ran up the stairs. She loved her mother's bedroom. The first thing she did was to kick off her shoes, run, and jump into the middle of her mother's king-sized bed covered with the embroidered pillows and a beautiful matching quilt of silver and blue.

"I hear you and Micah's wife were close. I bet you miss her, huh?" Anjuli asked Kali who was fidgeting in her seat like a nervous cat.

"What?" Kali glanced at the woman.

"Your sister-in-law? Ruby? I bet you miss her," Anjuli repeated.

"Yes, yes, of course."

"What was she like? I mean, Micah only gives me bits and pieces. I don't think he likes to talk about her much even though she's been gone over three years now. You would think he could talk about her a little."

"One, he's a man. They don't talk about such things. Two, he loved Ruby. It probably still hurts to talk about her. And three, where the hell is everybody?"

"Is that her pin on his lapel? I mean, it's a woman's pin. On Artie's lapel?" Anjuli asked.

"What?" Kali stopped fidgeting for a moment and turned to her.

"I smoothed Artie's lapel down and felt a pin. When I looked at it, it looked like a very expensive piece of women's jewelry on the bottom side of his lapel. When I asked him about it he just walked away."

"Yes, it's hers," Kali sighed, now the conversation had switched to Artie, adding another reason she didn't like the woman to her list. "I put it there. I put it on all his suits when he wears one. We haven't discussed it in a long time. I just automatically put it there."

"What does it mean? I mean, why?"

"Ruby used to say a man who wore a suit everyday was a successful man. And, she wanted her son to be a successful man. She wanted him to wear a suit every day. So, I told him that story and I put that pin on the underside of his left lapel to remind him his mommy expects him to be a successful man one day. He's never turned it down and I have never stopped making sure it was there."

Kali checked her watch again and none of the Sperlings, brothers or children, had returned. She couldn't bear anymore mindless banter with Anjuli. The woman was creeping her out but, while Anjuli was questioning her, she had figured it out partially. It was the voice more than anything. Anjuli's voice reminded her of Ruby's, even more than her eyes, but she wasn't as refined, not as pretty. This one woman was a little rough around the edges. Jordan would never have approved of her for Micah, not like he did Ruby. Kali certainly didn't.

"We should probably go ahead upstairs. The others will catch up when they see we aren't down here," Kali said, wondering how long Kacie would take in the bathroom. She hoped she was okay.

"You go ahead. I'll find the kids for you," Anjuli offered. "I'll bring them up."

Kali hesitated for a moment, but she wanted to put her arms around Katie. "Okay."

As she walked through the lobby to the elevator Kali looked around. There were no signs of Ash or Kacie. She wondered if Ash had taken Kacie with him. Or better yet, may be Kacie was already upstairs with Roderick. She stood in front of the elevator hesitating before pressing the button. As she was about to turn to go back to the lobby to check the bathroom, she felt his hand on her arm. She didn't have to check to know who it was. She could smell him. It was Micah.

"We need to talk a minute," Micah whispered in her ear.

"About Chico's investigations?" She wasn't ready to hear any bad news. Being kept in the dark until after Katie's celebration was going to be fine with her.

"I talked to Lazarus." Micah was leaning over close to her ear, but was interrupted by his girlfriend, who leaned in close to their faces.

"I checked the bathrooms. She is not in either of them. I didn't see Ash or Roderick either. Do you think they are already upstairs?"

"Let's hope," Kali said, pressing the elevator button. It opened right away. Artie and Adam, appearing out of nowhere, both brushed against her, excitedly jumping inside the doors. Kali held her breath as Anjuli moved inside the elevator, too. Micah guided Kali in, still holding onto her arm.

The adults rode up the two floors silently, while the boys joked with each other, one of them even breaking into one of the songs Katie had performed.

Again, the boys rushed past the adults when the elevator doors opened. Micah still held onto Kali's arm.

"I'll be there in a minute," he said to Anjuli. "A minute."

Anjuli exited the elevator and Micah pressed the L button for the Lobby to close the doors, then he pressed another button. When the elevator stopped, he pressed the red one to put it out of service.

"What's going on?" Kali reached for his tie and smoothed it. She had asked the question, but she didn't want to know the answer. They stared into each other's eyes for a moment. Then he kissed her. Her heart fluttered a little bit; maybe the news wasn't bad after all. Then he stopped and his eyes looked sad.

"We are on high alert," Micah said, pushing the rogue curl from her eyes. "We have to get all the kids in one place. I have sent Mr. Brown, Kacie's usual bodyguard so she will know him, over to the penthouse to pick up the wanderers. My men could only account for those two," he nodded toward the elevator doors. "At least, I hope that's where Kacie and Ash are, along with Roderick. No one has seen him either. I kind of feel responsible for that kid."

"What are you saying, Micah?"

"Chico was right. The girl who was working as Lazarus's housekeeper was murdered and butchered while he sat in the airport."

"What does that have to do with us?"

"Lazarus thinks it was someone gunning for him, at least in a way to make him hurt."

"Chico mentioned a baby."

"Don't go there. It wasn't his."

"But, you asked, didn't you?"

"I did, because I knew you would. He's concerned. He thinks he knows who was married to Redd and he thinks it's someone from our past."

"Who?" Kali said as she heard Ms. Elle's voice ringing in her ears.

"Lazarus wants me to look up a guy named Jack Pulaski. He thinks he was going by the name Jocko over there."

"Do you think," Kali almost choked on the words, "that…he's Jordan's little white boy?"

"That's the only Jack he knows who would have any reason to hurt him."

"Because he was Jordan's grandson?"

"No, I'm afraid there is a lot more history to that. Don't worry, I didn't alert Reck. After you told me about Mama, I sent Reck on a different assignment. He is probably sitting at the airport waiting to pick up Lazarus."

"Is he coming?"

"No, but Reck doesn't know that, not yet."

"But, if it was Reck, he couldn't have killed that girl. He was here."

"Ever heard of killers for hire, Kali?"

Micah pushed the button and the elevator started moving again.

"Together. Once we get together, we stay together. No stragglers. I have called in some additional bodyguards. No ducking them."

"But, we checked Reck out. His whole history."

"Maybe Reck just looks like Jordan's little white boy; but, I find it very odd that my mother reacted so strongly, don't you?"

Kali looked down at her purse thinking of the bracelet and looked up at Micah.

"I will call Brown to see if he's made it to the penthouse yet."

The two of them stepped off the elevator and Anjuli was hugging the wall directly in front of it.

"Everything okay?" Anjuli asked a little too sweetly. Kali suspected that, for Anjuli, everything was finally falling into place. The way Micah touched her freely was more than a brotherly touch, but she didn't care. She didn't have time for jealous women who were a flash in the pan to the men in her life.

"Everything's fine," Micah answered, kissing Anjuli on the cheek. "I do need a favor though."

"Whatever you need," Anjuli answered.

Kali sighed and walked away because she couldn't bear listening to any more of Anjuli's fake attentiveness. She then found Katie surrounded by the press asking her questions. Her baby was shining, freshly dressed without the crazy stage makeup.

"There's my mom," Katie shrilled. Everyone turned toward her and a few came rushing toward her.

Someone stuck a microphone in front of her and asked her if she thought her husband and his grandfather would have been proud. It had been over a decade since Jordan, Philly's most famous jazz saxophonist, had passed, but the newspapers still mentioned him more often than she liked. He was the elite of Philadelphia back in his day, and then Ashton's brief rise to notoriety as a mayoral candidate who had once served time kept him in the news as well. The press seemed to love him and his family even more when supposedly he was assassinated during his campaign. What a mess, but Kali smiled and hugged her daughter and then joyfully told everyone how proud both Jordan and Ashton would have been, especially Jordan with one of his descendants following in his footsteps in entertainment. Kali didn't want to disrupt Katie's special moment but, the whole time she was talking and waiting, her heart was leaping out of her body. Where was Kacie and where was Ash?

She didn't know how much time had passed when she was finally able to pull away from the madness. The stars of the play were taking pictures back down on the set. It was going to be awhile. She walked back into the lobby area and spotted Anjuli still holding up the wall.

"Where is everyone?"

"Micah is somewhere on the phone. Artie is in that stairwell talking to one of the young dancers. Adam is over there," she said, pointing to a section with a couple of benches. He was talking to another girl. "Ash is down there watching them take pictures."

"What?" Kali's headache rushed across her forehead so fiercely, she almost lost her balance.

"Down there." Anjuli walked toward a rail that overlooked an open area. "See." She pointed to Ash who had one arm wrapped around a strawberry blonde dressed in all-black.

"How long has he been down there?" Kali asked, her eyes beginning to feel as though they were going bulge out of her head.

"Are you alright?"

"Yes, yes. I'm fine. I need to go talk to Ash. Have you talked to him? Did he tell you where Kacie was?"

"No, I just saw him a couple of minutes ago. Micah left me in charge of those two." She pointed to the stairwell door and the sitting area.

"When was the last time you laid eyes on Artie?"

"Two minutes, three minutes, tops."

Kali headed for the stairwell and caught Artie in an awkward kiss. Neither kid looked as if they knew what they were doing.

"Back inside. Stay near Anjuli or go sit with Adam. That's an order. No questions. Just do it. Now," Kali said in a manner that made Artie get up and help the young lady up immediately. Kali stood on the stairwell until they went inside with Anjuli. She went down a flight and found Ash.

"Have you talked to your uncle?"

"Which one, Mom? I have three around here somewhere."

"Don't get smart. You know which one I am talking about."

"I haven't seen him."

"Where's Kacie?"

"Oh, yeah. About that. She and Rod aren't back yet?"

"Back from where?" Kali asked sternly.

"The penthouse. She wanted to ride with him. I didn't think it would hurt."

"But, I sent you, not Rod."

"He volunteered," Ash answered still holding onto the girl in black.

"Get upstairs. Stay close to Anjuli. If I find out you wandered away, you will pay," Kali whispered in her son's ear to keep from embarrassing him too much, although her presence didn't seem to disturb either of them at all. Neither one tried to hide that they were all hot and bothered. She recognized the look and the feeling in the air. She was going to have to ask Micah if he was still having those talks with the boys.

Kali dug in her purse, found her cell phone and dialed Micah who didn't answer. Then she dialed the penthouse. Maybe Kacie would answer the house phone. Now she was feeling bad that she hadn't given her baby a phone yet. She was making her wait for her birthday. The way Kacie was always surrounded by her siblings, her bodyguards, her parents or guardians, Kali didn't think the need was urgent. It was bad enough trying to limit her Internet and television access. Kali had wanted to hold out just a little longer with this one. But, she was ten, soon to be eleven. She should have had a phone. Kali thought about Roderick, but she would have to interrupt Katie to get his number. She watched her son go up to the floor where Anjuli was and then she headed downstairs straight to the street. She was going to the penthouse herself.

Kali let herself inside the penthouse. Not seeing anyone right away, she headed for the stairs. But, as she passed the opening to the living room, she saw Mr. Brown kneeling over someone lying on the floor. Her body stiffened mid-step; for a moment, she thought she had twisted her knee. Her eyes zoomed in on the light gray jacket. It belonged to Ash, he had been wearing it at the play. Did he have it on when she just saw him? Stunned, facts muddled in her mind as she tried to make sense of what she was seeing.

As she started walking toward the two, Reck stepped out of the dining area, gun pointed. He shot Mr. Brown point blank in the head. Kali screamed and tried to turn around to run, but she stepped on something, the little Tiffany box. That caused her to reel a little. As she tried to regain her balance, Reck grabbed a handful of her curls and jerked her head back.

"You Sperling women are some of the nosiest bitches I have ever met. You don't know how happy I was when you people killed off that fucking bitch, Ruby." He pushed her toward the door as she kicked him in his calf with her pointed toe shoe. For a moment, she thought she was getting to him, but he regained his balance and punched her so hard she dropped down to her knees. *Where's Kacie,* she thought as she began to black out.

Reck lifted her and threw her over his back. He took her back through the kitchen to the rear door leading to the garage elevator. As soon as they arrived, he threw her in the trunk of Jordan's old Mercedes. He sped the car out onto the street and headed for Vine Street as quickly as he could.

"Bitch," Reck screamed into the windshield as he drove the car over the Franklin Bridge toward South Jersey. "Bitch. Why couldn't you stay the fuck away?" Reck glanced at the speedometer and realized he needed to slow down to keep from bringing any attention to himself.

"What are you doing?" Reck said, talking to himself aloud. "You are so off schedule. Off plan! Damn it. What did you just fucking do?" He started to drive aimlessly around in Jersey trying to think things through. Was the house ready? he thought. It wasn't meant for Kali, but things could still work, possibly even better. Reck began to calm down and began to drive more deliberately.

"Maybe. Just maybe. He's still gotta come home. He will be here. I have her. So, he will be here. He is definitely coming now."

PART TWO

CHAPTER ELEVEN

S O MUCH HAD happened within the last 48 hours that Lazarus' mind was still on spin cycle. Natasha was dead. Her baby boy was alive and the hospital had released the child to him as the father, based on the dying woman's word. He heard the child cry and saw his former executive assistant and the woman he trusted like a mother jump into action. Tawny Elliott, affectionately known to him as Elliott, was the first person he had called before leaving the hospital the day Natasha died. Elliott and Ray, her husband and the only person Lazarus called friend, were getting ready to board a plane to Philadelphia to attend Katie's play. But, instead, they boarded a chartered plane and flew straight to London.

Lazarus had had no one else to turn to at that moment. Kali had her hands full with Katie's play, Micah was going to have to jump into action to find Jack Pulaski, and he was stuck in England until the police investigation into Nat's murder set him free to leave the country.

From experience — but he never *knew* how he knew — Elliott, whom he had hired as a personal assistant years ago would always pull things together and make everything all better. She did it with such ease. If only she could do that with the rest of his life, he thought, as she sped into his bedroom to take care of little Aaron. Elliott had seemed very happy about the name, a little too excited about it at first. But, that was Elliott. She always supported him in anything he wanted, including keeping his identity a secret, and now she was going to do that for this child. He was sure of it. Lazarus had never discussed the name with her, but thought it appropriate to keep the A's going in his family as part of his own family tradition, even if this child wasn't his blood, and Elliott agreed. He was going to take care of him, always, no matter who the child's biological father was. Just like his grandfather, Jordan, had wanted to take care of Jack Pulaski when he was a child, had felt responsible for him. The thought saddened him. He hadn't thought of Jack in years, but now he had no choice but to be obsessed with him.

"Here's a list," Elliott said, handing a sheet of paper to Lazarus.

"You need to go out and get these things immediately."

Lazarus looked at the list. "There is no need for furniture, Elliott. I'm hoping we'll be on our way back to the States in a couple of days. At the very least, you and the baby."

"Buy the damn bassinet or something like it. The child cannot sleep in a drawer for much longer. Plus, he needs clothes. Don't act like you don't know how to buy baby clothes. I was there when you took care of the twins by yourself, remember?" Elliott put one hand on her hip while holding the child in her free arm. The little boy was whimpering.

"He needs the right bottles and formula, too. We are going to run out soon. The hospital only gave you, maybe, a day's worth of food and diapers. Plus, you are in dreamland. They are not letting this child out of the country without a passport. We need to go apply for one tomorrow. And, don't think Micah is going to snap his fingers and get everything speeded up. We are going to be here for a few weeks, at best."

Lazarus kept looking at the list and absorbing the fact that he was now in an even more complex situation.

"Move," she commanded.

He stood up quickly like a little boy. She had that effect on him and he didn't know why, but he was going to follow her instructions. Within twelve hours of his call, she had come all the way to London to help him out, along with Ray who was a retired sheriff in Colorado. Lazarus had been responsible for bringing the two of them together and he couldn't have been happier for both. Though he still thought it kind of odd that his friend had fallen for a woman at least ten years his senior. But, there was no doubt Ray was in love with Elliott and she with him. You could feel it in any room they occupied. He thought about Kali; he wondered if their love could still fill a room like that.

"She does have you trained," Ray laughed.

"Like you aren't," Lazarus retorted. "I saw you dragging all that luggage off the plane. All she had was her purse."

"So what's the plan with this Jocko character? Any news from Micah?"

"Nothing yet. It's been quiet. Waiting to hear from them to see how Katie's play went. I'm going to run out to get these things before Big Ma comes back and smacks me." The men laughed in agreement.

Lazarus looked at his watch. His real family was six hours behind him. The play was probably over and they were partying somewhere. He wondered if Kacie was still awake. That kid could fall asleep standing up, he thought. She would be extremely active one second and the next sound asleep. He wished he could pass out like that. Now, it was almost six o'clock in the morning and he was being sent to find one of those 24-hour stores to buy diapers and formula and whatever the hell else was on this list. Within two days of his life, the brand-new resident of the world had already been kicked out twice: once out of his mother's womb and then out of the busy hospital.

Lazarus walked out onto the well-lit street toward his car when, out of the corner of his eye, he saw someone darting across the street into a stairwell next to his home. He took a few steps and decided to cross the street for a better vantage point. Were they following him or was the figure just a figment of his imagination? He crossed the street and started back toward his home just as the figure came out and ran up the stairs to his door. Then the figure started fumbling as if she, yes she — he realized it was a woman digging in her purse. Whoever this person was, they weren't being that careful. He ran back across to his side of the street and up the stairs, surprising her. She tried to scream but he muffled her mouth with his large hand. As soon as he looked into her frightened eyes, he knew who she was.

"Marja, what are you doing here?"

"Don't hurt me. Don't hurt me," Nat's sister protested as he removed his hand from her mouth.

"I'm not going to hurt you. What are you doing..." Lazarus stopped mid-sentence. Marja had Natasha's purse.

"I come see if Natasha alright. She no answer phone. She leave purse."

"Then why didn't you just ring the doorbell?" Lazarus asked while pulling out his own keys.

"I didn't want wake her."

"You lie." Lazarus opened the door and waited for her to follow him in. "Upstairs. My flat is upstairs."

"You supposed be in America."

"Obviously, I'm not, and for obvious reasons. What were you planning to do? Steal her stuff?"

"No, why would I steal from Natasha? She give me what I want."

"She would have." Lazarus opened the door to his place finding Elliott and Ray sitting on the sofa talking to the baby.

"Natasha had baby? That's why she no answer phone." Marja sound excited for a minute. "Where Natasha?"

Lazarus stood over her studying her. She was rail-thin with dirty, greasy white-blonde hair with black roots. As she talked, she shifted from side to side, scratching her bare arms one at a time.

"Can I hold baby?" Marja started toward Elliott who jumped up and gave her a wide berth before going into the bedroom, shutting the door hard.

"Excuse me a second," Lazarus said to Marja and then looked at Ray for help.

"Why don't you have a seat here on the stool at the counter?" Ray said, pointing to the three stools that looked over into the kitchen. "Let me get you a cup of coffee."

Lazarus went into the bedroom where Elliott sat on the bed next to the drawer that served as the baby's bassinet. She had lined it neatly with the plush towels out of the linen closet to give the baby some support and comfort while he slept.

"She's filthy. I'm not letting her touch this newborn. I'm still in shock they released him from the hospital so quickly. I bet that woman has fleas or lice or something. Get her out of here," Elliott said in a coarse whisper, not to disturb the sleepy-looking child.

"I will. I will, but I need to ask her a few questions first. Why don't I give Ray the list and directions? I will ask her some questions and send her on her way. She probably knows how to find out who killed Nat."

"I don't care. Just don't let her touch this child. Who knows what she is infected with."

"Got it," Lazarus said, letting himself back into the living area and kitchen. He figured Ray must have been thinking the same thing because the woman was on a wooden stool next to a granite counter and all food items had been moved to the inner kitchen. So, whatever she touched could be disinfected easily. No wonder Ray and Elliott got along so well.

Lazarus walked into the kitchen area and asked her, "Are you hungry?"

Marja nodded, so he opened the refrigerator door for the first time since he had come home with no Nat and his heart hurt. Each container was filled with something Natasha had cooked. He pulled out the first container and opened it. It was the tasteless chicken fried rice she had made. He heated it up in the microwave.

"Why are you here, Marja?"

"I want to see Natasha. She no call me back. I think, I think she in trouble."

"Why would you think she was in trouble?" Ray asked and Lazarus suddenly remembered the list.

Marja looked back at Ray suspiciously.

"He is my friend," Lazarus said, taking the list out of his pocket heading toward Ray.

"Natasha say you have no friends. She your only friend."

"It may have seemed that way," Lazarus answered and slipped Ray the list and some money.

"Really?" Ray asked.

"Your wife will kill me if we don't get this stuff now," Lazarus said as Ray crumpled the list a little. "You married her."

"You introduced us."

"Didn't mean you had to make it permanent." Lazarus smiled as he took a pen out of his pocket and jotted down the directions to the store. "Please."

Lazarus went back to the small kitchen to retrieve the food as Ray went out of the door.

"Okay, here's something to eat and my friend is gone. Why did you think Nat was in trouble?"

"He look for her. He call her, tell her come now. Then he give me something. When I wake up, Natasha purse in chair. I call her. She no answer. So, I wait and wait for her come back. He no come back. She no come back. I think she in trouble with him. But, she have baby," Marja smiled and took a few bites of food.

"Who is he? I have to thank him for getting her to the hospital."

"You don't want talk to him. Not very friendly. Very mean."

"I bet he likes cash." Lazarus pulled out a wad of pounds. Marja smiled.

"Yes, he love cash. Takes from me every time I get some."

"Let me guess. Is he Jocko? Natasha's old pimping friend?"

"No, no that one in America."

"Where in America? For how long?"

"Big Jocko in America long time now. Come here long enough to get Natasha with baby and then go back. He leave Jocko Jr. in charge. He real mean. Meaner than Big Jocko. Likes play games on phone with each other. They call it three-way. They three-way Natasha to make it sound like Big Jocko here. But, he not here."

"Where can I find him? Where does he live?"

"Big Jocko in someplace he call Philly. He born there. Junior from Munich."

"So, it was Jocko Junior that hurt Nat," Lazarus said out loud, pulling out his phone. Big Jocko was in Philadelphia. The whole Sperling family was there.

"I need to call my friend in the States," he said, dialing Micah again. Still no answer. What was it with him and Kali not answering their phones?

He put the phone back in this pocket. "Where did you say Jocko Junior lived?"

"He don't live in Brixton. He live near you in North London somewhere. Used meet Nat at store."

"What store?"

"Starts with a T or something. I hate shopping."

"Tesco. Are you saying he would meet her at Tesco?"

"Yeah, that could be it. He live near there."

"What does he look like?"

Marja had finished her plate and was looking at it longingly. Lazarus dumped the rest from the container on the plate and she dug in hungrily. Nat had been right. The woman was starving.

"He look like Jocko."

"Big Jocko?"

"Yes. Weird-looking blond with bright blue eyes. Except Big Jocko cuter than Junior. Junior could look cute, but he just look mean."

Lazarus dialed Ray and walked away from Marja.

"Do you have drink?" Marja called after him. Lazarus came back to give her some water, but as he did, he caught a glimpse of Nat's purse. He picked it up and took it with him to the window.

He went through the purse and found the money he had given her, so it was obvious the killer wasn't trying to rob her, and then he found a receipt for Tesco's. That's where she had been yesterday morning. He wondered if she had encountered him there.

As Ray walked toward the car, a man hurriedly moved down the street and then bumped into him. Ray raised his hands in disgust thinking the man would, at least, pause to apologize but, instead, the man continued to move almost running. "Jeez, they are just as rude here as they are in the States," he complained to himself as he looked for the car that Lazarus had described parked on the street four houses down.

Ray found it and looked at the small car. The first thing he wondered was, how in the world did Lazarus fit in it. As he peered into this possible transportation, he noticed that it was a stick shift. How the hell did Lazarus expect him to sit on the right side, drive on the left side, and remember how to drive a stick to go on an errand in a city he was not familiar with at all. He pulled out the list and flipped it to read the directions.

But, then, looking straight ahead, he saw the same man who had bumped him standing about a block down, shifting a little as if he were cold. Ray was suspicious. Why was he in such a hurry to stand in one spot? Being a former law enforcement officer, his gut was telling him that the guy was up to no good because that spot didn't look like a bus stop. At least, there was no sign indicating it was. Ray reminded himself that this wasn't his turf and he had long ago turned in his badge. All he could do was observe.

Ray opened the car door and slid into the seat trying to get comfortable. He fumbled a few seconds with the keys and stuck one in the ignition. Then, he noticed the man again. He was still standing in the same spot. Ray decided to sit there a second longer to see if the man was meeting someone or trying to catch a cab. A few taxis had already passed him. This is silly, Ray thought, and put his hand on the key when his phone rang. He searched his pocket and answered it.

"Ray," Lazarus said as he walked toward the window with Nat's purse still in his hands, "I need you to keep an eye open for a tall, blond guy."

"Why?" Ray asked, his eyes still fixated on the guy down the street. He was blond, and he was tall.

"I think he's the guy that killed Natasha. Apparently, he lives around here somewhere."

"How do you know that?"

"Marja. She's giving me little bits and pieces."

"Ask her, ask her if this guy wears a big, light brown leather jacket." Ray took his hand off the key and began to open the door to the car as he heard Lazarus asking the question. Then he wriggled his way out of the car and started running toward the man. The man just stood there, looking in his direction. Ray ran faster. When Lazarus arrived at the window, he saw Ray running. He dropped the purse and began to run for the door. Before he could get down the stairs, he heard the loud explosion followed by screams from the baby and Elliott.

By the time Lazarus reached the street, his car and a couple of cars nearby were engulfed in flames. He found Ray on the other side of the steep apartment steps lying face down. Lazarus ran to him and covered him with his body.

"Get off me," Ray said, "I'm fine."

"Things are still flying. The other cars are going to catch."

Lazarus grabbed hold of Ray and they ran up the stairs before two or three more blasts went off.

"Is there a back door, man? The houses are going to catch fire if this keeps up. We have got to get everybody out." As they left the building, there were two more explosions. What a welcoming for little Aaron. Lazarus wanted to make this Jocko pay now in the worst way. They stayed in the backyard of the home as they heard the fire engines and saw their neighbors doing the same. Everyone was looking confused about what had happened, but there was no doubt in Ray's mind. The man who had bumped him had just planted a bomb and he would have been toast if Lazarus hadn't called.

CHAPTER TWELVE

T HE PAIN CREPT up the side of her face with an explosive force, jolting her into consciousness. As she lay there in the darkness giving all her attention to the pain, her left hand dropped down onto something hard. It made the sound of a loud thud. Now pain shot through her knuckles, too. She winced as she tried to lift her head, but the pain weighed it down like an over-sized bowling ball. Tears flinched outward from her eyes as if a pebble had splashed into a warm pool of water.

Taking deep breaths, she willed her right eye open realizing her left eye was not going to cooperate. The deeper her breaths, the more she began to smell the thick, musty odor of her surroundings. Wherever she was, this was not her nice clean, fresh-smelling bedroom in the penthouse. And that was not her nice thick comfy mattress beneath her. She opened her hand and felt a coarse, bare material beneath her, occasionally snagging on what felt like loose threads. As she moved a little more, she began to realize her body was on the hard coils of an uncovered cheap or old mattress. It creaked loudly with her every minor move.

This was not a dream. There was light coming from somewhere. She turned her head trying to ignore the extreme discomfort and noticed it was coming from underneath a doorway. Kali rolled her body toward the light and fell a few inches, striking the floor with another loud thud. No sooner than had she hit the floor, she heard heavy footsteps moving hurriedly and closer. Her greatest fear — feeling vulnerable — kicked in. She pulled her knees up to her body and used her hands to get some balance to shift herself up into a sitting position. Her head wanted to take her back down, but she refused to let it. Kali waited as she heard the jangle of keys, the unhinging of locks, and the twist of a doorknob. The door opened slightly and then a light switch went on. Her right eye, its sight blurred, tried to adjust to the figure darkening the door. It was him, she thought, as her head carried her forward and back into the darkness.

CHAPTER THIRTEEN

K ALI REALIZED SHE had passed out again. But, this time she awakened without the fuzziness. She groped around in the dark, found the floor and crawled toward the light under the door. When she reached the door, she pushed herself off her knees into a standing position, immediately swaying toward the wall for support. This time though her head didn't want to take her forward and down.

How long was she out was her first thought as she began to feel around the room for a light switch? The light bulb above her blinded her at first. She shielded her eyes as she felt the headache returning. Which one, she didn't know: the one that had been present for the last few weeks or the one that was caused by the blow to her head? She put both hands on her face and felt it, pressing her fingers lightly against every bone and cartilage, every inch of skin. Except for the slight swelling on the left side, she was fine. She could even see out of both eyes now.

Leaning against the wall, she took in the slight, ugly gray stucco room wondering if this was where Reck lived as a child. She remembered a few stories about a little white boy, but only vaguely. The stories had something to do with Jordan wanting to adopt him, but they wouldn't let him because he was black. Back then, that was unheard of and he had been blocked whenever and wherever he tried to make it happen. But, other than the fact that Ashton didn't like the kid, there wasn't much she knew, except Elle's intense reaction meant this was not good. Who was she kidding? THIS was not good.

What she did know was that she had to get home, she had to find out if her baby was okay. Whether she was asleep, dreaming, or awake, all she could see was Kacie's sweet little face. Where was she? Had he killed her, too?

Kali took a few unsteady steps toward the doorway with no door. She had to pee. She made it across the little room and almost tripped over the mattress which took up most of the floor space. Catching herself at the door frame, she leaned in for a view, but it was dark in there. She reached in and found a light switch. It didn't work.

What she could see from the light of her new bedroom was a toilet with no seat and no lid. Then she saw a bathtub and in it faded spots ringed with rust, where the faucet and the shower head used to be. There were no curtains or curtain rods either. Above the sink was an empty hole in the wall where a medicine cabinet once had hung, probably with a mirror on the outside and a light fixture above it or as part of it. The next thing she noticed was what she was wearing. Where were her clothes? Her violet and black designer suit had been replaced with a pair of cheap scrubs. She peeked inside the pants. As she suspected, she was panty-less. Bra-less, too.

Kali pulled down the scrub pants, squatted over the toilet and peed as if she had never peed before. She reached to push a handle to flush, but that was missing, too, then she reached inside the reservoir up top and realized there was no water and no mechanical devices to flush. Everything in this place had been stripped of anything she could use to defend herself. He hadn't even provided her with toilet paper, let alone soap.

Kali left the bathroom and began to feel the walls. She had no idea what she was looking for and she had no idea if she was alone. That thought startled her. Where was she? She stopped and started listening. Dropping down on the mattress, Kali pulled her legs close to her and backed up to the wall. What could she hear? Nothing.

At first, she heard nothing. That was odd. Carefully, she listened for traffic. There was a slight hum. There had to be a main street somewhere but not too nearby, perhaps a highway. She took a deep breath and tried to think of things she should be hearing. Buses? Where were the buses? In Philadelphia, no matter what street you lived on or walked on, a bus wasn't too far away. So, she sat there, listening for a bus. Nothing. No buses. Where would you be if there were no buses? Jersey, she thought, South Jersey. Where they had lived, there were no buses and no major highways or streets nearby. They were in an isolated area, off a two-lane highway in the country. Was she in the country? No, she ruled that out. She could still hear the low hum. Maybe there were no buses nearby, but there was a street with cars, but not this street. Still listening, she finally heard a car. Her ears perked listening for another. It took a while, and then she heard another one. The street must be small. Wherever she was, she concluded she was not in Philadelphia. But, another sound made her stomach tighten, footsteps.

Behind the footsteps coming toward her room, she heard the soundtrack of the news. A television was on. What news was on? Was it the morning, afternoon or evening news? Or, was it a special report, she thought as the keys jangled and the doorknob turned once again.

"Awake, I see." Reck let himself in and stood with his back to the door. "You had a really good nap this time."

"Your amenities are outstanding," Kali said, wrapping her arms around her knees.

"Don't worry, your majesty. I am not going to touch you. I have already had a feel or two while changing your clothes." Reck winked, disturbingly so.

"What? Didn't want to see the blood stains? Or, maybe you couldn't stand the reminder of killing a child? I hope you copped a good feel. But, I am sure it wasn't good enough to make you forget," Kali countered wiping the snicker off his lips. "What did you do to my daughter?" she asked, letting go of her knees.

"Your daughter?" Reck looked genuinely surprised, for a moment giving Kali a little hope.

"She wasn't who I tripped over, was she?" Kali remembered turning to run and then losing her balance, a balance righted by his fist full of her hair.

"You tripped over your son's legs," Reck said, but the look on his face told her different. She knew him that well, at least.

"My son? Or my daughter's boyfriend? It's on the news by now, isn't it? Who else did you kill, Reck? Why did you kill in the first place? What was the point? What are you so angry about that you would kill a child? And Mr. Brown? You could have left. We didn't see you. You could have disappeared before the police checked the surveillance tapes. It's all on video, you know. Probably audio, too, if there were still any listening devices in the place."

"Why do you ask so many questions?"

"You once called me nosy, remember? I want to know. Wouldn't you?"

"Ask your husband."

"That would be difficult to do. My husband is dead."

"You sit there lying to me, or to yourself?" Reck asked and slid down to a squatting position. Kali wondered if she could take him if she attacked him in that position.

"What are you holding against my dead husband?"

"Why don't you ask him?" Reck asked. He was surprised how beautiful she looked even when she was unkempt. Her hair was standing out all around her face looking like an out of control bird's nest.

"Okay, don't tell me. Tell the universe. I'm sure his spirit is out there somewhere."

"Funny. Very funny. I know Lazarus Smith is really Ashton. I have known all along. I was part of the crew in the know. Me, Ruby, Redd, his own twin brother, and his poor old friend Brady. I have got to give it to your husband though. He was a lot more devious and lot more dangerous than I thought him capable of being. He was such a pansy growing up. Jordan gave him everything. He never worked for a thing."

"Wow, I think we knew two different people. The Jordan I knew didn't hand out anything easily."

"You think you knew Jordan?" Reck leaned his head against the door and rolled his blue eyes. "You didn't know Jordan."

CHAPTER FOURTEEN

RECK WENT INTO the living room and sat down on the old green sofa, creating a whirlwind of dust as it flew up into his face. It had been years since he had set foot in this place. That is, until he had come up with the bright idea to hold Ashton captive there so he could torture him. Before that, the place had been left in the hands of a rental agent who hadn't rented it out in the last two years. No one had wanted to live in a downward spiraling subdivision with access to nothing.

Reck wasn't about to give up totally on his plan though; maybe that could still happen, he thought, as he remembered dropping Kali in the room instead. He wondered if Micah or Ashton would even bother to look for any properties he owned. Would they even think to search for him in Burlington Township? Heck, they had no idea what name to search under. Trying to track a property owned by Jonathan Reck or Jack Pulaski would lead them nowhere, he laughed.

When Reck was only eighteen, Jordan had transferred the deed to the house to a ghost corporation he had set up for Reck. That had been Jordan's subtle way of getting rid of him. After that, Jordan had given him enough money to live off until he could find a job. Then he made it official by kicking him out of the penthouse, all because of his shining star, Ashton. Reck had been smarter than Jordan had given him credit for being. He had rented it out through an agency and joined the Army until they kicked him out years later while serving in Germany. But, Reck had never sold the house because he knew, one day, he'd be back to settle things with bratty boy and he would need a place to lay low.

That day, the day that changed everything, was still etched in his mind. Some might say, he should have been too young to remember all the details of that day, but he did. The little boy, who he would find out later was Ashton, had run out in front of him at lightning speed. The wiry little kid was following an escaping ball when an exiting patron had opened the door to the little restaurant that he and his mother used to pass often. The three-year old's eyes were fixated on that ball as it bounced toward the street. Reck's mother had dropped her bags and lunged to grab the little boy before he stepped off the curb. That was what had caused his mother's accident. Ashton had tried to pull away from her, causing her to lose her balance and fall into the street. She had gotten hit by a car that had been meant for Ashton. Because of that one instance, not only had his mother's body been confined to a wheelchair but her mind as well. Marianne Pulaski took to that wheelchair like a special lifeline because it had opened doors for her that she had never known existed before.

Reck didn't care about the dust; he lay on the couch that had belonged to an old tenant, resting his head. Kali Sperling was right. It was all on video. He knew that. That's why his original plan had been to be clandestine, like he had been three years ago when they had almost killed Ashton the first time. At least, he smiled, they had brought him down. But, not down far enough. Ashton was healthy again. He'd seen pictures of him with Natasha. He was obviously trying to make a comeback. Reck couldn't allow that, now could he?

Reck felt as if he had lost too much because of that idiot and Ashton had lost too little to call things even. It didn't matter that he was hiding behind the identity of a man with no memory, calling himself Lazarus Smith. He looked like Ashton again, and Reck knew what that meant, even if no one else did. Ashton was getting ready to come out of hiding. He was going to fight to get his family back. Except, Reck planned for Ashton to come home and witness losing his family members one at a time. Then he would put him in a grave right next to the rest of them.

At first, Reck had been excited to go to the airport to pick him up. He was ready to act right then and there, hoping by the time Ashton recognized him it would be too late. Reck imagined drugging the big guy and delivering him into the very room where Kali was now. He was going to show him videos of his family dying one by one.

"Whoo Hoo." Reck sat up and clapped his hands at the thought, and then remembered who was in the other room.

He was at the airport when he had gotten the call from his son, the product of one of his German whores. The women who had worked for them called the boy Jocko Jr., not only because he looked exactly like his father, but because he had helped with the orgies in Germany as soon as he was old enough. That is, before the authorities started sniffing them out and disrupting their traveling parties. Reck had decided then to leave his Jocko moniker and profession behind before he ended up in a German prison. He had been okay with turning away from that trade and that country because, by then, he had Redd and a beautiful little boy. The boy was sickly but, at the time, they had no idea he was going to become terminal. They moved to London where Reck started managing a few women, just like Jordan had. He knew, without a doubt, that would have been one way to make Jordan proud of him.

While he sat in the airport waiting for Ashton, Jocko Jr. had given him the news about how badly things had gone with Natasha, causing him to move the schedule up based on panic: now Ashton had his child and was still in London. Not only that, because of that old Sperling witch, he was probably under suspicion meaning he would no longer have access to the family. Why else would Micah have sent him on a wild goose chase?

The information his son gave him in that moment spurred a type of indecision and spontaneous anger that had never happened to Reck before. Or had it? Reck punched the couch pillows trying to find a comfortable spot and glanced toward the door. A memory of himself as a kid answering that door flooded through his mind. It was as clear as if it were yesterday.

The doorbell rang and eight-year-old Jack ran as fast as he could to answer it. He knew who it was. He and his mother had only one real visitor, the one visitor that always walked in like sunshine rushing in with him. He and his grandson would always arrive with arms loaded. At first, Jack was excited to see the little fellow. He would take Ashton by the hand and lead him to the ugly sofa that sat in the middle of the living room floor facing a big, console television that Jordan had bought them. They would watch cartoons while Jordan put away groceries and fixed a meal to die for. Sometimes Jack would be so anxious to eat that he would run in and out of the kitchen for an inspection and a taste test. He would take a few morsels back to share with Ashton.

Jack looked up to Jordan, the tall, dark Negro man that he loved and couldn't understand why other people didn't like him. That's why Jordan had them moved to Burlington Township. The houses were further apart and no one paid too much attention to the tall Negro going in and out of the house with a single white woman in a wheelchair and her young, impressionable son. Jordan had been met with a lot of hate and confrontations going in and out of their little apartment in South Philly. It was as if their neighbors thought he was carrying some deadly disease, all because of his skin color. Even though some of them recognized who he was, they didn't want him near poor, crippled Marianne Pulaski. Not that any of those concerned neighbors cared about her before she became a cripple. Most of the time, they wouldn't have even talked to either of them.

But, when he was twelve things started changing, even in Burlington, and he wasn't ready to change with those things.

"Where's your mother, Jack?" Jordan and Ashton walked through the doorway with their usual bounty. Ashton sped by Jack and plopped on the sofa, putting his feet up on the coffee table.

"Get your feet down, boy. You and Jack put those groceries away," Jordan said as he walked down the hallway of the one-story home, heading for the master bedroom.

Jordan knocked on the door lightly and then opened it.

"Damn, woman. Don't you ever get out of this bed? You have a son in there who needs your attention. Get up and clean this smelly house. This is pathetic."

"Don't start with me, old man. You the one stopped the housekeeping. I can't get up and clean this place. I can't reach half of what's in here. You promised to make it handicap friendly," Marianne complained. She was sitting in her bed covered with magazines and discarded food wrappers. The smell was disgusting.

"Have you shit on yourself?" Jordan asked.

"No, Jordan, I need a bath. Nobody been here to help me take a bath."

"Marianne, I have known you for six years now. Been taking care of your every need, but you are passed all of that. There are plenty of people in wheelchairs who not only work, but who take care of their families, and they don't sit in bed feeling sorry for themselves, drinking all day."

Jordan walked around the bed, picking up tissues and napkins tossed around the floor. "Until you start making some kind of effort to better yourself, I'm not hiring another soul to set foot in this house. Your bathroom has guardrails. Get up and get your ass in the bathtub. Take a bath before I leave here. If you fall, I can pick you up. If you don't, as much as it would hurt Jack, as much as it would hurt me to hurt Jack, I will walk away. I have done all I can for you. All I can. It's over, Marianne." Jordan put the trash in the wastebasket and left Marianne sitting in the bed wiping tears from her puffy, red face.

He was tired. He had tried to keep his promise. She had saved Ashton's life, and that was the most heroic thing anyone had ever done for him or his family. He had every intention of making sure that the two of them were well cared for. But, there was a limit. Marianne just sat there getting fatter and fatter, drinking more and more.

"Who's buying her the liquor?" Jordan walked into the kitchen to find the two boys silently putting the food away. He was having to drag Ashton across the bridge now. Ashton complained of the smell, said his clothes smelled like them hours after he left. Plus, he didn't like the shows Jack made him watch. It had become a struggle for both of them, but Jordan couldn't let Jack completely falter with such a whacked-out mother.

"The librarian," Jack answered.

"The who?"

"My mom had to go to school with me one day because all of the parents had to be present. I pushed that wheelchair all the way to school, Jordan. She didn't even try to wheel herself," Jack complained. "Why is she like that?"

"I don't know." Jordan shook his head. He had disposed of a few women just like her in his stables. But, he couldn't do anything to Marianne. She hadn't been in his stable and she had a son who needed her. He wondered what Jack would have been like if she had not fallen in front of that car keeping Ashton from getting hit. Immediately, he figured the boy would already be living a life of crime. Right now, though, his grades were good and, from what Marianne had told him, the teachers thought well of him. He was courteous and he did seem to try to take care of his mother. But, he knew the boy was lonely. Who could take him to his friends' birthday parties or watch him play in a baseball game? Jordan had done what he could and showed up to see what he could do, but he had to be on the road most of the time. Plus, Jack wasn't his, could never be legally, according to Billy who was now a lawyer. Some way, somehow, he had to get Marianne off her ass.

"Does he bring it in the house or leave it on the doorstep?"

"Both. He has been coming by more and more often."

"Do me a favor. Call me the next time he comes over here. I want to talk to him. Can you do that for me?" Jordan was serious. He had had enough. The woman was useless and he was going to stop giving her a pass right now. He thought about putting Jack in a private school away from this. He ruffled Jack's spikey blond hair.

"You need a haircut," Jordan laughed. "After we eat, let's get it cut."

Jack didn't have to call Jordan. Before they could get back from the barber shop and a movie, Claude Wilson had brought Marianne some more liquor and, since she had taken a bath, he was sharing her bed.

"Listen, darling, did you cook all of that food out there?" Wilson asked

Marianne as he got dressed. She had already told him that Jack would be back soon.

"No, my manservant does that for me. You know the one I told you about," Marianne cooed in her deep, South Philly accent. Her mother had been Italian and her father had been Polish. After her father was killed in the war, her mother had moved them back to the Italian haven of South Philadelphia. She thought manservant was a great term to describe Jordan. She had heard it used in one of those 1940s movies that she loved so much. Wilson kissed her and made her squeal.

"You mean that nigger fellow that keeps coming in and out like he owns the place?"

"Yes, he means well," Marianne answered. "He thinks he is helping out, but you see this place. I could use a real man in here to help with that wild son of mine."

"Don't worry about that, sweetheart. I can be here for you. I just don't want to deal with no crazy niggers coming in and out though. I know you saved his grandson and all, but you need to put a stop to his visits. You do that, and I will move in. I will keep you well taken care of and that son of yours, too. He needs a real man in here to discipline him, like you said." Wilson looked at his watch and decided to leave before the others got back. He winked at Marianne and blew her a kiss. She caught it smiling and decided she had had enough of Jordan and his demands. All she needed from him was a check, she didn't need his visits. And now that she had her own man, she didn't need him around to do things for her. She was going to let him know as soon as he got back.

Jack had never been happier. He loved going to the movies with Jordan. Not only did he see the latest movies, but he could get popcorn, candy, sodas and hot dogs, whatever he wanted. Jordan had left Ashton in the car half asleep. What they found when they walked in the house confounded them both. Marianne was dressed, sitting in her wheelchair watching television in the living room. The place had been picked up, slightly. At least, it was looking a little better. She was sitting there with a big grin on her flushed face.

"Well, look at this," Jordan said cheerfully. "I bet you are feeling a lot better, aren't you?"

"Well, you are right, I do feel much better," Marianne said, brushing a few crumbs from her lap. She had ventured into the kitchen and found Jordan's buttermilk biscuits he had made for Jack's breakfasts.

"Now, all you have to do, Marianne, is to do this, the same thing every day. You'd be surprised how much better you will feel. You'd be surprised by the things you might become interested in doing. One step a time. And, by the way, you look very nice."

"Thank you, Jordan." Marianne smiled up at the man she used to wish was her man. But, she knew that wouldn't work, him being colored and all, and especially since she couldn't travel around with him in her wheelchair. She had seen the newspapers and magazines about the places he traveled and the people he met. Nobody knew how well he took care of her when he wasn't doing all those glamourous things with those glamorous people. But, she sighed, she had a man now, a white one, not famous, but one who would help to take care of her. She took a deep breath to make her announcement.

"Jordan," she said, reaching for his hand. He let her take it. "You are right, Jack and me need to take care of ourselves more without depending on you for everything."

"All I am asking, Marianne, is for you to take more responsibility for yourself, your son, and your surroundings. You can't sit in bed all day expecting him or anybody else to wait on you. You have run that well dry. Get a job. Get out of the house. Pay Jack some attention," Jordan said, taking his hand back. He knew that look in Marianne's eyes. What was coming?

"I don't need a job," Marianne said. "I have a man now, a real man. He's going to move in to help me and Jack. All that he asks is that you don't come over to visit anymore."

"What?"

"He's not comfortable with a Negro man hanging around me and my son. I know he's wrong. You have never done anything other than be good to us. But, he has to get used to you. So, I am asking you not to show up unannounced 'til we can work things out." Marianne tried to grab Jordan's hand again, but Jordan stepped back, sat down on the ugly plain sofa he had bought because that was what she had wanted, and glanced at the television set that he had let Jack pick out.

"Do you like this man, Jack?" Jordan looked at the little boy whose eyes were bulging from the news.

"No, no. I hate him. He's greasy looking. His teeth are broken, and he's a horrible teacher. Nobody likes him. That's why they made him a librarian," Jack said, repeating middle school gossip. "And, and…he comes to school drunk and he comes here drunk."

"No such thing. No such thing. You lie Jack. Why you lie?" Marianne protested.

"He can't be too far off track, Marianne. Most of the time I come over here you are sitting in your bed drunk. You smell like alcohol now and supposedly you have had a bath." Jordan sat forward, putting his hands on his knees.

"Don't listen to her, Jordan," Jack pleaded. "Don't stop coming."

"I won't, Jack. Does this man know that he is planning to move into a house that I own? Does he know that he is trying to ban me from my own house? I bet he thinks you own this place."

Jordan stood up. "Marianne, if you want to live with this man, you can live with him under his own roof, not mine. You are a grown woman; I can't tell you how to raise your son. But, I recommend waiting until he gets to know Jack and waiting until he marries you before living with him. With that said, I can't stop him from visiting you, but if I find out he's living here, I am going to have to evict you. I have talked to your physical therapists, your doctors, everybody whom I have paid to take care of you. The only thing holding you back is your lack of desire to do anything for yourself. I suggest you start doing as much as you can for you as soon as possible. Your ride here is dead ending.

"I've got to go." Jordan looked at his watch. "Ashton is sitting in the car half asleep. He's been out there too long by himself already. Walk me to the car, Jack," Jordan said, putting his arm around the boy's shoulder.

"Jordan, you can't mean that," Marianne whined. "You promised to always take care of me and my boy."

"Taking care of you did not mean waiting on you hand and foot." Jordan opened the door and let Jack out first. They could both hear Marianne crying loudly behind them. Neither of them turned around. Her shrill whining was a norm, hard to take seriously for any reason.

Jordan hugged Jack thinking he was going to talk to Billy again about adopting this boy or setting it up somehow where he could legally care for Jack. If that wouldn't work, he was just going to have to take him and pay someone to act as a cover. All he knew was that he had to get Jack out of that woman's reach. The boy had been tainted by her long enough.

"It's going to be alright, Jack." Jordan kissed the boy on top of his head and left. Jack stood there watching as Ashton's head lay against the window of the brand-new Mercedes. If Jack could have had his way, Ashton would have been in the back seat and he would have been in the front seat driving away with Jordan. Jack closed the door and went back into the living room. His mother had already wheeled herself out. He turned on the television and put his feet up on the coffee table. He had to get away from his mother, one way or another.

CHAPTER FIFTEEN

RECK HAD GONE out into the hallway and leaned against the wall outside his mother's old bedroom. No matter how many times he had set foot in that house since he was twelve, he could never bring himself to step into that room. Maybe it was because a part of him thought she was still in there, waiting. Waiting for him to come and apologize for what he had done to her.

It had been as if an atomic bomb had exploded within his chest that day. He could remember watching that big, black Mercedes pull off with Ashton in the front seat asleep, drooling on the window of the passenger side. He remembered trying to imagine what his and his mother's lives would have been like, if she had just let that little bastard run into the street and die. At that moment, he wanted Ashton dead, somehow believing if Ashton was dead, his mother would regain her legs and they would be living somewhere in South Philly and doing…nothing; he had finished his thought.

Even at five years old, he knew his mother was trash. Jack had no idea which one of the men who spent nights and — sometimes days — with his mother in her bedroom for hours at a time was his father. Maybe none of them. Sometimes, she would come out and put a box of cereal and some milk on the table. She would flip on the television as loud as it would go and tell him to be a good boy and don't bother her. Then one man would leave and another would come. They would all look at him strangely. A couple of them tried to touch him, but his mother made a big enough fuss for them to leave him alone or just leave. That wouldn't have changed. Jack had realized that by the age of 12. He had heard boys talking about women who put out for money. Jack would never say anything, but he remembered money on his mother's bedroom table that usually wasn't there before the male visitor came. He got it. That was how she earned her living.

But, then there was the accident and Jordan. His mother no longer had to work on her back. And Jack had everything he could dream of, except to live with Jordan. Sometimes, Jordan would take him to his house in Germantown and then later to that tall apartment building in Center City. Those days were filled with excitement and joy. A few times, he had even spent the night across the hall from Ashton's bedroom in a big bed of his own. It would have been a dream come true, if he never, ever had to set foot back in Jersey again. But, he had to go back to take care of his mother. She was a woman who was too darn happy about the attention she was getting from the nurses, housekeepers, and physical therapists Jordan had hired. She had stopped doing anything for herself, literally, until now. Jordan was finally tired of paying for all those amenities since everyone reported Marianne wouldn't lift a finger to help herself, at least when they were around.

Jack's legs moved stiffly, his mind seething with rage. Fireworks were bombarding his young nerves at once. He had wanted to scream. As he reached his mother's bedroom door, the doorbell rang. For a second, calm entered his mind. He thought Jordan had come back for him. He ran and opened the door to find that greasy pig his mother was calling her man at the door. The alcoholic stench was too much. Jack tried to shut the door. The man stopped it with his foot and used his weight to push it all the way open.

"Move out of the way, boy." Claude shoved Jack out of his way. The boy was such a lightweight, he barely felt him. Claude laughed as the boy's back hit the wall inside the doorway.

"My mother's gone to bed," Jack yelled after him.

"Good thing. That's where I am going," Claude said, not bothering to look back. He was on a mission. He had seen the car pull off and knew Jordan was gone. He couldn't wait to get back in to see how things had gone.

Marianne was struggling to undress herself as he walked in.

"There's my lovely lady," Claude said, stumbling a little toward her and noticing the scuff marks from her wheelchair along the wall. He was going to have to tolerate this filth for a while. "Did you give that nigger his walking papers like we discussed?"

Claude began to help her out of her clothes and out of her chair.

"We talked," she said, putting her arms around him. She lay her head in the cusp of his neck as he lifted her into the bed.

"And...?" Claude began to peel out of his shirt, revealing his beer belly and his incredibly red, hairy upper torso.

Marianne reached over and let her hand run across his pink nipples which stood at attention. He took her hand and kissed it.

"Home." Claude kissed her on the cheek. "I'm home. I will bring my things over tomorrow."

"Well," Marianne began to say and then hesitated. "Maybe we should wait a little while. Jordan thought we should consider Jack. Jack is not all too happy with us right now."

"Fuck, Jack," Claude said. "He's a fucking kid. He knows nothing at this

age. You yourself said he needed some discipline. I can give that to him."

"Well, you know Jordan thinks a lot of that child. I don't think he would go for you punishing Jack. I mean, if Jack tells him, things might not go the way we want them, too."

"Did he threaten you? I don't care who the fuck that nigger is, I will kick his ass. Did he threaten you?"

"He said if you move in with me, we all have to move." Marianne tried to put her arms around the thick torso lying next to her. He pushed her away.

"What control does he have over you? He can't tell you to move out of your own house." Claude sat up at attention. He had been counting on selling this house to help get him out of debt. Why else would he be interested in this unkempt, ugly cripple?

"It's his house. He had said he was going to put it in my name, but he hadn't gotten around to it yet. He travels a lot you know."

"I know who the hell he is. You're telling me you don't own this house? That's not what you said when we met, bitch."

"Claude, don't be rude. Eventually, he's going to give me the house. Don't worry. Come on. It will just be a while before we can live together. Besides, he's right. You and Jack need to get to know each other. I'd be a terrible mother if I didn't consider Jack."

"You are a terrible mother, bitch. A terrible lover, too. You must have been a terrible whore. You can't do a damn thing for yourself and here I was…here I was about to marry your dried-up ass," Claude said as he got up and searched for his shirt and belt. He was glad he hadn't removed anything else. His head was spinning.

"Don't be like that, Claude. Don't say such hateful things. You go sober up and come back tomorrow," Marianne pleaded as Claude stormed out of her bedroom slamming the door behind him.

Marianne reverted to her usual loud wail. Jack was sitting on the sofa watching television with the volume low enough to hear what the adults were saying. He didn't budge when he heard Claude bumping into the walls as he stormed down the hall. For a moment, Claude stopped and looked at the back of Jack's head. He had the urge to go punch it, but tempered himself. He couldn't sell this damn house. He was going to have to keep working until he found himself another helpless woman. If he hit Jack now, he would probably lose his job.

"Bitch," Claude stopped and yelled as he was exiting the front door.

Jack got up and turned off the television. He wanted to call Jordan, but realized that wouldn't do any good. Jordan had called someone on the phone about rehearsal tonight for a television show. Jack could never get in touch with Jordan when he was rehearsing or when he was on the road or in a show.

He sighed and sank as deep as he could into the couch hoping it would eat him. He put his hands over his ears to silence his mother's screams of distress. She had lost two men in one day. Jordan was visibly angry when he left. Jack wasn't used to seeing that look on Jordan's face. It kind of made him feel special, feel stronger seeing that Jordan was not a man to take lightly. He was going to grow up to be like Jordan, kind but strong as hell.

Finally, Jack's mother's cries drifted into silence with a slight whimper here and there.

"Jack, Jack," Marianne called. "Bring me some water, Jack," she said between loud, gross sniffles. "And some tissues," she yelled.

Jack got up and filled up a glass with water in the kitchen. Then he went into the living room and grabbed a box of tissues from the coffee table. Before going in, he stood outside his mother's door hitting himself in the head with the box. He hated her. The last thing he wanted to see right now was her, lying in that bed, drunk, crippled, and pathetic. The very image of her on the other side of that door detonated that atom bomb once again. Jack opened the door and was standing next to his mother, surprised he had even entered the room.

"Don't spill the water. Help me drink," Marianne said, not even attempting to lift her head off the pillow.

Jack put down the box of tissues and the glass of water. He sat on the bed next to his mother and lifted her head.

"The water, Jack. I really need the water," Marianne said as her eyes looked over at the glass of water.

"Sure, mother. Let me get another pillow to prop up your head. I can't manage your head and the glass like this," Jack said in his most adult voice. He was practicing as he needed Jordan to be proud of him for his maturity and trust him enough to take him home with him. He leaned over his mother and picked up a pillow from the other side of the bed. He lifted her head for a moment and then dropped it back on the pillow.

"Jack, stop playing. I'm thirsty. I've cried out all my water. Be an understanding young man," his mother said with her arms lying limp next to her plump body.

"I'm not playing, mother," Jack said as he took the pillow he had picked up and put it over his mother's face. Her arms immediately went into action, but he pinned them down with both of his knees as he straddled her. For a moment, he thought he felt his mother's legs move behind him. He looked back and they were.

"She's a lying, bitch," Jack said to himself as he stared at the headboard waiting for his mother to stop moving. When she finally did, he stayed put for a little while longer, not wanting to take any chances. After thinking it was probably long enough, he got down off the bed and stood there. Looking down at the floor, he saw Claude's belt. Jack, remembering how the criminals covered up their acts on television, grabbed some tissues. Then he picked up the belt with the tissues and put it around his mother's neck, taking care not to touch it as he put the belt through the loop where the buckle was. He pulled hard until his mother's head jerked. He thought he may have even heard a snap. He got off his mother again, went into his room and fell sound asleep.

The next morning Jack stuck his head into the bedroom and saw Marianne lying there with the belt still around her throat. He smiled. After pouring himself a glass of juice and making a bowl of Rice Krispies, he went to the phone in the living room and called the police screaming that something had happened to his mother. She looked dead. He was afraid to go into her room, but it looked like there was something was around her neck.

"She won't answer me," he cried into the phone. "There's something on her neck."

The woman on the phone had told him to go sit on his front step until the police arrived. He did exactly what she told him to do. Everything was working perfectly, except for one thing. He forgot to call Jordan.

Reck tried to rest, but he couldn't. Nothing was going the way he had imagined it. Kali Sperling was right about something else. In his haste, he had killed the wrong boy. It was not only all over the news, but so was his face and the fact that she had been kidnapped. Thanks to the security cameras inside and outside the penthouse and thanks to his inside alliance, the police would eventually have access to audio of what took place, too.

There was no coming out of this one unscathed. Micah had already given the police enough information to be looking for Jack Pulaski as well as Jonathan Reck. Both of his names were all over the news. But, he would be damned if they were going to catch him. He was determined not to serve time for anything less than Ashton's cold dead body in the ground. Reck had fantasized about Ashton coming home to witness the death of his family, not family friends. He wouldn't be satisfied until he had executed his plan to make Ashton suffer as much as he had. All because of Ashton, he had lost his child, his wife, and the dream life he should have had with Jordan. It wasn't fair. He should have been heir to some of that money Jordan had left behind.

His phone began to ring and he answered it with shaking hands, surprising even himself. Nothing ever shook him before. Not like this. He took a deep breath.

"Did you get my son?" Reck asked the caller without giving him a chance to say a word.

"No, I almost got your Lazarus, though. I blew up his car."

"You did what?"

"I figured he would need the car to go get things for the baby. I told you he checked him out of the hospital. Right?"

"You did what?" Reck rubbed his head.

"Look, it was an easy plan. I sent Marja in to see the baby, to get the baby. Since he has no one else here, I figured he would let her take care of the baby while he got some supplies. I was right. He came to the car, but he got out just before the car blew up."

"Did you kill him?"

"No, but I think he's hurt or he could be dead. Someone dragged him into the house." Jocko Jr. hesitated and then added, "But the house caught fire. No one came out."

"You idiot. You idiot. All I asked you to do was to keep Natasha with you until she had the baby, not cut the baby out. And, I never asked you to kill him. Nor kill my child. Don't you ever listen to me? He was supposed to be in the States by now."

"You were upset he had your baby. I could hear it in your voice. I came to get the baby back. Plus, Natasha was going on and on about it being *his* baby, not *yours*. She said you would never see your baby. I got angry. So, I decided, if it wasn't your baby, you would want it to use against him. I didn't think you cared about Natasha. She was an evil woman."

"You believed her?" Reck asked pacing the floor. "You are dumber than I ever thought. That is my child. I'm upset you put Lazarus in the position to get his hands on my child. He was supposed to be in the United States where I could deal with him personally." Reck cut off the phone and started to slam it into the floor, but he stopped himself. He needed it. This was the only phone they couldn't trace. He had already gotten rid of the other phones, his and the one belonging to Kali.

Reck sat back down on the sofa and dropped his head into his hands. He had surrounded himself with imbeciles. How could that idiot expect Marja to walk in there with any credibility as someone who could care for a child?

CHAPTER SIXTEEN

KALI LAY ON the mattress curled up into a ball trying to get warm in the chilly room. She was scared. Coming up with a way to escape was beyond comprehension as she looked around the bare room. His height and his weight were an advantage, but she wasn't going to let that stop her from fighting to the end, if necessary. Suddenly, there were a lot of angry noises coming from somewhere else in the house. Reck had lost it.

She got up and started touching the dingy colored walls hoping for a hollow sound or for something that she could put her foot through. But, what then? If she could break into another room, would it at least have a window for her to escape? She felt the door. It was solid wood, the kind they used to put in older homes. Letting her fingers run across the deadbolt and the doorknob, she tried to give herself some hope. She traced the wall back to the bathroom with the missing door and the missing hinges. She went into it and looked under the sink, but the only thing there was the metal pipe welded into the sink and into the wall. She didn't have a wrench. Even the contraption to close the sink to keep the water from flowing out was missing.

Kali was going to have to fight; she had to. Closing her eyes, Kali tried to blot out that nagging mystery headache. Fighting him would be tricky enough; he was the one who taught her most of the martial arts she knew in the first place. He would know what to expect from her, but she had to force those defeating thoughts out of her head. Biting his balls off was not beneath her, neither was gouging out his eyes. Whatever it took, she had to get home to Kacie. Trusting, loving little Kacie who had held them all together, who had been the glue to keep their family whole and complete. Kali needed to wrap her arms around her, hold her. Where was she? Kali's heart ached from the unknown. Had she tripped over her baby?

Reck tossed and turned on the sofa as long as he could. He had to decide. If any part of his plan was going to come to fruition, Ashton had to come home soon. Jocko Jr. had created even more of a mess in

London than he had counted on or planned. And, if he knew anything about the authorities, which he did know too well, they were going to keep Ashton from leaving London until they were perfectly sure he was clear of having had anything to do with Natasha's murder and now the bombing.

He picked up his phone and called another London associate. Reck asked her to call the police and turn in Jocko Jr. for both the murder of Natasha and the bombing and blame it on his obsession with Natasha. Then he called Jocko Jr. and told him to meet Marja at their apartment in Brixton. His son had begged his forgiveness over and over hearing the disapproval in his father's voice. Reck had promised him he would consider forgiving him and then convinced his son to find Marja, take care of her, and then go back to Munich. Jocko Jr. had agreed willingly. Now Ashton would have no excuse for not leaving London. But, how long was it going to take now that he had custody of the baby? He got up and went into the kitchen. The television was still on.

"Tragedy strikes the descendants of Jordan Banks once again, as if all that is left behind of his long, stellar career in the music business is a doomed and very unlucky family. Just under four years ago his son, Billy Banks Sperling, was found murdered in his home, followed by a very public assassination of his grandson, Ashton Taylor Sperling who had just thrown his hat into the mayoral race. A very popular candidate, everyone had expected him to win. Now this, a friend of one of Ashton Sperling's daughters was found murdered in their home.

According to sources, Mrs. Sperling walked in on the murder scene and was kidnapped by the alleged killer. A region-wide search is now on for a Jack Pulaski, Mrs. Sperling's personal bodyguard, also known as Jonathan Reck. The Sperling family owns PDSI, a nationally-known security firm, offering personal and corporate security services and products. Since Mr. Sperling's murder was never solved, the family had beefed up their own personal security, but it appears that their security measures failed when they vetted this employee. All that is known about Reck is that he is a former career Army man, born in Philadelphia as Jonathan 'Jack' Pulaski, and was adopted by a family in Linden, New Jersey, whose last name was Reck."

The reporter was still talking when Reck punched the power button on the old television set that sat on the counter in the kitchen. He had found it in the garage and was surprised it even worked since it was something else another tenant had discarded, like the couch he went back to sit on.

He brushed off more dust as it popped up around him on the sofa. A silly thought about firing the rental agency overseeing the property raced through his mind. It was obvious they hadn't been doing such a great job and it was a wonder the neighbors hadn't complained. But, why would they? At least, the grass was cut. That thought made him feel normal for a few minutes as did another thought that the house still looked good on the outside. Maybe the agency was worth a little of the money.

His thoughts were now pummeling his mind as if they were trying to normalize his situation. He laughed at himself, knowing that he would never be paying them or anyone else again. His chance to be just a businessman or a legitimate investor was long-gone. Whatever happened now would be the end of the road for him, be it death or prison. For a fraction of a second, he experienced sadness and a regret he didn't realize existed until her face flashed in his imagination. Its name was Kali. But then, there were other regrets. Like there would be no one inheriting anything he left behind, neither this house nor his savings, nothing. And no one would be standing at his graveside either. Just like he had imagined no one standing at Marianne Pulaski's graveside.

"What now?" he asked himself looking back toward the kitchen. He needed to feed her. There was no doubt she was hungry. If she had stuck to her schedule, she hadn't eaten anything in over 36 hours. He looked at his watch. Heck, even he was hungry.

CHAPTER SEVENTEEN

KALI JUMPED WHEN she heard the keys in the lock. Reck opened the door. She heard the crumpled plastic grocery bag in his hand. Something was in it.

"I brought you a few apples and some bottled water. Thought it might help you get through the rest of the day." He set two bottles on the floor next to the mattress and threw three red apples onto the mattress.

Kali looked at her "gifts"; she was starving.

"What's the matter, Reck? Don't have the stomach to kill a woman with an empty stomach?"

"I don't worry about stomach contents when I kill, but if you would rather starve to death waiting for your man to come, be my guest." Reck looked around the room. Kali wondered what he could possibly be looking for since the room was bare and obviously, with its faint color of gray puke, not freshly painted.

"Afraid I may have missed a potential weapon?"

"There isn't anything useful in this room to you or anybody else. That's why you are in this room," he answered in a melancholy tone.

"Is it getting to you now? Killing an innocent child?"

"That innocent child was fucking your daughter." Reck grunted half a chuckle that Kali had never heard before. She used to like it when he laughed.

"Well, great, stick around and I will have you murder all the men that fuck my daughters." Kali had moved to the other side of the mattress and stood up as the water and the apples began to tempt her. Dropping to her knees, she crawled toward one of the apples, picked it up and started examining it.

"Don't worry, Mrs. Sperling. I'm not the one poisoning you. Heck, by the time you get out of here, your body may have eliminated what's left of the toxins," he said, putting his hand on the doorknob. "Not that it really matters now."

"Poisoning me? What are you talking about?" Kali asked as she rubbed the apple on her pants leg.

"The headaches. The headaches have a source. A little of cup of tea, of source." Reck smiled at his own gibe.

"What are you saying, Reck?"

"I'm saying you drink a lot of tea," he said as he opened the door and left.

Kali examined the apple to make sure there weren't any tiny holes or pricks. She took a bite as she thought about her personally delivered morning cups of tea.

"No, no way," she said, taking another bite out of the apple. It was old, she could tell by the toughness of the peel. She wondered how old it was and, as she continued to eat it, she considered her tea. Reck was right, Kali was in the habit of drinking tea before she imbibed anything else almost every day. And almost every day for the last month or so, her sweet nephew had delivered his special blend of home-grown tea.

"Auntie, look what I have. Can you taste it? Let me know if you like it." Artie had knocked on her door one morning.

"I love it. What is it?"

"It's an herbal tea I grew in the greenhouse. Wanna come see?"

"Sure," Kali grabbed a sweater and tried to keep up with Artie and his long Sperling legs. It was still chilly outside, even though it was late Spring. They went downstairs to the kitchen to another set of stairs leading up to the roof of the building. Up there, Micah, Artie, and Adam had spent most of the last summer building the greenhouse from scratch. Kali had watched them with joy, and Ash with much disapproval. He did everything he could to keep from getting his hands dirty. That boy was too much like his father. Though Ashton had fun getting dirty with the kids when they lived down in Jersey, normally he wouldn't do anything that would get him too grimy. You could always count on his hands being clean; he washed them incessantly.

But, Ash had complained about everything to the point that the other boys had kicked him off the roof. Kali had been proud that Micah wouldn't let Ash help them celebrate when it was completed, something that had an actual impact on the boy. He had seemed jealous when the other boys went to Great Adventure to celebrate and he had to stay home with the girls.

"Look at all the neat things I have grown." Artie led the way into the greenhouse. He began to touch the plants as he passed them.

"I know how much you like tea. The one you tasted was lemon balm. This one. I have grown some mint for you, here. Some chamomile, here." Artie was

excited and animated as he touched each plant he named. "And look, I have herbs to cook with, too. The chef is going bonkers, coming in here all the time to get stuff. Look, I have rosemary and thyme."

Kali smiled. He was happy and that made her happy. Last year, in one of their many lengthy and serious conversations, Artie said he wanted to be a botanist or a farmer. Kali had gone straight to Micah with her idea of a greenhouse, except she was thinking of something on a much smaller scale. This one was big enough to be seen from an airplane.

"But wait, Auntie, come here." Artie went into the rear corner and waited for her. "This is just for show, Auntie. It's poisonous. All of the plants in this area, don't eat or drink, okay?" Artie then bounced to another area of the greenhouse.

"Sure, but put a sign or something up," Kali said, stopping to sniff one of the plants. "Let everyone else know these things are poisonous and to be careful. Not that I think anyone other than the cook is coming up here to go grocery shopping."

"Ta Da," said Artie, holding up his hands like Vanna White on that game show where people had to guess the words from a few letters. "Look, Auntie. Tomatoes. These are my tomato plants. And these are my peppers. And these are my beans. Isn't this cool?"

"So cool," Kali said with as much excitement as Artie's, honestly feeling it with him.

"Would you like some more tea?" Artie asked.

"Yes, I am dying for more." Kali gave him a big hug and they went back to life as normal, with one exception. Every morning thereafter, Artie brought her a cup of tea.

Kali curled up on the bare mattress and stared at another apple. She couldn't stop thinking of Artie. He wouldn't be the only child in her household capable of murder. Ashton never spelled it out for her, but there was enough evidence in the way he and Micah treated Ash after the supposed assassination that made her think it was Ash who had pulled the trigger that night. And, at the time, he had been only fifteen. That's how old Artie was now. She wondered if Ashton was that old when he had made his first kill. That was a story she knew she would never hear, not from his lips anyway. But, why would Artie want to kill her? As she tried to come up with one reason, she remembered a day when she had been angry with Micah. But, not just Micah, she was just plain angry — and reckless.

"What are you going to do, kill me like you did Ruby?" Kali had shouted at Micah. It had been their first argument over Anjuli.

"What the…." Micah was furious. He went to the bedroom door and slammed it shut. "Are you trying to broadcast that shit to Ruby's son? The one that you claim to love like your own? Besides, you don't know what I did."

"I'm sorry. It just came out. I'm tired. I can't think. You are bringing that strange woman in here and around my kids. Around your son. I don't like her. You shouldn't either."

"Do you want me and Artie to move into one of the other apartments in the building? I have been thinking maybe we should. It's time we branched out on our own again."

"No, Micah," Kali said, sliding down onto the sofa. She couldn't believe she had said that aloud after all those years. Ashton had said it was done to protect her, the family, but that was something she would carry around like a dead weight for the rest of her life. There had to have been a better way. With all her flaws, she loved Ruby.

"You can move, but you can't take Artie. You are not disrupting his life so you can get some regular nookie from someone other than me."

Micah touched her lips and then leaned in as if he were going to kiss her. "I warn you, Kali," he whispered. "Don't you ever do anything to hurt my son. I don't think I could ever forgive you." He then left the room without another word.

Kali shook her head. Artie couldn't have heard the conversation. Or did he? Nothing had changed between them. Nothing that she had noticed.

Chapter Eighteen

MICAH FELT SO sorry for Katie. What a way to end a night she had been looking forward to for so long. When Brown had failed to answer and when Micah couldn't locate either Kali or Kacie, he had jumped in a cab himself and went to the penthouse leaving Anjuli with strict instructions not to let the remaining children out of her sight. He had sent two more bodyguards into the theater. No one was to move from that spot until they received the okay from him and that meant even if Katie had to miss the cast party.

"Any demands yet?" Troy startled Micah, walking up behind him as he stood in the foyer trying to think.

"Nothing yet." Micah looked at his phone. He had a couple of missed calls from Lazarus while he was trying to get the children situated in his apartment downstairs. He couldn't let them walk into their home with two dead bodies and a blood-splattered living room.

"Where's Kacie?"

"She's at the hospital. Ricky and Chico are with her."

"Have you talked to her yet?"

"No, I am going to see her as soon as I finish talking to the other kids. Ricky said Kacie wasn't talking. She's in shock so I am going to give her a little time."

"You think that's wise?" Troy pushed. "Maybe you want to try to get her to talk before she completely shuts down."

"The other children have to know what's going on before they hear it from someone else. Katie is already upset about missing her after-party. They know something's wrong because Anjuli has confiscated their phones and won't let them watch TV. You know they are scared to death anyway because their mother isn't with them. And," Micah shook his head, "Katie keeps asking for Roderick."

"Okay, I got that. But, can you speed it up?" Troy stood eye to eye with Micah. "Why are you still here?"

Micah walked away from Troy and went into the study. It was the same as he had left it when he had made love to Anjuli in it only a few hours before. He sat behind the big wooden desk and toyed with his phone. He was going to have to call Lazarus who was already dealing with his own drama in London.

When Lazarus answered the phone, Micah could hear sirens in the background.

"Where the hell are you? Are you still at the hospital?" Micah asked because the noise was so loud.

"I'm kind of busy here, Micah. Can you call me about the play later?" said Lazarus as he watched flames and sparks jump up from the other side of his building.

"This is kind of important," Micah said. "Kali's been kidnapped. Katie's boyfriend and one of the bodyguards have been murdered, and we think Kacie may have witnessed it all."

Lazarus couldn't find any words worthy of a response. If only he had just gotten on that plane, and walked away from this. He looked down at Elliott who was cradling the baby in her arms, rocking him. The poor little fellow was probably in a diaper filled with poop, but he wasn't crying. Lazarus reached over and touched the baby's cheek and thought, there were no tears left for him to shed. Nothing in London was going to keep him there. He was going home to get his wife and his life back. It didn't matter how.

Shortly after the daring rescue of three-year-old Ashton, the relationship between Jordan and Billy had taken an even darker turn than usual. By the time the twins were five years old, Ashton's twin, Asa, was living with his father, Billy, in the old house in Germantown and Ashton was living with Jordan in Center City. But, the twins still went to the same schools and spent every weekend together, most of the time under Elinor Rutherford's watchful eye. She was a mean one and very strict on the twins except, occasionally, she did seem to have a sweet spot for Asa. But, Ashton believed she downright hated him.

When Jack came back into their lives, the identical twins were just old enough to start catching public transportation on their own. Ashton was filling Asa's head with stories about the grungy, streetwise kid who had moved in with them. He hated Jack and that made Asa hate him, too.

One day, the three of them were on the subway platform. Jordan had given them money to show Jack around, so they had decided on a movie up on 69th Street. They were waiting for a connection to the El train when Jack, supposedly playing, nearly shoved Asa in front of an oncoming train. Ashton didn't know how he did it, but he grabbed his brother and snatched him back onto the platform, just in time. When he saw the look on Jack's face, he realized then that Jack had thought he was shoving him in front of the train, not Asa. In return for the deed, Ashton and Asa beat Jack down, stomping him and kicking him until a police officer pulled them off and dragged them all down to the precinct. It was Ashton's first taste of a police station and he had vowed it would be his last.

Ashton had never seen Billy or Jordan as furious as they were when they arrived to pick them up. For the first time in his life, he was afraid of Jordan. Jack's face was one massive bruise, but there was a smirk of pleasure on the boy's otherwise sour face. It was as if he was celebrating that, finally, he had shoved a wedge between Ashton and Jordan. But, that wouldn't last too long.

"Papa." Ashton had run into Jordan's room about a week or so later. "You have got to see this."

Jordan was at the piano in the music room making notes on his music sheets. "Ashton, I am busy."

"This is important, Papa," Ashton pressed.

"What is it?"

"You have to see it for yourself, Papa." Ashton stood in the doorway waving his grandfather toward him. Then he pulled out a set of keys and went down the stairs, a few steps at a time.

"This had better not be a wild goose chase." Jordan didn't like interruptions when he was working on his music.

"I came in here to see if I had left my white jacket down here last week." Ashton was talking about the apartment next door where Jordan held parties for some of his special acquaintances. He hadn't purchased the building yet, but he was renting the only two apartments on the top floor. Jordan followed Ashton into the apartment.

"I guess somebody figured no one would be coming in here, if there wasn't a party going on."

"Somebody?"

"Jack, Papa. I don't think Jack realized this was not just for parties every once in a while."

"Get to the point, Ashton."

Ashton increased his speed and went to a bedroom down the hall. He opened the door and the odor was immediate and unmistakable.

"Is that reefer I smell?" Jordan walked into the room and found remnants of joints in a big ashtray.

"That's not all, Papa." Ashton opened the closet door and picked up a small *duffle bag.*

"Look." He put it on the dresser and opened it up for Jordan. It was loaded with packs of marijuana. Jordan reached in and touched it. Then he looked at Ashton, anger in his eyes.

"You are not setting him up, are you?"

"I don't believe you, Papa, why would I do that?"

"For one, you accused him of trying to kill you and almost killing Asa instead."

"That's not an accusation, Papa. I know he knew what he was doing. I could feel it. And, you, you always tell me to follow my gut, don't you?"

Jordan nodded and looked back down at the evidence. He took the bag and zipped it up and headed for the door.

"That's not all, Papa. There's more."

Jordan sighed and stopped. "What else?"

Ashton motioned Jordan toward the closet. There were a lot of things there that shocked Jordan. He picked up his old saxophone. It had been stored in the back of the music room closet. He hadn't touched it since they had moved into the penthouse. Then, there was the gold-veined vase, one that had been given to him by a prime minister because he had commented on its beauty. Both items were worth a lot of money. He wondered what else was slowly leaving his house. Jordan held on tightly to the duffle bag.

"Put every one of those things back where they belong," he told Ashton. "Let me know the minute Jack walks in the door. Here or there. It don't matter. You keep an eye out for him."

Jordan had gone back to the penthouse and straight to Jack's room where he recovered several more items that shouldn't have been in there. He meticulously packed Jack's clothes and everything else he owned and sat them, bags and boxes, by the bed. Then he went back to the music room and started a new sheet of music. He wanted to write or, better yet, hear something angry.

Jordan had given Jack the keys to the old house that night, cab fare back to Jersey, and enough money to live on for a month. Then, though it hurt him to do it, he had asked the boy never to darken his door again. That was a few months before Jack's eighteenth birthday.

But, he didn't listen. Never did because he did darken Jordan's door again maybe 15 years later. Jack sat across from Ashton in the penthouse study just months after Ashton had started his security firm. At that time, it was called Sperling Enterprises. "Jordan thinks my military experience would be really helpful to you right now. He said Micah was still tied down with your father in his law firm.”

"This isn't Jordan's company," Ashton had said, annoyed that Jordan was still trying to help this creep.

"You and I both know how Jordan is about family," Jack said, nervously biting his bottom lip.

"I know Jordan still thinks he owes you something, even though the last time you were here you stole from him."

"I was a kid. I'd been on my own too long. I didn't know how to appreciate Jordan's hospitality. I admit that. But, I went into the military as soon as I could and I have grown. I have grown a lot."

"You haven't grown that much. You had to come back to Jordan to help you out financially."

Jack straightened up and stared at Ashton who continued to drive the point home.

"I take care of Jordan's finances now. I know what comes in and what goes out. He's given you over $100,000 this past year. You should be on your own feet by now. Why would I want you to come in here and destroy what I have?" Ashton pulled out a cigar and lit it. Normally, he would have offered his guest one, but this was no guest.

"Well, I guess it shouldn't surprise me that you are still a snobby bastard. Haven't changed a bit. I told Jordan you wouldn't hire me."

"Maybe Jordan can forgive you for what you did to my brother, but I will never, ever trust you. Nor am I going to give you a chance to get another cent or steal another item from my grandfather. So, why don't you crawl back under whatever rock you climbed out from under and get out of here? I don't have to restrain myself anymore for anybody, but I would rather not upset Jordan." Ashton stood up and blew smoke in Jack's face. Jack didn't flinch, but he did get up and leave. Later that day, Ashton had to lie to Jordan. He had told him Jack had received another offer in another state and wouldn't be coming back for a while. He did his best to hide his growing agitation over Jordan's gullibility when it came to Jack Pulaski. But now that Jack knew he wasn't going to get any more money, maybe he would stay away for good.

That had been the second time Jack had shown up after his first disappearance. The first time wasn't his fault. The authorities had removed him from his home in New Jersey after his mother's murder. By the time Jordan had gotten the news, the boy had been shipped to a foster home in North Jersey; and, since he wasn't a relative, they wouldn't give Jordan any information on him. No one heard from Jack again until he showed up at the penthouse when he was sixteen years old. He looked like a boy who had been living on the streets. Jordan had welcomed him into his home with open arms and an open bank account.

Lazarus didn't have any of the feelings that Jordan had had for Jack. Jordan had been obsessed with Jack because of what his mother had done for the child Ashton. He was okay with that, even grateful, but only to the extent that was understandable by anyone with any common sense. But, no, forgiveness was not a strong trait in his own genes, especially for Jack. Lazarus reminded himself that he was in no position to judge anyone else for their deeds. He, too, was going by another name, hiding out now from his own actions. But there was no way he could think of anything he would have done differently when it came to Jack. That's when Asa crossed his mind. How in the world did Asa forgive Jack? How could he have worked with Jack against him? That had been one of the things that he and Asa had kept in common, their total disgust when it came to Jack Pulaski. Then he remembered how gullible his brother was when it came to Redd. She had led him down that path. It certainly wasn't Billy's doing this time, his father hated Jack as much as he did. If Jack had come back for a final fight, he was going to give him one. And God help him, if he laid one nasty, crooked finger on Kali.

CHAPTER NINETEEN

THE KIDS JUST stared at him. He had hugged each one and each one had half-heartedly hugged him back. He couldn't blame them. What now? It had taken another three days to get out of London, but he was home.

"We are going to get your mother back," he said as he sat there looking from face to face in Micah's living room a few floors down from the penthouse. Any room his kids normally occupied was usually filled with laughter or the occasional kid-conflict over a game or an opinion. But the only sound you could hear now was the silent hum of the heating and air system.

Lazarus opened his arms toward Kacie who was staring at him the hardest. When she didn't get up to come to him, he went to her.

"Mommy's a fighter, she will be home," he said, picking her limp body up into his arms. This one hurt him the most. The children didn't say it, but they were angry. He had abandoned them and now the only constant in their lives was missing.

"Lazarus," Micah said, standing in the doorway motioning for him. The kids looked at Micah, too, with disappointment.

Ash stood up and took Kacie from his father's arms. Kacie wrapped her arms around her older brother and buried her head into his neck.

"Tough crowd," Micah said closing the door behind the two of them. "We need to go upstairs to the study."

Lazarus followed him.

"The house in Burlington — no records of Papa owning anything over there. If he did, he must have used a bogus name. You know, back then it was hard for a black man to buy in certain neighborhoods. Are you sure, it was Burlington?"

"Yeah, I am sure. Burlington Township." Lazarus glanced toward the living room. "We need to find that address, if you really think that's where he would have taken her."

Workers in the penthouse had ripped up the carpet from the floor and were painting the walls.

"Have the children seen this yet?"

"I haven't let them set foot in here. I wanted it to look like the way they last saw it, not like this. And not with all that blood."

"Kacie. Did she see it?" Lazarus stopped and noticed the large stain on the wooden floor where the carpet had been.

"No," Micah shook his head. "She says she didn't."

"Did she know what happened down here while she was here? I mean, at the time?"

"She knew something was wrong," Micah answered. "She's like her mother though. Strong. Defiant."

Kacie had been lying in the middle of her mother's bed when she heard the first shot. She didn't know what it was, the loud sound. At first, she thought Roderick had knocked something over so she dismissed it, still lying in the bed bringing her mother's pillow to her nose. The smell of it made her feel safe and happy. But, she began to feel guilty about letting poor Roderick wander around by himself downstairs since she hadn't even looked for that bracelet yet. She left her mother's room to investigate the noise and even tease the boy if he had broken something. Walking slowly down the hall, she noticed a different feel and smell in the air. It was almost smoky, like one of her dad's cigars.

As she neared the landing at the top of the stairs, she saw Mr. Brown coming through the front door. He held up his hand and waved her back. Stopping for a second to figure out what he meant by the wave, she waved back but the look on his face was serious. He mouthed the word 'run' and she did. She ran back down the hall to the music room and hid in the closet that held her great-grandfather's old things. She climbed over the stacks of records and moved as far in the back as she could. That's when she heard another loud noise. There was a cape of some kind folded neatly on the shelf above her. She picked it up and covered herself. She stayed there for what seemed a lifetime until finally she heard her uncle's voice calling her name.

"Kacie, Kacie," Micah called to her as he walked through the upstairs of the penthouse.

"I'm right here." Kacie stuck her head out of the closet. She ran to her uncle and jumped into his arms. He held onto her so tightly she thought she would stop breathing, but she held onto him with all of her 60-pound strength. Micah carried her into her mother's room and deposited her on the bed.

Finally, he said something. "Are you alright?" His eyes were red and worried looking.

"I'm fine, Uncle Micah. What happened?" She asked.

"Don't worry about it, Sweet Pea. I just want you to stay put until someone in the family comes for you. Only a family member, do you understand?"

Kacie nodded.

"Lock the door," Micah told her as he exited her mother's room. Kacie ran to the door and secured the lock.

It wasn't long before she could hear a lot of people moving around in the penthouse. She squirreled herself away under her mother's cover, smelling her mother's scent and wishing she had never followed Roderick to pick up that stupid bracelet.

Someone knocked on the door calling her name once again. It was Anjuli. At first, Kacie ran to the door to unlock it, but then remembered her uncle's words 'only a family member' and Anjuli was not family yet. So, no matter how many times the woman called her, Kacie refused to unlock the door. She went into her mother's dressing room and sat at her vanity searching for the bracelet. This time she was going to listen and follow directions.

Micah came and called her name twice and that's when she jumped up and ran to the door. He picked her up and kissed her several times.

"Bury your head on my shoulder," he said. "Close your eyes. I am taking you downstairs to my place, okay? Anjuli is going to stay with you, alright?"

Kacie nodded and leaned her forehead into her uncle's neck. It was warm and slightly sweaty and he smelled like her dad. Anjuli walked up behind them, took off her jacket, threw it over Kacie's head as they descended the stairs. But Kacie saw Roderick's feet as the jacket flapped. He was lying without moving on the living room floor and there were policemen everywhere.

"Where's mommy?" she whispered.

"Mommy's fine," Micah responded and almost ran to the door with Kacie in his arms. He carried her all the way to his apartment door and then handed her to Anjuli who carried her into the apartment where the rest of her siblings sat staring in shock. They all ran to her and kissed her. Ash picked her up and carried her into the kitchen.

"We have got a lot to talk about, kid," her big brother said. "But, first, are you alright?"

Kacie shook her head and covered her eyes. But, when she opened her eyes again, she could still see Roderick's feet on the floor. That's when she started sobbing uncontrollably and her words stopped coming.

CHAPTER TWENTY

AFTER A USELESS exercise of ploughing through Jordan's records for the deed to the house, Lazarus returned to the apartment downstairs. He found the children, all five of them, in a huddle. They were sitting in the middle of the floor like a massive human ball. Their arms, legs, and heads were touching each other somehow. Afraid to break the silence and the moment, he slid down to the floor and crawled over to them. Reaching into the middle, he touched Kacie's head; she flinched without even looking, she knew it was him.

"I'm sorry," he whispered to them and the ball of Sperling children began to break apart. Artie was the first one out of the door.

"Wait, everybody, wait. We need to talk," he said to his children who were almost three years older than when he had left them. They weren't babies anymore, especially Ash.

"Please, listen to me. Come back and sit with me," he begged as he folded his legs beneath him and looked up at them. They were all standing and they all looked to Ash for his approval. Ash nodded his head and went back to sit directly in front of his father. They all followed obediently letting Lazarus know who was in charge now.

"What do you want, Lazarus?" Ash asked as Kacie climbed into his lap, laying her head on his shoulder. She looked toward the other side of the room away from her father.

"I want to come home," Lazarus answered.

"You don't have a home here," Ash answered. Looking down he saw a tear slide down Kacie's face. He wiped it with his thumb.

"Home is where the heart is," said Lazarus, using the cliché he hoped would at least make Katie, his young actress, listen. She had taken a position directly behind Ash with her eyes focusing on the floor.

"Yada, yada," Adam was still standing with his hands deep in his pockets.

"How come you never came home to visit, or have us visit, like you said you would?" Adam's voice was low, but it boomed, surprising Lazarus. The boy's voice was changing or, in his absence, had it already changed?

"I had a few health issues. I thought I was going to die, and I didn't want to burden you," Lazarus said, slipping out of his shirt. Pointing to his new scars he explained, "I had to have a couple of gastric surgeries to replace my stomach and my intestines. The first operation didn't work, so I had to undergo another one. I was sick most of the time I was over there. Almost from day one."

Lazarus was happy to see the girls lean toward him and his scars.

"You don't look sick, now, Dad," Adam said. Everyone looked up at him.

"Look, it's no secret in this family who you are. And, it's no secret that you are a murdering son-of-a-bitch who abandoned us, either," Adam said as his eyes met with each of his siblings.

"We know. We have seen the news and we have seen all the old stories on the Internet. We have figured out a few things. Heck, we are Sperlings, or Banks. Whatever. We are your blood, remember? We know bad things happen in this family."

"Are we really cursed, Daddy?" Kacie asked.

"No, sweetheart, no." Lazarus reached for her but she held onto Ash with all her might. Ash hugged her back tightly.

"Then why do people want to hurt us?" Katie asked. "If Roderick hadn't looked like Ash, if Roderick hadn't been wearing Ash's jacket, he would be alive, right? Whoever it was, he wanted to kill Ash, not my Roderick." Tears flooded Katie's face and she tried to hide them by leaning her face onto Ash's back.

"We don't know that." Lazarus said.

"Oh, yes, we do. And, if we know it, you know it."

"What would make you come to that conclusion?" Lazarus asked his oldest daughter who was now leaning her chin on Ash's shoulder.

"Roderick was wearing Ash's jacket," Kacie said as she gripped Ash's shirt and twisted it. "He looked just like Ash from the back and a little like him from the front. He even had the same haircut."

"Is that so?" Lazarus gasped as Kacie nodded her head. "Did you tell the police?"

"Yes, Daddy. You are late," Katie answered. "Kacie is having nightmares that it's Ash that's dead. I'm having nightmares that I put a target on Roderick's back. I'm the reason the only boy I ever loved is DEAD."

"Kacie is seeing a psychiatrist," Ash blurted out. "They kept her in the hospital for two days. She just got home this morning. Two days, Dad, two days that you weren't here. Two days and our mother has been missing for over three," Ash bellowed in anger. "And, Katie, look at Katie. They considered putting her in the hospital, too. She had a meltdown when she found out about Rod. She didn't eat or speak for a whole day. She's scared. We are all scared. Heck, they are all sleeping with me every night. YOU weren't HERE. And, Mom. Who knows what she is going through or went through," Ash's voice softened with a saddened look on his face.

"Don't say that. Don't say 'went,' your mom is going to come out of this. She's a fighter. She will come home. And I would have been here if I could have. One day, I will explain it to you. But, it won't do any good now. You have to trust me. There was a very important reason I wasn't here. But, I'm here right now and I am going to help bring your mother home."

"How?" all four children asked in unison. Lazarus sat there, helpless. He didn't know how.

"Either of you ever spend any time with Reck? Or, heard your mother talk about him at all? I need to know anything special or unique about the man. How did he make you feel when you were in his presence?" Lazarus asked, leaning forward. He touched Kacie and she didn't flinch. Then he tugged at her arm and, with relief, she let go of Ash and crawled into his lap. He picked her up and held her close. He couldn't stop kissing his baby girl. She began to giggle. Before he knew it, he was getting a kiss from Katie and then hugs from both of his boys. I'm home, he thought.

"I think he knew Troy," Artie said walking back into the room. He had been lingering outside of the door to the living room. Lazarus reached up, grabbed the boy by his shirt and pulled him down with the rest of them. He kissed Artie on the forehead.

"Hi, Uncle." Artie reached up and touched his face. Lazarus kissed the back of his nephew's hand.

"Hi, Art Man." Lazarus rubbed Artie's head. "What would be so weird about him knowing Troy? Doesn't Uncle Troy still come around?"

"Not much," Ash answered. "Not after he finally convinced Mom to go out on a date with him. I don't think it went the way he expected."

"It wasn't a date," Katie added. "He kept asking Mom and I heard Uncle Micah tell her to go just this once as a friend having dinner with a friend. He said maybe Uncle Troy would get her out of his system."

"Out of his system?" Lazarus laughed. "Was he obsessed or something?"

"Or, something," Ash said frowning a bit.

"Really?" Lazarus wasn't sure why he was surprised. Troy literally drooled when Kali walked into a room. Not only that, Troy had been a bit over-protective when he thought he, as Lazarus, was getting a little too close. But, he had chalked that up to Troy's overblown loyalty to his former self. Troy was still blaming himself, rightly, for almost getting Ashton killed in prison.

"So, Artie, was there something odd about him knowing Troy?"

Artie shrugged his narrow shoulders. "I don't know. I mentioned it because it just felt funny."

"Funny like what? What kind of funny feeling did you have? Was it like they were up to something when they were together? What? Describe your funny feeling for me," Lazarus asked as all eyes went to Artie.

"I was coming down the stairs in the back. I had been on the roof watering my plants in the greenhouse. We still haven't put in the sprinklers yet. Dad keeps promising me though." Artie looked over at Adam expecting him to make his usual dig about the greenhouse, especially the sprinklers, but Adam was silent.

"Anyway Unc, Reck and Uncle Troy were standing in front of the rear elevator. Reck was leaning down a little over Uncle Troy like he was whispering something in his ear. Uncle Troy was listening to him, but when he saw me coming he stepped back and told Reck he would see him later. Reck looked at me kind of funny like I messed something up or something."

"Was that the only time you saw them together?" Lazarus asked

Katie spoke up. "I saw them, I saw them talking to Anjuli down near the reflecting pool in the park. I was coming home from rehearsal. Mom was driving. She didn't see them, but I told her it looked like the three of them."

"What did she say?"

"She said, *'that was interesting'* but that's all she said." Katie took her place next to Lazarus and playfully poked Kacie who giggled once again. Lazarus noticed that all the children's eyes lit up when Kacie giggled.

"I wonder why your Mom thought that was interesting. I'll see if she mentioned it to Micah. Anything else?"

"Uncle Micah has a girlfriend," Kacie sang. "Mommy doesn't like her."

"Now that doesn't surprise me," Lazarus laughed. "Your Uncle Micah has your mommy spoiled."

"Uncle Chico and Uncle Ricky, too," Adam chimed in. "The men in her life can't do anything but keep her happy."

"Or, the men in her life can't do anything but keep her in a bind." Katie pushed herself up to her feet and looked down at her father. "I'm going to lie down. I don't want to talk about Mom anymore. I just want her to come home, Dad."

Lazarus left the kids, suggesting they go to bed. They had been up all night and morning was going to be there soon. He went back upstairs to the study. Micah was sitting behind the desk on the phone again so he plopped onto the sofa like everyone else usually did.

Lazarus put up his feet and waited patiently until Micah finally hung up the phone. "Who is Anjuli? Is that the new flame?"

"Why are our conversations so one-sided?" Micah laughed. He couldn't remember if he had ever told Lazarus Anjuli's name or not. "Yes," he said answering Lazarus's question, looking a little sad. "I was planning to propose to her this weekend. I had even told Kali about it, though your old woman wasn't too happy about it. I think she has gotten too used to being the only woman in the Sperling family."

"Let's hope she still is, right now," Lazarus said sighing, trying to think of one thing he could do.

"Did Kali mention a confab between Troy, Reck, and Anjuli in the park recently? One night, when she was driving Katie home from the theater."

Micah sat there a moment. He started rubbing a circle with his finger on the desk, a habit he usually had when he stopped to think about something specifically.

"Not a confab, but she said didn't know Anjuli knew Troy and

Reck. And I told her I didn't either. I was going to ask her what she was talking about, but then we were interrupted by one of the kids. Yeah, that was last Tuesday or Wednesday. Artie and Adam got into a fight over a video game. We had to put them both on lockdown. They are doing that a lot lately. Fighting."

"Those two? They had always been like peanut butter and jelly."

"Batman and Robin, remember?" Micah said, nodding his head.

"I remember. What happened?"

"The truth is, I think Adam was starting to miss his dad. Remember, you have spent more time with AJ and Katie, and then Kacie, than you ever have with Adam. They didn't start fighting until after Artie asked to build this damn greenhouse. Man, you gotta go up and see it. We did a bang-up job. I'm proud of us. Artie, Adam, and me. We built it from scratch. I think that made Adam feel as if he was missing out on having his real father here. I was just a poor substitute."

"You were the man," Lazarus said. "I'll never be able to repay you for taking care of my children. And, my wife."

Micah looked as if he wanted to respond to that, but stopped. Lazarus knew there was a tight bond between his wife and his brother, but then wondered if he had stayed away too long. How tight was that bond now? Why was Micah suddenly getting married again?

"I have an idea," Micah said with a nod and a smile. "Let's go for a ride."

CHAPTER TWENTY-ONE

"WHERE'S MY DAUGHTER?" Elle asked Micah as he walked in the door. She was fully dressed with a tray table before her and on it a breakfast that was steaming hot. She tried to look around him to see if that spunky little thing was behind him. She loved it when he and Kali came together. More than that, she loved it when Kali walked into the room. She made the place feel festive.

"She's not here, mother," Micah said with a worried look on his face. "I hope you don't mind, I brought you some company." Micah looked back as Lazarus stepped inside the door. They both looked at Elle for her reaction. She smiled and waved him to her.

"Good morning, Ms. Elle." Lazarus leaned forward and hugged her. She surprised him, holding on to him tightly as if she didn't want to let him go. Then she rubbed his head. His eyes almost teared up; she hadn't done that since he was a child. He pulled back and looked at her. He was shocked by his reception and, for a moment, he thought he saw sadness in her eyes.

"You are back," she said, again trying to look past the two tall men for the door. "I may be a little crazy and sometimes I forget. But, I remember a lot, too." She leaned the other way.

"Where is she?" Elle said as she grabbed Micah's sleeve. "What have you done to her?"

Both men shared a stare.

"Where is she?" Elle began to wipe her eyes. "Did you hurt her?"

"Mother, I would never. Lazarus," he said touching his brother so his mother would know to whom he was referring, "would never hurt her. But, she's why we are here to see you. She's been…" Micah wasn't sure how much he should tell her. But then, he just said it. "Kidnapped. Kali was kidnapped three nights ago. We are trying to find her."

"Jordan's little white boy?" Elle asked, startling both men with her immediate assessment.

"I told you I am not crazy, just get a little lost some time," she said, pulling Micah closer. He pulled the white ottoman up next to her chair and sat on it. Lazarus sat on the floor in front of her and crossed his legs. He suddenly remembered that vantage point, too. But, she was much younger then. Why was he having such a rush of childhood memories in her presence?

"She's my baby, you know." Elle smoothed out her skirt and then pinched the material. Kali had bought her that, too. Kali had bought just about everything in the room.

Micah touched her hand. "Mother, the other day you thought you recognized Reck. Who do you think he is?"

"You know who he is," Elle said, directing her gaze at Lazarus.

"Ashton, you and him used to run all over the place. He was mean to you, though. Real mean. I never liked that boy. Not even when he came back. He's got my baby?" Elle cried.

"Yes, ma'am," Lazarus answered and swallowed hard trying to keep his own emotions in check. He started to tell Ms. Elle not to call him Ashton, but it didn't seem to make any sense. Who would she tell he was home? And to hell with anyone who overheard.

"Mother," Micah tried to find the words but they left him; he had to refocus, they were looking for a lead.

Elle reached out and touched Lazarus on the shoulder.

"When that gal walks in, my heart just leaps. It almost leaps out of this frail old body. Does that surprise you?"

Lazarus nodded yes. He remembered how much Elle hated Kali at one time.

"Want to know why?"

Both men nodded.

Elle reached for a tissue from her junk table. That's what Kali called it. She made sure Elle had everything she needed within reach on that table, including an elegant cover for a box of tissues. Elle used the tissue to dab at her tears.

"I had a daughter once. She would have been older than Kali. She was older than you and way older than Micah. Didn't make it to her first birthday. But, she was a little doll. I will never forget her. She would smile the biggest toothless grin you could ever imagine. But, I lost her and I always wanted another child. Years later, I had this little boy," she said, patting Micah's bald head.

"Then one day, Micah brings, or should I say drags, Kali to the old place where I was staying and she just started taking care of me. I mean taking care of me like I was her mother. She would get me out of bed and take me for a walk. She'd comb my hair. And, she would talk non-stop. Just never stop talking, and she would sound so good. I started imagining what it would have been like if my daughter had lived. Would she do what this woman was doing for me? Would she have the heart to take care of the woman that threw her under the bus?" Elle dabbed her face with the tissue again. "Cause that's what I did. I thought she was just another one of those gals that Jordan would be selling to his special clients. I didn't think about her at all. I never thought about any of them really. I was a hard woman," Elle said, folding her hands in her lap and looking past the men now. "I had to be. That's how I protected myself from them."

Elle sighed deeply. "But, you know what I realized — on my good days, that is — she needed her mama just like I needed my baby girl. Some days, she walks in that door without a word. She just comes in and sits right there." Elle pointed to where Micah was sitting. "Not on that thing you are sitting on. She sits on the floor and leans over and puts her head in my lap. Then we just sit here. I stroke her head and she lets me. Sometimes she just cries her heart out. Uses up a whole box of tissues. Then she cleans herself up, kisses me, gives me a big hug, and walks right back out that door. A few days later, she will come bouncing in with all kinds of bags and boxes of beautiful clothes. She knows how much I love beautiful clothes. She keeps me covered in the best," Elle said and tightened her hands. "How did you let that man back into your life, Ashton?" There was anger in Elle's voice. "He never liked you, not even as a child."

"Who is he, Mother?" Micah asked.

"You weren't even born when that boy walked into our lives," Elle said. Turning to Lazarus, she said, "Do you remember the way it happened?"

Lazarus shook his head, and said, "His mother was in a car accident."

"Not just any kind of car accident," Elle said. "I will never forget that day. You come this close to dying. Somehow, you ran out of the café Jordan owned on Ridge Avenue right into the street. Or, almost into the street, and that woman saved you. Well, the way it was told, she was trying to save you and lost her balance. She fell in front of a car trying to keep you from running in front of one." Elle shook her head.

"Her little boy was with her. Jordan took to caring for them. She was confined to a wheelchair. He paid for her medical and living expenses, but that wasn't enough. Had to move her to Jersey because it was getting crazy down in South Philly when he tried to visit her. So, he bought a little house over there. You and him used to go over there a lot in the beginning. Then, I think Jordan got tired of the whole situation. But, he loved himself some Jack. He doted on that little white boy. But, there was just something about that child that just didn't sit right."

Elle leaned forward and grabbed Lazarus's face, cupping his chin but digging her hard, narrow fingers into his cheekbones. He remembered her clearly from that angle. He remembered that stern face except, he realized, it wasn't as hateful a face as his grandfather had told him. Jordan had turned him against Elle. Possibly, rightly so, because she had been the only reason he hated going to his father's house every other weekend. The weekends he skipped going to Billy's was when Asa came to Jordan's house. At least the two men had agreed to let the twins be twins on the weekends. But, her face had the sternness now of someone who gave a damn.

"Ashton and Asa are dead." Elle squeezed his face tighter. "Remember that, Lazarus Smith. I know you have a lot of questions and I am going to try to answer some of them today while I am with you," Elle laughed. "Some days I can't tell you who my own child is." She winked at Micah, who was five years younger than Ashton, and her only child.

"Your Mama had three babies. You weren't twins, you were triplets, identical triplets," she said as a little grin lightened her face. "But only two of them lived and everybody was surprised that Billy kept them. Rightly so, he was an angry, hard father. He was jealous of you, Ashton. I think he saw that Ashton got the best half of Jordan's life. And the best part of Jordan's heart. The old man softened as he got older. That's the only reason Kali survived him and you," Ms. Elle winked. "For that, the more Billy drank, the more he hated you. He influenced Asa against you and then you put the cherry on top by stealing Asa's woman, that ratchet, hateful, red-headed, selfish bitch, Redd. I never knew what either of you saw in her. I figured she must have been really good at giving head. A man will do anything for a woman that's good at that, you know," she said, still holding onto his face. She leaned forward and looked into his eyes.

"Mama, what are you saying," Micah asked. "I thought you didn't come into Daddy's life until much later. I mean, I was four when we moved in with Daddy, right?" Micah sat down contemplating what his mother was telling Ashton. His entire life he had thought his mother and his father had tried to hide him from Jordan. If what she was saying was true, she knew Jordan before he, Micah, was born.

"I knew your daddy long before he and I moved in together, before we even had you. Long before I began to help Jordan run his girls. I had been one of his girls. I just left for a while, or tried to is a better description after your sister died. But, let's stick with how to help Kali today.

"Your daddy was the one that set it up so Asa's first death looked real. He paid off a lot of people, swapped his body out in the morgue with some poor homeless soul that, to this day, I think was killed because he looked enough like Asa. He's the one in that first grave. Then Billy tried to send Asa to Germany." Elle nodded seeing the lights go off in Lazarus's eyes. "You know who else ended up in Germany? From what I heard, it didn't work out though. That bitch wasn't going to take care of anybody but herself. Asa was angry, but he sat in rehab center down in Brazil until he got better. Being alone can make people angry and bitter. And that man had sat down there stewing about everything while that bitch was over in Germany stewing, too."

Lazarus nodded. Redd had ended up there and since Asa had come back with her, they must have worked something out, like a common enemy. Otherwise, what place would Asa have in Redd's new relationship with Jack? Maybe that's what he had been trying to do; Ashton had never stopped trying to understand what Asa had done to him and his family. Maybe he was trying to justify his presence with Jack and Redd. Why else would Asa have been willing to team up against him to kill him?

"Back to Ashton," Elle said, getting his attention again, she could almost see his mind in overdrive. "He died on that stage and there is no resurrecting him the way Lazarus was resurrected out West. Do you understand me?"

Lazarus nodded as the old woman spoke.

"You will not put your family through any more shit like this. They won't be able to survive anymore of this nonsense. You put a stop to it right now. Don't make your children suffer the way you, as Ashton, and Asa and Micah did," she nodded toward her baby boy. She could see his mind working hard to piece the story together. She prayed she would remember to tell him the truth one day.

"I want you to tell your mama a story for me." Elle said as she squeezed Lazarus's face tighter to keep him from speaking. They didn't have time for him to protest that he did not know who his mother was. "Tell her that I said it. If you tell her *I* said it, *she* will say it. Trust me. Tell her that you know, that you know she didn't have twins that cold winter morning in one of the backrooms of the house in Germantown. Tell her you know she had triplets. She had triplets. Do you hear me?"

Elle let go of his face, but not his gaze. It was frozen onto his face in a head that looked as if it had been stacked on his body, easily knocked off by the flicker of a child's finger. Elle smiled down at him. He understood her; he was taking it in like he was supposed to, without missing a thing. Somebody had to shake up these Sperling men into right action for a change and she was the only somebody left to do it.

Elle let her fingers glide down his cheek and continued, "Ashton was born first, screaming and hollering like a mad man wanting to go back into the womb. Asa came out squirming like a little lazy worm. They had to tap his behind a couple of times to make him cry. And, the last one, I believe, she told me she ended up naming him Aaron. I asked her why all the A names and she said something about the order of the alphabet. Her second child and third child would be a B and a C name. She was a silly girl, very intelligent though. I think that's why Billy and Jordan liked her. Think about it," Elle sighed, "the women who survived them were very smart, intelligent women."

Lazarus heard his heart pumping in his ears. Had Elliott planted the name Aaron in his head when he had told her about Natasha having a baby? That was months ago, but the name had stuck and he had tried to convince Natasha to name her son that, instead of George.

"At first, they thought Aaron was dead," Elle said, closing her eyes for a moment. "He was the smallest of the bunch. He wasn't moving or crying. Somebody put him in the bathtub, that cold, porcelain bathtub, and he didn't protest. But I did. I went in there and picked that child up. I massaged his little body until he coughed. He coughed up a plug of something and then starting squealing for dear life. But, Jordan thought he was going to be a slow child. Said he could tell just by looking at him. That's when he decided Aaron wouldn't be staying. He took that child from me and walked out of the room. The next time I saw him, he was lifeless. Jordan had killed that innocent child.

"You see, Jordan made the decisions about all the babies born in his house or in his domain. The girl babies didn't make it. Billy had hid me and your sister, but then when Jordan found us, she suddenly became ill and died," Elle gulped as she released Lazarus's face and touched her own. "There was no place for girl children in his life. Just like there was none in his own father's life. His father was from one of the islands where women had no rights at all. That's why Jordan never respected women. He was taught they were tools, toys, useless things to sell like dry stock. But, he liked your mother a little. Maybe she was the first one to see even the slightest hint of kindness in him, like Kali did.

"Sure, he was charming. He would smile in your face while he dug the dagger deeper and deeper into your back. I feared him. That was the only reason any of us stayed. We knew if we stayed, we lived. We leave, or even try to leave, we were sure to die. You both taught Kali that early on, that's why she never ran. I know you warned her. I know you found out in your teens, why his women had real reasons to fear him."

Lazarus nodded. He had helped Jordan to dispose of a woman's body when he was fifteen. But, who was his mother? He tried to remember the women who had come and gone in his life. Who was he supposed to tell this story to? Right now, there were only two women left who were important to him. One was being held hostage and the other was.... No. No, he thought, as he could feel one of Jordan's daggers digging into his heart.

"He tried to send her away, but she was stubborn. She wanted so much to be a part of her children's lives. She was a Philly girl, so it wasn't hard for her to just show up. She had shown up at the café to help Billy that morning when you ran out in the street. No one knows what happened to the third child or that there even was a third child. No one knows still. But, your mama does. She can testify for you, if you need be. I don't know how all that works. But, as far as you are concerned, all we know is that a man without a memory showed up on a park bench in the Square and that man's DNA showed a high probability that he was the missing triplet. You know how generous the Sperling men are. They welcomed him into their home and their lives.

And Kali, well, she fell in love with him and so did her children because, as it turns out, memory or not, that Lazarus Smith is a good man."

Lazarus swallowed hard exchanging a stunned glance with Micah who was still processing his own history. Was Miss Elle implying he take on this other brother's identity? Was any of this true?

"Now, you go tell Tawny Elliott I said that," Elle said. For a moment, she thought Ashton had stopped breathing and to her left she could almost hear Micah breathing heavily as if he were trying to inhale and exhale for Ashton. "You tell her where no one else can hear. She has lived all these years watching you and loving you. Sometimes, I used to let her see you boys, especially if I happened to have you on a weekday when school was out. She worked at the telephone company in Center City. So, we would rendezvous at a restaurant in Suburban Station. I'd find a table for four and she would come over like she and I were old friends. She would talk to you boys and your eyes would just light up. I want you to know, Ashton, she was never too far away. And Jordan knew it. And, for some reason, he never chased her away completely. He was surprised though when she applied for the job at your new company. I wasn't. I told her to do it. I knew you would hire her."

"Ms. Elliott is my mother?" Lazarus asked. Every part of him, every molecule had tightened up into a hard ball. He couldn't move. He didn't know whether he was angry or relieved. Why hadn't she confessed it after all these years? She was already close to him, even closer than his wife. He was still talking to her often even when he wasn't picking up the phone to call Kali. She was even closer to Kali, acting as the surrogate grandmother and confidante to help raise the children. What did she have to lose by telling him after all these years? What was she still hiding? Jordan was dead. Billy was dead. What would she have lost by telling him the truth?

"Yes. Now, when you get Kali home, you tell her, too. You marry my baby girl again and you keep her safe. Promise me that." Elle leaned over to him with her arms open. He leaned into those long, skinny appendages and remembered the reason why he was there. He had to save Kali.

"We can't find any records of the house in Jersey. Did Jordan own it? Where was it?"

"It was in Burlington Township. Not a very ritzy area, but back then it was hard for black people to get a real estate agent to sell them anything in an all-white neighborhood. So, Jordan sent one of his record people to buy it. They put it in a company name. The name of it was something like Twin Arthur Properties or Arthur Twins. It's been a long time, but I remember him using his middle name and I remember it had something to do with twins. That was around the time those two devils separated you two and started pitting you against each other. You almost survived it. You would have, but you couldn't keep your hands off Redd." Elle tapped him on the head three times as if she were knighting him in a royal ceremony.

"Now, what is your name?" Elle rested back into her chair as if she had hiked a few miles. She was exhausted.

"My name is Lazarus Smith." Ashton almost choked on the words. His dreams of reclaiming his identity had just ended, falling from the lips of an old woman suffering from dementia. But even now, there was one thing he knew about Elinor Sperling: she was usually right about everything.

"Now go bring me back my daughter," Elle smiled and then looked at Micah. "What a beautiful man you are. What's your name again?"

CHAPTER TWENTY-TWO

THE ROUGH STUCCO-textured wall hurt her back, but it didn't matter. She wanted to feel something. Letting go her legs with one of her hands, she touched her face, wondering what it looked like. The swelling had gone down some and, though she was sniffling a lot, she didn't think her nose or her jaw was broken. She could still talk, but now her head hurt even more. Maybe she was suffering from a concussion as well as from being poisoned.

Desperation wasn't her usual style. She looked around the room again hoping she had missed something important. Kali's body began to rock. This was it. She was sick of men. The ones in her life were huge, dangerous babies. All of them. Her father had murdered her mother. Ashton had seduced her into a relationship with his grandfather, and then he had stolen her babies and tried to kill her. As if that wasn't enough, Asa had beaten and raped her multiple times. Then Ashton, whom she thought had come to his senses and cherished her, had ended up abandoning her. And now Micah, the one man in her life who had lulled her into thinking that she mattered, was running away from her as fast as he could. Maybe this would make him happy, even make Ashton happy. Neither one of them would have to worry about her anymore because another man in her life was planning to kill her and he had been hired to protect her. Why he wanted her dead, she had no idea. All she knew was that, obviously, he hated Ashton. Why does everybody hate Ashton, she whined to herself as she crawled onto the nasty bed.

The partial light from beneath the door gave the room an eerily surreal ambience. The perfect place to die, her thoughts whispered. Both of her hands went up to her hair as she tried to run her fingers through her tangled curls. She was on her back, the way the Sperling men seemed to like her. What about Reck? She had seen how he looked at her, especially when she was walking toward him. It used to make her smile thinking that he was having fantasies about her. She tossed to her side: what kind of fantasies was he having though? He may have been imagining killing her instead of kissing her. What was she to do? He was tactically and more physically able to subdue her than she was able to subdue or even hurt him. Sure, she could do some damage, but that wouldn't give her the freedom to leave this room. She needed to leave this room, if for nothing else other than to get the lay of the land. Where was she?

"Mrs. Sperling," Reck said as he opened the door to the room. Kali saw the key hanging in the top lock.

Gold, she thought. It's a bright and shiny gold.

"More water?" Reck flung the water bottle and she flinched. It landed beside her.

"I know you are probably hungry. I will bring you something else soon," he said, reaching into his pocket pulling out another apple that looked more wretched than the others he had brought the day before. How old was this food?

"You are probably hungry, too," she said. "Do you have an accomplice to bring us something? Something good now, I'm starving. Please tell whoever it is that I would like a full, hot meal. Although, I would prefer to eat out. A nice restaurant like Ruth's Chris would be acceptable. I'm sure the outfit I wore to the play would be more than sufficient."

"I am sure by the time I return you will eat whatever I bring you." Reck stepped back through the door and she heard the locks drop. All she needed was the shiny gold key to unlock the top lock on this side of the door. She didn't have to worry about unlocking the doorknob, not from inside. The key was hanging from the top. She jumped up and tried the knob. It didn't turn.

"Don't worry. It will be over soon," Reck yelled through the door. "Ashton is home."

Listen for the jingle, she said to herself, not letting the doorknob deter her hope. Which pocket man was Reck? She tried to imagine him when he accompanied her places. Did he drop the keys in the left or the right pocket? Then she rolled off the mattress excitedly. Reck was left-handed so he was a left-pocket man. Kali wasn't sure how she was going to get that key, but she knew she was going to get it. Running her hands through her hair again, she realized it needed a comb and a wash. There was no comb and no water, but what man was opposed to some dirty sex? Maybe she would use a little of the other kind of hand-to-hand combat to get her hands on that key. Reck was no fool though; he would recognize the ploy if she came on too strong. She was going to have to seduce him and make him think it was his idea.

Kali found Luther Vandross deep inside her for that moment and she started singing one of his love ballads that she and Ashton used to play while making love. She knew exactly what she was going to have to do. She couldn't wait for Ashton or any other man to sweep in and rescue her. Her baby was waiting for her. She knew Kacie was longing for her because she was longing for Kacie with her entire being. Her arms were empty and restless. Putting them around her kids was what she needed and what they needed. It wouldn't be the first time she had succumbed to a brute. But, it was definitely going to be the last.

Reck hung up his cell phone as he sat in the old Mercedes parked in the dark garage. He confirmed what he had already told Kali. Ashton was on his way, if he hadn't already landed. The police had followed his friend's tip and had arrested Jocko Jr. as soon as he had arrived at Marja's. Except there was no Marja. It didn't matter though; the druggie had served her purpose. He no longer needed her like he no longer needed his Nazi son. He had never loved him anyway. For a moment, Reck imagined his Junior spilling every detail of their businesses so they would come after him. But then again, the younger man was blinded by his love and loyalty to his father. There was no use in worrying, he thought. The young idiot was probably sitting in a cell blaming Marja, instead of him. God forbid, they let him go. Marja would never be safe again.

Reck couldn't take the risk, not yet, of driving the Mercedes out of the garage. Everyone in the tri-state area was looking for it. Kali had been right. His pictures and hers were everywhere. Reck put on a baseball cap and a pair of sunglasses, he lifted the garage door and started walking. They needed food.

Kali heard the jingle again as she stepped out of the bathroom. She was detangling her hair with her fingers, and trying to braid it when she heard that gold key in the top lock again. She watched him drop it in his left pocket as she lowered herself to the mattress and shifted the too large shirt down and frontward, exposing more of her breasts. He had one of those vinyl 99 cent shopping bags you buy at the cash register in a chain store. It had a Wawa symbol on the price tag, still attached by the nylon string.

"I brought you a change of clothing, some fresh fruit, some other stuff, and water. Oh, and some crackers," he said, putting the bag on the mattress. Kali noticed him biting his bottom lip. Her breasts had stirred something in him, good or bad. She would find out soon enough.

She plopped onto the mattress and crossed her legs, then leaned toward the bag. Reaching in, she pulled out a new pair of scrubs. That wasn't a good sign, she thought. Why would she need to change clothes? Like he said, there were a few food items, and a box of tampons. She pulled the box of tampons out of the bag and looked at him.

"You are due, aren't you?" Reck leaned back against the door.

"How would you know?"

"I could always tell."

"How. Do I smell?"

"Maybe. Maybe you smell different during different times of the month," Reck answered, shoving his large hands into his pockets. The keys jangled again.

"What else have you noticed about me, Reck?"

"Oh, I notice everything," he said as he slid to a sitting position with his back still to the door.

"I noticed you watching my pockets," he said.

"It's not your pockets. It's what's bulging between your pockets," Kali said as she dropped the tampons into the bag. "You knew the right brand."

"That was actually a wild guess." Reck had laughed at himself as he took the tampons to the counter. He had expected the young boy at the register to smirk, but he hadn't. The kid was busy listening to something in his ear buds and didn't even see Reck.

"Well, good wild guess. And depending on how long I have been in here, I have at least a week before my period. That is, if you are wondering." Kali said looking back in the bag and finding a sandwich, a little smashed for wear, but it was there.

She grinned up at him, "Thank you. Thank you."

She began to unwrap it and looked up at him staring at her. "Would you like to share?"

He shook his head no.

"I don't think you planned this, Reck. And I know a few things about you, too. You don't carry cash. You can't expect to use plastic in this situation now, can you? I'm willing to share, if you are hungry."

"I'm not hungry. I have a sandwich in the other room and you had plenty of cash on you. We should be able to survive for a few more days off the grid. Thanks to you."

"Glad I could help," Kali said, taking a bite out of the soggy turkey hoagie. Someone had soaked it in too much oil and vinegar, but she didn't mind. Her stomach was happy. Anything more than a stale apple was absolutely welcomed.

"So," Kali took another bite and savored it for a moment, "what brings us to this dark, dark place? Could I, at least, have a blanket? It gets cold in this little room. And some water to wash with, some soap, and some toilet paper."

"I will put that on your wish list," Reck replied.

"That would be greatly appreciated," she said savoring another bite.

"Why?" Reck asked, both of his hands flat against the floor. She wasn't sure if he was getting ready to boost himself up or if that was just a comfortable position for him, but she noticed. She noticed the veins bulging in his hands. She noticed a twitch in his right eye, and she noticed he was biting that bottom lip more often than normal.

"Why what?"

"At some point in time, you had the opportunity, the freedom, to just walk away from the Sperlings. You were accepted more than any woman had ever been in that family. They hold you in awe, they respect you. I don't get how that happened. What's worse is, I don't get why you stayed. You were a sex toy. Women try to get out of that situation. Don't they?"

"It's complicated," Kali answered truthfully. She should have been frightened and angry. Instead, she had started feeling as if she was in control of everything, at least off and on. She was not in control now, obviously.

"You were a whore. How complicated is that?" Reck suddenly looked at his hands as if he were surprised to find them on the ends of his arms.

"So you know my history with the Sperlings, with Jordan? What's yours? There is a reason we are here. There is a reason you hate Ashton so much that you have transferred that hate to poor Lazarus."

Reck laughed heartily. "You can stop the charade. There aren't any bugs from your policeman friend hiding around here."

Kali pushed the bag aside. "What else do you know? You knew the penthouse was bugged."

"I'm on your security detail, right? Micah kept us informed on what to look out for inside the house and out. I want to know why he didn't remove them. That would have made more sense."

"Only if you didn't want to find the source." Kali stuck up for Micah's plan. That's why additional cameras had been added and that's why Reck's face was probably all over the news by now.

"There were other ways."

"Did you tell Micah about them?"

"Why would I? I could care less whether you and your family were protected. Hell, the more of you that keel over, the better." Reck got up from the floor and put his hand on the doorknob. "Forget your seduction plan. Remember, I already copped a feel or two when I changed your clothes. As a matter of fact, you should have awakened with a wet pussy. I stuck a couple of fingers inside for a taste," Reck said, sticking a finger into his mouth.

"That's very sick of you," Kali said, wiping her mouth with the back of her hand.

"It was a lot of fun, trust me," Reck said.

"For you." Kali put her sandwich back in the paper wrapper and began to wrap it carefully.

"So, who the hell are you? Are you Jordan's little white boy like Mama Elle said?" Kali asked, carefully putting her sandwich down in the bag. She arranged the food items inside and put the box of tampons on the other side of the bed.

"Hmmm. That old bitch isn't as crazy as you think she is. Yes, I am Jack. Jack Pulaski. My mother was Marianne Pulaski. This was our house. Is my house."

"Then we are in Jersey," Kali said, remembering bits and pieces about Jordan's little white boy. Jordan had wanted to adopt him, but for some reason it never happened.

"Yes," Reck swayed a little.

"Was this your room?"

"No, I had a window. This was the guest bedroom."

"It was ugly," Kali said, walking across the mattress to the area against the wall. She wanted to sit up with back support.

"Everything back then in this house was ugly. Still is." Reck slid down the wall again to a squatting position.

"Why do you hate Ashton?"

"Where do I begin?" Reck drew his knees close to his body and bounced his forehead on them for a second or two. He reminded Kali of a small, frustrated child, but there was nothing small about him and his frustration was dangerous.

"Just begin." Kali followed suit and drew her legs close to her body. She hugged them and placed her chin between her knees. Their eyes met for a moment that hung heavily in time. She wasn't walking away from this one, she thought. He made Jordan, Ashton, Asa, and Billy look like fireflies.

"My son is dead because of Ashton," his voice said harshly. "My wife is dead because of Ashton. I didn't get to live a normal life with my mother because of Ashton. Jordan died thinking I was a useless piece of shit because of Ashton. Do you want me to keep going?"

"How is Ashton responsible for the deaths of your wife and child? I mean, I know a little, some of the history between you and Ashton and your relationships with Jordan. And your mother, of course. She was the one who saved Ashton's life, right? When he was three?"

Reck nodded his head and begin to right himself up again. He was restless.

"Redd and I got married in Germany. We had a boy. She came over here to ask Ashton for some money to help care for him. The kid was chronically ill and we couldn't afford the care he needed. She thought Ashton was going to help her."

Kali started laughing. "Oh, is that why she kidnapped him, punctured him a thousand times, and threw him over a cliff? That was asking for help? That is what you are talking about?"

"I had no idea she was that far gone," Reck snapped. It was true. He had no idea about the plan until afterwards. And that plan hadn't developed until Asa had found her again. The two of them had always been a dangerous combo, adding a big element of stupid. Asa was too dumb to recognize him and realize he was Jack and, eventually, had tried to act as if they had been friends all their lives which surprised him greatly. Maybe he was the one with lost memory, or maybe his hate for Ashton was even stronger than his. Either way, he hated Asa and hated him even more when he realized how much he had helped Redd go completely over the edge.

"Well, I knew Ashton. If only she had asked for the money to help with your child, he would have written her a big fat check."

"Believe what you want, but I was there. I was there down in Brazil when he killed her." Reck failed to mention the whole story. Redd did die, but only because he had let her.

Reck had followed Redd and Ashton to the mountains that morning. Having parked his car a couple of miles away, he had walked through the rocky thicket to the bottom of the cabin's driveway. This was finally going to be his opportunity to finish off what his wife and her ex-lover had started. He was going to take Ashton down completely. Asa had already alerted him that he thought Ashton had morphed into this new identity calling himself Lazarus, and then there he was, showing up in the same bar as Redd while Reck sat in the corner watching. That wasn't a coincidence. He had come down to Rio to get her to come home. Their son was failing and she was running all over the place trying to get her career back on track to earn the money they needed. But, who wanted a spaced-out, aging model with a taste for Special K and a craving for vodka and cocaine?

Reck was on his way up through the trees to invade the cabin when he saw Ashton come out and switch the jeeps. As soon as saw the way Ashton had parked the second jeep, he knew something was wrong with the brakes. He had stopped it next to a large stone. Anyone who drove it would have to back up and then leave. Reck could have revealed himself then, but he didn't. For some reason, he had decided to hold back to see why Ashton was going through the trouble. Then, he had a second thought. If that jeep was meant for Redd, he was going to need to stop it, so he went back down to the end of the driveway to prepare.

An hour later, Redd came stumbling out of the cabin, yelling. Ashton was talking about money. He lifted a duffel bag and put it in the back seat. She snatched the keys from his hand and jumped in the jeep. Just like he thought, she had to back the car up to go around the rock. It was easy for Reck to tell she was drunk as a skunk. He had seen that wobbly head up close and personal for over ten years now.

He watched Lazarus turn and go back into the cabin. He ran down the driveway in the open, because it was a shorter path to the bottom. He was not surprised to see the car stopped by the line of rocks he had put at the end of the driveway. She was swearing loudly and getting ready to back up the car and try to speed over them when he grabbed the passenger door.

"Stop, Redd. Turn the car off," Reck had yelled. She had looked at him with her bloodshot eyes and obeyed.

"What are you doing here?" she sighed, shaking her head in frustration.

"I'm here to protect you from yourself. I told you who I thought this guy was. Why did you come out here with him?"

"It's him," Redd said as tears started to appear on her splotchy, reddened cheeks. She wiped at them and he noticed her cracked, red nail polish. There was a time in her life when that would have been unheard of. Seeing her this way made him a little sad but, more than that, angry.

"What's in the bag?" He looked in the back and picked up the duffel bag.

"Put that down. It's the money he said he owed me. Me, you dirty bastard. I don't need you. I'm going back to Europe and put my son in a hospital that will fix him. Put that money down."

Reck unzipped the bag and saw neat rows of stacks of $100 bills. He zipped it back up and threw the bag into the woods.

"Give me that back," Redd yelled. "You fucking low-life, I regret the day I ever laid eyes on you." She started sobbing. "If you hadn't been playing your games in Munich I would have been home. I could have stopped him from leaving me. I loved him. I never loved you. Never. You were just there, you and your warped mind. Obsessing over me the same way that pathetic Asa used to do. I would have been better off without either of you. That could have been me," she cried aloud. "He loved me first. She was just some whore Jordan threw at him. Kali Sperling, Kali Sperling. I'm sick and tired of hearing about her. Her life should have been my life. Give me back the money."

"I will make sure Robbie is well-taken care of. If I let you keep this, you will lose it or spend it. Now get out of the car. Mine is parked back there." Reck pointed toward the woody path he had taken to get there.

"No," Redd screamed. "I'm tired of taking orders from you. I am tired of you."

"You are high, too high to be driving. You can't drive down that mountain. Robbie needs you to come home. I need you to come home. Let's take this money and just go home," Reck pleaded honestly. The money had been the answer all along. This was a big duffel bag. The first row of cash all by itself was at least $100,000.00.

"Come on," he held out his hand. "Get out of the car. We can get on a flight by the end of the day to go see our son."

"Just give me the money and I will see you in Germany."

"You are not making any sense." Reck took a few steps back. "I am not giving you this money to goof like you did with the rest of it. Where is the rest of it anyway?" Reck pleaded.

"Asa has it, or I think he does. He said Ashton and Micah took some of it back. I don't know. Go get yours from Asa," Redd said, shifting the gears in the jeep.

"Back up, turn the car into that little ditch. Put on the parking brake, I will move the rocks." Reck stared at his wife. She was already dead to him. To his surprise, she followed his directions and the car sat still in the little indentation in the ground without rolling forward.

He moved enough rocks for her to get through. She gave him the finger. He reached in his pocket and pulled out a wad of cash and handed to her.

"Take the first flight home. That's what I am going to do," he said, wanting to kiss her for the last time but deciding instead to remember her underneath him and happy, instead of stinking with vodka and sweat. She took the money, stuffed it in her purse beside her, then backed up the car and maneuvered through the rocks. Reck stayed long enough to move all of them from sight. As he began to weave back through the woods, he heard the other jeep. It was Ashton. He stopped at the end of the driveway and looked both ways, then pulled out onto the two-lane highway in the same direction Redd had just gone.

"So you are following in Ashton's footsteps. You are going to kill his wife and children?" Kali asked looking him in the eyes. He didn't flinch.

"I'd rather kill him first," Reck said, walking out of the door.

"I'd rather kill you first," Kali whispered as the room darkened. The bright light from the hallway went out, and she sat completely in the dark.

"You could have at least turned on the light, damn it," she yelled. "I can't see a damn thing in here."

The hallway light went back on and she heard his feet moving about. The door opened again and the light suddenly switched on, shining brightly. She deflected her eyes for a second.

"Thank you," she said, getting up from the mattress. As she moved toward him, he moved toward her with a swiftness that shocked her and before she knew it, she was on her back. He began to struggle to remove her pants.

"Let me," Kali said, breathlessly noticing the door was standing wide open. "I want this. I think I have always wanted this."

"Shut up, bitch." Reck ripped the pants off, hurting her as they tore into her skin. She screamed. He plunged inside her and bruised her delicate skin, tearing the tissue between her legs. She screamed and tried to gouge his eyes. He pinned her arms beneath him. She had sworn, after Asa, that she would never be raped again, but there she was underneath his weight and his strength having to endure his brutality.

"Who do you see, Reck? Are you fucking me or Ashton? Is that it, damn it? Do you have a little thing for Ashton?" Suddenly he stopped and looked down at her; his penis drooped and he rolled away.

Reck struggled to his feet and stumbled out of the door slamming it, but Kali didn't hear the lock. The bright hallway light was still on. She reached into the bag and found the new pair of pants. She slid into them and went to the door to listen. She couldn't hear anything so she turned the knob as quietly as she could and opened the door. Was this a trap, she thought, as she stepped into the hallway. From where she stood, she could tell there was an opening on the right, maybe a living room or something. Moving as quietly as she could she peeked around the corner and saw no one, just a big empty room with a sofa and a television. But her heart jumped, it was daylight and she could see the door to the outer world.

Kali hastened her steps and made it to the door. Even though she was afraid she would open it to find Reck, she didn't feel she had a choice. Easing it opened she saw the typical suburban Jersey home across from her. She stepped out and pulled the door closed behind her. The way the entryway was made, it hid her on both sides. She peeked out from the sides and looked both ways. There were no cars and no people. She stepped out onto the hard pavement and started walking fast, listening as she walked. She heard traffic to the right of her, so she turned right at the next block, still walking fast, wondering if she should knock on a door, but no one looked at home anywhere. The place was as dead as a Twilight Zone scene, so she kept walking.

The sound of the traffic picked up and her heart raced, though her feet ached from stepping on pebbles, and trash along the way up the hill toward the traffic. Then she saw a Wawa chain store with a small parking lot, sitting next to another little building that looked like a little strip of offices. No one was parked in front of either. She hoped, at least, the Wawa was still opened. She walked inside and the ringing bell made her jump. A young man stood behind the counter.

"I need to call the police, or you call the police. My name is Kali Sperling. I was kidnapped. Please help," she spilled the words fast, still not believing she had gotten this far.

"Oh, my God. You are her," he said and almost ran in a little circle. "Yes, yes, I will call," he ran to the back and then back toward her again.

"Come on back here with me," he said waving as if he were cheering her across a finish line.

Kali followed him, noticing the digital clock on the wall read 7:15 a.m. Sunday. No wonder the neighborhood had been so quiet. She limped toward a chair in the cluttered office, sat down, and listened to the boy make the call.

"He wants to talk to you," the boy said and as he handed her the phone, the bell ringing as the door to the store opened.

"I will be back," he mouthed the words walking out of the room proudly.

"Hello," Kali put the phone to her ear.

"Mrs. Sperling?" the voice asked.

"Yes."

"Mrs. Kalina Sperling?"

"Yes.

"How are you?"

"Alive," Kali answered, tears beginning to pour down her face.

"Our patrol is being dispatched to your location and the Philadelphia PD is being notified as we speak. Do you feel safe?" the man asked as Kali heard a gunshot. She dropped the phone and looked toward the door to see Reck coming toward her.

"He's here. He's here," she started screaming at the phone on the floor. Reck reached out and grabbed her by her curls and then shoved her toward the store. She slipped as she was going past the counter and looked down to realize that she had slipped in a large pool of blood.

"Why did you hurt him?" She tried to turn back to see if she could help the young man, but when she saw his head, she knew there was nothing she could do. As Reck sent her crashing to the ground outside in the parking lot, all she could think was another mother was going to be grieving tonight because of her, because of the Sperlings. How could one family create such a legacy of hate and despair? Kali turned and used her arm to block his fist going toward her face. For a moment, she thought he had broken it, but he twisted her, picked her up, and threw her in the trunk of the old Mercedes and slammed it shut.

Reck was angry at her, at himself, at Ashton, and at everything in his sight. Everything was in a red haze. Why was he doing what he was doing? Why did he rape her? Better yet, why did he let himself get so frazzled that he left everything open? Reck had rushed out the door, disappointed in himself, and had gone into the garage to calm himself down by getting into the driver's seat of the Mercedes. This Mercedes was the only link he had left to a normal life.

"A normal life," he laughed as he merged into traffic on highway 130 heading south. "Jack Pulaski never had a normal life."

Kali kicked at the trunk as hard as she could. This car was old and sturdily built. The trunk wasn't even getting a dent in it. She bounced around, trying to hold onto the sides to keep from getting hurt even more. Whenever he had to slow down, she would feel around to find anything that would help her escape. There was nothing. This car had been built long before there were latches inside to help you escape a trunk if you were locked into one. This car was vintage and not a lot of them on the road. All she could do was pray that someone would recognize the car. At least now, the police knew where to start looking for her. Poor kid, she thought, wanting to cry for the child on the floor in the Wawa, too. But, tears weren't going to help now. This man was insane.

CHAPTER TWENTY-THREE

KALI REALIZED THEY had left the highway by the increased number of bumps at a slower speed. At the speed, they were going she suspected that they had just gotten off 295 or 95. Unable to tell which direction they were traveling in, she continued to try to steady herself. She wouldn't be surprised to find her body covered in bruises the next time she had a chance to look at it. Then she thought about his gun. She wondered how many bullets he had left. She closed her eyes trying to picture it, but she couldn't. If he didn't have a refill it could be three left, or it could be many, many more depending on the type of gun. She had been too shocked to pay attention. She had never seen him carry a gun, not once, unless he holstered it in the back under his jacket. She hadn't wanted to be around guns, nor did she want any of the guards around the children with guns. Unaware if they were just humoring her by not letting her see them, she couldn't be sure what each man would carry. But, Reck had a gun. Her body shivered at the thought. And he was getting real used to using it.

The car began to slow down more frequently; perhaps he was getting caught up in traffic, she thought. She started kicking. Every time they came to a stop, she screamed and she kicked, trying to find the tail light and kick through.

The car slowed down in the lane closest to the sidewalk. A vendor who had been selling fresh produce all day was standing idly by on his phone. When he first heard it, he thought it was coming from one of the cars' radios.

"Hold on, man," the vendor stood there looking at the line of cars at the red light. "No go ahead, I thought I heard a woman scream."

"No, you want to hear a woman scream, buddy," the other guy on the line joked and then the vendor heard it again.

"No, it's real man." He started walking toward the cars as he heard the kicks and the screams getting louder.

"Hey, yo man." The vendor walked up to the passenger side of the Mercedes. "Yo man, is that your radio or is that somebody in the trunk of your car, man?"

Reck smiled at the man and lifted his gun. He shot him point blank in the face and drove up on the sidewalk across the man's body. The car crossed the curb into a large parking lot of what looked like an abandoned Walmart strip mall. He crossed the parking lot at the highest speed he could muster and dropped into the flowing traffic on the other side.

"Damn bitch," he screamed. "Now I have to get a new car right away. Bitch. I should come back there and shoot your ass right now."

Reck knew this area of South Jersey well. He took back roads and streets as long as he could before he pulled out onto Delsea Drive. He picked up speed again until he was just outside of Vineland. He didn't want to draw the cops' attention out there. They were always looking to pull someone over.

Nerdy Nick had been listening to the radio all morning about the black vintage Mercedes and the famous kidnap victim. He had never been so excited, especially when he heard from a friend that someone had just been shot outside the old Walmart and witnesses were describing the old Mercedes.

"Yippee," he had yelled as he hung up the phone. Nerdy Nick, was nicknamed that by his siblings because that's what he was, the family nerd who was obsessed with video games, comic book heroes, and mystery novels. Nick had always wanted to be a hero. He jumped into the old Chevy Malibu he had inherited from his grandfather and headed out, taking Landis over to Delsea Drive.

"Now which way would I go?" Nick asked himself as he sat at the light. "South. Too much traffic north of here. How would I stay off the radar? Maybe I would go down to 70."

Nick was still talking to himself 20 minutes later when he saw the vintage Mercedes go by, not in too big of a hurry, and turn onto a small street.

"Ah, you know about the speed traps. But, don't you know your car is being broadcast all over the world," Nick said as he clapped his hands over the steering wheel. He picked up his cell phone and called 911.

"I see him." Hurriedly, Nick told the operator who it was he saw and where he was heading. "Do you want me to follow him?" Nick asked, already turning his car down the street, realizing too late that it was a dead-end country street with only a couple of houses at the end of a little cul de sac. Nick was getting ready to back out when a tall, blond man appeared at the side of his car with a gun pointed toward him.

"Get out," the man said. Nick's hands began to shake badly as reached for the ignition to turn off the keys. "Leave the keys. Leave the car on. Pop the trunk."

Nick popped the trunk.

"Get out."

"Yes, sir," Nick said trying to think of a superhuman trait he could morph into in a few seconds to save the woman's life. It was then that he heard her screaming and kicking.

"Give me the phone." Reck held his hand out and Nick put it in his hand. The 911 operator was still on the line. Reck looked at the phone and then at Nick. He pulled the trigger. Someone in one of the houses screamed and Reck took two shots at the window. Then he went to the Mercedes and opened the trunk. He held the gun in Kali's face as he dragged her to Nick's car, making her step over Nick's body. Reck shoved Kali into the trunk, slammed it shut, and got into Nick's car.

He plowed across the yard of one of the houses through its backyard, through another yard in a house located behind it on a separate street and headed to parts only known to him. He had planned that route a million times. He had to thank the boy for a non-descript car. He figured he could get to where he was going on these back roads in little more than a half hour. He knew how and where he would hide the car. The rest would be easy. Reck smiled, he couldn't wait to see Ashton's face when he set eyes on his dead wife. But, it had to be just right.

Reck picked up the phone while trying to focus on the twisting two-lane highway. Someone had surely called the police by now but, by the time they identified Nick and started searching the airwaves for this phone, he would have gotten rid of it. He pushed the numbers as he slowed for a stop sign. Someone answered on the third ring.

"Phase Two. Almost there," he said as he hung up the phone, then banged it against the dashboard before tossing it out of the window down into the road. He was hoping another car completed its destruction. It was now early Sunday afternoon and most people were just starting to move around. There were only a few cars on the road. He doubted anyone passing him was on the lookout for him. He was heading for an area where people didn't care what was going on in the rest of the world.

CHAPTER TWENTY-FOUR

OTH MEN GOT into the black SUV without uttering a word. Micah put the key into the ignition and let it hang there like the rest of his life, uncertain.

"What now?" Micah asked, glancing over at his older brother who could have impersonated one of those blow-up balloons waving around at a car dealership. His whole demeanor was deflated or, at least, the air in him was seeping out at a fast pace. For the first time, Micah noticed how deep the crow's feet around Ashton's eyes had become, or maybe they had just appeared after talking to his mother.

"Do you have men protecting your mother?" Ashton asked.

"The car in front of us has one. There should be another one in the building. You think he will try to hurt her?"

"She recognized him."

"Damn, he never let go of the family."

"No. And I bet you a dime the reason Daddy didn't relay the messages about Redd and Asa being stuck in Germany was because he knew who they were with. Probably some sort of sick game he and Jack were playing with them. Daddy was probably already turning on Asa then."

"Damn all of them. Daddy got what he deserved though, didn't he? Damn, what a sick family we are. Mother's right, we must protect our children from this type of life. Hell, I can't take much more of this shit myself. My mother's a cunning woman though, isn't she?" Micah said. "What a fantastic cover story. I mean, it was so detailed. We had talked about a variation of that, remember? Making you a long lost relative or something, but that story was a good one. You think Ms. Elliott will go along with it? I mean, what would that do to her family if she backs you up on this? You know the press still likes a good Jordan Banks' crazy family story."

"Elliott is my mother," Lazarus said, gulping down the huge lump of truth in his throat.

"You believe her?"

"I remembered the lunches in Suburban Station. When Elliott came for the interview, she looked familiar. Real familiar. And the way it felt just being in her presence, kind of felt right. Your mother was right; I couldn't help but hire her. The minute she walked into that suite, I wanted to hug her for some reason. She was like an old friend and I didn't realize why."

"That still doesn't make her your mother."

"Have you ever watched her with my children?"

"Yes, I have always marveled at how good she is with them, even with Artie."

"She is their grandmother. She has been acting like a grandmother from day one. Heck, they refer to her as their god grandmother."

"Then why not tell you? Jordan's dead. Billy's dead. My mom is freaking crazy one minute and lucid the next. And she was freaking lucid today. Or was she? And why today?"

"Well, there are one or two reasons. The lucid part wants to save Kali. We all want to save Kali. Or, your mom's not crazy. Maybe acting like she lost it was the only way she could get away from Billy. I mean that, in itself, was a risk. The Billy we knew could easily have just killed her off and been done with it."

"No, Billy wouldn't have gotten his own hands dirty. Our father paid other people to do his dirty deeds. Chances are, since he put mom in such a downtrodden place to begin with, he didn't have the funds to hire someone to do it the right way, without it pointing back to him anyway. He didn't have an Asa to manipulate to take the fall regardless of whose decision it was. I contacted the FBI agent assigned to Kali's kidnapping while you were still talking to Mama. She has someone researching the address. In the meantime, we can drive over the bridge in that direction. Or, do you have something else we need to do first?"

"Let's take the Tacony Bridge over. That's how Jordan used to drive over there. That's one of the things I do remember about going to Jersey. The loud sound of the bridge as the tires went over the grids. I remember I used to get so happy bouncing around on the car seat, jumping up and down yelling Tacony, Tacony. What a stupid kid I was."

"We were all stupid kids, Ashton." Micah gripped the steering wheel tighter. "I guess that should be the last time I can call you Ashton," Micah said as he was patting his jacket. He lifted the compartment next to the driver's seat. "Shit, where's my phone?" I need to run back in the apartment to see if I dropped in there."

"What is it with you and your phone? Am I going to have to glue it to you?" Lazarus complained.

"I don't know," Micah answered sheepishly. He had missed some very important calls lately. It was so unlike him to be careless about anything, especially his phone. As he got out of the car, he saw one of the men who worked for him running down the stairs.

Micah started walking toward him.

"Your mother tried to leave her apartment. When I stopped her, she said you must have dropped it when you hugged her. It's been ringing," the guard said. "I think you better call them back right away, sir. There's something on the news, too. I just got a call looking for you."

Lazarus was anxious. They weren't moving fast enough.

"What are we doing, Lazarus?" Micah asked his brother, avoiding calling him Ashton again. He didn't want to slip up at the wrong time. After this morning, he was going to have to talk to the children about that again. No more daddy slip-ups.

"I am going to get my wife," Lazarus answered.

"Why do you think he's going to take her to the house in South Jersey?"

"Because that's where she was happy, where we were all happy. And, if I know Kali, that's what she had told Jack. You said she talked to him freely, didn't you?"

"Yeah, I used to think she spent too much time with him. He was always there. Which is where he was supposed to be, but I don't know." Micah's voice trailed off, angry with himself because he wasn't making any sense.

"You were jealous," Lazarus explained it. "You fell in love with her."

"Naw, naw," Micah shook his head, shamed by the fact that a lot of what he felt was jealousy when he saw Kali and Reck together laughing, sharing a secret joke.

It had even bothered him that Reck would ride alongside Kali in her car. Why wasn't he shadowing her like the other guards, he would ask her. *'I don't know,' she would answer. 'He keeps me company, I guess.'*

"He does know everything about us, then. Doesn't he?" Micah

said more to himself than to Lazarus, refusing to admit his feelings about his brother's wife.

"Yeah, not just from Kali. He learned everything he could about us through Redd, even Asa. Then he planted a woman in my household in London. That is, if he is Jocko. And I bet my life that Jack Pulaski is Jocko. Think about it. Jocko the DJ. Jack loved listening to him."

"He's lived a tangled life trying to keep up with you, then." Micah could almost understand the man's motives. Ashton was that much like their grandfather. He could bring out the best in people and he could bring out the worst, without any intention on his part of doing either. Redd had had a sick obsession with him and so did Asa, Ruby, even Troy.

"You know why your mother was afraid of Jordan's little white boy?" Lazarus said, rolling up the window so Micah could hear him.

"Why?"

"Because she didn't believe he was orphaned twice. You see, the guy, the librarian that supposedly killed Jack's mother was still swearing his innocence when he died. He kept saying she was alive and well when he left her. They even had this in the newspapers. I found an article Jordan had saved. It reported that the guy said they should be looking at her twelve-year-old son."

"My mom thinks he killed his mom and his adoptive parents, too?" Micah asked. He hadn't been privy to that story before.

"Yeah, well, supposedly his new parents died of carbon monoxide poisoning from either a backed-up furnace, or one that was improperly stalled, or something to that effect. Anyway, they died in their sleep on a night when Jack was at a church sleepover for kids, after which the state tried to place him in another foster home, but he ran away. That's what he told Jordan and me when he came back. I bet if you traced that story his new name was Jonathan Reck, like it says on his application. I'm guessing Jonathan is his real first name, not Jack. Jack was probably just a nickname. He knew that. He knew we wouldn't know. We didn't discuss names when he came back, at least I only knew him always as Jack. We didn't cross that line, a lot like we haven't been discussing my name. Stop calling me Lazarus, son, my name is Ashton."

Micah looked at Ashton again, taking his eyes off the road a little too long.

"Stop, son," Ashton called out, reverting to his old lingo he had picked up from his grandfather growing up. It had come out naturally as he was beginning to feel like he was home again and Micah had come dangerously close to rear-ending the car in front of him. Call it instinct.

Micah instantly regained control of the car and blew out a long whistle.

"Are you serious?" Micah asked his brother.

"Yeah, what am I supposed to do? Tell me. Walk around with a big beard and contact lenses, hiding beneath hats and crap? I was careful as hell when I killed Scully," he said referring to the prison guard he had vengefully murdered with his bare hands before his ex-wife had tried to do the same to him. "Someone planted that evidence. And since Redd and Asa showed up to kidnap me the next freaking day, Reck or one of them had to have had something to do with that evidence. It wasn't me. Besides, the fingerprint was on an old prison ID badge, not his new one, not the prison where he was working currently and where he was headed that morning. That would have been the badge he had worn. That shit was planted."

"By whom? That's the only way we could get you out of being a suspect. We would have to have the 'who and who' motive?" That was what the two of them had been supposedly working on when Ashton had left for Europe. They had to clear Ashton of any possible murder charge before he could resume his identity. Once the news got out that Ashton was alive and the actual fingerprint matched the right brother, Troy, with his overly defined sense of justice, would be the first to want to arrest him. This time if he went to prison, the sentence would be justified. It would be a crime he did commit.

"The only possibility, the only person left has my wife and is waiting for me, "Ashton answered. "He's going to kill her. You know that, right? He wants me to hurt. He wants me to hurt real bad. He knew how bad I would have hurt had that boy he killed been AJ. He knows now that it wasn't AJ, so he will hurt me where it hurts worse. He's going to kill Kali," Ashton said and looked at the trees they were passing on the side of the road. This was as helpless as you could get, he thought. If only he could put his hands on him right now, he would make sure Jack would never breathe again.

"When was the last time you heard from my old friend, Troy? Is he still trying to pin my own death on me?" Ashton asked.

"That, and still trying to woo Kali." Micah said with a half-chuckle.

"You mean to tell me he hasn't figured out yet how much she hates him?" Ashton shook his head.

"Which brings me to a subject we haven't discussed yet." Micah said as he took the next exit and began the trip of winding, two-lane roads down toward Cumberland County.

"You screwing Kali?" Ashton asked. "I already knew about that."

"No. No, we haven't discussed it. There's no need, there is no us. No Kali and me. We, we just needed each other momentarily, "Micah answered, saying what he knew his brother needed to hear. He and Kali had never hidden their affair. There had been no need under the circumstances. "It's probably not a real secret either. Before the murder and the kidnapping, though, the penthouse was bugged."

"By whom?"

"We left the bugs there trying to trace them. I had a team working on it and, well, I didn't like what they were finding. Fortunately, they weren't taken down before the kidnapping. At least, the police didn't have to search too far for evidence outside of our own video of who kidnapped Kali and killed the kid. Hmm," Micah swallowed hard. "They even had audio."

"The police? Are you saying the police?"

Micah answered slowly, "That's what I am trying to tell you. It was Philly PD that was listening to our daily lives, not the FBI, or some crazy man."

"Police? Why would the police have the family under surveillance, especially the police? Supposedly, I'm dead. The Ashton me that is. And Lazarus, well, that side of me was keeping my distance. I'm sorry, I am trying to make sense of this. What did they know?"

"There is only one person that keeps using his resources to keep tabs on us. That's that loyal friend of yours who wants to send the Lazarus side of you to prison. I think he knew that you were coming back to Philly. Figured you would be sniffing around Kali again."

"Did you tell him?"

"No, we told the other board members you were coming and we told security, which included Reck. Reck was supposed to be picking you up from the airport, you know. We didn't tell the kids until this week because we didn't want to get their hopes up too high. They get a little hyper when it comes to you."

"Were they calling me Daddy?"

"No, we curbed that pretty well. We even took them out of the house and schooled them on the bugs. Told them we were doing our best to trace them. Your kids have learned how to lie pretty well." Micah pulled onto another highway as Ashton checked his watch. "Must be in the genes."

"I didn't ask for this."

"Neither did they. Thirty minutes. It should take less than another 30 minutes."

"I am assuming Troy knew about the house in Burlington. Did you tell him?"

"Two days ago. I didn't know what town, but I gave him enough info to look."

"How long do you think he's been working with Jack?"

"Long enough," Micah answered as the digital speedometer began to increase.

CHAPTER TWENTY-FIVE

T HE CAR HAD slowed and was dipping over uneven terrain. Kali bounced harder when the car dipped harder. She figured they were off the highway. Wherever he was taking her, they had almost arrived. She could feel it in the deliberateness of each hump as the car went up in absolutely no hurry at all. Then she realized the car was backing up. She heard doors — and then she heard the whinnying neigh of a horse. She was home. He had taken her back to her home in Jersey. Without seeing where she was, she knew he was backing the car into the side area with the stacks of hay where the kids climbed to play hide and seek when they were growing up there. It was a funny thing. Immediately, she began to smell the hay, the horse dung mixed with the fuel from the car so strong she almost gagged. She hadn't noticed any smells until now.

Kali tried to position herself so she could get in a kick or two when he opened the trunk. No matter what, she wasn't going down like a wuss. She would scratch him, bite him, claw him, kick him, whatever it took until she could get away from him. His footsteps moved around the car hastily, she expected the trunk to pop open any minute and it didn't. She lay there looking into the darkness and then thought about a safety latch. She started feeling around for one, but it was either missing or she just couldn't find it.

She heard the footsteps again walking past the car, but this was a different set of footsteps. Kali jumped, bumping her head. The other voice sounded muffled and farther away, but it was a voice, a male voice and he continued to move farther away. Kali tried to put her ear to the top of the trunk to see if she could hear better. It didn't work, it muffled the voices even more. Kali lay back down and tried to be completely still so she could hear better, but then the other voice was gone and a set of footsteps came back hastily toward the car.

"Well, well, well." The trunk popped open and he lifted the lid higher at the same time. "How was the ride back here? I hope you found it comfy," Reck laughed viciously, as he held the gun close to her face. "Come on, get out. You can do it. You need the exercise. Come on." Reck waved the gun toward the side of the car.

Kali struggled to get her footing as she stepped out of the car. The tossing and turning had made her a bit punch drunk. She stumbled toward him; he took a few steps back. She leaned over and put her hands on her knees and began to throw up.

"Trying to make me feel sorry for you?" he said, poking her with the gun. She took a swing at him. That made him laugh.

"Do you think you could take me, Mrs. Sperling? Really?" Reck threw the gun and it went into the stall of one of the horses, making it jump and neigh.

"There, now we are even." Reck stood back in a fighter's stance with both of his fists up. She dropped to her knees, keeping her head down between her legs. Her world was dizzy.

"I thought so. You are just a little pussy." Reck laughed at his own joke. "Let's get that exercise."

Reck grabbed her hair and pulled her upright to her feet. She clawed at his hands to no avail as he shoved her toward the door of the stable. Kali was glad to see it was a beautiful day. If this was to be her last day, that, at least, was something to be thankful for. She set her eyes on the blue sky and thought maybe her babies were looking at the same sky. She stumbled through the grassy wetlands they used to call their backyard. There was a time when they would cut the grass out this far, but now they only worried about keeping it cut close to the house since they were never there.

"Keep walking. You know where we are going, don't you? You told me about it, right? The little place that you hated. Wouldn't go down there with Ashton because you thought it was too dangerous for the kids. You didn't think I would remember, did you? When you told me about it, I couldn't help but think what a perfect little getaway for us. I love little caves."

Reck shoved her again. She stumbled forward on her rocky legs again. Why was she feeling so out of it, so groggy? And then she remembered the fumes she smelled in the car while it was parked. She could have easily been unconscious or dead when he had opened the trunk. It would have all been over. She wondered if he would have been disappointed.

"You don't know who you are messing with," Kali shouted and then stopped in her tracks holding her head, the veins inside were beating insanely as if they were trying to escape her skin. Kali took a deep breath and it relieved the pain only slightly. She realized she needed to buy herself some time if that was even possible. She went face down flat into the grass.

"Don't play with me, bitch, I'll crush your ass." Reck placed his big foot on the small of her back. Kali kept her face buried into the dirt and grass. "Get your ass up," he reached down and flipped her over.

Kali looked up at him with half-closed eyes. She breathed in deeply through her nose.

"I said, GET UP." He stomped the ground next to her. She flinched and rolled slowly the other way.

"Then crawl, damn it," Reck shouted.

Kali moved forward once and then dropped. She moved forward again, pushing a leg behind her for traction. As she lifted her arm to move again, she felt her body being tugged upward. Reck picked her up and threw her over his shoulder. He began to walk fast toward the sound of the water. But, in the meantime, she breathed as deeply and evenly as she possibly could. The deep breaths were waking her up. She offered no resistance at all, other than the resistance it took to fill her lungs with oxygen.

The hike to the waterfall was farther than Reck had expected. He was beginning to tire under Kali's weight. She wasn't as light as she looked.

"How much farther?" He stopped and dropped her to the ground, almost knocking the air completely out of her.

Kali turned her head and saw the single oak tree where the horses would stand while the kids ran wild. You would have thought it would have been the other way around. But, those were her kids. For a moment, she heard their joyful giggles, their feet running through the grass, the outdoor smells of their bodies as they rushed into her arms and gave her big hugs and kisses. The tears caused by a bruised knee or a scraped shin. She could even hear Ashton's voice as he complained that no one was listening to him and the kids making loud noises to prove his point.

She looked at Reck and smiled. No matter what he did to her now, he couldn't take that away from her. She reached up to him and he took her hand and pulled her to her feet. She turned around trying to get her bearings. There was the tree. She pointed past the tree and her knees began to buckle.

"Oh, no you don't. This is one plan you are not going to ruin," he said, giving her a small shove this time.

She made her way forward and stopped about ten feet from the edge of the ravine that hid the cave.

"You have been here before," Kali said as she realized how deliberate his path to this ravine had been. "You were the one who was working with Redd and Asa, weren't you? You were the one who planted the duffel bag with Brady's wallet and the cash near the riverbed?"

"If I were, I would also be the one to hear Lazarus confirm he was Ashton, and to see Ashton kick Brady over onto the bed of rocks near the waterfall. Now that would be a big coincidence, wouldn't it?"

"No, not a coincidence, a shame. It's a shame, Reck. I always liked you. I even trusted you." Kali let her body go limp again. He caught her and pulled her close to him as he moved them closer to the edge of the ravine. Kali could see the ledge below that had barely caught Ashton long ago. When they had been alone that night, he had finally admitted to her that he had fallen. He hadn't wanted to frighten the kids. What was it about him and ledges? She thought of the tree that kept him from going over a ledge in the Rockies. She hoped she would be as lucky.

Then, she kicked her leg between Reck's, mid-stride, causing him to lose his balance. As he started falling forward, she jumped onto him and they both went flying over the edge toward the ravine. They landed on that ledge maybe an inch from going over into the bed of rocks below. He lay beneath her.

The fall was farther than she had anticipated. All she could remember was Reck's arms trying to grab her and the air at the same time. They were having a hard time choosing which one to do while she almost sat on top of his chest as if she were riding a sled going downhill midair. Her whole body shuddered with pain. She was afraid to move, so she lay there unable to lift her head, listening to the sound of the waterfall.

She had no idea about the time or about how long they lay there. But, Kali was determined to remain aware as long as she could. She started cataloging what she could, one by one. One. She could breathe. It hurt, but she could breathe. That meant she was still alive. Two. She could move the fingers on her left hand. She wiggled them and felt part of Reck's arm beneath them. He moaned when she touched him. She let her hand drop from his arm to feel where it would go. On him, they were stable, off him was air. The problem was, she didn't know how much air. It could be a lot of air between her hand and the ground, she thought and decided to try to move to her right.

Three. She started with the fingers on her right hand and gasped when she could not feel them at all. She tried to wiggle. Nothing was acting as if it was there. She tried to lift her right shoulder and excruciating pain shot through her whole body. Finally, she opened her eyes wide and realized she was correct in her first assessment. To her left was at least a hundred-foot drop; to her right was the rest of the little ledge that had just saved her. She used her left hand to find some leverage on Reck's body to push her to the right. Reck moaned again. As she began to move over him, she realized something very disturbing. Reck's bones, his mass moved beneath her like jelly.

"Why?" Reck gurgled the word. Kali could still see the side of his face. A little stream of blood was pouring down the side of his mouth as his head pointed toward the sky. His eyes were open.

"I could ask you the same," Kali said and winced from another sharp pain, her body still vibrating from the crash. As she lay beside him now, trying to breathe deeply enough to focus on something other than the agonizing pain, she glanced at his chest. It was sunken in and trying to heave upward. Realizing it was her weight that had crushed him, she imagined that the granite below them had stopped him faster than it had stopped her. She tried to inhale deeply again, but the deep breath caused her more pain.

"I, I would never have hurt you," Reck said, wanting to believe that he wouldn't have gone that far. All he had wanted was Ashton and now Reck was lying there without any feeling in his body.

"Go ahead, lie to yourself on your death bed. You already hurt me," Kali said, her words shooting out in spurts with a different kind of pain accompanying each one.

"You have to go to the cave." Reck's words, filled with a regret he had never experienced before, were struggling to escape his lips between breaths.

Kali's head fell toward him heavily as she had no control. He was trying to turn his head toward hers.

"Cave. Safe. He thinks you know. He thinks. You know. What he did," Reck said, his head finally turning toward hers and a brief thought of what could have been raced across his mind.

She watched as the light left his eyes and his chest stop moving. "Who's coming back?" Her brain was scrambled. Those words should mean something. What did he say? She thought, as her eyes began to close.

"Do it," Kali heard a voice and forced her eyes open. Reck's lifeless eyes were staring into hers.

"What?" she asked Reck, though a part of her knew he was dead. But, another part of her was clear that she had heard a voice, a voice that had reminded her of Jordan's. With an effort that felt as though it was taking forever to accomplish, she turned her head to look upward. She darted her eyes to either side of her and saw no one. She strained to see the ledge above them and it was just a dark piece of stone jutting out over her blocking the morning sunlight. Between the part that jutted out and the side of the little cliff was the path down to the ledge, with stones melded in place by time, creating little steps down to this ledge that hid the cave.

"Rollover," the voice said. Kali's good arm went up fighting the air. Who was talking to her? She wanted to shoo him away.

"Move, Kali," the voice said again. "You can do it. Move. Go into the cave, little girl."

Kali almost sat up, but the discomforting feeling made her lie back down. She reached out again, and this time grabbed hold of Reck's arm. Was this some sort of joke? Her hand kept grabbing at Reck, and eventually fell onto his pants where she felt the outline of another gun. No wonder he so carelessly threw away the other. It was probably out of bullets. She tugged at it, hoping she wasn't about to shoot herself. Grabbing hold of it, she laid it on her stomach and looked up at the sky. Still no movement or any sound from the man lying beside her.

"Are you dead?" she asked Reck and didn't get a response.

"Move." She heard the voice again and this time she recognized it.

"Jordan?" she called helplessly. "Jordan, is that you?"

Kali steadied the gun and found the ground beneath her with her hand. She used it for leverage and shoved herself only a few inches away from Reck. For a moment, it excited her that she did it. She moved. A powerful ache followed causing her to close her eyes in agony.

"Move," the voice said again, so she shoved herself a few more inches. Kali moved an inch or two whenever the voice said to do so. Inch by inch, she shifted her broken body to the mouth of the cave.

"What if they can't find me?" she asked the voice, referring to Micah and Ashton.

"Move," the voice said, this time in a whisper, cajoling her as if she were a small child. Kali moved again until her head was inside the moist cave. It sent a chill through her body. What was she doing? "He's coming back," the voice said, and this time she knew what Reck had meant. He had been talking to someone outside the stables. She rolled toward her good side and almost lost the gun, but she caught it and readjusted. Using her hand and foot to gain traction, she descended deeper into the cave as she crawled behind a boulder where the kids used to sit and eat a snack as a reward for coming down there to camp all day. Though she had initially fought the idea of bringing her babies down into such a dangerous little alcove, she had given in because that was what Ashton wanted. He had been determined that his children would not be afraid of anything.

CHAPTER TWENTY-SIX

T HE ROCK WAS cool and moist beneath her right cheek, but her face was warm and moist from tears on her left cheek. Kali positioned herself as best she could with her broken body and listened for Jordan's voice again. It was silent. But, the sounds of water dripping into the cave and her heart pumping briskly in her ears were dreadfully loud causing her to think of what it must be like for a prisoner of war to experience water torture.

She moved the gun gingerly between her body and the rock wondering how well she would be able to use it with her non-dominant hand. With her right hand, she was damn good at firing a weapon. After all the attacks on her and her husband, she made sure she was skilled in self-defense at every level imaginable. Too bad, it had been Reck who had taught her hand-to-hand combat. She was sure he must have left out some important stuff but, then again, he weighed twice or more what she did and he was even more skilled than she had any interest in being.

"Don't go to sleep," she told herself. "You may have a concussion. Don't sleep." She stroked the gun lightly with her fingertips. "Think of something nice. Something exciting. Something good."

Kali tried to adjust her body to find a comfortable spot and knew with every move how impossible that was. She thought about meditation. Could she put herself in a meditative state? Then she thought about how many times she had fallen asleep at some point during her long attempts at meditation. So, she imagined being interviewed by a TV news reporter saying, "How did you survive the kidnapper?"

"I thought about my children and how much they needed me," she replied. And then she hesitated. Where was Kacie? What had happened to Kacie? Had she seen what had happened to Katie's boyfriend? Was she hurt? How was Katie? Was she traumatized by her boyfriend's death? The questions about her children wouldn't stop.

Kali tried to concentrate and replay the interview again, but her eyes were getting too damn heavy as if someone was pressing them down. The darkness in the cave wasn't helping so she looked toward the mouth of the cave and stared at Reck's body until it began to fade behind her eyelids.

Kali awakened to his lips on the back of her neck; she tried not to respond. Having no idea what time it was, her body knew it wasn't time to get up. Then his tongue flickered and he began to suck on her neck gently, making her turn toward him.

"Ashton, stop it. What time is…" he stopped her sentence midstream as his mouth took over hers while he rolled on top of her. She kissed his luscious lips back. He was going in deep as if he were trying to suck the breath out of her body. Finally, she came up for air.

"Let me sleep. I want to sleep," she protested as his hands removed her nightgown inch by inch lifting her toward him.

"Ashton Taylor Sperling, this is no time for Taylor," Kali said, referring to Ashton's nickname for his penis. He liked calling her sweet vagina, Niecy, for her middle name Denise. She tried too late to pull her gown back down as he had it over her head in a second or two. That was the problem with loving such a big, powerful man. Her strength was no match for his. He would fling her over his shoulder like a rag doll and run down the stairs with her a few steps at a time without effort. He loved to do that, to hear her squeal and make the children squeal, too, to see their parents having fun, their dad being so devilish.

But, this was his spot, getting his early morning nookie. No matter how long they had been together, this would never change. It didn't matter if early morning to him was at 3:00 a.m. because he had a six o'clock flight. Ashton's Taylor was going to plunge into Kali's Neicy hungrily and brilliantly hard the way she loved it.

"Ashton," she pleaded again trying to move his big head which had taken up residence on her breasts, sucking her nipples one at a time. Her back arched as his hands began to find the center of her universe. His forefinger rubbing gently and then swiftly, as another finger tried to find the opening to her rectum. She squirmed and squealed at the same time. It didn't matter the time, she had to muffle her squeals and soon-to-be screams with a pillow which she grabbed. She had already been asked once by little Kacie if she had had a nightmare. Her baby told her she had heard her scream one night. Thank God, Micah was walking down the hallway and grabbed the potential little intruder in time to take her back to her room. He had been the one to plant the nightmare idea.

Kali tried to turn away from him and he flipped her back onto her back and began to suck her belly button.

"Boy," she said, popping his head lightly and then letting her fingers run through his silky, curly hair. It was slightly damp, smelling of the strawberry vanilla oils he liked to use all over his body, a ritual his grandfather had introduced to him. Whatever time it was, he was getting ready to leave for the day. She tried to remember if he was going on another business trip or just to the office. Between him and four kids, it was hard keeping up with their schedules.

She put the pillow over her face and bit hard, as he went down deep between her legs with the same intensity as he had kissed her mouth. Her body exploded over and over, and no matter how hard she tried to escape his feast, he held onto her with his powerful grip. She tried to pry her legs from beneath, but his weight pinned her down. And, then it happened, the big explosion inside of her that made her think she had ripped the pillow in two. She heard him laugh his low mischievous giggle as he flipped her on her stomach like the wind flipping a feather and entered her. She bit the pillow again. She lay there as he rhythmically began his entry and stayed at that pace for a long time and then he peaked, ramming her with all his might, picking her bottom up in the air with the rest of her body following. She sat in his lap while he held onto her breasts and bounced her rigorously until he detonated inside her. Then he dropped her onto the bed and slapped her behind playfully. She threw every pillow she could get her hands on at him as he tried to dress quickly.

"All right, woman. If I wasn't already late, I'd do you again. You keep that up and I'm going to…" he ended by jumping on the bed as she crawled to the other side, laughing. He pulled her into his arms and planted light kisses all over her face.

"Do you need to hear me say it?"

"Say what?" Kali kissed his nose and let her hands rest on his massive chest.

"I love you, Kali girl." He leaned in for a kiss and when he lifted his head, there was a scar on the left side and his face was drawn thin. His hair was still bouncy and clean, but her hands rested on his chest covered in lots of keloid scars that looked like little rain drops. His shoulders and his arms had shrunk. He looked like a stick man. She pinched his nipples and made his sad eyes smile. He leaned in for another kiss, a pleading, sad kiss but deep. She hungrily accepted his savory tongue.

His body was rail-like, but he was still strong. He lifted her up high and slid her down onto his stone mountain. Neicy wrapped around it and clung to it as it gently intruded into her universe. He placed his hand in the small of her back and shifted the angle to make sure she would climax with him. She buried her head into his neck and kissed it. Her tears flowed as she ran her hands through his hair and nibbled on his ears. What more could she do to help him? He was lost. She turned his head toward hers to take his mouth again but his lips had changed. These lips were full and brown and juicy. They grabbed her lips, gently bit at her lips, and made her giggle as he threw her down on the bed.

Micah's body was magnificent as always, a deep chocolate brown with not a blemish or a flaw in sight. Everything about him was perfect, even his bald head that she loved to rub and kiss. "Where's Lazarus?" she asked giddily, realizing now was not the appropriate time to ask about another man. But, she thought, wasn't he just here?

"Nowhere to be found," Micah turned her over and bit her butt checks playfully. She squealed, not worrying about waking the children. It was obviously in the middle of the school day and they had the penthouse to themselves. Kali attempted to crawl away and he pulled her back to him entering her doggy style. That was his favorite position, she thought. He was always bending her over something and taking her at his will. The two of them spent a lot of time working from home as they would tell everyone and then let their calls rollover to voicemail.

Kali finally pulled away as he came, and fell on her back to playfully put her foot on his chest. It was big, but not as big as Ashton's. She loved big men. They made her feel safe, but it wasn't Micah's flawless body that her foot landed on, it was Troy's. She yanked her foot back and pulled at her clothes to make sure she was completely covered. She had never let that man touch her, not that she could remember. Jordan had drugged her and given her away a few times for punishment in the beginning. She suspected Troy may have been one of those men she had been gifted to by the way he looked at her. He frightened her, not just for her own physical safety, but for Ashton's as well. He talked about his loyalty too damn much and he was always offended by not being included in the family. He wasn't her family, never had been. His relationship with Ashton had been damaged years ago. Kali knew that Ashton pretty much just tolerated him and didn't trust him anymore. Kali went behind the desk in her office and sat down.

"What can I do for you, Troy? What brings you to PDSI today?" she asked, watching his mouth answer, but she couldn't understand what he was saying. It was his voice, but the words weren't matching his lips. She squinted her eyes to make sure she was fully aware of what was happening and then she heard him, she heard him clearly.

"Jack, Jack." She heard the rocks move above as if someone was coming down the path. It was his voice. It was Troy, Troy was calling to Reck, wasn't he?

Kali focused her eyes on the body to see if it would move, but it didn't, and watched as Troy's legs came into her view. It was him, she would recognize those pants and shoes anywhere. The man had no sense of style. Whether he was wearing the same clothes or not, they were always the same style and the shoes always looked a little too worn. She thought he took gumshoe to heart too much. Just because he was a detective didn't mean he had to look like an outdated slouch. Troy knelt and touched Reck's throat and then picked up his hand and checked for a pulse.

"Damn, Jack, what the hell happened to you?" Troy wiped his face in frustration. He stood up and looked around.

"Kali, Kali," Troy began to yell. Troy looked over the ledge where the small waterfall ran violently over the rock bed below. He put his hands on his narrow hips and stood looking out at the river.

Kneeling again, he checked Reck's clothing.

"You couldn't wait, could you? What the hell did you do with her?" He got up and turned around.

"Kali, Kali," he yelled again. She still didn't answer. Kali didn't even know if she had the voice to do so and, even if she had, she wouldn't. She was still trying to process the name Jack.

Troy looked down at the ground and swept his foot across the dirt. Then he looked directly at the mouth of the cave. Kali's good hand gripped the barrel of the gun and started feeling for the handle. She was not about to let him touch her. As he neared the cave, she heard more movement.

"Troy!" Kali thought she heard her husband's voice. Her heart almost stopped as she saw Troy's hand move toward his holster.

"No," she tried to yell, but the words choked in her throat. She coughed instead.

Troy heard her and dropped his hand to his side.

"Down here," Troy yelled up. "I think she's down here in this cave."

"I'm coming down," Ashton yelled over. "How is she?"

"I don't know yet," Troy answered and then kneeled to peer into the cave. He saw part of Kali's right leg.

"Are you alright in there?" Troy called.

Kali just lay there still gripping the gun with her left hand, in case she needed it. There was something wrong, very wrong. Troy called

Reck, *Jack*. How did Troy know Jack? Damn, she thought foggily, as she fought to keep her eyes open.

CHAPTER TWENTY-SEVEN

ASHTON HAD MUCH to atone. His family was in shambles because of all the lousy decisions he had made. He had to get it right this time. He and Micah drove silently into the driveway of the old Victorian spread they had called home for ten years. He had had it all. Life had been good here. But he couldn't let go of a grudge, the grudge he held against the men who had tried to murder him in prison. One by one he had eliminated them. For the very first time, he was regretting it.

"The horses, we need the horses. You still have them?" Ashton had asked as Micah drove the car over the large green landscape, getting off the driveway.

"Yeah, but horses make noises." Micah kept heading through the grassy landscape.

"And this car doesn't?"

"No, listen." Micah rolled down the window. He was right. The car was quiet, except for a few gravelly sounds here and there.

"That's what I like about this babe," Micah smiled at his brother. "She's quiet enough to sneak up on people. You should see how many pedestrians I have startled." He patted the steering wheel.

"I bet," Ashton answered, leaning forward to get a glimpse of the cliffs he and his children had run around. They were still about a half mile away.

"Stop," he said. "Stop, right here. I have an idea."

Micah stopped the car and pulled over near the tree where they used to leave the horses.

Ashton touched his brother's hand and said, "Call the police."

"We don't know that she's here," Micah said.

"Yes, we do." Ashton pointed down the hill toward the edge of the cliffs. There sat a black sedan gleaming in the sunlight and in the open for all to see.

"I'll be damned," Micah said, recognizing Troy's car. "Artie was right."

"We should always listen to our children," Ashton said. "What about that girlfriend of yours we left with the children? Who is she?"

Micah pulled out his phone and called the police. Then he called Anjuli.

"Hi Baby, how are the kids?" Micah asked.

Anjuli was sitting in the kitchen of Micah's apartment. It was much smaller than the penthouse, only four bedrooms as opposed to the twenty-plus rooms upstairs with all the suites and the bathrooms. She had always thought of his place as more than large enough, but it didn't seem that way with five anxious children in it. She wanted to run.

"They are fine. They are pretty much sticking together. I think they are even going to the bathroom with each other. They are a pretty tight crew," Anjuli answered, wanting a cigarette for the first time in years.

"Are they with you, right now?" Micah asked.

"No, they are in the living room trying to watch a movie that none of them agreed to watch. Ash is making them, I think. It's amazing how well he controls them — to a degree that is. The boys push back at him more than the girls."

"I need to ask you something, Anjuli," Micah said, walking away from Ashton and putting some distance between them. He wanted to do this on his own.

"What? Has something happened? Did you find her?"

"Did you know Troy or a man named Jack before you came to work for me?" Micah asked. He wanted her to say no immediately, but she didn't. So, he went over to the tree waiting for her answer.

"Troy Lucas?"

"Yes, Troy Lucas."

"Of course, yes. He's your family friend and he works for Philly PD. Remember, I was working for Philly PD before you hired me. Is something wrong?"

"How well did you know him?"

"Where is this coming from, Micah? He was an acquaintance. I knew him. Not well. We have talked here and there. No real kind of relationship, if that's what you are asking."

"What about Jack?" Micah pressed as he could feel a void growing between them and it wasn't just the distance in their locations.

"Jack who? I know and have met a lot of Jacks in my life. You have to be more specific."

"What about a Jack who was posing as Reck?"

Anjuli gasped and looked at the phone. "What the hell are you talking about? What are you insinuating?"

"One of the kids saw you talking with Reck and Troy recently down in the Square. I need to know what you were talking about."

"Well, Kali, of course," Anjuli sighed. "She has always been a handful, you know."

"Anjuli, answer me honestly, please. Did you have anything to do with the bugs in the penthouse?"

"The what?"

"The surveillance equipment someone installed."

Anjuli leaned back in her chair and put the phone down for a few seconds. She stared at the wooden cabinets with their intricate handles. They had always intrigued her. For a moment, she wanted to touch them the way she always did before opening the cabinet. It had made her wonder if Ruby had picked them out. That was one of the silly questions she had always wanted to ask about her sister. But, she was afraid to ask, and more afraid that she was going to give herself away.

"Did I ever tell you why I wanted to become a forensic psychologist?" she asked.

"No," Micah answered and almost dropped to his knees. Instead he leaned against the tree and watched his brother crawling around the edge of the cliff.

"I wanted to find out what had happened to my sister," Anjuli paused and then said, "Ruby."

"Ruby? My Ruby? Ruby was your sister?" Micah put his hand on his forehead and glanced over to see his brother moving closer to the path down into the ravine. "Ruby never mentioned any sisters."

"I bet Ruby never mentioned any family. But yes, she was my sister. I came looking for her, but it was too late," Anjuli confessed.

"What did Troy tell you?"

"He said that Ashton killed her. He said that Ashton was a serial killer and that he needed to be brought to justice."

"And Jack, or Reck — whatever you called him?"

"He said he needed to bring Ashton to justice, too."

"What about Lazarus?" Micah asked. "What did he say about Lazarus?"

"Troy said he couldn't prove it, but he thought Lazarus was Ashton. Either way, Reck said that he was going to help Troy ensure that Ashton would serve time for all the murders he had committed, for all the lives he's messed up. He claimed Ashton was not only responsible for his wife's death, but his kid's somehow."

"And you believed him?"

"I just wanted answers," Anjuli whispered into the phone.

"I just have one more question," Micah said, "are you going to hurt our children?"

"Never," Anjuli answered. "Never. I would die for these kids."

"Remember that," Micah said. "If a hair on any one of them perishes under your watch, you will die." He hung up the phone and caught up with Ashton who was kneeling from a covered vantage point. He was looking over into the ravine where the jutted ledge was. He pointed to the top of the path and Micah moved over and looked down. He saw Reck's body lying still and broken. Then he saw Troy getting ready to move toward the mouth of the cave.

"Kali, Kali," Micah yelled startling Troy. The detective's hand even went to his holster for a second. Micah looked back at Ashton who was getting up, but he held out his hand for him to stay back.

"I think she's in the cave," Troy said, pointing to the cave.

"I'm coming down," Micah said as he stopped and fumbled openly with his phone where Troy could see him. Then he started down the narrow, rocky path holding onto the wall of the cliff.

"I called the medics. Someone should be here to help us soon," he said as he made it to the ledge. "Kali," Micah called again.

"There's her leg," Troy said. "Can you see it?"

Micah got down on all fours. "I see her. I don't think I can fit in there. How about you? You're pretty narrow."

"Let me see." Troy moved down to his hands and knees and started to enter the cave.

"Get away from me," Kali said, her voice barely audible, "don't touch me."

Troy began to back out of the cave. "I don't think she's alive," he said and got to his feet quickly. "Where is he? I know he's in town. Did he send you out here by yourself?"

"No, he didn't," Ashton said, sliding down the last of the path.

"Well, well, well. Reck was right." Troy said as he stood face to face with Ashton. "The dead man has arisen. Too bad your wife won't rise."

Ashton looked at Micah who was still down on his knees. He reached into the cave and found Kali's right leg. It shuddered with pain in his grip. Micah looked up at Ashton, his eyes smiling for a second. He took off his jacket, leaving it behind Ashton on a rock. Ashton picked it up and put it on the top of the cave mouth.

"Does that make you happy? It sounds as if that's what you wanted," Ashton asked Troy before leaning down toward the cave. He called to his brother. "Can you get to her? Let me try."

"It's too late, Ashton." Troy's hand went toward his holster again. "It's over man. Why don't you just come on up out of there and take responsibility — for your wife, for Ruby, for Redd, for Scully? Hell, even for my sister. She would have never died had it not been for you. Not to mention your wife's ex. Heaven knows who else. I heard you learned a lot from your grandfather. Hell, I could probably write a book about that old man's dirty laundry, including his missing whores, the ones that disappeared bit by bit down a garbage disposal. Yeah, Reck filled me in on those, too.

"And yeah, I know you killed Scully, your old prison guard and partner in selling your contraband. Yeah, I know about how you survived in there, too. At least until Scully and his boys decided you were more valuable dead than alive. And you survived, you could have let it go. But, true to you, Ashton, you couldn't let go. You had to have your revenge. You always thought you were smarter than everybody else. But, here's the thing. No one can't deny the evidence at Scully's murder scene. But somehow, I knew somehow, you would get away with that one, too. It's that rich boy magic still following you because, as usual, you were saved, this time by your stupid brother's fingerprint. Reck helped me fill in the blanks on that one, too. Damn, and I used to want to be a part of your family. Jordan Banks left a hell of a sick legacy. Glad I never made the cut."

"And you believed him? Reck, Jack? What was his name?"

It looked as if Troy stopped breathing for a second. He turned to see the man lying on the ground behind them. He had first introduced himself to Troy as Jack and that's what Troy had called him until he helped him get the job close to Kali. Troy turned back to Ashton and almost stuttered, "Not. Not at f-f-first, not until he proved to me you were in Brazil when Redd died. Then I started retracing your steps. Now look at you. You are not the drawn and skinny, mysterious

Lazarus anymore; your face isn't scarred. You are not wearing contact lenses to hide your evil eyes."

"And, I am assuming, there is no one left except you who wants Ashton dead now?" Ashton answered trying to gauge the right time to admit that he and Lazarus were the same.

Troy chuckled and rested his hand on his gun. Their eyes met in silence. Ashton tried to recognize his old friend in these older eyes. Where was the friend he once trusted with his life? Behind him, he could still see the long, lanky body of Jack Pulaski. It would have been easier to recognize those eyes filled with hate, if only he had just come home.

"Is that why you bugged the penthouse to entrap the Sperling family?" Ashton asked.

"You have trained your children to lie very well. Not one little slip-up. Nobody claimed you. Hell, it was almost as if you were forgotten until Kali got mad at you for not showing up for Katie's play. Even then, she didn't reference you the way I would have wanted, but I knew she was talking about you."

"Are you sure this isn't all about her?" Ashton glanced over to see where Micah was. His legs were sticking out of the cave now. "You know she never liked you for setting her husband up to go to prison for your sister's death," Ashton said as he tried to stay in character for Lazarus. But, he knew Troy was no fool. Other than Kali and Micah, Troy knew him better than anyone.

"My sister would still be alive if it weren't for you. Your brother, Asa, was trying to kill you and your family. Not Rita, not Kali's little fly-by ex-husband, Marcus. They were in the wrong place at the wrong time."

"Which Ashton had no control over, from what I am told. Do you think he would have put them on that plane if he had known it was going down? Hell, if you think he didn't care about them, what about his friend? He was the pilot. I heard he and Ashton went way, way back. Long before he met you in a fucking dorm room."

"Real nice, Ashton, still talking about yourself as if you aren't you," Troy said, his hand still on the gun.

"My name is Lazarus Smith. I was found nearly dead hanging from a tree in the Southwest. The doctor named me that because I had no, and still have no, memory of my life before then. And I heard the theories, the same theory you heard that I am Ashton Sperling. I can't deny that may be me. I don't know. I do know there is a grave marker with his name on it. But, what do I know for sure? Nothing. Only what I have heard and read about the man. And, from that evidence, Ashton wasn't a murderer. So why don't you give me some evidence to prove he was a murderer, or get out of my way and let me help Micah remove Kali from the cave."

"Oh, that's an easy one," Troy answered. "Your fingerprint was on Scully's badge, the badge they found on him."

"Yeah, about that. I did some digging of my own. Funny, I got a copy of the police record of when Ashton was attacked in prison. When he was found, he had Scully's badge in his hand. And it's even funnier that Scully had a new badge and a new job. But the old badge that had been in police custody up in Harrisburg showed up at his murder scene in Camden, New Jersey. What do you think happened there, Troy? Were he and Ashton discussing old times? Had Scully recovered his badge for old time's sake, maybe? I have looked over and over those records and there is no explanation of how that badge ended up in Camden, New Jersey. Can you explain that?"

"You think you are so smart. Scully would have had to get a new badge after the incident in prison. That is, if he lost the first one. Who knows, maybe they gave it back to him," Troy said as his hand lightly touched his pistol again.

"True, but I'd be interested in knowing if that original badge is still in an evidence locker somewhere. Do you think you could check for me?" Ashton glanced down at Troy's hand. He let it drop again to his side.

"Brazil. Redd. Someone matching your Lazarus description was seen talking to her in her favorite bar. The bartender even said she arranged to take a trip with you the next morning."

"Sounds like I was in two places at once when she died. Somebody who looked like me went to visit his friend, Ray, and Ray's grandson, Bobby, that week. Someone who looked like me had a tryst with Mrs. Kali Sperling at a hotel in Las Vegas before he returned to Philadelphia. That was when Ashton informed me he was contributing to Redd's funeral. No, I wasn't in Philly when she died, but that doesn't mean I was anywhere near Brazil either.

"Did you ever ask any of them where I was that week? Did you ever check the flights to make sure if I was on them or not?" Ashton pointed to Reck, "No, you took that guy's word for it, didn't you? Why? Who did you believe he was, Troy? How do you know him? How did he get hired at PDSI without us picking up something, anything? There should have been a red flag. I don't recognize the name Reck, but from here he looks like Jack Pulaski, the dude who was kicked out of Jordan's house and who reportedly hated Ashton since he was a kid. There are pictures, if you need them for identification. And then, there is Micah's mother. She recognized him the day he kidnapped Kali and murdered that child."

Micah crawled back deeper into the cave after figuring out how to maneuver the opening again. It had been a long time since he and Ashton had camped with the kids in there. It was roomy once you got past the entrance. Kali could have moved further back had she had the strength. The only thing he was focused on now was getting her to safety and fast. Ashton was going to have to take care of Troy who was looking for a reason to pull his firearm, that was obvious.

For a minute, Micah had a little empathy for Troy. He knew how lonely he was and how committed he was to bringing everybody to justice, even if it meant breaking the law to do so. Troy was in love; at least, he believed Troy had thought he was. The poor guy had fixated on Kali. He himself could understand that more than any other. She was his brother's wife and he was in love with her, too. Too bad for all of them though, she had become jaded from all the trauma and lies inflicted upon her. Micah wasn't sure if Kali could even share her love with anyone anymore, let alone with this man whom she openly hated and, for some reason, Troy couldn't recognize that hate. Now that this has happened, her children had been put in danger and she had been kidnapped. Well, she was going to be even more unbearable and even more distant now and with good reason.

Micah crawled up beside her and brushed her hair from her face.

"Kali," he whispered. "It's me. I'm here. We are going to get you home."

"The kids? Kacie?" she answered in a broken whisper.

"Alive. Well. Wanting their mother. All of them. Kacie especially."

Kali reached for Micah's hand. He squeezed hers lightly but she pulled it in the direction of the gun. She wrapped his hand around the barrel.

"Is this Reck's?" Micah asked, gently prying it from between her and the rock to keep from firing it accidentally.

"Yes. Micah, he told me to go into the cave. Reck didn't name him, but he said he was coming. He knows Troy. I think Troy was already here when we got here, but he had to leave or something." Kali shivered from another sharp pain as she spoke.

"It's all going to be over very soon. Hang in there. I'm going back out to see what kind of progress we are making."

"I'll be here," she said heaving from the pain of Micah sliding past her.

"Are you boys still playing name games?" Micah crawled out head first. He noticed Troy touching his gun again.

"Nervous about something, Troy?" Micah pulled himself upward and grabbed his jacket.

"Why would I be nervous?"

"Kali's alive. You just told us, she wasn't," Micah said, stepping aside for Ashton who was moving toward the cave.

"Stop. Stop right there," Troy said, lifting his gun.

"Why? What are you doing?" Micah said, holding his hands up instinctively.

"I know you two. You are going to try to involve me in all of this. When it was you all along," Troy yelled anxiously.

"What does Kali know that you don't want her to tell us?" Ashton asked.

"Lower the gun, officer," a voice above them said. "You are Troy Lucas, from Philly PD, are you not?"

Troy lowered the gun and holstered it. He looked up shielding his eyes from the afternoon sun. He could see the light bouncing off a badge.

"That's me," Troy said.

"I'm Officer Clanton. I'm with the Cumberland County Sheriff's Department. Do you mind placing your gun on the ground for me, please sir?"

"What's this all about officer?" Troy tried to fake a smile.

"Well, I am about to send some medics down this rocky path and I don't want anything accidently happening to them."

"My gun will be in the holster."

"Sir, I would feel more comfortable if the gun was on the ground away from any of you gentlemen. How about you gentlemen come on up and give these men some room to get down there?"

"Of course, of course."

"The FBI is coming up the hill. I'm sure they have a lot of questions for all of you and they are going to want their forensics team down there quick."

"FBI?" Troy was shocked at how soon everyone had arrived. Micah had just made the call and they were miles away from civilization.

"Yeah, Mrs. Sperling is a kidnap victim across state lines, is she not?"

"Yeah, yeah." Troy looked at the two brothers standing at the mouth of the cave. "I guess I will go up first."

Ashton started to drop to his knees to go into the cave.

"Sir, all of you. I need all of you up here. Thank you," the officer said. Micah moved to the bottom of the path to wait for Troy to move upward.

"She's in the cave. She had taken the gun that man used to hold on her. I just took it out of the cave. It's in the back of my waistband." Micah showed the officer both of his hands and turned his back to show him the weapon.

"Come on up, sir." Another man took a step up and stopped beside the officer. "You wait," he said, pointing to Ashton.

Micah climbed up the path and the new man turned him around, removing the weapon.

"You got a weapon?" the man asked Ashton.

"No sir."

"Then come on up." The man waved upward.

"The medics may have to move that boulder. I can help with that," Ashton called up.

"Come on up, sir. You can go back down if they need you."

Ashton nodded and started up the path just in time to see Troy walking away with two men cresting the cliff's edge. Then he looked back down at Jack. Until now, he hadn't gotten the chance to take a good look at him. When he saw the jaw and the wide, blue eyes, Ashton wasn't sure how he felt. Ms. Elle had been so right; it was Jordan's little white boy lying down there with a sunken chest and a large pool of blood around head and neck. Another victim of the Jordan Banks' curse, he thought.

Someone grabbed his shoulder and guided him out of their way. He moved further down the lower side of the grassy cliff listening to the rushing water just beneath him and kept his eyes on the men below him. He wanted to see them bring her out, wishing he had been the one to reach her in the cave first. He had to say he was sorry, so sorry. He wanted to say that he was sorry for her life with the Sperlings; they had given her nothing but grief since she was 17 years old and now this.

"Excuse me, sir?"

Ashton turned to see a short woman in a black pant suit and who appeared to be of Mexican descent.

"Yes, ma'am?" he answered.

"Could I have your name, please?" The woman asked.

Ashton looked at her and then looked down just in time to see a man sliding out of the cave with a stretcher. He could see Kali's bare feet.

"It depends on who you ask," he answered.

"Sir?"

"My name. It depends on who you ask," Ashton said again.

"I don't follow you, sir. What is your name?"

"Do you have time for a long story, ma'am? Right now, you can call me Lazarus Smith. At the end of the story, you may want to call me Ashton Taylor Sperling," he answered, his eyes glued to his wife now. He could see she was injured by the way her body lay in what seemed like disarray. Her right side appeared mangled. There was blood on her, but her eyes were alert. She was searching the area with her eyes, until they landed on him.

"Call me, Ashton," he turned to the woman and looked her dead in the eyes. "My name is Ashton Taylor Sperling. And, that's my wife," he said pointing down to Kali as they began to tie the stretcher up to lift her out. A helicopter appeared suddenly. It must have drowned him out or maybe the woman wasn't sure she was hearing him right.

"Repeat that sir," she said, with her pen hovering over a small pad, reminding him of the officer in London.

"My name is Ashton Taylor Sperling."

PART THREE

CHAPTER TWENTY-EIGHT

ASHTON WAS STILL in disbelief as he sat in the hospital room waiting for Kali to open her eyes. He wasn't under attack. He hadn't been arrested. No one was even questioning him; he was just sitting there. He had told the FBI agent his real name and the woman hadn't flinched. Maybe she had no idea that he was supposed to dead. Maybe she had no idea that his name had popped up several times as a suspect in Scully's death. All he knew was that both he and Micah had been allowed to leave in Micah's car to chase the helicopter taking Kali to Cooper Hospital. The medic had said she was lucky to be breathing and would be even luckier to make it to the hospital. But, here she was, in that bed, with all those tubes, surviving a major operation to her chest and having her limbs prodded into place with casts while she lay unconscious. How much more trauma could she take? He couldn't even imagine the pain she would experience when she woke up, if she woke up. And, he knew that kind of pain in the worst way.

Micah knocked lightly on the door before he entered. "They said I could come in for a little while."

"Have they talked to you?" Ashton stood up over Kali, looking down at her. He leaned over and kissed her lips hoping she would open her eyes. She didn't.

"A little bit."

"Were they able to hear our conversation?"

"The sheriff said they heard enough to feel like things were going to get a bit dicey. That's why they intervened when they did."

"He should have let it. He should have let Troy go ahead and shoot me," Ashton said, pushing Kali's curl from her face. "I was dead anyway."

"Yeah, about that," Micah said. "The FBI is opening another case."

"What kind of case?"

"Your kidnapping."

"My what?"

"Apparently, there was a kidnapping report made on you and then you denied it. Said you had to take some time to yourself."

"What?"

"Someone reported seeing you thrown into a vehicle, a few days too late I guess, but no one corroborated it and you showed up about the same time unharmed. The FBI even spoke to you."

"They spoke to Asa?"

"They spoke to Asa."

"Why didn't you know about it?"

"I guess because it didn't involve me directly."

"What about Kali?"

"I don't know. We have to ask Kali." They both looked down at her waiting for her to speak. Micah walked over to her and kissed her forehead.

"The kids?" Ashton asked pulling his phone out. He hadn't had the heart to tell his children that he had let their mother down again.

"On media silence. No telephones, no television. Only video games and movies. But, they are suspicious."

"Still with your girlfriend?"

"With her and three guards."

"Where's Troy?"

"Out there. Lurking. We can't leave her alone for a second. Kali said he was already there when they got there."

"Was she sure it was him?"

"I think she was."

"Why was he there?"

"You know as much as I do. What did he say while I was in the cave?"

"Same finger-pointing without anything concrete. But, he seemed hell-bent on believing Jack."

"Are you sure that's Jack?"

Ashton nodded. "I would know him anywhere. That's him. Did they confirm him dead?"

"Yeah, that was pretty much a no-brainer. One of the medics said she was probably on top of him when they fell."

"They fell?" Ashton remembered when his horse threw him over the cliff. He had had the presence of mind to catch onto the wall and slow his fall enough to not get too injured, just shook up. His knees had ached for days. But, they had fallen out over the ledge, near the edge. That was a pretty big drop for that.

"We need your girlfriend, Son." Ashton reached out, touched Micah's head and then brought forward his own forehead. Micah nodded. Anjuli was their only hope in bringing the missing pieces all together.

"Sure, I will be there," Anjuli said into the phone, looking at Kacie playing in Katie's short hair. Katie was staring out into space from the living room floor, sitting between her younger sister's legs, letting her go crazy with a comb and brush and all kinds of gooey hair care stuff. That's how they were coping. Anjuli wondered how she and Ruby could have coped together when their parents had died, one by one leaving her behind, alone. By the time she found Ruby the first time just after their mother's death, she had been distant and unwilling to even acknowledge her as her little sister. Then, before Anjuli could reach out to her again to give her the news about their father, she was just gone. Ruby was already buried by the time she had reached Philadelphia, so Anjuli had stayed and gone to school there since there was no one back home in Jersey to even care where she was.

She put the phone in her pocket and went to look for one of the other guards. The tall one who reminded her of Micah was in the foyer looking very stern.

"Mr. Sperling has asked me to come over to Jersey. The girls are in the living room. Do you know where all of the boys are?"

"Kitchen with Higgins," the man answered.

Anjuli walked through the apartment and found the three boys sitting at the kitchen table. Higgins was setting plates of food in front of each of them. She stood and watched the little scene. These boys were used to being served. Just like the rest of the Sperling men. That angered her a little bit. Were they always supposed to get what they wanted when they wanted it?

Micah had been very closed mouth about what had happened in Jersey, and the news reports were very scarce on details. Funny how power and a little money could have the local news stations stand down long enough to suit the people who had the money and power.

"I'm going out for a few hours," she spoke to Higgins, who didn't look too happy about his role as a cook and a servant. But, he was doing what he had to do to take care of the Sperling bunch.

"Where are you going?" Ash asked, getting up from his chair and walking toward her.

"I'm going to run an errand for your uncle. I will be back," Anjuli said, backing out of the door. Ash was the intense one who creeped her out a little bit. There was something very dangerous about that kid. She wondered if Reck could have gotten the drop on him as easily as he had on Roderick. Maybe Reck should have counted himself lucky for taking out the wrong kid.

"Rules still apply," she said to Higgins. "No media."

"What's happened to my mother?" Ash was still following her as she entered the living room. He looked back over his shoulders to make sure Artie and Adam hadn't followed.

"What have you done to my mother?" Ash grabbed her arm and leaned toward her, neither his face nor the expression in his voice changed. He was as calm-looking, and his voice was as courteous, as always. But, there was a darkness in his eyes that sent three very noticeable and consecutive chills down her spine.

"I have done nothing to your mother. Why would you think that?" Anjuli removed his hand from her arm and almost sprinted toward the foyer. She could feel his body close to hers following her.

"What's the hurry?"

"Your uncle needs me," Anjuli said as she walked over to Sanchez, the guard in the foyer.

"Media silence. No one leaves this apartment."

"Yes, ma'am," Sanchez answered and opened the door for her, blocking Ash from following her.

"Next time you talk to my uncle," Ash shouted between the opening and closing of the door, "tell him, we are not stupid. He needs to talk to us. To me, at least."

Now there it was, Anjuli thought, the anger that should have been in his voice days ago, the anger that the other kids should have been showing as well. Even some type of fear should have been exhibited. Sure, they had mourned and worried, but only to a very sedated degree. There was something missing. These kids weren't normal, they were super-jaded she thought, as she entered the elevator. What did those little brats know? What else have they been exposed to? She was beginning to rethink her opinion of Kali. Maybe there was a reason she had built a solid wall around her.

CHAPTER TWENTY-NINE

KALI MOANED A little and both men jumped to her side. "Oh, my God," she said, shivering from the pain. "Where am I?" Looking upward and seeing the cords gave her an immediate clue.

"You're in Cooper Medical Center," said Ashton, leaning over her so she could see him, but she appeared to look past him. "Hey." He leaned down to kiss her cheek and she turned her head. "Kali," Ashton whispered. "Kali."

Kali's heavy head rolled to the right making her feel as if her bones were going to jump out of her body. She saw Micah.

"Children?" She managed to say without wincing again.

"The children are fine. They are down in my apartment right now. The penthouse is being cleaned up, so the living room will be white again," Micah said and gave her a curt smile before his eyes turned gravely dark. "You?"

"Apparently alive. All of me broken?"

"No, but right hip, right ribs, right arm, shoulder, clavicle. Doctors say it's a miracle you didn't crack your skull, too."

"Reck's name is Jack."

"We know. Jack Pulaski. Jordan's little white boy. How did you know? Did he tell you? Did he tell you why?"

"No. Well, yes. My head hurts," Kali said, trying to reach for her forehead unsuccessfully, "Reck kept talking about making Ashton suffer like he suffered," she sighed. "He told me he was Jack, but I got confused when Troy called him Jack. Troy wasn't around then, was he? Did Troy know all this time? I told you I never trusted that man."

Micah looked across Kali at Ashton who was still in shock from his wife's rejected kiss. He was staring at the two of them talking as if he weren't in the room. Micah had forgotten his brother momentarily. The second Kali turned to him for answers, he was too relieved for words to be talking to her at all. He took her left hand and squeezed it.

"Someone has come a long way to be here by your side, Kali." Micah kissed her hand. "After the two of you talk, you need to rest. I'm going to get the nurse. But, I will ask her to give you five." Micah held up his five fingers for his brother to see.

Kali straightened her head as her eyes began to focus on the other face in the room. She grimaced and then closed her eyes.

"Kali, are you alright? Do I need to get the nurse now? We can talk later, especially, if you are in a lot of pain. I understand, babe, I do. I should have been here. I know you are angry." Ashton stopped talking and went to her left side so he could touch her hand without moving her or having to reach across her body. "I'm here. Whatever you want me to do, I'll do. I have already told the authorities I am Ashton. No more Lazarus. I can't do it anymore. I can't let anything else happen to you or my babies anymore. I'm back. I'm home. I'm here," Ashton swallowed so hard it hurt. He took her hand into his. He was hopeful when she didn't snatch it back.

"Who is Jack, really?" Kali asked. "Was he still just an angry kid inside wanting revenge? He blamed you for everything."

"Anger. Jealousy. False entitlement. Jack wanted to be me is all I can think of. And, if I hadn't been in his life, he would have found someone else to blame for his shortcomings." Ashton was being honest. That had been the thorn in Jack's side. Jack had wanted to be the center of Jordan's attention, but he couldn't be as long as Ashton was there. That's all it had been, plain and simple. The problem was Jack had issues with seeing things in a logical and reasonable manner. Now that Ashton could reflect on it, Jack had been dangerous since Ashton was three years old. Many times, Jack had pushed him off the sofa, off the bed, put him up on top of tables and then acted as if he had accidentally knocked Ashton off something, sometimes on his head. But, it was always attributed to being rough little boys. Jack had been more than rough. Looking at Kali, Ashton believed Ms. Elle and Billy's theories that Jack had murdered his own mother and his adoptive parents.

"Then it's all over," Kali sighed.

"I wish." Ashton kissed her hand. "There's still Troy and maybe Anjuli."

"I want to talk to Anjuli." Kali took her hand away and touched her head. "I need to talk to Anjuli."

"Why?"

"According to Reck, someone's been poisoning me. I need to

know if it was Artie who was bringing me one of his herbal teas every morning, or if someone was using him.”

“Anjuli?”

“I couldn't think of anyone else. And, I can't believe Artie wants to hurt me.”

“I'll talk to Micah,” Ashton was saying as a nurse strode in.

“You have to go,” the nurse said looking at Ashton sternly.” The doctor will be here in a minute. Let's see how this beautiful, young woman is doing after all these horrendous things done to her.”

“I'm fine,” Kali lied, not wanting to be interrupted. She watched Ashton as he was leaving the room and, for the first time, she noticed his face was full again. No wonder he wasn't denying who he was. She could see who he was now and anyone else who knew him would recognize him, too.

Kali wanted to see her babies, but she knew she didn't want them to see her in this condition. She must look like a hot mess, she thought, fighting to keep her eyes open. Were they coming back? The nurse had joggled her more than she had desired, and then stuck a needle in her IV. She knew it was a pain med because she became groggy immediately. That was the last thing she wanted. Kali fought hard to stay awake, but her eyelids won and shut her down into darkness while she listened to the faint beeping sounds of the machinery in her room.

As the melody of the beeps lured her into a totally relaxed state, she saw him, his eyes twinkling. It was the first time she had laid eyes on him and he was ignoring her on purpose.

“Big boy,” she reached out to touch him and he disappeared. Her hand waved through the air as she turned to see Micah, the disco ball's light in Jordan's nightclub was bouncing off Micah's bald head. Micah was dancing with Ruby and she was happy, until her eyes met Kali's.

“What did I do?” Kali asked, but Micah swung Ruby around, her back to Kali. “What did I do?”

Kali heard her bedroom door open and Artie entered with a steaming hot cup of tea. “This one is lemon balm. Smell it. Doesn't it smell great?”

Kali took the cup and sniffed in the aroma.

“Love you, you are such a great botanist. I bet your greenhouse is so full, it's about to explode. I will come up tomorrow to see it again, okay?”

"No need, Auntie. I'm going to burn it after you drink this last cup of tea," Artie said with an odd smile on his face, but his eyes looked like his mother's had on the dance floor.

"What did I do?" Kali asked him as she sipped the hot tea.

"The same thing as Uncle Ashton." Artie patted her on her cheek. "You lived."

Kali almost spilled the tea in her dream as her body jolted with pain. She jumped, jarring her already jarred bones. She automatically tried to turn, becoming fully awake with even more pain. She looked up at the ceiling and then immediately knew someone else was in the room. A warm, soft hand picked up her wrist, and then let it down gently next to her body.

"Are you alright?" Anjuli pushed Kali's hair from her face and looked down at her and then up at the machines.

"They have you pretty restricted, but you were moving quite a bit. Bad dream?"

Kali nodded. Looking up at the woman, she could almost believe she was concerned for her.

"Where's Micah?"

"Right here." Micah moved close enough for her to see him. For some reason, that didn't make her feel any better or worse for that matter. She kept her eyes on Anjuli.

"Micah says you want to talk to me," Anjuli said, pulling a stool next to the bed closer and sitting down.

Kali lifted her head to see more of Anjuli's body. Not that it mattered whether she was wearing a firearm or not, there was plenty the woman could do to her lying in this bed like this. She looked over at Micah who was looking apprehensive. She knew what he was thinking. Was he going to have to kill another woman that he loved to keep his brother's wife alive?

"Just us, Micah," Kali said. "I need to talk to another woman, if you don't mind."

"Kali, I don't think…." Micah began to say and then he looked at Anjuli. "Okay, ladies. I will be right outside this door."

"Where's Ashton?" Kali asked.

"He's with the FBI. They will be in here to see you soon, I'm sure."

"I don't think I'm going anywhere. Am I, Anjuli?" Kali tried to smile as she said that, but she couldn't help but wonder if she had just signed her life away by sending Micah out of the room.

"I'm not taking you out of this room," Anjuli said, shaking her head. Both women watched Micah go out of the room as if he were moving in a series of still photos.

"The children are fine, a little frighteningly fine," Anjuli said and touched Kali's hand. "I mean, they are almost normal, but I know they are really worried about you. All they know is you are fine, but unable to come home now. That's it. So they are scared, but…."

"They are Sperlings," Kali said. "They are used to having their world being turned upside down. They are used to death, violence, and lies."

"That's what I was afraid of," Anjuli said, looking back at the door.

"Do you love him?" Kali asked. "The rest of our conversation will depend on whether you really love him. Do you?"

"Yes," Anjuli said. "I understand now why she did. There's no other explanation why she never came back. She could have. Couldn't she? She could have just walked away one day."

"She? Ruby?" Kali said. "You knew Ruby, didn't you? Are you related to her? You are, aren't you? That's why you gave me the creeps. You sort of look like her."

"Yeah," Anjuli stifled a sob.

"So, I am right. You knew Ruby? She is the only other woman that I know that loved him."

"Did know. I didn't know her well at all. I was ten years old when she ran away from home. Saw her only one time after that. She is the reason that I wanted to become a forensic psychologist in the first place. I wanted to find her."

"You found her?"

"Yeah, but she didn't want anything to do with me. At first, I thought she was being highfaluting, you know, her being part of this wealthy, prominent family and her little sister coming across the bridge from Camden to look her up. Little too hood, some might think."

"A little rough around the edges, but I thought you were from North Central Jersey. Linden, right?"

"Went to high school there. My mother's sister lived there. My parents wanted to give me a chance to escape the Camden life."

"Looks like it worked."

"Yeah, I ended up at Rutgers, finished up at Drexel, and the rest is history, I guess. I work for you. You pay me very well. I mean, I ended up with a dream job, right?" Anjuli sighed.

"So what was the other reason?"

"What?"

"If Ruby wasn't being highfaluting, what was she being?"

"I don't think she wanted me to find out about her past."

"That's silly, don't you think?"

Anjuli looked at Kali questioningly.

"She was a whore; I was a whore. Neither of us by choice. We ended up in the service of an older man who was very charming and very manipulative. I didn't see it coming. I'm guessing she didn't either. Not before we were permanently trapped. For some reason, though, he decided to raise us up to a level above his other whores. We were his private property or, I guess I should say, for private use only. I guess the good thing about it — if there was a good thing — was that he was a man who was very aware and concerned about appearances. He couldn't have us appearing or acting like common whores, now could he? So, he educated us, dressed us in fine, expensive clothes, put us under expensive roofs, and gave us to his spoiled little grandsons to play with like toys. For two of them, good or bad, we became their favorite toys."

"Micah didn't love her?" Anjuli wondered aloud.

"Micah loved Ruby with all his heart. He's been an empty shell ever since she passed. Why wouldn't you come to him with who you were? Does he know now?"

"Yes, I told him. He didn't tell you?"

"I just woke up. We haven't talked at length yet," Kali said trying to raise her head. Anjuli jumped up and adjusted her pillow slightly elevating her head.

"Is that okay?" Anjuli asked as she sat back on the stool.

"Okay." Kali stared at her. She needed to know more about this woman, but what could she believe? The woman was being kind and solicitous toward her now. But, there was always a "but."

"Is this some sort of act?" Kali blurted out.

"What?"

"You are being nice to me." Kali watched as Anjuli opened her mouth and then closed it and opened it again, tilting her head.

"You aren't used to people being nice to you, are you?" Anjuli asked.

"Not unless they are getting paid to do it, I guess." Kali looked back at the ceiling again. She had never thought about that. People were nice to her, strange people that she didn't know and family members, of course.

"Have I ever been anything other than nice to you?"

"I don't know, are you poisoning me?"

"What?" Anjuli asked, pushing the stool back from the bed.

"My nephew, your nephew is bringing me tea every morning. His herbal teas from his greenhouse up on the roof. Have you been up there? Have you given him wrong information about his plants up there? Funny thing. My headaches faded when I was away, at least the intensity of them anyway. And your friend, Reck, said it was because I was being slowly poisoned by someone. He said something to the effect that I should stop drinking tea."

"You think Artie is poisoning you?"

"I can't believe Artie would harm a hair on my head. But, I can believe he can be swayed or misinformed."

"Not by me." Anjuli sat back down and scooted the stool closer to Kali.

Holding her hand close to Kali's face Anjuli asked, "May I?"

Kali nodded and Anjuli lifted her eyelid.

"What are you looking for?"

"I don't know yet," Anjuli sighed. "I don't see any discoloration, other than strain. Why don't we ask for some tests, toxicity tests? The FBI would happily run them if they think it's related to the case. Tell them you think Reck was poisoning you."

"Okay, I will do that," Kali answered, then asked, "What do you think? Do you think Artie would harm me?"

"He adores you. He's under you more than your own children. You pay him a little more attention either because his mother's gone or because of your relationship with him period. I think he genuinely loves you and wouldn't cause you any harm."

"I have thought that of other people, too, though." Kali looked back at the ceiling. "And they have hurt me just the same."

"Why did you call Reck my friend?"

"You tell me. You are both from the same area in Jersey. He is older so I don't think you went to school with him. Or did you? How did you cross paths? Rutgers?"

"No, your office. I was sitting in your office behind your desk. Micah had me working on something, a case. The hard copy files were in your office so we went in there. I took my laptop and he told me to sit at your desk. Then he left to grab us something to eat."

"And Reck approached you?"

"Yes, he approached me."

"Making any leeway, my dear?" Reck said as he entered the executive suite, closing the door behind him.

"Excuse me?" Anjuli looked up from her laptop. She had seen the guy many times lingering nearby as most of the Sperling bodyguards did. But, this guy was always around. "I assume Mrs. Sperling is around here somewhere." Most of the guards were usually silent, lurking, looking, and doing what they were hired to do.

"Yes, she is, actually. She is over in marketing. Something calamitous or important is going on in there. She actually doesn't need me anymore today. I thought I would stop in and check on her office. Make sure it was secure, and look who I find sitting at her desk." He smiled, and then took a seat across from her.

Anjuli sat back in the chair and closed her laptop. "That's unusual, isn't it? For us to be in her office without her."

"Not really, especially when you need to recover a listening device." Reck stood up and moved Kali's designer stapler. "This is a very expensive item that she never uses. She once told me she liked the look of a few old desk items on a desk to make it look used. I don't know how you are supposed to make a desk look used. But, when you have the kind of money she does, you can buy gold-plated staplers."

"Looks more like bronze," Anjuli said, watching him remove something from the bottom of the stapler. "Did she know that was there?"

"No," Reck shook his head. "Plus, it hasn't been really useful. One, she is rarely in here and, two, when she does talk in here, she is on guard. Mr. Sperling is, too. What I need them to talk about, they never discuss here. They are pretty damn boring, you know. All business all the time here, at least. I need a new tactic, a new lodging place for my devices." He got up and removed another device from a picture frame of one of the photos on the dark wood file cabinets lining the wall.

"How many of those things do you have in here?"

"This was it. I was just testing the waters. Would you like to help me test

them in the penthouse?"

"Why would I do that?"

"Oh, maybe, just maybe they might have a conversation or two about how your sister really died?"

"Excuse me?" Anjuli was shocked.

"Ruby, your sister. She and I were friends. She told me about you. You showed up once, a few years before she died. I assumed you were here to get the real truth about your sister's death. I'm right, aren't I?"

"I don't know what you are talking about." Anjuli looked to the door hoping Micah would come back and interrupt the questioning.

Reck looked back at the door, too. "He's in marketing. Lots of brouhaha going on in there. Don't know what it's all about. Can't be anything my old friend Brady can be blamed for anymore. He was the first VP of Sales and Marketing around here, one of Ashton's so-called friends. But, he's dead, too. Lot of people die around here. You and I have to be on our best behavior, so we don't end up on the deceased list."

"Who are you? What do you want?"

"I want you to help me bug the place to keep a check on the Sperlings. You are not the only one you know. These devices, and the others I have, come from the Philadelphia Police Department. I have a friend over there that thinks the same way I do about the Sperlings."

"And what do you think?"

"I think they are murderers," Reck had said as he left the office and Anjuli, her mouth wide open.

"You bugged the penthouse?" Kali asked.

"No, I decided to find out on my own if you were murderers, if someone had murdered my sister. And the more I got to know Micah… well, I couldn't believe he would hurt my sister. Did he?"

"I think you should ask him yourself, because nothing I could say would make a difference," Kali said as she began to feel more pain. "But most importantly you should ask, what would Micah have to gain from killing Ruby? He loved her. He loved his family. Can you imagine wanting to raise your child without his mother? Micah is not that kind of man. Do you think you can ask them to get me more pain meds?" Kali waved her hand in distress.

Anjuli jumped up and went to the door. Kali watched her and

wondered if her pain was returning because she was lying to Anjuli. Then, she thought about the day she had thrown that truth up in Micah's face. Had Artie overheard her? Maybe he was capable of hurting her. After all, Micah did kill his mother.

"She's coming, but she said I can't stay much longer. You need your rest."

"Then you have to come back, so we can finish our conversation."

"Sure. In the meantime, I will check out that greenhouse." Anjuli got up to leave the room as Kali's nurse entered it.

Kali wasn't sure what the conversation had accomplished. She was still on the fence about Anjuli.

CHAPTER THIRTY

TROY BANGED HIS head on the back of his car seat. He was under scrutiny from all angles now. His Captain had just informed him he was on suspension and the FBI had indicated they had more to discuss with him. That woman agent, Sanchez, kept asking him the same questions over and over expecting him to give a different answer. Troy had been the questioner for a good twenty years; he knew how to answer questions. He was not going to slip up. The only thing that frightened him now was Ashton. He was out, fully out, but he was still feigning loss of memory and Troy wasn't buying it. Ashton's amnesia was as temporary as it could get. Maybe in the beginning he didn't know who he was, Troy could buy that piece. There was something different about him when he had returned and it wasn't just his appearance. It was the way he carried himself. But, Troy had watched him move around on that ledge. That was Ashton. Jack had been right about that.

"Damn, Jack." Troy hit the steering wheel. "Why the hell did you have to drag me back into the *past?*"

It had been an accident, a simple accident. It had been an accident that would change his life forever and, as fate would have it, it was an accident that indebted him to the wrong man. Jack was with Jordan that evening at the nightclub. Both had drunk a little too much by the time he'd arrived. Jordan was trying to convince Jack to apply for a job with the Philly PD since Ashton wouldn't hire him in his new company. Troy hadn't been surprised. Ashton hadn't offered him a position either. The company was so brand new that Troy wouldn't have taken it anyway. He was a man that needed stability.

Jordan had invited Troy over to help him convince Jack that it would be the right route to take. Troy had been cautious about meeting Jordan because his two previous calls hadn't turned out well. So, he was doubly relieved when he realized the call was no more than a social call. For the first time, Troy had felt flattered to receive a call from Jordan.

The night grew older as the three of them sat in the back of Jordan's club and laughed at the plight of the women that circled them regularly, trying to get their attention.

"Back in the day, I might have folded some of these young women into the business. Look at them, I wouldn't have to advertise their wares. Most of them don't wear much to hide much anymore." Jordan lifted his glass as a young girl with her breasts bulging from her low-necked shirt walked by and smiled. Everyone knew Jordan owned the club, and most of the men he hung out with had money, pretty much like himself. The women that paraded near them didn't care or maybe they had no idea the danger they could have easily put themselves in. Jordan was not a man you wanted to toy with, no matter his age. Troy could attest to that.

As henchmen go, Troy had never aspired to be anything except a lawman. He grew up on Westerns and Elliott Ness. He was always pulling for the good guy. Then, when he went off to school, he thought he would become a lawyer. He had gotten the degree, but couldn't pass the bar. He'd given up after the second try and decided to stick with carrying a gun, maybe moving up to the ranks of Captain one day. All Troy knew was that he was going to be a good guy, a guy that delivered justice, and he was going to clean up the neighborhoods. He was going to make sure, single-handedly, that the world was a better place. He would be a superhero cop, if needed.

But, that didn't quite work out. Troy had a lot of debt, especially student loan debt, so when Ashton's grandfather had asked him to do some extra work for him, he was happy to oblige. After Troy had met Ashton at his grandfather's in his uniform one day, Jordan had become real friendly, even asking for his phone number when Ashton was out of the room. Troy hadn't noticed that it was intentional — until Jordan had asked Troy not to mention their arrangement.

There were three on Kali's detail. They rotated watching her go back and forth to school every day. Poor Kali thought she was being trusted, but Jordan knew better. You can't abuse a woman and expect her total allegiance, not if she doesn't believe there will be consequences. Troy had caught Kali trying to run and Jordan had rewarded him with her sweetness, but it hadn't ended there. When Jordan felt confident that Kali was not ever going to run again, he had taken Troy off the detail. But, he still had work for him.

The first time Jordan contacted him was one night around 3:00 in the morning. He wanted Troy to be quick and quick he was. That was when he found Jordan dismembering a woman in his bathtub in the apartment adjacent to his penthouse. Troy threw up in the nearby toilet while Jordan continue to dismember.

"Take the pieces down and start the garbage disposal," Jordan motioned to a

dishpan of chopped body parts. "Hurry up. I want to put some of these pieces in outside garbage. Trash pickup is around seven for those dumpsters out back. Some of the other pieces, we will just transport. But, start these little pieces in the garbage disposal. Hurry up, now," Jordan said as if he were giving directions to a child to take out the kitchen trash.

Troy looked at him, "You do realize I am a cop?" Troy was still stunned that Jordan had called him.

"You do realize what you did to Kali is considered rape?" Jordan asked and then motioned toward the dishpan again.

"You do realize that this is murder?" Troy retorted.

"I didn't kill this bitch," Jordan protested. "One of my clients got a little too amorous and she stopped breathing. My clients don't pay to sleep with dead girls. And I am not going to be dragged down by some slutty run-away. Garbage. Disposal. Do you hear me?"

Troy thought about the rape charge and his reputation. As far as he knew, Kali didn't know that he had ever touched her, but there was no doubt in his mind that Jordan could easily get her to speak up. The last time he had seen her, he could see the fear in her eyes when Jordan would call her name. He didn't know the exact tactics Jordan had used, but whatever he did, she respected that he would keep his word and possibly kill her. Maybe he had shown her body parts like this one. He didn't want to know what kind of tactics Jordan used, so he picked up the dishpan and went into the kitchen.

The second one was even worse. Jordan didn't feel like chopping that one up; he made Troy do it all. Those two were between him and Jordan, but not the third. There had been this one chick that just wouldn't stop trying to get their attention. It was almost as if she was asking for it, though Troy felt guilty about his stereotypical thinking. He knew better and he should have made sure the young girl had left the club safely that night.

Her name was Cherry or, at least, that was what she told them. She had walked up next to Troy at the bar and asked him to buy her a drink. He did, and she followed him back to their table. Jack and Jordan were grinning from ear-to-ear, asking the young woman question after question, making her blush one minute and giggle the next. Troy had sat back and listened to the seduction. Even though Jordan was in his seventies, he was still good at picking up women. He was smooth, and Jack wasn't bad either.

"You see this gentleman, right here," Jack said to Cherry. "The reason we are out here tonight is because this is a lonely police officer. His girlfriend just dumped him because he is sort of married to his job, to justice. He's looking for a new

girlfriend. I think you are prettier than the last one. Don't you think, Detective?"
Jack said elevating him from his lowly patrol officer role for the evening.

"Don't put her down," Jordan added. "She was a good woman. Troy only
likes good women, don't you, Troy?"

Troy nodded and noticed that the girl was looking at him differently now. He
was an upstanding man with a job, not just some guy hanging out in a nightclub.
She smiled at him and leaned over her drink giving him a better view of her cleavage.
He smiled back. Jordan nodded his head and downed his scotch.

"Why don't the two of you get to know each other? It's loud in here. Why
don't you go to my office? You might be on to something," Jordan said, reaching into
his pocket giving Troy the key.

Cherry stood up before he did with her drink in her hand. "Lead the way," she
said, lifting her right shoulder and winking her right eye at him.

"This way," Troy had said as Jack and Jordan howled behind him. He had
no idea what he was doing or why and couldn't believe the young woman was
following him so willingly. He should have shooed her away, but the loud pounding
funk music only made him bolder. Troy was going to find out or die. The two of
them walked into the office where a long, leather sofa sat against the wall where one
of Asa's paintings of a nude woman hung.

"That jacket doesn't look too comfortable," Cherry said and began to peel
Troy's jacket off. He smiled down into her eyes trying to see if her pupils were
dilated. She had to be tipsy. What woman would follow a man into a private room
and start peeling his clothes off. He started laughing. This had to be one of Jordan's
girls. This was some sort of joke, he thought, as he leaned over to kiss her. Cherry
kissed back and wrapped her arms around him giving him the courage to go further.
In an instant, he was inside of her on the sofa listening to her scream with delight
until he rolled off her.

That's when they discovered Jack and Jordan had joined them. Cherry started
pulling her clothes together when Jack grabbed her and ripped them off. He bent her
over the desk and plunged inside her. She screamed in pain, but no one outside the
office heard. The funk music sounded as if it had been pumped higher and there was
sudden urgency pumping through Troy's veins because, as Jack finished, Jordan
began, and when Jordan finished, Troy found himself riding her once again. Cherry
did her best to fight back and at one point she almost gouged Jordan's eye. Before
Troy realized what he was doing, he punched her in the face. The punch killed her.
They had to lock the body in the office until the next day when the club was closed to
dispose of her body. This time, Troy was the killer, a fact that Jack had kept to
himself until he returned to Philadelphia, this time as Jonathan Reck.

Troy was pissed, more than pissed. He had spent over a decade bending over backwards trying to make up for what he had done to Ashton. They had been close once. Heck, Ashton had been the only person left that he considered family after Rita had died. They had still been friends, but things were never the same. He understood that a little. Ashton had suffered traumatically in prison, almost losing his life. But, when Scully was found dead, that was it. Troy's sense of justice was resurrected.

Troy had been tracking them one by one. The other four inmates involved in the attack on Ashton were dead, and then Scully. No matter how much he loved his friend, he couldn't let him get away with it. Not anymore. Who knew who would be next? Then, Troy received a phone call from an anonymous, concerned citizen that placed Ashton on the scene. Troy knew he would never be able to live with himself if he didn't take some sort of action. So, he had made sure that the badge found between Ashton's hands, when Scully and crew almost killed him, found its way into Scully's murder evidence box. No one knew where it came from and no one seemed to care, but it was too late. Someone else had taken Ashton's identity and the thumbprints no longer matched. That should have been his first clue that something was terribly wrong in the Sperling household.

Troy was beside himself. He had been that close to making Ashton pay for a crime and it didn't stick. He had almost let it go, but then Ashton himself called saying that he feared for his life. Troy didn't know that it was Asa masquerading as Ashton. And then only a few weeks later, Asa was dead, shot by a trained assassin — one bullet through the head and, then, a second one right through the first one, missing Lazarus. That sharpshooter could have easily taken out Lazarus if he had wanted to do so. That didn't sit right or fit for Troy, so he had kept Lazarus on his radar from that moment on, even more so because the fake Ashton had pointed the finger, the source of danger, right at Lazarus.

Then, it all became clear when Jack Pulaski knocked on the window of the very car he was sitting in. The tall dude with the graying blonde crew cut smiled and re-introduced himself as his own cohort in crime. He said he wanted to help bring Ashton down and it would help if he could become Kali Sperling's bodyguard. On the one hand, Troy took that as a sign that he would be doing the right thing; but, on the other, he was more afraid of what would happen if he didn't help Jack with his agenda.

At first, they tried to convince each other it was all about Kali and the children's safety, which wasn't too far off the mark. Troy had prayed many times in the early days about freeing her from Jordan and the Sperling boys. But, he couldn't because he was busy salivating over her all by himself. Troy wanted her bad. And, if she had been set free, he knew he would never see her again.

Troy rubbed his chin as he remembered following Kali from school one day. She was enrolled at University of Penn and Jordan had given her free rein to take the bus home every day. At first, Jordan would have her driven to school and picked her up the minute she walked out of her last class. She hadn't earned his trust yet. But, it had been a few months and it was Spring. She was given permission to travel on her own, so she could go to the library or a school event without worrying about coordinating getting home. It had been important to Jordan that the girl receive an Ivy League education.

But, Jordan still only trusted her but so much. He had hired Troy and two other officers to watch her when they could. This particular day was Troy's watch. He cruised by her as she stood at the bus stop that would have taken her into Center City where they lived. But, as the bus came from another direction, she crossed the street and immediately boarded the bus.

"What the hell?" Troy remembered thinking. He pulled over his patrol car and let the bus pull in front of him. He followed it. "Where the hell are you going, Kali girl?" Troy stopped when the bus halted near 56th Street and hoped she wasn't noticing the police escort. She didn't. She jumped off the bus and went straight down Lancaster, walking fast. Troy held back, holding his breath. He knew the house where she was headed. It was a safe house for abused women. She was running, getting ready to escape Jordan's grasp. Part of him wanted to root for her, but the other part of him was sad. If she walked through that door, he would never get to see her again and she was the most beautiful woman he had ever seen. Troy sped up the car, pulled over to the curb and jumped out. He grabbed her by the arm just as she was about to ring the doorbell.

"You don't want to do that," Troy said and tugged her arm gently. She had looked up at him with defiant eyes filled with tears. "You and I both know that it

won't end well for you or those people inside. I know you are afraid, but think of what you will put them through if you walk through that door. They can't help you, Kali. Jordan is a powerful man. Let me take you home."

That was the reason she hated him, he knew that. I bet she had played that scene over and over in her mind a million times. What would have happened if she had fought him and went inside that house? She probably would have walked away free of Jordan, free of Ashton, and would have gone on to live a normal life. He had taken that away from her, just so he could see her face from time to time.

Jordan had been thankful and had sent Kali to her room to prepare herself. When Troy heard those words, he realized the life he had doomed the young girl to and he wanted to take it back, take her back. But, what happened next wiped out his remorse completely. Jordan had given Kali something to drink to calm her nerves. He had stood next to her, pushing the cup gently to her lips to make sure she drank it all.

By the time Jordan had taken him to her bedroom, she was completely in another world, nude, freshly bathed, freshly scented and fully loaded. Jordan told Troy to feel free to spend the entire night and he did. He explored every inch of her and prayed for the opportunity to do it again. He was hooked, even obsessed. But, what disturbed him was that the tonic that she drank before receiving him had left her oblivious to how much fun she had had with him. She had been so lively and so ready for sex with him, he would have bet his life that she knew what she was doing and who she was doing it with.

But, Jordan had awakened early the next morning and removed anything of him before she awakened. He then explained to Troy not to mention that evening to her or anybody else, and especially not to Ashton. Troy swallowed hard, on the fence because of what he had just experienced with her. Then he decided, for her, he would take that incident to his grave. But, then the real Troy, the policeman Troy, the Troy that prayed for justice in the world, would never forgive himself because of what he had done: he had seized the opportunity to plunder her. And he had enjoyed every taste, every thrust, every touch of her flesh. He left nothing to his imagination anymore. He knew her even more than in the biblical sense and every time he saw her or even smelled her after that, he could almost feel her underneath him.

Troy pulled into the parking lot of his apartment building in Chestnut Hill. The complex was a cluster of three-story buildings that created a square with the parking lot inside and a swimming pool next to it. He walked through the gate to the pool and sat on one of the metal benches. It was scorching hot. They were finally having a real, late-Spring day. Why would someone put metal in the freaking direct sunlight, he thought, but he stayed there as the metal began to cool against his skin.

Aloud, he asked himself, "What have I done?" The FBI was involved now. That was probably the reason Lazarus came clean as Ashton. The FBI wasn't going to be looking at events through the eyes of separate police departments anymore. They were going to be bringing all that evidence of everything Sperling together in one spot. He wondered if it would go public that Jordan Banks had been a pimp. Not that it mattered anymore. What did matter now was his connection to Jack and why.

It wasn't just the history between the two that brought him onboard. Jack had a line of stories that had clicked, though he had offered no real evidence. Jack had accused Ashton of murdering Brady, Ruby, Redd, and Scully, and then had accused him, as Lazarus, of murdering Asa as Ashton. All the stories lined up. It all made sense, especially since he had already become suspicious when Scully died. But now, now he was confused, now he wasn't sure if he had believed Jack because he had wanted to believe him or believed him because he knew it was all true. And now, the FBI had all that surveillance equipment that he had funneled to Jack to bug the penthouse. Not only that, they had the video and audio capturing Jack murdering that boy and the kids' bodyguard just before kidnapping Kali. How was he to explain that? How was he to explain he was in cahoots with a ticking time bomb that couldn't freaking wait for Ashton to come home and confess? Instead, the idiot ended up dead. And not only was Kali seriously injured, but most likely she was aware of Troy's true link to Jack. Jack had implied in the stables that she knew everything, every last detail. Troy stood up and stepped out of his shoes. He ripped off his shirt and tie. Pulled the belt out of his pants and dived into the pool.

Troy swam as if he were escaping to Cuba. He needed to escape this mess he had put himself in. His intentions were good, they were justified. The man he had looked up to since their college days was without a doubt a murderer, whether he was killing using his own hands or paying someone to do the killing for him. The inmates and prison guard murders were all connected to him. They had all died so conveniently, so logically spaced apart, one this year, one another, but all gone. Everyone who had had a hand in that brutal attack on him in prison was gone. Troy stopped swimming, wondering if he had fit into the plan, too. After all, Troy had blamed Ashton immediately for his sister Rita's death and had led the charge to take him down. He swam over to the ladder and came up for air and, as he ascended, he saw his old friend's face squinting in the afternoon sunlight.

"Couldn't go in and get your trunks first?" Ashton asked as Troy stood up in his drenched slacks. "Looks like you wet yourself pretty bad, Son."

"Ha Ha. What are you doing here? Am I next on your hit list? Time for me to go?" Troy started picking up his shoes and the rest of his things.

"About that," Ashton leaned over on his long legs, "why are you after me, Troy?"

"I'm not after you, Ashton. What are you so paranoid about?"

"Funny, I was going to ask you that. What are *you* so paranoid about?"

Troy limped barefoot across the hot pavement but his body was shivering, a reflection of how his life seemed to be going. Confusion. Chaos. None of this made any sense. He turned when he heard Ashton moving behind him.

"Where are you going?" Troy asked.

"Aren't you going to invite me in? Don't you think it's time we sat down, man to man, to discuss what's happening here? You owe me that much, Troy. Don't you?"

Ashton was standing as tall and confident as he had the first day he had met Troy in a Cornell dorm room. He was older. They both were, but Ashton's body hadn't aged. His arms were still massive and muscular and his abs were still streamlined. Troy sucked in his little belly. It wasn't protruding that much, but much more than it had when they were younger. Troy went to the gym often, but he didn't look anything like Ashton, not that he ever had.

"Come on." Troy led the way up the backstairs two flights to an apartment on the end. Ashton followed him in.

"Nice," Ashton said as he noticed the wood parquet floors and the open kitchen space with a solid granite bar separating the living room from the kitchen.

"Not too bad for a public servant," Troy said. "Or, one with no badge and no gun.”

“They suspended you?”

“Yeah, a couple of hours ago.”

“Sorry, man. I know that hurts.”

“Like you care.” Troy started down a hall. “Occupy yourself for a minute. There’s beer in the fridge. I have to take a shower.”

“Okay.” Ashton sat down on the large, navy blue sofa. It was comfortable. The whole place was comfortable and he liked it. He had half expected it to be bare, with bits and pieces of cheap furniture, like Troy’s personality.

There was a stack of magazines on the coffee table. He counted them, ten: two of each issue of *Newsweek, Time, Ebony, AARP*, and *Rolling Stone*. There was a current and a previous month of each one. Ashton smiled. Troy was still a methodical dickhead, always had been. Ashton started leafing through the magazines to catch up on the news stateside.

“You are looking too comfortable there,” Troy said, handing him a bottle of beer.

“We are still friends, aren’t we?” Ashton asked.

“You tell me.” Troy sat down across from him in an oversized matching chair facing him.

“Do you own this place?” Ashton got up and looked out the window. It had a good view of trees. Little patches of roofs from neighboring homes peeked through here and there.

“That much about you hasn’t changed. You are trying to size up my financial status. If I tell you this is a condo and I own it, you will ask me how much I paid for it. If I tell you it’s an apartment, you will think I have squandered all my money. Then you will wonder how a single man like myself could live all these years without a savings.”

“You think too much, Troy. Is that why Kali almost died?” Ashton plopped back on the sofa and slid out of his loafers. He put his feet up on the coffee table near Troy’s beer. Troy moved it and sat it on the floor next to his chair.

“Why are you here?” Troy took a long swig of his beer.

“For answers. For both of us.”

“Then tell me the truth,” Troy said.

“The truth is, I am a man with bits and pieces of a memory of a past life. A man who has been living the life of someone else, afraid that someone from his past life was still trying to kill him. Not too far off, am I? They tried to kill my wife and son. Go figure. Problem is, I don't know why. Can you help me with that?"

"Why do you think I can help you?"

"I think you were suckered into something and you know it now. I think you wish you could get a do-over," Ashton paused and let that sink in. "If someone would tell me what I did, I would do a do-over to save my family from all this trauma, to save myself from being a target. Am I still a target?"

"Why are you asking me? Why don't you ask yourself?"

"Bits and pieces, Troy." Ashton wasn't completely lying. There was still a lot missing from his memory banks.

Ashton pointed to his head. "When I woke up in that hospital bed, after the other Ashton was killed, I began to remember bits and pieces. Before that, I didn't remember anything. All I knew was what I heard people whispering about and intimating that I was the real Ashton. I could remember nothing. It started coming in bits and pieces and then I left. I left to keep the family safe. I figured if I lived as Lazarus, whoever was after me would let me be. They would think I was dead and leave everybody alone. But, that didn't happen, did it?"

"What do you remember?"

"Stupid shit," Ashton laughed. "I was looking through pictures last night trying to trigger something and I saw a picture of the two of us in front of a big, green foot."

"The Statue of Liberty," Troy smiled, nodding his head.

"What the hell?" Ashton laughed again.

"You found out I had never been to the Statue of Liberty. I had a paper to write that day, but you convinced me to take the ferry and go over there. You said I was too intense, too nervous to write a good paper. You paid my way. You were always paying my way somewhere. You almost put me through school," Troy laughed. "That's why I always tried to look out for you. You looked out for me. And then I made a mistake."

"Troy, my brother tells me you are a man of justice, sometimes blind justice, but he says you are after justice like a hound dog after a bloody cat."

"A what?" Troy laughed again. "You still have a weird way of looking at things."

"So, is he right? Are you involved in seeking some sort of justice for Ashton or for Lazarus or for whomever?"

"Are you wired?" Troy asked downing the rest of his beer.

"Do you want me to strip?" Ashton stood up and was about to take his shirt off.

"I will pass, thank you." Troy waved him back down. "I didn't know about Asa. I didn't know he had kidnapped you and taken your place. I didn't know any of that until a few months ago."

"So a few months ago is when you realized Lazarus was me?"

"Not at first. He gave me bits and pieces," Troy shook his head.

"He? Jack? Reck? Who is this guy? I mean, I know who I think he is, but who is he? I was in Europe trying to find out who Redd was married to and I found out that she married a man named Jocko. No last name, no marriage records in any European country that I had access to. He lived in Germany but supposedly he was an American. Circumstantial nonsense is all I have. But, Jocko is a real close moniker to Jack and Kali said you called him Jack."

"Maybe they didn't get married in Europe. You said he was American. Maybe they were married here or in New York. And, maybe his name was Jack. Who's your Jack? Who do you think he is?"

"A Jack Pulaski, a kid my grandfather wanted to adopt, but things never worked out for either of them. He lived with us for a while. Most of my memory of him was as a kid. My grandfather used to tell him, boy, you are going to be taller than me. You are all legs and arms. Get in that kitchen and eat something. You need to fill out the rest of that body. I remember running into the kitchen behind Jack to make sure I filled out my body, too."

"I could see you doing that." Troy got up and put two more beers on the granite counter. "Be right back."

Ashton put his feet down and leaned over his long legs. He started restacking the magazines noticing the date on one of them. It was Aaron's birthdate. What was he going to do about the baby? He pulled out his phone and texted his brother, Chico: GET KALI'S CLOTHES. GOING TO NEED DEAD GUY'S DNA.

Troy walked into the room with his laptop. He went on the kitchen side of the counter and opened it.

"What was Redd's name again?"

"Mary Elizabeth O'Reilly," Ashton said.

"You remembered that?"

"Maybe, maybe not. There is a copy of my marriage records in Jordan's old office."

"Both of them?"

"Ha. Ha," Ashton said, sipping his beer and watching Troy's narrow fingers type on the laptop.

"New York City. They were married in New York fifteen years ago."

"She had moved on then," Ashton said, shaking his head.

"What brought her back?"

"Money. She came back for money. Money I would have given to her had she asked. I am sure I would have. All she had to do was ask but, instead, she and Asa came in with agendas and guns."

"She couldn't walk back in the door with your dead brother, now could she?" Troy still couldn't believe Asa had come back.

"Why bring him? I thought he was dead. I had no idea Asa and Daddy had cooked up a plan to keep him out of jail for murdering your sister, Marcus, and Kenny. Remember Kenny? He was Kali's best friend, used to be one of Jordan's flunkies? They found him in a car at the bottom of the river. I'm surprised you weren't in on that, too."

"Funny. Do you want to know his name?" Troy was still staring at the clunky computer screen.

"Let me guess, Jack Pulaski?"

"No, Jonathan Reck."

"Reck? Jonathan?"

"Reck. He took his adoptive parents' surname, looks like Jack's real first name was Jonathan in the first place." That much Troy had learned directly from Reck.

"Do you think Redd knew his connection to me? Did she know he was Jack, Jordan's Jack?"

"Who knows? He was a very convincing man. He convinced me that you were a murderer. Maybe he convinced her, too."

"And Brady and Ruby?"

"And Brady and Ruby. Brady had a bone to pick with you anyway. Maybe you don't remember, but you kicked him out of PDSI over a woman."

"Really? Was she good looking, at least?"

"She was hot. But, whatever you said to him when you kicked him out had him running scared. That's probably why he teamed up with Asa, Redd, and Jack to bring you down."

"Don't forget you and Ruby," Ashton chuckled and drained the beer bottle.

"Yeah, I am the only of them left standing. How can I forget?" Troy closed the laptop. "Really, Ashton, what are you doing here?"

"Honestly, I just want to know what you know. I know whatever part you played in this you thought you were doing the right thing; but, not knowing what part you played in this frightens me. It frightens Kali. You see, someone was poisoning her. We suspect Anjuli. We suspect Artie. I suspect your hand may have been in it. Maybe even Jack's. I just want to know something from your lips, something that will make me feel like my family is finally safe. I don't care about me. I never cared about me. All I know is what I feel. I don't feel as if I did anything to warrant having them put into harm's way. I feel that you would do nothing to put them in harm's way. But, what I am feeling could be wrong so I want you to tell me that, tell me what my feelings are based on, Troy. Tell me you weren't going to hurt my wife down in that cave. Tell me why you said she was already dead when she wasn't. Tell me something that makes me think somehow, someway you are still my best friend. Tell me that it wasn't all a lie."

"Then tell me you never lied to me, Ashton." Troy leaned toward him. "Tell me I wasn't some sort of joke to you. Someone your wife toyed with, someone you hid important facts from about your life."

"My wife never toyed with you, Troy. I don't think she could have been more clear about anything other than her dislike for you. Hell, let's be honest, she hates you. She could never understand my continuing my friendship with you. I used to explain it to her and she would reject it. So, I would try to lighten it up and say I keep my enemies close. Was that it, Troy? Were you the enemy all this time?"

"You stopped trusting me, and when Asa was pretending to be you, he let me back into the circle. It felt good. He needed my help to bring you down. I didn't realize he was the one I needed to bring down. If I had known, I would have helped you, but you lied to me."

"I didn't know who I was then. Like I said, it was all innuendos and whispers."

"Why didn't they tell me?"

"Kali didn't trust you, which meant Micah wasn't going to trust you either."

"So here we are. Lack of trust still abounding. You wanna take off that wire?"

Ashton stood up and began to strip down to his boxers. "You wanna look inside these."

Troy walked around the counter and looked inside.

"Okay," Troy said. He picked up Ashton's pants and examined the pockets. He went over to the magazines and flipped through them. Then he felt under the table and examined the lamps as Ashton put his clothes back on.

Troy went to the refrigerator and pulled out two more beers. "This is how it went down."

Chapter Thirty-One

ASHTON RETURNED TO his car almost unable to breathe. He had wanted to know and now he knew. Devastation didn't fully describe it. Once again, his world had collapsed into senseless chaos. He reached over to the glove compartment, opened it and saw his gun. At first, he reached for it; then, changing his mind, he slammed the little door shut. What was he supposed to do now? Killing himself or his brother was not an option anymore.

His phone rang. He looked at the Caller ID and turned the phone downward. He wasn't ready to talk. There wasn't even a time he could fathom having that conversation, not after what he had just learned. Suddenly aware of the belt he was wearing and the small buckle that he had carefully laced into it before visiting Troy made him feel even guiltier. The only thing in sight for him to hit was the steering wheel and he hit it so hard it bounced. Ashton leaned over into the steering wheel and cursed his own life.

A light knocking on the window startled him. Half expecting to see a gun pointed in his face, all he saw was the bulky class ring on his friend's finger tapping on the window. Ashton turned the key in the ignition and let the window slide down all the way.

"You alright, man?" Troy asked, standing there looking a little tipsy.

"I'm alright," Ashton lied. His condition right now was anything but.

"You are going to be able drive back into Center City okay?"

"Yeah, Son. I got this," Ashton said, hating to meet Troy's eyes.

"It's okay, Ashton. I know I have done a lot of things that I am going to regret for the rest of my life. I'm okay with that. That's why I am going to walk down a couple of blocks here and pick up two more six packs. I plan to down them all before your boys from the FBI show up to take me away. Hell, they are going to have to carry me out of the place," Troy chuckled.

Ashton looked up at him questioningly.

"Don't worry, I know you recorded me or bugged me somehow. I don't know how. Maybe I should have looked up your butt cheeks," Troy laughed. "Trust me, I know that look. It's the same look you used to give those girls you used to introduce to Jordan so he could seduce them into the lifestyle. You would be smiling goodbye, pocketing his money, but your eyes would be saying I am sorry, I am so sorry. Just like they did when you said goodbye to me a few minutes ago. Hell, I thought you would be gone by now."

"Troy," Ashton said in a low whisper.

"What man?"

"I have a gun. It's in the glove compartment."

"I don't have a gun on me, man. Are you going to shoot me?"

"No, I want you to take the gun and shoot me," Ashton replied. "Just put me out of my misery. Put me someplace with a real headstone."

Troy started laughing and began to back away. He had a beer bottle in his hand. When he turned to walk, he threw the beer bottle crashing into the sidewalk in front of the parked cars.

"I have always wanted to do that," Troy laughed turning around with the joy of a mischievous little kid. "It went crash." Troy laughed harder, backing away from Ashton so fast it looked like he was skipping, and then it happened. Troy stepped into the entrance of the parking lot just as a car sped into it, throwing his body high and toward the gates surrounding the parking lot.

Ashton struggled to get out of his car and then ran to Troy who was lying against the steel fence, his eyes still open.

"Troy, Troy, are you alright?" Ashton asked, knowing all too well that Troy had left that body in that instant. Blood was coming out of his mouth. Ashton felt for a pulse, but it was already gone. He sat down on the ground and slid Troy to a lying position. He heard two women behind him screaming. One was screaming at the other that she told her to slow down. It didn't matter, he wanted to tell her. Troy wouldn't have survived prison, even if it had been a short stay with only a slap on the hands. He was all about justice and there were too many men in prison to whom he had already served justice.

Ashton got up and walked to his car. He picked up his phone to call 911. There were six missed calls from Micah. That conversation was going to have to wait a while. He called Chico.

Ashton was sitting in his car again when another tapping on the window aroused him from his thoughts. He looked out to see his younger brother, Chico.

"Trying to kill yourself sitting in this hot car like this?" Chico opened the door and Ashton's head fell toward him. Chico grabbed his big brother, tugged him out of the car, and pulled him into a big bear hug. "Come on. I'll send someone for your car. Get in mine. Let me drive you down to the house in Olde City. I still have the keys." Chico led what appeared to be a devastated and confused Ashton to his car and put him in the passenger seat. He strapped him in like a doting mother buckling in her child. He patted Ashton on the head, and then got into the car.

The wreck had been moved and so had Troy's body. Police tape was still up and children were riding past on their bicycles while a cleaning crew was already removing Troy's blood from the scene. All in a day's work, he thought, as he drove through the neighborhood looking for Stenton Avenue. It was the only street he knew well enough out there to get him back to Broad Street. He wanted to ask Ashton why he called him. Whenever there was trouble, Micah was always on his speed dial, but Micah had called him saying something had happened and Ashton wouldn't answer his calls. It was as if neither of them wanted to see each other and that wasn't good.

They arrived on the small, neat one-way street in walking distance to South Street. Chico helped Ashton into the little row house, hoping he didn't slip on the cobblestones getting him out of the car. He had never seen his brother look so weak. He stood under his brother's shoulder and led him to the glistening black door of the house that Ashton had bought for Kali before the twins were born. Kali still owned it and said she never planned to sell it. Sometimes, Chico or Ricky would use it for their guests; sometimes Micah and Kali had used it to play without the kids in sight just like she used to with Ashton when they were once happy. The place that was barely big enough for more than two normal sized adults was well kept with a regular housekeeper, so the place was clean, and there was food in the pantry and the refrigerator, though, he didn't know how old it was. Chico got busy making coffee in the compact, but stylish kitchen. Kali had seen to that. He looked in the cupboard, found a couple of cans of chicken noodle soup and heated them up. Going back in the living room to check on Ashton, he found him curled up on the large, tan leather sofa in an almost fetal position, so he pulled a blanket out of an upstairs closet and threw it over him. Then he stood back and watched the strongest man he had ever known cry like a baby beneath the blankets.

Chico's phone rang.

"How is he?" Micah asked.

"Not good," Chico answered. "What's going on between you two?"

"We just need to talk," Micah answered. "Can I come over?"

"No, not yet," Chico said, worried that Ashton was not in a space to be logical right now. "Can this wait until morning?"

"I would rather not wait that long," Micah sighed. "He and I really need to talk."

"He's not really lucid right now. He's pretty melted down."

"He needs to hear my side of the story," Micah said. "I can't let it just fester. It's only going to make matters worse."

Micah was standing over Kali who was sleeping soundly. "I'm coming over now. It would probably be best if you left. I will be there in an hour."

He kissed Kali's head, and then smoothed back her hair. As he was about to back away from her, she grabbed his hand.

"What's going on, Molasses? What's wrong with Ashton?"

"Troy's dead. Hit by a car," Micah said. "Chico sounds like everything's finally hitting home with Ashton. I need to go see him."

Chico waited until he saw Micah parking his SUV behind his own little sports car, a reminder how different he was from his older brothers. Ashton hadn't touched the coffee or the soup; he was lying there still, in a ball, staring into space. At least, he had stopped bawling like a baby.

Chico met Micah outside as quickly as he could. "I'm not so sure this is a good idea. He is in some sort of state like I have never seen him in before."

"He's hurting. I'm the only one who can help him whether he likes it or not." Micah tried to step around Chico, but Chico wouldn't move.

He had never fought with any of his brothers, but he was ready to now, if need be. He tried hard to stand taller.

"I'm not leaving. I don't know what the two of you have done this time. I really don't want to know the details, but I am not about to leave and let you kill each other. I'm just not going to do it," Chico said, still looking up at Micah. He hated being the shortest brother, but he wasn't going to be bullied by the giants in the family anymore. He wasn't about to watch these two go down and leave him responsible for the pack of urchins back at the penthouse. He knew his brother, Ricky, would just leave him hanging and responsible. "I'll stay in the kitchen or go upstairs in the bedroom. But, I am not leaving."

"You don't want to be here, Chico. Trust me," Micah said and moved his brother aside.

"You are right. I don't want to be here, but I have to be." Chico stayed on Micah's heels as he went into the house to keep him from locking him out. Surprised that Micah didn't attempt to do so, he followed him through the foyer and found the sofa in the living room empty.

"He was right here," Chico said walking toward the kitchen. "Ashton, Ashton."

"I'm right here." Ashton came down the stairwell. He had washed his face, his wet hair was pushed away from his face, but it was still red and distressed looking.

"Look who I found outside," Chico looked back at Micah and then back at Ashton who was still coming down the stairs. He was waiting for the explosion, an eruption of whatever was hanging in the air.

"I'm not going to fight Micah, if that's what you are worried about. I want you to call Ricky and AJ. Get them over here. We all need to talk this thing through. Today."

"Go make the calls. And get us something hard to drink." Micah put his arm around Chico. "Trust us, this is something we can work through. Still standing."

The brothers watched Chico close the kitchen door behind him and they sat on the big L-shaped sofa that seemed to fill the whole room together, facing each other.

"Was the FBI really listening?"

"No," Micah shook his head. "I am going to let you make that decision." Micah pulled out a small recorder and handed it to Ashton.

Ashton pushed a button and they both stared at it as Troy recounted what he knew about Micah's part in the events.

"So they don't know everything yet?"

"Not unless you tell them. I don't plan to share. Do you?"

"Why, Micah?"

"She was going to bring us all down, Ashton. She missed you so much, her lips were loose. When she shouted at me for killing Ruby, with Artie only a few doors away, I knew I was going to have to do something about her. I killed Ruby for her, and she was getting ready to destroy my son, her children, and you with her mouth. She was getting out of control. I needed to control her and I couldn't."

"So you brought in Anjuli to antagonize her even more? She was dependent on you. You were pulling away from her."

"I was afraid Artie was going to find out and he was going end up just as dangerous as Ash, as you, and as me. I couldn't bear that. I didn't want to hurt her. But, I wasn't poisoning her. I had tried to get her to go to the doctor, even to Chico or Ricky for depression. She wouldn't admit it, but she was depressed. And it was getting worse. So, I started slipping her some Nardil. When she finally calmed down and seemed to be getting better, I stopped. I think the headaches were a result of withdrawal. I was afraid to own up to it, but I was going to tell Chico.

"For the most part, it worked. She had calmed down quite a bit. I don't know if it was because of the… because of what I was giving her or because the reality of what she was doing had set in. She wasn't screaming anymore. I had stopped over a month ago, but, she was still complaining of headaches. She was planning to go to Chico for blood tests the day after the play. I heard them talking."

"What were you giving her again?"

"An anti-depressant called Nardil."

"Enough to damage her organs?"

"No, no, I don't think so. I had done my research. The only side effect she was showing was the headaches. I'm the one who introduced them into her tea and other food when I had the chance. I followed a regimen. A pharmacist I know helped me with the dosage."

"Why didn't you call me?" Ashton asked a little too calmly. Micah froze. "If you had called me, I would have come home. If I had known you could only think of drugging her…You could have killed her, Micah." Ashton shook his head. "Just like Ruby. I never asked you to kill your wife. Never."

"You killed yours," Micah answered, referring to Redd, "but that was not my intention."

"Redd did her best to kill me. It was always going to boil down to me or her. One of us was going. Besides, from the way Troy tells it, Jack put the finishing touches on it. He was the one that let her go down that mountainside in a car with no brakes. He tried to stop her at first, but then she went into one of her Redd rages, so he let her go. I always wondered why it took her so long to get down that mountain. I had stayed behind cleaned up and everything, but there she was sailing over the mountainside right before my eyes. It was a beautifully frightening sight."

Ashton reached over to touch his brother's knee. "Am I supposed to forgive you for being stupid?"

"I don't know," Micah said. "I don't know. I know I wish I hadn't done it. I regret it, Ashton. I love Kali, I do. I just couldn't face the hurt it was going to cause my son one day."

"So you almost took two mothers from him and expect it not to affect him at all?"

"I thought about that, but you weren't here. You didn't hear her. You didn't see her. She was getting completely out of control. And she was talking, talking to that bodyguard, Reck. She was really losing it, Ashton. I couldn't call you home. Hell, you nearly didn't talk to me when I did call. I thought you were just withdrawing from us so I had to keep the 'us' that was here together."

"Without their mother and their father?"

"Without their mother," Micah shook his head. "I have been their father. Where the hell have you been?"

CHAPTER THIRTY-TWO

THE SPERLING MEN

CHICO WAITED UNTIL the doorbell rang. He brought out a tray loaded with short glass tumblers, the kind that fit real nice in a big man's hand. He sat the tray on the coffee table with a large bottle of Maker's Mark. Micah reached for it and started pouring, filling each glass half-full. Ricky walked in with Ash in tow, looking apprehensive seeing his father and his uncles cramped in the small living room that he only visited once or twice a year. Ashton patted the sofa next to him and Ash squeezed in between him and Micah.

Ashton picked up a glass and raised it up. "Here's to the Sperling men." The brothers and his son followed suit. They clinked their glasses together and downed the strong brown liquor. Ash started to cough. They all watched him as he tried to regain his composure. Ash looked at them waiting for the sarcastic and humorous remark to come. But, instead, they put their glasses back down and Micah poured another round.

"To survival." Micah raised his glass and the men clinked the glasses again followed by another draining of the glasses. Ash mimicked the Sperling men but began to cough again. The men waited silently as he regained his composure. When he saw his Uncle Micah reach for the bottle again Ash wanted to run. Micah poured and then Chico stood up from his chair. His eyes met those of each of his brothers.

"We all know how we were raised. We all know how responsible we are for the next generation of Sperlings. The tide has changed. As we grew up, there was only one woman allowed in the family and that was Elle. Now we still have Elle and we have Kali, and we have two daughters, Katie and Kacie. The legacy of the Sperlings has changed for the better. We almost lost the one woman that held us together. We almost put the younger women in our lives in danger. You can go ahead and tease me because I am gay. But, I am still a man, and the women in our lives require our protection. Kali, Katie, and Kacie as well as Ms. Elle and Ms. Elliott must be treated like priceless treasures, not to be toyed with. I raise my glass to say that we, as the men in their lives, should start getting it right. We can't let outsiders like Jack Pulaski and Troy Lucas bring any more chaos into our lives. We all must be on our watch. Ashton, you, especially, and Ash, you especially. Ash, you are responsible for the next generation. We charge you with this today."

The men clinked their glasses and drank down the shot. Ash wanted to keel over from suddenly feeling out of sorts and halfway from wanting to break into laughter. But, he looked at their faces and they were serious as Micah poured another round.

This time Ricky held up his glass and snickered, "I don't know what the fuck we are doing here. But, it's about damn time. I have missed my brothers more than you can know. I am gay. I am a man. And I never knew the details, nor did I ever want to know the details, of what you dangerous motherfuckers were doing. Thank God for being the youngest," he said, chuckling, but continued. "All I know is I loved my grandfather, his legacy be damned. I loved my father who was kick-ass in the courtroom and kick-ass with us. I pledge my life to my brothers; I don't care what the hell you have done. So, I raise my fucking glass to all the dead because of you and pray there will be no more. All I know is one thing for sure: I am a Banks. I am a Sperling. I am a man, and the females in this family will continue, even if I have to join the ranks of the murderers in this room. I love you bastards! But, please keep your asses out of trouble and stay alive, cause there are no fucking tears for dead men."

All the brothers stood up. Micah and Ashton lifted Ash to a standing position and they clinked their glasses one more time before they yelled 'Sperling.' Then Ash crumbled back onto the sofa laughing hysterically.

"I think he got the picture." Micah rubbed his head.

"Let him sleep it off. Pour us another round." Ashton smiled. He was home.

CHAPTER THIRTY-THREE

THE BABY

ELLIOTT GAVE THE baby another big hug and kiss before putting him in the car seat in a rental car.

"You act as if you are never going to see this child again. Why are you so attached?" Ray asked Elliott for the millionth time. He had watched her fuss over the child while they were in London waiting for his papers to come through, and then when she brought him home to Buenos Secos, she barely let the child breathe without hovering around him. Ray was getting worried. The woman was obsessed. Now they were leaving the airport, and she was going to have to leave the child with Ashton. What was she afraid of?

"I'm just going to miss him," Elliott answered and that was no lie. She had never raised a child of her own. She had helped her sisters with their kids, but her own two boys had been out of reach, and her womb wasn't accepting anymore boarders. She was considered sterile after her babies were born. She was sure it had something to do with the way they had been delivered. She wouldn't have been surprised if Jordan's hand was in that as well. But, now she had one. She could still smell him, and his name was Aaron. He was the replacement child, if such as thing could exist, for the one who had died at Jordan's hands, the one who had haunted her entire life.

Maybe she was getting old, and crazy, for wanting to hold onto this child, or maybe she was just afraid to talk to Ashton. He wanted to talk to her and the tone in his voice unsettled her. When he called, he spoke to her less and less about the generalities of life and only, specifically, about Aaron, as if he was really trying to avoid talking to her at all. But, then he would get on the phone with Ray and talk freely for long lengths of time, like he used to with her. Maybe that was why she wanted to hold onto Aaron, a part of her was feeling as if she had already lost Ashton. She never thought that even possible. He had stayed in touch with her as Lazarus, even when she knew he wasn't talking to Kali or Micah.

He had let her know before his wife, that he was Ashton. There was a mother and son bond there between the two of them that she thought could never be broken. At least, not until, she had let Asa chase her out of their lives. Elliott took in a deep breath. That was it. There it was. The guilt. Guilt because she had known it was Asa who taken Ashton's life, that it was Asa who was sleeping with Ashton's wife, was torturing Ashton's children, and who had threatened to kill her if she uttered a word. What else was she to believe? He had killed Billy, and he had even admitted to killing Jordan. So, she had remained silent, even when Ashton had come home. Even when she knew Asa was dead, she had remained silent. What did Ashton know?

Elliott was surprised to find the entire Sperling family sitting in the dining room waiting for her, Ray, and little Aaron. Ashton had met them at the door and was leading them into the huge room with Aaron snuggled up in his arms. The baby latched onto Ashton's hair and started trying to eat a few strands as he sat down at the head of the table. Kali reached up from her chair, untangled his little fist, and took him in her arms. Elliott's heart sank at the sight. Her grandchildren oohed and aahed at the infant who was sitting confidently without any back support. He was three months old. Until now, he had been all hers.

"Ladies and gentlemen," Ashton spoke dramatically as a couple of his children giggled, "I present to you your new brother and nephew, Mr. Aaron Elliott Sperling." Everybody clapped and Aaron giggled playfully.

"As you know, Aaron's mother and father are both deceased. His mother helped me more than I can tell you. If it weren't for her, I wouldn't have been alive to return home to you. She's the main reason I have decided we are going to raise this child as part of this family. I owe her that. Now his father, well, you know now that his father was the man who kidnapped your mother, murdered Roderick and several others with the intent to murder the rest of us. I don't ever want you to hold that against this child. He had nothing to do with that, neither did his mother. His father raped her. And the people who were born of bad unions like that should not be punished for the parents' actions. Let them stand on their own character throughout their lives. I am telling you this, because I am charging you with making sure he is loved and treasured, and not burdened by the past. This family has carried too many burdens from the past as it is, and today we are letting go," Ashton continued, but he looked directly at Elliott who was holding her breath and fighting back the tears.

"So, who is going to welcome him first?" Ashton had to move fast to dodge both Katie and Kacie running for the baby.

"I think that was a welcome," Ray laughed and made his way to the food that was waiting on the table.

"Elliott," Ashton nodded toward the door and left. Elliott followed him down to the study wondering if this would be her last time in the penthouse, the last time seeing him.

She was surprised when he didn't take his usual seat behind the desk. Instead, he sat on the sofa under the spiral staircase and bookshelves in the study and patted the space next to him.

"I know it's been a few months. It's a conversation that I have been dreading. You know that, right?"

"No more than me," Elliott said.

"Why, Elliott? Why haven't you ever told me that you were my mother?"

Elliott shook her head. "I didn't think I deserved you."

"What?"

"I couldn't protect you. I couldn't save you. All I could do was to make your life as easy as I possibly could. You didn't need a mother," Elliott said, wiping her face. "Then when Billy died, I thought, it was possible. But, then, then, you started acting crazy. Like a man I didn't know, and then I figured out it was Asa and not you."

Ashton jumped up. That was the last confession he had expected. He took a few steps back and sat on the desk.

"You knew Asa was alive?"

"Billy had tried to get me to take care of him when he was injured. I said no. I told him to turn Asa into the police. That was the same day the police found him in the cellar. I had no idea before that and, like you, I thought he was dead. I had no reason to think otherwise and I guess, since I suggested turning him in, Billy didn't trust me with knowing otherwise."

"Why did you quit PDSI? Did you know it was him then?"

"Yes, and I was going to tell Micah, but he threatened to kill us one by one just like he had already killed you, he said," Elliott said, still sniffling. "I was going to try to figure a way out. The best I could do to keep everyone from harm was to keep moving your money. He called me a few times trying to figure out your system, and I would tell him I had no idea, but then I would give him a false hint to keep him interested, to keep him busy. All I could do was play cat and mouse with him. I couldn't help Kali or the children."

"What were you going to do when he got tired of chasing the money? Didn't you realize he was going to go after the insurance money?"

"He didn't think you had insurance money. I told him you had decided that you had more than enough to pass onto the children and to Kali. I told him the only insurance was what was covered in the banks. He seemed to believe me. I moved the insurance policies out of his reach. I know everyone thought I had left Philadelphia, but I was only out in Collingswood. At night, I used to catch the train over to Suburban Station and let myself into the office. I would undo most of what he had done during the day, finance-wise anyway."

"Why didn't you tell anybody?"

"I didn't want anyone to die. But, I was afraid if anyone found out I didn't tell, they would discard me. I would lose my family, the only family I had left. Then you came back, and I got so excited, but you didn't remember me. You didn't remember anything and I thought disclosure would make it even more dangerous for you and the family. So I kept quiet some more, but this time I took my hands off your money and Asa started making pick-ups. That's when I alerted Micah that somebody was playing with your money. I was hoping that would trigger something, that someone would find out who and what and you did."

"And then Micah said you needed me, you, Ashton," Elliott sighed. "I was happy and scared at the same time, but I was going to do everything I could to guide you. You know how much it hurt though? You were both my sons."

"Did he know that you were our mother?" Ashton said the word 'mother' harshly.

Elliott shook her head. "I was afraid it would give him even more ammunition. I thought everybody would be safer, if I just kept quiet and in the background."

"Did you know about Jack?"

"Hadn't heard that name in a long time. Don't think I would have even recognized it. I was there the day of the accident that brought the families together, but after that I was banished. And rightly so. You should never have slipped out of that café, let alone almost get hit by a car. I was supposed to be watching you boys. Billy had fought the old man on that and was winning until that day."

"What about Elle, did she know Asa was alive?"

"I don't know. Elle and I have not spoken in years. I do know she was more and more of afraid of Billy when I did speak with her. She said he was about as murderous as Jordan was. I didn't know what she meant by that and I didn't want to find out."

Ashton nodded his head. "You will understand if I give you some space for a while. And it would be helpful, if you give us all a little space, please. Let us get settled with the baby. I'm still trying to win my family back. We are not over the hurdle just yet. I'm still fighting to be Ashton and not Lazarus, too. So, give me some time. Some time to think. I understand what you are saying, but my I'm feeling too much right this minute to even figure out what it is I am feeling. Maybe, maybe when I am ready, I can introduce you as my mother, my kids' grandma. But, not today. Today, I have to get passed the past and start a new chapter for Aaron," Ashton said and held up his hand. "I'm having a hard time with the name right now, as you probably can tell. Don't be surprised if I change it. Stay as long as you want. I don't want to upset the apple cart. Spend time with Kali and the kids, but when you leave, give me some space. Give us some space. Okay?"

Elliott nodded her head.

He bent over and kissed her on the cheek, and then walked out of the study where she broke down into a torrent of tears.

EPILOGUE

KALI CHECKED HERSELF in her dressing room mirror again. She saw the walker in the reflection and sighed, "Goodbye to you, baby."

She moved it out of her view and checked herself again. Then she stepped into heels for the first time in a long, long time. They felt good, a little awkward but good. She moved over to the vanity and put on more lip gloss. She puckered her lips and blew herself a kiss.

"You shall overcome." She hummed the tune of the old civil rights spiritual. She had overcome and was ready to move forward. Kali walked out of her bedroom without stumbling, not even a little. A feeling of power swept through her as she closed the double doors to her bedroom. When she reached the landing to go downstairs, she stopped to touch Jordan's portrait. This morning his eyes were twinkling.

"I did it, old man," Kali whispered. "I'm still standing." She said to the life-sized painting that Asa had created years ago, doing such a great job that Jordan's eyes changed with the dominant emotion in their home. "It's all good." Kali smoothed her skirt and held onto the bannister. She was taking a big leap, not only by leaving the walker behind, but by wearing three-inch heels down a flight of stairs.

"Mom, mom, mom," Ash was calling her from the bottom of the stairs. "Mom, nobody's mom is supposed to look that good."

"Stop it, Ash. Don't distract me." Kali took each step carefully, one at a time. She didn't want to greet her son by rolling down the stairs on her Independence Day.

"Mom," Ash said, starting up the stairs with his hand reaching up for her.

"Go back down, Ash. I'm fine," she commanded and he obeyed. Patiently, he waited but his eyes never left her.

Kali stopped about three steps from the bottom so she could look her son in his eyes. He was so much taller than she. She touched his face and kissed his forehead.

"Good morning," she said as he grabbed her around the waist and gently lifted her to the bottom of the step.

"Did I hear the doorbell earlier?" Kali asked.

"Yeah, I was about to come and get you."

"Who is it?" Kali asked, starting toward the kitchen. Ash grabbed his mother by the shoulder and redirected her.

"They are in the study," he whispered. "Both of them."

"How timely," Kali said standing up taller.

"You want me to come with you, Mom?" Ash asked.

"No, I will call you if I need you."

"Mom." Kali turned to see Katie coming through the living room with baby Aaron in her arms. "Mom, I have got to run and the nanny had to run an errand," Katie said handing Kali the baby. Now she had to power walk with little Aaron in her arms. Ash snatched up the little one and led the way down the hall to the study. He waited at the door with the baby as the little one kept trying to put his fingers in Ash's mouth. All five kids had accepted the baby into the fold and Aaron was flourishing and healthy.

Kali opened the door and found the Sperling brothers sitting on the sofa. She stepped down the couple of steps into the study and then turned to reach for the baby.

Ash relinquished him to her as she shifted him to her right hip and strode to the desk taking the tall chair behind the desk.

"Gentlemen, how are you this morning?"

"Good," said Ashton. "Real good. How are you this morning?"

Ashton was the first one to join her at the desk. He reached over and grabbed Aaron's little hand.

"He looks more and more like Nat every day. Can I hold him?" Ashton reached over the desk and the baby started reaching back. Kali stood up and handed him over. Ashton rubbed his fingers through the baby's light-colored hair.

"I think he looks more like Reck myself," Kali said. They had gotten the DNA tests done when Elliott and Ray had brought him into the States confirming the boy was Reck's. She had consented to raising him since they couldn't find any other family that was worthy of caring for him on his mother's side. But mostly, she wanted to make sure he didn't grow up wanting to murder all of them one day like his father. She knew she had to open her heart to the little fellow, which she did much to Elliott's dismay. Kali knew Elliott wanted him, but Elliott was aging and didn't need that extra hassle. That she and Ashton had agreed upon, though they still had not come to terms on what family meant these days. But, she made a deal with Elliott for visits whenever and wherever she and Ray wanted. That seemed to satisfy mostly Ray. He was less enthusiastic about raising another child, as opposed to Elliott, who was ready to rise to the challenge though she seemed to be more missing in action these days. It was getting harder and harder to nail her down on the phone or to schedule a visit.

"What are you planning to tell this kid when he figures out he's white and we're black? What are you going to tell him about his parents?" Micah asked as he took a seat next to Ashton. He took the baby's hand. Aaron was a friendly little thing. All smiles. That was because all his adopted sisters and brothers carried him around all day or whenever they were in the house. It was as if the baby had become the family therapist.

"The truth," Kali said, "that his mother and father passed shortly after he was born. I will tell him we knew and cared for both of them and that's why we kept him and adopted him. That's not a total lie. There was a time I really liked Reck. I thought he was my friend. And, well, his mother was more than just housekeeper, wasn't she?"

"He will find out the truth one day. And this could start all over again," Micah said, still playing with the baby.

"We could ask the same of our children, can't we? When they find out their real history? If they find it out," Kali answered. Though the only thing the toxicity tests showed was that she had had too much caffeine and the antidepressant Micah had finally admitted to giving her without her knowledge. She wasn't sure if she would ever trust him again.

"Besides, as the two of you keep telling me, let the past go." Kali leaned back in her big chair. Struggling to keep her feet on the floor, even in those heels, she was glad her body was hidden behind that big, old desk that had been occupied by all those long-tall men in this family for decades. It was a good feeling to be in control now. Holding all the cards was something she could get used to easily.

Kali smiled at her son still standing guard. He had sat down on the stairs listening intently.

"I am okay, Ash. I will call if I need you," she said. He was leaning forward on his knees. Kali smiled as she noticed that he and his father had the exact same expressions on their faces.

"Baby, I promise. I'll call you if I need you. One thing though. Could you take Aaron, please? He has that look on his face as if he is about to…"

"Eew," Micah and Ashton both said. "He just pooped."

"I thought he was looking a little too pleased with himself. Ash, please?"

"Yes," Ash answered as he walked over and removed Aaron from his father's arms. "Come on stinkpot. Let's get you cleaned up."

"He's pretty good with him, huh?" Ashton turned to Kali with pride. "Maybe he will be a good father, like his old man."

"I hope he does better than his old man," Kali said opening the drawer and pulling out a flash drive. She was putting it into the laptop when she heard Micah sigh.

"What's wrong, Micah? Wedding getting to you?"

"No, it's not that. It's this," Micah said spreading his arms wide. "You are making me feel like a stranger. This is my home. You are the best friend I have ever had, besides him. We have to get past all of this."

"Micah, I've told you that I forgive you and I meant it. It's just that I can't live with you. I can't even work with you. You and Ashton should be happy. I have stepped down and away from PDSI which is what I had planned to do before all of this happened. The company is yours to do with whatever you want. Go for it. Besides, Artie is still here. He's not going anywhere unless you decide to make him move downstairs with you and Anjuli. Anjuli, by the way, is driving me crazy about helping her with this wedding. You have created a monster, you know. But, that's all on you, too." Kali turned her attention back to the computer. "By the way, boys, the numbers look good. You can actually take me off the distribution lists though. I don't need to get any reports from the company anymore."

"No, I need you to keep an eye on those reports. You know how you used to pick up on any variances or discrepancies. Keep looking, please," Ashton said and leaned on the desk. "What's this meeting about? Don't tell me, you got all beautiful to just meet with us. You look outstanding by the way. Is that the first time in those heels?" he added, getting up to look over the desk. Kali stuck her feet farther under so he couldn't see them dangling.

"Sit," she said and turned the laptop screen toward them. She pushed play.

"I wanted the two of you to know what I have done," she said. Both men hushed and focused on the video playing. It was Kali talking to the screen as she walked through a group of women in a setting that neither of them recognized.

"The Jordan Banks Foundation?" Ashton asked.

"Yeah, I have created a foundation to help end domestic violence and sex trafficking. I thought naming it after Jordan was sort of a cute twist," Kali said as she watched the men's expressions, "given that he was the king of both."

"You make it sound worse than it was, Kali," Ashton said.

"Really, from where I sit, it couldn't have gotten any worse. How do you think we got to this point?" Kali waved her hand demonstrating she was in the big chair and they were in the smaller ones.

"I think you are blowing this out of context," Micah argued. "I'm not sure this is something you should be drawing attention to, I mean it could draw closer attention to us. Listen, Ashton has been going through hell these past months to get his identity back. Don't you think we should be laying low, right now?"

"Oh, I see. You are afraid I will talk or something and send both your asses to jail for good. I have given you my word that I wouldn't do that, unless I die before you do. You know the kind of death I am talking about, Micah. I have forgiven you, but I will not forget what you have done."

"And me?" Ashton tried to touch her hand and she moved it.

"You are the master of domestic violence. Did you forget what happened when the twins were born?"

"I promised you on our wedding day, before and after, that I would never lift a finger to harm you ever again. I was in a different place then. I was really stupid, I know that, and I haven't, have I? Ever done anything to harm you?"

"No, but I have been put in harm's way too many times because of you."

"Not my doing," Ashton said and then glanced at Micah.

"I'm out. I can't support this foundation idea," Micah got up.

"No problem. Wasn't asking for your permission or your help. Was just keeping you informed. By the way, your fiancé is onboard.

She's helping me. I was thinking of even appointing her to the board."

"I thought you didn't trust her," Micah said, narrowing his eyes.

"I don't, but she is doing her best to be my new best friend. I'm giving her the benefit of the doubt, though I am not eating her food either," Kali said, turning the computer back around. "This video is real slick though, don't you think?" she said to Ashton as Micah walked out the door.

"I have to agree. It is real nice. As usual, you look stunning in it." Ashton leaned on the desk with both arms.

"Sit up, and get off my desk. Jordan would never allow you to do that." Kali closed the laptop. "You think if you keep telling me how good I look I will soften up."

"Well, you know and I know that we still have this thing for each other."

"Ha. Ha. I'm tired, Ashton. I have spent my entire life being battered by a Sperling man or a Sperling envy."

Ashton licked his bottom lip and smiled, "I can't argue with that. I wish I could do a do-over and make your life happy and drama-free."

"Oh, you wish you never met me?"

"Hell, no, little girl. Some way, somehow, fate was going to bring us together. Don't you know that?"

"I know you frighten me," Kali said, folding her arms.

"I know you lie." Ashton sat back in the chair and folded his arms. "You are just mad. You say you are not, but you are angry. I stayed in Europe because I was sick. And, because I was sick, I kept forgetting things. Because of my condition I thought you and the kids would be better off without me so I withdrew. Dumb, now that I think about it. But, that's all that was going on."

"So it didn't occur to you to call me, to let me or Elliott come take care of you instead of letting some whore into your house that was connected to someone who hated you."

"Didn't know it was going to pan out like this. But, if I had to do it over again, I would have given you a call."

"You didn't."

"And, you are pissed."

"Hurt." Kali put it into the word she knew best because it hurt her to sit across from him this very minute.

"I hurt your feelings."

"Yes, you hurt my feelings."

"I'm sorry."

Kali was stunned to hear those two simple words not surrounded by a million more. For the last four months, those two words were embedded in excuses. But, now those two words just hung in the air with a sincerity that wrenched her heart in another way.

Before she knew it, her feet were dangling higher in the air. Her husband had reached across the desk and picked her up as if he had reached across the table and picked Aaron up out of his high chair. He held her up high so that she could look down into his face. She grabbed it with both hands.

"I hate you," she whispered.

"You wish you did," he whispered back and gently bit her bottom lip.

"Stop," she answered weakly as he let her slide down his body to her feet. He used his leg to push away the desk chairs and sat her on the desk.

"I need to ask you something," he said, pushing the chairs further apart and then getting on his knees. He let his head fall in her lap for a moment and then he looked up at her with glistening eyes.

"Mrs. Sperling, would you consider giving me at least another ten years of pure bliss to rival the ten we had in New Jersey?"

Kali took two handfuls of his silky, graying hair and sighed, "I can't go back, Ashton. We can't go back."

"Mrs. Sperling," he persisted, "we definitely can't relive our mornings filled with screaming little kids running and jumping in the pool, chasing a dog trying to play dress up, or sitting in the mouth of a cave roasting marshmallows. Nor can we recreate making love in Olde City leaving Micah and Ruby with the kids here in the penthouse. Those days are gone. Most of the people in our lives are gone. What's left is a lot of new experiences to be had. Lot of women to be helped. I agree, naming the foundation after Jordan is apropos. And you need to start by finding your cousin, Alina, and rescuing her from that nut she married," Ashton said and took a moment to kiss her on the knee. It made Kali realize that her legs were parted on either side of his large shoulders. She shivered.

"I have already thought about that. Get up," she said, pushing his big shoulders; but they didn't move, he didn't move.

"You know I am not getting up until you tell me I can come home," Ashton said. "I will spend the rest of my life, whether it's five, ten, fifteen years, whatever, I will spend every minute making you feel safe and loved and spoiled rotten. Whether you view Jordan as a batterer or a lover, he spoiled the heck out of you and I'm going to make you even worse." He pulled her head to his and began to kiss her deeply.

"Only on one condition," she said. "You take your mother back into the fold. She misses you," Kali said thinking about the last time, she had seen Elliott. The woman had hugged her tighter than tight, as if she would never get a chance to hug her again. And she did the same thing with each of the kids. Kali was worried about her, and at that time Ashton hadn't share the news of their relationship, so Kali had no idea why she should be worried.

Ashton was quiet. He put his head in her lap and she stroked it.

"It's okay to forgive her, Ashton. How many times have I forgiven you? Heck, you are in the process of raising the son of a man who spent his life wanting you dead, it seems. Call your mother," Kali whispered.

"If that's what you want," Ashton lifted his big head and smiled. "Kali gets what Kali wants," he said as he grabbed her face and brought it back to his again.

She tried to squirm away from him but her body was turning into jelly. He got up off his knees and leaned over her causing her to lie back awkwardly over the desk. He felt around for the drawer and then pulled out a little remote control. He used it to lock the door.

"I have a meeting, a real meeting," Kali was saying as she tried to check her watch. He didn't give her a chance to see it. He picked her up and was removing her skirt and her panties all at once.

"You will make the meeting," he said, as his big head took up residence on her breasts. She tried to push his head up and it went down instead. She almost screamed, but remembered the kids were home and could be in the rec room next door. She bit him on his shoulder leaving lipstick stains on his white shirt. She didn't care. His tongue was inside her digging for gold and sending high energy beams from her body out into the universe. Her whole body shook with pleasure. The last thing she was ever going to admit to him was that, every night since the day in the cave, she had been dreaming he would do what he was doing right now. It would never escape her lips that the thought of having sex with him had kept her semi-conscious.

Kali had no resistance left, she was just as wild as he was and devoured every inch of him that she could. The next thing she remembered was lying in the middle of the floor next to the sofa with his nude body on top of her nude body. Their clothes had been strewn all over the room. They both started laughing. Then someone knocked on the door.

"Mom, mom, mom," Ash called. The two of them sat up stifling their giggles. Kali ran around the room picking up her items of clothes while Ashton tried to get into his.

"She's in the bathroom," Ashton yelled as he was stuffing his shirt into his pants. He couldn't find the tie he had on, but he slipped into his jacket anyway. As he was about to open the door, he saw the tie under the desk alongside Kali's panties.

"Your mom and I are having a very serious discussion. She had to go to the bathroom. What is wrong?"

"Nothing's wrong. She has a meeting in a half hour. She's going to be late." Ash dodged his father and made his way into the study.

"Mom, mom," Ash yelled.

"I'm in the bathroom, Ash. I will be out in five minutes, ready to go. Did you take care of the baby?" Kali hoped that would annoy him enough to leave, but he knocked on the bathroom door instead.

"Ash, I am indisposed, but I am fine sweetheart."

"I will wait here, right here until you come out, mom," Ash said, glaring at his father who was looking too happy about something. And then it hit him. There was an aura in the room that he knew. Whether his parents knew or not, he was having sex now, regularly. It hit him: his parents had just finished doing the dirty deed. He almost ran out of the room and, as he looked back, he saw the tie and the black lace panties lying under the desk.

"Oh, my God," Ash said as he left the room hurriedly.

Ashton locked it back again and went to the bathroom door. "I think our son is having sex with somebody."

"Why do you say that?" Kali said, smoothing her hair back from her flushed face.

"He had that look of recognition on his face when he left," Ashton laughed.

"Oh, my God. When did he start? Oh, what am I saying? I am not surprised."

"Oh, I will find out," Ashton pulled her into his arms. "Tell me something."

"What?"

"Does that foundation have to be based here in Philadelphia?"

"It can be based anywhere," Kali answered.

"Good," he grabbed her hand, "because I plan to sell it all: the penthouse, the rowhouse, the house in Jersey. Anything linking us to the past, to this city.

"Wait," she said. "I'm missing something."

"Under the desk," he teased. He went over got their missing items which they put on in haste. "Come on, you have a very important meeting, I hear. Mind if I come with you?"

Kali shook her head and let him take her hand again. What was she getting herself into now?

"Kids, kids. Everybody in the kitchen," Ashton called as he walked through still holding onto her hand as if it were a lifeline. Kacie noticed first and ran to put her hand over theirs.

"Everybody here? Where's Katie?"

"At the theater," Artie answered as he walked into the room followed by his father.

"We have an announcement," Ashton said looking down at his baby girl who was smiling up at him. Kacie had never stopped loving him, he thought, even in his absence. He let go of Kali's hand and picked her up. She squealed with delight.

"Let me guess. You are back together," Micah said sourly.

"Well, you might say that," Ashton said and surveyed the room.

"We are moving," he said. "Me, Kali, and all of the kids." He looked around the room of stunned, silent faces.

"We are leaving the penthouse?" Adam was the first one to be able to fathom the thought and say it out loud.

"Yep, I have been busy with some folks down in Atlanta. Since the memories in New Jersey and here have been tainted, I want to start some new ones in a new city. Anybody interested in taking on the Dirty South."

"I don't think that's such a good idea." Micah put his arm around Artie. "Artie will miss the kids. You can't separate them."

"You are right, little brother. That's why Artie can come with us, that is, if that's what you want, Artie. I can make sure you have enough property to build a brand-new greenhouse, even plant stuff outside of the greenhouse, and your dad can come visit whenever he wants and you can visit him whenever you want. Heck, Micah, you and your new bride can move up here into the penthouse. I bet she would like that.

"What about PDSI?"

"We have offices in Los Angeles and Miami. Why not Atlanta?"

Micah let go of his son and slid into a chair. "What do you want to do, Artie?"

"I'm going to Atlanta," Artie sang.

"We are going to Atlanta," the rest of the kids started singing.

"Atlanta?" Kali was in as much shock as Micah, but when she looked at his face, she knew she was moving to Atlanta. Time was what they needed, not bumping into each other in the hallway. Not having to deal with him and Ashton being attached at the hip. Not feeling feelings popping up from when they were so dependent on each other and feeling unsafe for not knowing if he would ever harm her or drug her.

"Atlanta, it is," Kali said as the family moved into a group hug that hadn't happened in years. This was home she thought with all the warm bodies crushing her, Atlanta, Philadelphia, New Jersey, or wherever, right in the midst of this sea of Sperling babies was the only place she had to be.

Ash was the first to break from the group. He pulled his mother to him, moved her rogue curl aside from her eyes, and kissed her forehead. He wanted to tell her she was safe now, that no man would ever hurt her again. She was under his watch now. He held her in his arms and stroked her neck. He knew every vein that pulsed through it. Ash had been studying the human body ever since he had been tasked with his first kill. It was still exhilarating to think about, and that made him want to feel his next kill when the pulse is completely stopped, silently dead. He let go of his mom and smiled. She touched his face and smiled up at him. They both turned away. She followed the two grumpy men who were still debating whether it was or was not a good move for the family.

Ash thought about his twin sister and where she would live. Until their mother's kidnapping, they had been at terrible odds, always disagreeing, slamming doors, and pushing each other whenever possible. He didn't know why because they had always been so close, but it was back. He knew she wouldn't be able live in Atlanta with them full-time. Her reviews for the play were all five-star. She was going to be the special one in the family, and he could live with that as long as she was safe. His younger sister then broke his thought by touching his arm, he smiled down at her. At least, he'd be close enough to watch her for a few more years.

"Do you think the people in Atlanta want to hurt us, too?" Kacie asked, looking directly at Ash.

"No. The people in Atlanta don't even know us. They don't care about us. Besides, all of those terrible people that wanted to hurt us didn't. They are all tightly sealed in their own little graves suffering in their own little hells. You are safe now," Ash said, using the word he couldn't stop thinking of when he looked at the women in his life. He was the head of the next generation, and he was going to do a better job than his father and his uncles, his grandfather and his great-grandfather. The legacy they had left was not the legacy he planned to leave for women, especially these women.

Kacie giggled as Artie picked her up and twirled her around. Then Adam grabbed her and kissed her before telling her their mom was looking for her.

"I never want her to grow up," Artie said, watching his younger cousin bounce away.

"She has already changed," Ash said. "Some of that bubbliness is now an act. We are all an act."

Adam shook his head as he watched his father and his uncle talk animatedly in the dining room. He felt sorry for them. They were so out of touch, he thought, as he turned back to his cousin and his brother. He wondered how they would react when they discovered the new generation's plan. They were already moving forward. He was learning everything he could about cybersecurity. He wasn't going to let anyone attack them on that front. Artie was going to be ready for anything biologic. That boy knew his plants, his poisons, and his antidotes and was learning more every day. But, those old men should already know Ash was the real killer in the family and he wasn't about to let their mother get hurt one more time. Safe. Huh, he thought of the word that they had tossed around all day, every day since the kidnapping. Those old men weren't safe. He caught his dad's eye; Adam waved and gave him a thumbs-up. Safe? Dad and Uncle Micah were far from safe.

Dilsa Saunders Bailey
Books

Fiction

Non-Fiction

Available at Amazon and other online retailers.

www.simplydilsa.com

www.twitter.com/simplydilsa

www.facebook.com/dilsasaundersbailey

simplydilsa's

Master Mind Group

A special thanks to the ladies who have supported me
and kept me motivated over the years. Your
encouragement is greatly appreciated!

Alicia Butler Pierre

Betty Saunders

Carolynn Rainey

Chandra Thomas

Donna Wise

Faye Reid

Lynn Suruma

Sara Lucas Williams

And

Many More!!!!

THANK YOU SO MUCH!!!